To my frien.
joins me
you'll enjoy the yarn!

GRAY RAIDERS, GREEN SEAS

The further adventures of Rory Dunbrody, CSN,
and Tobias St. John, USN

second in a series
cordially,
by Les Eldridge

Les Eldridge

ii

Printed in the United States of America.
ISBN# 0-9794847-0-7.

To the memory of Willard R. "Wede" Espy, who would frequently remind me, "Remember, Les, it's just a yarn!"

AUTHOR'S NOTE TO THE READER:

Gray Raiders, Green Seas is fiction, but most of its characters actually existed. I have tried to be true to their characteristics as we know them from history. They were involved in most of the events that take place in the novel, but occasionally I have collapsed time (and merged the accomplishments of characters) in the interest of the story.

The dialog of the historical characters is fictional, except for a few quotes from contemporary sources.

For the reader who is not a sailor, nor Irish, nor yet Hawaiian, it may help to scan the glossary.

As the story tracks two often-separate story lines, the chapter list identifies the primary character (Rory, Tobias) in each. To further aid the reader each chapter heading will display a harp for Rory, and a sextant for Tobias.

ABOUT THE AUTHOR

Les Eldridge has retired from careers as a college administrator, county commissioner, corporate executive, mediator, and administrative law hearings officer. He was co-author of The Wilkes Expedition, Puget Sound and the Oregon Country, a history. His first novel in this series, The Chesapeake Command, was published in 2006 by Broadsides Press.

ACKNOWLEDGEMENTS

My special thanks to those critical readers who read the complete manuscript, Sherie Story, Don Law, Dick Van Wagenen, Charlie McCann, Jack Howard and my wife, Mary Eldridge, and those who read portions, Tom Rainey, Rudy Martin, Lowell "Duke" Kuehn and Don Lennartson. Mahalo to my kumu, Laulipolipo'okanahele (Nova-Jean Mackenzie) for her continued guidance. Thanks for the help and advice of Jan and Justin Lewis, Bob Peck, Pat Soden, Chuck Fowler, Jane Laclergue, Kay Bullitt, Dean Foster, Denny and Paula Heck, Steve Skelton, C. David Hughbanks, Pam and Sturges Dorrance, Kathy Lovgren, Jose' and Christina Valadez, David Johnson, Tom Bjorgen, Marcela Gama Filho and Mary Lou Dickerson.

My friend and photographer Lloyd Wright was indispensable. My pre-submission editor Heather Lodge greatly improved the portions of the manuscript she read. The Business Manager for the enterprise is Mary Eldridge. Leeward Coast Press, in the persons of Layout and Graphics Editor Patrick Eldridge and Publisher Robert Payne, made it all come together.

CONTENTS

Map #1) Chesapeake Bay

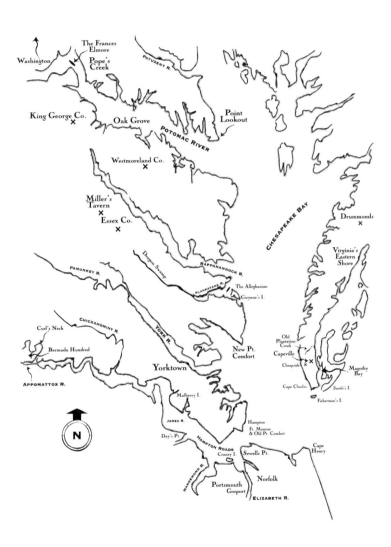

viii

Map #2) Charleston, Port Royal & The Savannah River

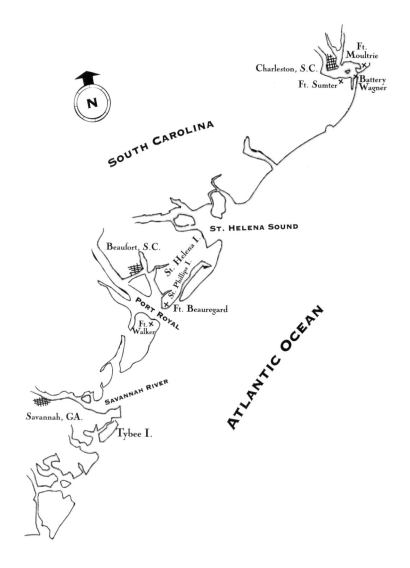

ix

Map #3) Broad River & Coosawhatchie

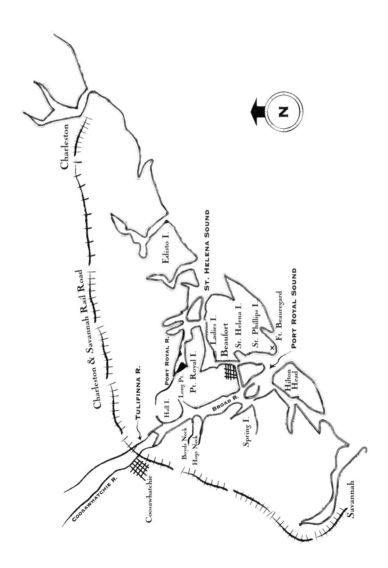

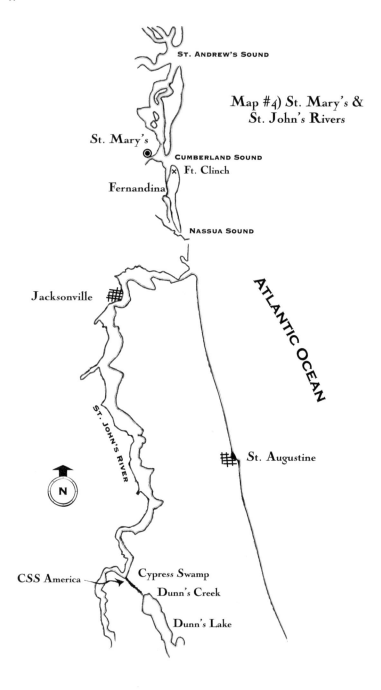

ST. ANDREW'S SOUND

Map #4) St. Mary's &
St. John's Rivers

St. Mary's

CUMBERLAND SOUND

× Ft. Clinch

Fernandina

NASSUA SOUND

Jacksonville

ATLANTIC OCEAN

ST. JOHN'S RIVER

St. Augustine

N

CSS America

Cypress Swamp

Dunn's Creek

Dunn's Lake

Map #5) Battle of Hampton Roads

8 MARCH 1862

9 MARCH 1862

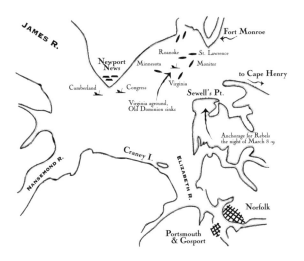

Map #6) Northeastern North Carolina

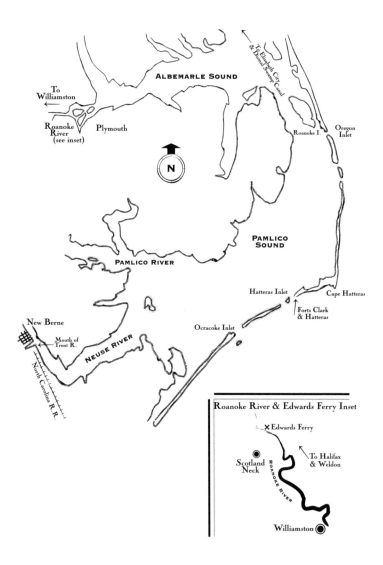

Map #7) Richmond & Vicinity, The York Peninsula

DREWRY'S BLUFF

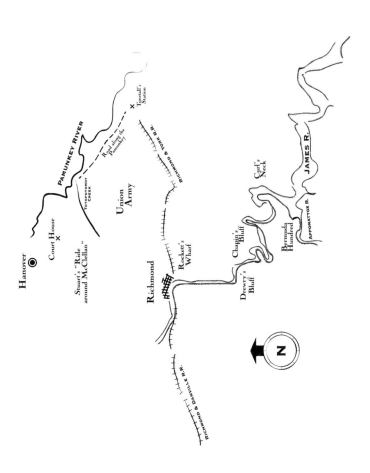

xiv

Map #8)
Northern Lesser Antilles

St. Kitts & Nevis

Antigua

Montserrat

Guadeloupe

Iles des Saints

Marie Gallante

Dominica

St. John's

ANTIGUA

N

Shirley Heights

Falmouth Harbour

English Harbour & Nelson's Dockyard

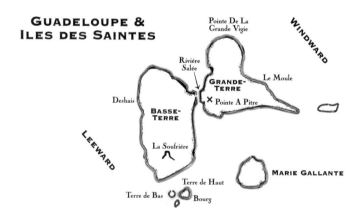

GUADELOUPE & ILES DES SAINTES

Pointe De La Grande Vigie

WINDWARD

Riviére Salée

GRANDE-TERRE

Le Moule

Deshais

BASSE-TERRE

Pointe A Pitre

LEEWARD

La Soufriére

MARIE GALLANTE

Terre de Haut

Terre de Bas

Bourg

Map #9) Cape Fear

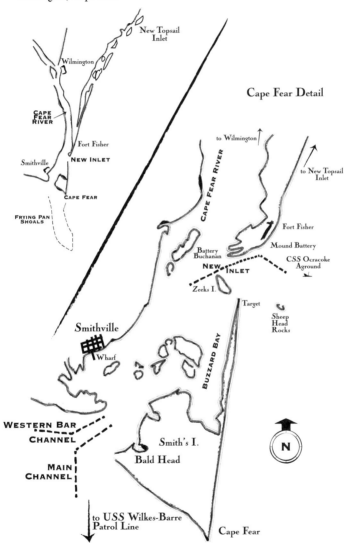

Wilmington/Cape Fear

New Topsail Inlet

Wilmington

CAPE FEAR RIVER

Smithville

Fort Fisher

NEW INLET

CAPE FEAR

FRYING PAN SHOALS

Cape Fear Detail

to Wilmington

CAPE FEAR RIVER

to New Topsail Inlet

Fort Fisher

Mound Battery

Battery Buchanan

CSS Ocracoke Aground

NEW INLET

Zeeks I.

Target

Sheep Head Rocks

Smithville

BUZZARD BAY

Wharf

WESTERN BAR CHANNEL

MAIN CHANNEL

Smith's I.

Bald Head

N

to USS Wilkes-Barre Patrol Line

Cape Fear

CHAPTER 1
ESCAPE FROM CAPE CHARLES

The armed tug *Old Dominion* labored through heavy seas, in the pitch black of a Chesapeake Bay night. Rory was experiencing an interesting rush of emotion. He was at sea, in the dark, and as ship commander, the sole responsibility for success was his. *God help me, I love it!* He smiled to himself. *Fancy that, now!* CSS *Old Dominion* rolled in the beam sea, but she was not rolling as much as Rory had feared. *Deep tugboat draft, big screw, low top hamper. We're doin' fine, by the Saints! Now, if only I can find those infantry trapped in Union territory!*

Confederate Navy Lieutenant Rory Dunbrody reached to slide the pilothouse door open. "Mr. Glendenning, keep our best lookout focused on spotting Fisherman's Island and Cape Charles. The war has extinguished the light on Smith Island. We're almost halfway, about four miles to go."

"Aye, aye, captain." Glendenning's tone was at a point midway between disdain and ennui.

The armed tug was Rory's first command. He had distinguished himself in action on Puget's Sound, off Hatteras Inlet, and on the Mississippi, but as a subordinate. He was more worried about his first lieutenant's thinly veiled insubordination than about the dangers of rescuing a "lost company" of Confederate infantry behind Union lines in east shore Virginia. *I'll either have to command Glendenning's respect, or scare the bejasus out of him*, he thought. Even his thoughts were rendered in an Irish brogue, Rory having been raised in Ireland after his North Carolina birth.

The army lieutenant, Drummond, was clutching the handrail

in the wheelhouse as the tug rolled and tossed its way across the mouth
of Chesapeake Bay. Drummond, a long-time Cape Charles resident, had
left with the bulk of the fifteen hundred-man Confederate force driven
off Virginia's eastern shore a month ago by Union troops, and was aboard
with his brother, a corporal, to guide Rory to the rear-guard company
left behind and now surrounded. Rory spoke to him. "Mr. Drummond,
when we're off Cape Charles, we'll be steering for Smith Island Inlet. I'll
be calling on you and your brother for guidance as we ease up to Magothy
Bay, south of Mill Creek."

"Happy to assist, captain. You sound like you know the area."

"I have a chart I can read. You have the experience to find our
destination in the dark, bein' an east shore native, and all."

Old Dominion eased up the inland channel, the dark loom of
Skidmore Island and the Eastern Shore peninsula to port. The tug had
made a perfect landfall at Fisherman's Island and Cape Charles, and,
bearing to starboard, had entered the narrow waters of Smith Island Inlet
and Magothy Bay, which the locals pronounced "Magotha". After several
miles, they were abeam of the village of Capeville, just overland to the
east, across the low and flat peninsula.

A leadsman stood by the starboard gunwale, chanting the depth
below the keel as he methodically swung the lead: "and a quarter less two."
Less than two fathoms - ten feet: only two feet of clearance under the
eight feet of water the deep-hulled tug drew.

"We're close to the cove I'm looking for, captain," said Lieutenant
Drummond.

Rory stuck his head out the pilothouse window. "Stand by the
anchor detail," he said in a hoarse whisper to Boatswain Edwards and the
men at the bow.

"There's the cove mouth, captain."

"Mr. Edwards, drop the hook, if you please." Twenty feet of
anchor chain roared out of the starboard hawsehole, followed by sixty feet
of anchor line. "Engine aback one third," said Rory into the mouth of
the speaking tube to the engine room, where Chief Engineer Mackenzie
carried out the order, repeated by Mr. Glendenning moving the big brass
handle on the engine room telegraph.

"Stop Engine." The tug swung to its anchor, and the boat crew lifted the gig from the deckhouse chocks by means of the crane on the short utility mast stepped abaft the deckhouse. A small steam winch controlled the line lowering the boat into the water.

"Mr. Glendenning!"

"Sir."

"Remember my orders. Four pickets along the shore, cutlasses and pistols, ten yards inland from the gig. I want the gig's crew also armed, and silent. Not a sound! It's midnight. If we're not back by daybreak at seven, up anchor and meet us at peninsula's end. Retreat at the first sign of Yankee cruisers; you'll be able to see their smoke if they're coming your way." Rory could see Glendenning staring fixedly at him through the gloom as Rory continued his orders.

"You'll have to make it six miles across before you're within range of our Columbiads at the Cape Henry battery. If you see my flare before daybreak, up anchor and use the same procedure for rendezvous. Tow the gig aft. Don't take time to bring her aboard. We'll need her if we meet you at Cape Charles."

"Aye, aye, sir. I'm more than familiar with your orders."

Rory could see Glendenning's petulant look in the dim light from the binnacle. "Not to worry, Mr. Glendenning," said Rory sarcastically. "I'm sure you'll find your abilities will rise to the task."

The pickets, Rory, and the brothers Drummond boarded the gig and were rowed into the cove. Rory carried his saber, and two "Navy Six" Colt pistols, light, small, and easy to use. The boat grounded gently in the soft yellow sand. The marsh grasses extended through a wetland toward a stand of timber a hundred yards back from the shoreline, the trees looming in the darkness. The brothers Drummond, lieutenant James and corporal Wil, led Rory up a path along a stream at the head of the cove, opening onto a meadow. The brothers' familiarity with the ground made passage quite rapid.

A farmhouse in a copse of trees loomed up out of the night. Dogs' barking was silenced quickly by James Drummond, who knew the hounds on a first-name basis.

A knock, and a light went on in the house. "Cousin Jonas, it's

Jimmie and Wil." Cousin Jonas, lantern in hand, peered cautiously out the window beside the door, and then opened it. A .36-caliber 1851 Navy Six pistol, which had been in his other hand, was now in his belt. *Truly, a popular weapon,* thought Rory.

"Cousin," said Lieutenant Drummond, "this here's Captain Dunbrody. His ship will take Bart's company to Norfolk and Richmond, if we can find them. Can you help us?"

"Tarnation, cousin," Jonas cried in recognition. "That's a hell of a way to greet a man after wakin' him out of a sound sleep." He nodded in greeting to Rory. "Yes, sir, I reckon I can locate 'em. Y'all fixin' t' take 'em out tonight?"

"Yes, sir," said Rory, "if you can help us find 'em, sure, we'll get 'em safe to Norfolk!"

Jonas spat indifferently in the dust. "Oh, I know where they're holed up, in the woods south of Cheapside. Let me get my coat and boots, and we'll get the horses and take a little ride." He grinned widely at his young cousins. "I surely do miss the days when I was younger and smugglin'. This will be like ol' times."

Four riders in the gloom of the East Shore night, swords and pistols by their sides, swept down the trail toward the village of Cheapside and reined in at a large stand of timber. Cousin Jonas provided a very passable birdcall, which was answered immediately from the woods. He called into the darkness. "Tell Bart it's Jonas Drummond, with good news, I think."

A call, *sotto voce,* went out from the sentry to the sergeant of the guard. After a brief wait, a man in the uniform of a Confederate infantry captain emerged from the piney woods. "Jonas, I hope this is important," he said.

"Important enough to get me up at midnight," Jonas replied. "Say hello to Lieutenant Drummond, your brother officer."

"Oh, hello, Jimmie, have y'all come to get us?"

"Yes, sir, Cap'n Bart. Cap'n, this here's Captain Dunbrody of the Confederate States Navy. He's got a tug over yonder on the Atlantic side, and wants to embark you tonight. Captain Dunbrody, meet Captain Bartholomew Nickleby, Confederate States Army."

"Sure, the pleasure's mine, captain," said Rory. "Could we be givin' ye a boat-ride, now?"

"We're grateful, captain. We're about out of places to hide, and there's a passel of curious eyes on us since the Federals moved in and started arrangin' for us all to be Marylanders. I can have us ready to march in fifteen minutes. Sergeant!"

Nickleby gave orders for mustering the company as the Drummonds mapped out the best route back to the tug. Rory was fascinated by the army's informality of address. Regimental officers were elected by their troops, rather than appointed by the Secretary's Office, as in the navy. It frequently led to troops addressing their officers by their first names, as in "Cap'n Bart".

At two in the morning, the forty men of Bartholomew Nickleby's company trudged and stumbled across the meadows and through the stands of wood and forest toward the *Old Dominion*, still at anchor in the secluded cove near the channel known as the Thorofare. As they came to a slight rise midway between their starting place and the Atlantic shore, the Drummonds looked eastward, and slightly north, in the direction of Old Plantation Creek. Nickleby trained a pair of binoculars on points of light where none should be.

"I'm lookin' at trackers examining a trail in the dark," said Nickleby. "Someone thinks we're in this direction strongly enough to have twenty cavalry out at this hour of the morning."

"Goddamn those traitorous Yankee-lovers," said Cousin Jonas. "Ever since Smith's Brigade disbanded, there've been damned turncoats watchin' your every move, Bart. Now that we're in Yankee territory, those worthless bastards are curryin' favor t'beat the band!"

"We're thirty minutes away from the tug, Bart, sir," said Lieutenant Drummond. "Those riders could catch up with us in half that."

"Captain Nickleby," said Rory, "the Drummond brothers and I could wait here. We'd be sheltered by the crest of the trail. If they come this way, we can ambush them. Sure, we can pin them down, dismounted, while we get to our horses and lead them south, away from your column. Just a five-mile ride, and we'll hold them off again, 'til you meet us aboard *Old Dominion*. Jonas, will your horses find their way home?"

"I reckon. They've done it many a time before."

"Well, now. You can lead the company to the tug while we lie in wait. You'll be in bed by sun-up!"

"Jimmie, your sailor friend here is the cheeriest feller I've ever met."

"So far, so good, Cousin Jonas."

"We'll do it your way, Captain Dunbrody," said Nickleby. "I hope you can ride!"

"Like the very wind, captain, as God is my witness, not t'mention Uncle Francis Xavier Dillon, who first put me in the saddle in County Meath."

The Drummond brothers and Rory chose firing points commanding the trail, and saw that their pistols were loaded and their horses handy. Cousin Jonas, Nickleby and the column resumed their march toward *Old Dominion*.

Twenty Union cavalry jingled and creaked their way up the trail from the Chesapeake side. They rode out of a stand of pines, and into a farm meadow, one of hundreds dotting the peninsula. When they were within forty-five yards of the rise where the three Confederates lay, Rory gave the signal to open fire. The Navy Sixes were not accurate at that range, but close enough to force the troop to dismount and return fire from the ground.

"Reload! Space your fire. When we've expended our rounds, get to the horses. Reload and ride. Jimmie, you lead. I'll ride rearguard." Rory fired his first pistol, paused to reload it, and then fired his second six shots. "Now, lads, to the horses!"

Off the three of them rode, due south, away from the trail of the "lost company", watching behind them. The Union cavalry came over the crest and paused. Rory turned in the saddle and fired two shots. He saw the troop swing to its right and take their trail.

"We've got them. They're following us!" Rory followed the Drummonds as they rode south. The Yankee cavalry began a third of a mile back, but were hampered by the darkness, lack of familiarity with the ground, and their own numbers crowded on a narrow track. The Rebels fired no more, but bore away toward Cape Charles.

At daybreak, the three riders came to a rise just upslope from the mild surf of Cape Charles' east shore. They paused to train binoculars on their pursuers, now two-thirds of a mile behind. "This rise should do well, gentlemen," said Rory. "If you look to the northeast, you'll see *Old Dominion* hull-up and steaming down the passage." He forbore to mention that he'd also seen smoke to the northwest, from Union cruisers coming south down the Chesapeake.

"Gentlemen, as they come within a hundred yards, we'll fire for effect. I'm hopeful that the Yankees will return fire. And sure, if my executive officer is as sharp as I wish, he'll see the muzzle flashes and give our Parrott crew a bit of practice."

As the Rebel pistol shots rang out, the Union riders dismounted, took cover, and began to return fire. Rory waved his hat at the tug, now abeam of the rise, four hundred yards distant and proceeding cautiously to the Cape Charles shore, north of Fisherman's Island. Her gilded eagle, wings upraised atop the pilothouse, glinted in the morning sun. With his field glasses, Rory could see that traditional tug boat symbol and the pivot gun crew as well, swinging the big Parrott rifle around to bear on the Union cavalrymen.

"Gentlemen, it's time we made our exit." Their horses had been let loose to return to Jonas a half hour before. The three Rebels ran down the slope and into the Atlantic, as the gig made its way through the surf, and the pivot gun opened fire on the Federals' position.

The Yankee cavalry included at least one resolute soul. A skirmisher flanked the rise that had sheltered the three Confederates, and as they entered the surf, he fired a round from his cavalry carbine. James Drummond's left leg crumpled beneath him and he fell, face forward, into the surf. Wil and Rory reached him as the gig, with Midshipman Ormsby at the tiller, drew up to the shore. Together they placed him in the boat as it backed water, and pulled frantically to the tug.

Rory was first over the gunwale to the deck of the tug. "Mr. Ormsby, put Lieutenant Drummond in my stateroom. Damn, I wish we had a surgeon on board." He turned. "Well done, Mr. Glendenning.

Maintain your fire on the cavalry until we're out of range, or until they disperse."

"Aye, aye, sir. Captain Nickleby's in the wheelhouse, sir. There're two Yankee ships at forty-five hundred yards, sir. I can see the smoke across the peninsula."

"Very good, lieutenant. Bring the gig aboard. We'll move west between Fisherman's Island and the Cape. Once over Latimer Shoal, hard a port and increase speed to all ahead full. We'll shift our target from the cavalry to the lead Union cruiser."

"Aye, aye, sir." Rory noted the change in Glendenning's demeanor, from disdainful to dutiful. *It must be the effect of battle action. Let's hope it lasts,* thought Rory.

The lead Yankee ship was a side-wheel steamer, with a big Dahlgren pivot mounted forward and four 32-pounders in broadside. At present, she was outside the limit of her range, but her advantage lay in the forward location of her gun, which was perfect for a stern chase. To fire at her pursuer, *Old Dominion* would have to yaw slightly before each round in order to bring her forward-mounted gun to bear on a ship astern, thus losing valuable ground in a chase.

A spout rose fifty yards aft of the tug, and slightly to starboard, as Cape Charles and Fisherman's Island receded astern. "She's firing round shot, sir, as you'd imagine," said Glendenning, his glass trained on the pursuing Federal ships.

The Dahlgren fired either exploding shells or round shot from its smoothbore muzzle. Round shot had the advantage of a ricochet in line with the direction of the shot, as opposed to shells, which struck the water and bounced in random directions, not always in the trajectory of the aimed gun.

"Carry on, Mr. Glendenning. Fire as rapidly as we can manage. We'll hope fortune favors the escapee."

Rory left the wheelhouse for his stateroom, to check on the status of Lieutenant Drummond. The forty men of the 'Lost Company' were on the deckhouse and the afterdeck, enjoying the chase. These were not the safest places on the vessel, as they were the most exposed, but the soldiers preferred open air to being confined below, even in the moderate sea buffeting the *Old Dominion* as it re-crossed the mouth of the Chesapeake.

Rory gave a sharp knock before entering the stateroom. "Sir, Jimmie's awfully weak. He's lost a lot of blood." Wilfred Drummond was beside himself with concern and helplessness. His brother grinned up at him from Rory's berth where he lay, a tourniquet on his left leg.

"I'm tougher than a Yankee carbine ball, Wil," Jimmie reassured him, weakly. "I'll be just fine when we get to Norfolk."

"Two hours, gentlemen," said Rory. "I'm coming to starboard a bit, and cut down our running time. That will reduce the range from the Federal cruisers, but it gives us a better angle on our pivot firing at them." He nodded at Jimmie. "We'll be there before you know it, lieutenant, sure as I'm a Dunbrody."

Rory left the stateroom and entered the wheelhouse. "Mr. Glendenning, come starboard to southeast, a half east, if you please. I'm going forward to lay the pivot myself."

"Aye, aye, sir. I estimate the range to the lead Yankee at a mile and a half."

"Splendid, Mr. Glendenning. We'll see if we can make his life more interesting." Rory left the wheelhouse for the foredeck. *The man's transformed himself! Voila! An ideal subordinate.* The big Parrott rifle was pointed at the lead Yankee, a fast side-wheel gunboat, now at a bearing just abaft the beam. Rory grinned at the gun captain.

"Gunner, your captain's feelin' a mite rusty in his firin' practice. Would y'be lettin' me have a shot or two?"

The gun captain, who had seen firsthand how well his captain could lay the pivot, grinned in return. "Aye, aye, sir, fire away. She's sponged and loaded."

Rory sighted down the barrel, and stood to the side, grasping the lanyard. "Prime." The gun captain cleared the vent and inserted the fuse. "Stand clear." The barrel was elevated only slightly, medium range for the Parrott. Rory waited as *Old Dominion's* bow plunged into the next wave and then began to rise. He pulled the lanyard and the big gun fired, smoke obscuring the target for the moment. The recoil was dampened by the big screw compressor to the side of the rifled cannon.

"Twenty yards right, sir, and fifty yards over," shouted Ormsby, who had his glass trained on the pursuers.

"Sponge," cried the gun captain, starting the reloading process.

"Depress one degree," Rory called to the gun captain, who raised the breech slightly by inserting a quoin, a wedged-shaped piece of iron, under the breech between the gun and the gun carriage, thereby lowering the barrel. "Come left half a point," Rory called. The crewmen in charge of the training tackle heaved the barrel around slightly to the left.

A great cascade of water erupted just alongside the afterdeck as the Yankees began to find the range. The soldiers aft were drenched.

"Gun loaded and ready, sir," said the gun captain to Rory as the crew rammed home the charge and the shell. Rory waited again for the roll and jerked the lanyard.

"Good shooting, sir," cried Glendenning from the deck outside the pilothouse. "It landed just off her bow and ricocheted into her port paddle box. Blew it to pieces! She's broadside to us and stopped, sir. The other Yankee's coming alongside."

The gun crew was cheering now, shaking their fists at the two Federal cruisers now falling rapidly away as *Old Dominion* sped across the Chesapeake. The soldiers aft echoed the gun crew. The smoke had cleared and Rory could see the two steamers.

"Luck of the Irish! Good shooting, gun crew, gun captain! Extra grog today, lads." Rory returned to the wheelhouse. "Bear up directly for Sewell Point, Mr. Glendenning, if you please. I want to land Lieutenant Drummond at the naval hospital in Portsmouth as soon as possible."

"Aye, aye, sir. Nice shot, sir."

Rory smiled. "Lucky shot, Mr. Glendenning, but you're very kind to say so. Still, I can't help wonderin' if we just did in any of our Academy classmates. Nonetheless, I'm going to indulge in a bit of celebration."

Glendenning looked puzzled as Rory stepped to the flag locker, and, from a back cubbyhole, extracted a green flag with a large gold harp in the center. "When I left County Galway for the Naval Academy," he said, half to himself, "after Da had secured my appointment, I promised meself if I ever commanded and won a victory, I'd fly the ould Irish Standard, for meself, for Brian Boru, and for my grandfather Fearghus and all the other Dillons who fought under it for France's Irish Brigade. Mr. Ormsby," he said to the midshipman, "run this up to the signal yard."

As the *Old Dominion* rounded Sewell Point and headed up the Elizabeth River, the harp of the 11th Century Irish warrior-king Brian Boru flew from the yardarm of the signal mast, stepped just abaft the wheelhouse. The new Stars and Bars, larger than the green flag, flew from the staff at the stern, with three bars, red, white and red, and a blue canton with thirteen stars representing the eleven states of the Confederacy, plus two unfulfilled Southern wishes, Missouri and Kentucky.

Glendenning gazed at the green flag. "Sir," he said, crestfallen, "I owe you an apology. I let a childhood prejudice color my assumption that the Irish could never lead or command. I was wrong. You've shown me that, and I'm grateful."

"I'm grateful, as well, lieutenant, for having gained the full support of a good officer. Let's say no more." Although danger was behind them, the rush of emotion that had carried Rory through the night and across the Chesapeake did not subside. He was determined that Drummond would not die before reaching the hospital in Portsmouth, and he willed the tug through the water at her top speed. Only after Drummond was in doctors' hands did he breathe deep, savor the elation of success, and allow himself a shiver at the memory of minie balls overhead in the East Virginia night.

CHAPTER 2:
OLD TALES RETOLD ON MULBERRY ISLAND
JANUARY 1862

The wardroom of the *Patrick Henry* was crowded. Lieutenant Robert Minor had reported back to the squadron from New Orleans. Rory had previously worked with him on an audit of the New Orleans Squadron carried out for Secretary of the Navy Mallory. Minor was to be transferred to the crew of the *Merrimack*. Lieutenant John Taylor Wood had been transferred from the Potomac River Squadron, and likewise had been assigned to the crew of the *Merrimack,* which was still in drydock, without a commander, and under direction of its first lieutenant, Catesby ap Jones.

They had both stopped on their way from Richmond to Gosport to say a hello to the James River Squadron commander, Jack Tucker, an old comrade in arms. Considerable merriment filled the wardroom. Minor and Wood renewed acquaintanceships with Rory. Wood had been a senior midshipman and later Rory's gunnery instructor when Rory had begun at the U.S. Naval Academy. Rory had entered the Academy upon his return to America from Ireland where he'd been raised by his uncles. Rory's father, a North Carolina shipbuilder, had arranged for Rory's Naval Academy appointment.

The gathering was a perfect illustration of a phrase in a later Naval Academy song, "Blue and Gold"; "and when just two or three shall meet, and old tales be retold."

"Bob," said Rory, "how did you leave things on the Mississippi?"

"A case of too little, too late, I'm afraid, my friend", Minor replied. "The materials available for the Mississippi ironclads are insufficient for two, and are sought after by all four ironclads being built, two in Memphis and two in New Orleans. Poor Commodore Hollins bounces back and forth between New Orleans and Cairo with his little squadron, like a man on a tin roof in August."

"At least you're on your way to that grand ironclad in Norfolk, Bob. You and Mr. Wood will have the Yankees all shakin' in their boots."

"If we can find a crew for the *Merrimack*, Rory," Wood replied. He clapped Rory on the back. "You must call me Taylor, as we're the same rank, now. And you have your own command!"

"Sure, Taylor, it's a little tug a-tootin' about the bay. I did greatly appreciate your letter to me when I was aboard *Active*, as we were both agonizin' over our resignations."

"As I appreciated your thoughtful response, Rory. I regret we had to make a choice, but I have no regrets now that we are comrades in this great cause. Which you, I understand, furthered considerably last month by saving an infantry company and damaging a Yankee cruiser."

"Damn fine job he did, too," Tucker declared. "What ever happened with the infantry lieutenant who took a bullet?"

"Well, now, captain," said Rory, "Lieutenant Drummond lost his leg but not his life. And who could be more deservin' of life, saving his company by leadin' three of us away from it down the Cape Charles trails, and trickin' the Yankees into followin' us instead?" He smiled. "And shouldn't we be addressin' you as 'Commodore', now that you've got *Teaser* and *Jamestown* in the squadron?"

"Ever notice, sir," said Bob Minor to Tucker, "that an Irishman answers a question with another question, at the very least?"

"Damn'd cogent observation, Mr. Minor. Could I trouble you for another glass? Gentlemen," said Tucker to his squadron officers. "Let me propose a toast to the James River Squadron, and to its next addition, the Confederacy's first truly great ironclad!"

Toast followed toast, to Academy days, to the pre-war lessons taught these young officers by Tucker on board the *Pennsylvania*, to absent comrades. "Captain Dunbrody," roared Tucker. "We need a song here! If my memory serves, you used to lead us aboard the old *Pennsylvania*?"

Others chimed in. "Yes, Dunbrody! How about the Mingulay Boat Song?"

"All right, lads," said Rory, "Four-part harmony," and they were wrapped within the strains of the song, listening to one another, hearing the parts join and echo, *"What care we though white the Minch is, what care we for wind and weather, let her go, boys, every inch is wearing homeward to Mingulay."*

As they broke up in the wee hours, Rory went on deck to bid farewell to the ironclad's newly appointed officers. Bob asked, "what happened to that blonde beauty over whom you fought to the death?"

Rory sighed. "Sure, Bob, isn't she right upstream in Richmond? And livin' with her mother, her brother, her aunt and her uncle. We saw one another at Christmas, under several sets of watchful eyes. I despair— and that's the right word—of ever bein' alone with her."

"Well, sailor, if I know you, you'll find a way."

"God save ye, Bob. Smooth sailin' to you."

CHAPTER 3
THE BLACK DISPATCH
FEBRUARY, 1862

Sailing Master Tobias St. John, USN made his way back to his berth aboard USS *Wabash*, Flag Officer Samuel Francis "Frank" Du Pont's flagship in the harbor of Port Royal, South Carolina, fallen the previous November to an overwhelming Union amphibious attack. Tobias had just impetuously volunteered for a spy mission to capture blockade runners behind Confederate lines. Du Pont and Allan Pinkerton, Union Secret Service chief, had welcomed Tobias' plan. After Tobias had been dismissed, Du Pont and the Glasgow native Pinkerton continued their discussion regarding newly-freed slave "contrabands", and their value to the Union war effort. "These contrabands are a real asset tae our side in this war, Flag Officer," said Pinkerton. "I cannae believe that we have some general officers who welcome southern slave retrievers into their camps, or who turn escaping slaves away, but we do."

Du Pont nodded in agreement. "Yes, Mr. Pinkerton, I've heard that of Generals Hooker, Buell, Halleck and W.T. Sherman. I agree, it's a great mistake. On the other hand, we have generals like Hunter, who are raising black regiments on their own. I'm afraid they're a bit ahead of national policy in that regard. Poor Mr. Lincoln, trying to keep a balance between the Copperheads in the north who favor slavery, and the abolitionists, who require him to emancipate immediately!"

"But," continued Du Pont, "in the generals' defense, the army has long had a color bar, unlike the navy. We're relatively free of blatant prejudice toward Negroes in this branch of the service. For years, we've had noticeable numbers in our crews. They mess together and work together, without segregation, at least on the lower deck. Admittedly, you'll find few petty officers, and St. John is the only Negro commissioned officer I'm aware of. St. John has come quite far, for a Negro. A combination of luck, talent and determination rarely equaled."

"I agree," said Pinkerton. "One of the reasons I sought ye out, sir, as an ally in this intelligence effort, was Secretary Welles' authorization to Flag Officer Goldsborough last September to enlist contrabands for naval service. Very forward-looking of the navy, in my judgment, and very useful to the secret service. Mr. St. John could turn out to be a real treasure for us. And with the courage and resourcefulness he showed in saving the *Vincennes* from destruction last year, there's nae doubt of his abilities."

The next day, Tobias traveled up the Beaufort River in the gig to seek out Isaac Tatnall. Tatnall was a young recently freed coastal pilot from a plantation in Georgia, and had arrived at Port Royal with a group of fellow freed slaves. He was currently helping more elderly freedmen work the plantations near Beaufort in the absence of the owners and overseers who had fled. After making inquiries at the Beaufort wharf, Tobias told the coxswain of the gig to stand by, and rest the crew in the shade, while he walked a red dirt trail north of town, 'til he came across Tatnall helping a crew of freedman laborers in a sorghum field on a nearby plantation.

"Isaac, a word with you, please." Tobias was in his winter wool uniform; his tunic slung over his shoulder and his white linen shirt a comfortable covering for his long walk. It was a clear day, and he wore his summer sennet hat instead of his uniform cap.

Isaac followed, and he and Tobias sat under a nearby oak. "I want your opinion, and perhaps your help, on a plan to help the blockade," Tobias explained.

"I'se interested in anything keep me free, Tobias." Tatnall laughed. "You a mighty-educated nigger, I bet it be some plan!" Isaac was taller even than Tobias' six-foot two, well set up, and strong. He knew every inch of water and narrow channel in the Sea Islands, from Great Tybee to Edisto Island. He was obviously comfortable in talking to Tobias, and rested his back against the oak.

Tobias gestured with his hand, determined to enlist this

resourceful pilot in his enterprise. "You know most of the tidewater pilots on the Georgia and South Carolina Coasts?"

Isaac leaned forward, a look of curiosity on his face. "Oh, 'deed I does, and some more in Florida, Wilmington, and de Cape Fear River, too."

"If you needed to, could you find out what day a blockade runner was sailing?"

Isaac nodded confidently. "Most of de time, I can ask an den get de answer, right quick!"

"Would most of the other slave pilots that far away help us find out sailing days? The local ones I've been working with here have done so."

"Long as they's careful, and don't get caught, sho'. They know which side makin' free men out of slaves."

"Could you start getting ship names and sailing dates from Charleston and Wilmington?"

"Oh, yes, but I like to row out to a picket ship at night and give it to you. Not quite ever'body stop talkin' to our ol' massas."

"How about once a week, starting in a week?"

"I can do that. Tell me where the ship be."

"Right off the point at Parry's Island, midnight, next Tuesday,"

"Okay, but you be de one. Nobody knows but you an de commodore. Some time people have secrets, show off by tellin' fren's, pretty soon, everybody knows, and we're in trouble." He leaned forward. "*I'm* in trouble!"

The two tall, striking black men nodded to each other and burst into laughter.

"Yes, mon" said Tobias, lapsing into his Antiguan lilt, "dat how it go. We keep it close, jus' you an' me!" Tobias and his father had been born into Antiguan slavery, and had left for New England after the British had freed their slaves in 1833. First the senior St. John and then Tobias had become New Bedford whalers. Tobias usually spoke with a Massachusetts accent, but could easily affect his native Caribbean patois and even a passable imitation of an upper class Englishman.

Upon returning to *Wabash,* Tobias reported to Flag Officer Du

Pont and Mr. Pinkerton. When he had concluded, Du Pont said, "Mr. Pinkerton, this seems an excellent expansion of our current effort. As commander of the South Atlantic Blockading Squadron, I'll be able to put the information gleaned to immediate use. You'll receive copies in Washington, of course, and be able to ask St. John and Tatnall to focus inquiries for you on particular areas of interest."

"Quite true, Flag Officer," said the detective. "I particularly like the direct line of communication. We've experienced too often that, when many know of the operation, much can go wrong. And when things go wrong in this business, it's often fatal! With that caution in mind, Mr. St. John, d'ye still wish me to look for an agent in place, and perhaps develop a scheme to take a blockade runner?"

Tobias swallowed hard, but replied, "Yes, sir, very much, sir."

"Carry on, then, Mr. St. John," said Du Pont. "I'll look forward to weekly reports. Of course, if our duty takes us from Port Royal, we'll designate another officer as contact. But the information will continue directly to me as flag officer. And St. John, you should know that I appreciate the unique talents you bring to this command. Your whaling background, your formal New Bedford education, and your ability to speak your native Antiguan patois make you a very versatile officer. Which leads me to assign one more task. You're becoming the squadron's 'on-shore, Port Royal' expert. Treasury Secretary Salmon P. Chase is sending us an investigator, Edward L. Pierce, to assess the situation here with the tens of thousands of freedmen, and recommend a Federal response. I think this can only work to the freedmen's advantage. Chase was known as the 'attorney-general of fugitive slaves' when he defended so many in Ohio, and Pierce has already put in place a system to physically aid and educate Negroes in the Fort Monroe area of Virginia. I'm asking you to be Pierce's guide and ambassador among the freedmen. He arrives tomorrow. You're dismissed."

"Aye, aye, sir. Mr. Pinkerton, sir, by your leave." Tobias left the cabin with the feeling that his role in the war had expanded to affect many more individuals than just the crew of the *Wabash*.

On the next day, Tobias was introduced to Edward Pierce. Flag Officer Du Pont excused himself for other duties, and Tobias and Pierce had the flag cabin to themselves, to exchange information and develop a plan of action.

Pierce, dressed in a gray pinstriped suit, leaned back in his chair and casually crossed his legs. Tobias had difficulty imagining him dressed as an infantry private. Pierce, a lawyer, had volunteered as a private soldier out of patriotic duty, and had served in the infantry until General Butler had chosen him to supervise "contraband" labor at Fort Monroe. Butler, an attorney in civilian life, had applied the word "contrabands" to freed slaves in what some considered a brilliant legal approach. Virginia slave owners, under flag of truce, had asked Butler to return runaway slaves then under Butler's control. "Will you rent them to the Confederate army to build fortifications?" Butler asked. Told they would, Butler declared the escaped slaves to be the same as captured ammunition or arms, "contraband of war" under the law, and therefore legally subject to seizure, and outside the purview of the law requiring runaway slaves to be returned. The term "contraband" soon came to mean any freed slave.

Pierce smiled at Tobias. "Mr. St. John, could you briefly describe the situation for the freed slaves here."

"Aye, aye, Mr. Pierce. There are roughly nine thousand freed slaves in the Sea Islands area surrounding Port Royal. The departing slave owners took as many able-bodied slaves as they could, but they left an equal amount of younger, stronger men and women here, as well as all the younger children and the elderly. I would summarize their attitude toward the change in their lives as being sure that life under the Union, as free men, could not possibly be worse than their lives as slaves."

Tobias continued. "They are enthusiastic about their new condition, but they need help. They're unused to thinking for themselves, and living without constant direction. They don't know how to maintain themselves effectively. Most of all, many want to help the Union in the war effort. They don't want to go back."

Pierce had a look of rapt concentration. "It would seem they need a corps of dedicated and capable people to provide that help."

"Yes, sir, similar to that which you created at Fortress Monroe."

"We had teachers and missionaries from all the states of the North, and many freed Negroes from north and south."

"I understand, sir," said Tobias. "I was raised and educated in the Quaker society of New Bedford. I'm sure that they and their denominational counterparts were and will be among the first to volunteer, and the last to leave."

"And, of course, their efforts will be compromised by those who take these cotton plantations, and various others, out of receivership. Entrepreneurs are there for profit, and not for enlightenment of the instruments of profit." Pierce sighed resignedly.

"'Twas ever thus, Mr. Pierce."

"I look forward to your guidance through the territory, Mr. St. John. You're obviously an officer of remarkable talent.'

"Thank you, sir," Tobias said with a smile. "It will be my pleasure."

And so was born the 'Great Port Royal Experiment', in which thirty schools serving two thousand pupils daily were operated in South Carolina by dozens of northern relief agencies, agencies which also distributed books, clothing, farm implements and seed, all supported by the U.S. Military Department of the South. Watching the newly-freed students, Tobias thought, *with just an opportunity, who knows what can be achieved.*

CHAPTER 4
ON THE EVE OF BATTLE, THE JAMES RIVER
AROUND FEBRUARY 1862

Rory's friends who were assigned to the *Merrimack's* fledgling crew were among the busiest Confederate officers in February of 1862. Taylor Wood had been given the task of recruiting a crew for the soon-to-be-completed ironclad. Officers were plentiful for the Confederacy because so many Southern officers had served in the U.S. Navy. Crews, however, were sparse. Most sailors were northerners, and most of the few sailors from the South had stayed in the U.S. Navy. Owing to long service, they considered the navy their home, much more than southern soil.

Wood beseeched General John Magruder, commanding the Rebel forces holding the York Peninsula, next to the James River, for volunteers out of his ranks. Some responded, and some few more North Carolinian sailors followed Rory's earlier recruits. The 9th of February had yielded a fertile North Carolina recruiting ground.

A combined Federal Navy and Army landing, under General Burnside and Commodore Goldsborough had taken Roanoke Island, bordering Hatteras Island on the Pamlico Sound side. The island's naval defenders had been sunk or scattered. Only the *Beaufort* and *Raleigh* escaped through the Dismal Swamp Canal to Norfolk, there to join the James River Squadron. The crews of the Confederate ships *Ellis*, *Appomattox*, *Fanny*, *Black Warrior*, and *Seabird*, the last of the "mosquito fleet", were free to make their way to Norfolk by land, if they chose, as all their vessels had been lost at Roanoke Island.

From this seagoing detritus and some army volunteers Wood fashioned the crew of the *Merrimack*, soon to be CSS *Virginia*. Wood, who had been assigned as gunnery officer by Lieutenant Catesby ap Jones, drilled them at the 32-pounder guns of the CSS *Confederate States,* at Gosport Yard. Until late 1861, it had been the USS *United States.* The big fifty-gun frigate was an effective training platform for the student gunners of the new ironclad.

On February 13th, the *Merrimack,* a "river" class frigate like the *Wabash,* was reborn with a slanted casemate of four-inch-thick rolled iron and launched at Norfolk. On February 17th she was rechristened CSS *Virginia,* though most sailors in either navy continued to call her *"Merrimack"* (and spell her name "Merrimac" after the river valley through which the Merrimack River flows). She carried eight guns in broadside and a seven-inch Brooke rifle at both bow and stern. She also had a 1500-pound iron ram below water at the bow.

One week later, Captain Franklin Buchanan, a venerable and respected former U.S. Navy officer, was named commander of the *Virginia* and flag officer of the James River Defense Force.

Rory stood at the rail of the *Patrick Henry,* talking with Captain Barney of the *Jamestown,* after a squadron 'captain's call'. "How do you think Captain Tucker's taking the news of Buchanan as flag officer?"

"My guess," said Barney, "is that he was ready for it. Dozens of senior lieutenants and commanders, like Tucker, were hoping for the appointment. I think Mallory had to find someone of Buchanan's stature so there'd be minimal grousing, and I think all of the hopefuls knew that."

"I agree," said Rory. "I'm certain 'Old Buck' will never shrink from battle. When I was at the Academy, they were still talkin' of him as the first superintendent. Got the institution goin' properly, he did. And Tucker didn't lose a thing, did he? He still has *Patrick Henry,* your *Jamestown, Teaser,* and *Old Dominion* under his command.

"Yes," replied Barney, "although he now reports to Buchanan, who also has *Virginia, Beaufort,* and *Raleigh.*"

The *Virginia* was far from being ready for action during the last week in February, and the same week, a squadron of French Navy ships arrived for a formal diplomatic visit. Ships on both sides of Hampton Roads, Federal and Confederate, were abuzz with excitement. The French, builders of the world's first ironclad, *La Gloire,* were there to observe the newest entry into the ironclad world competition, the Confederate States Navy.

The three-ship squadron had requested permission to anchor, and to pay formal visits to the commanders of both sides. The French flagship, the *Gassendi,* was allowed to anchor between Fortress Monroe and Newport News, a good vantage point for observation, should the *Virginia* attack the Federal squadron. The others anchored off Fortress Monroe.

Rory had brought *Old Dominion* down river for supplies on a late February day when the French and Union vessels were exchanging naval courtesies. The French flew the tricolor from the main and mizzenmasts, and the Stars and Stripes from the foremast of each vessel. The Federal squadron flew the reverse, with the French flag at the fore. John Marston, USN, captain of the *Roanoke* and senior U.S. officer present, had ordered a thirty-three-gun salute. Rory could hear the salutes, one for each state (including those which had seceded), bang out from the *Roanoke,* and then heard the *Gassendi* reply in kind.

The supplies for the James River Squadron were loaded, and Rory was preparing to give the order to cast off from the Gosport quay, when a courier from the *Virginia* came aboard. "Dispatch for Commodore Tucker from Flag Officer Buchanan, sir." The courier saluted and departed, and the tug made its way out the Elizabeth River and upstream to Mulberry Island. Rory noted a French captain's gig leaving *Virginia,* and pulling down-river for the distant French ships, the crew decked out in smart naval uniform shirts with the distinctive red collar trim and the French naval caps with the red pompoms atop each sailor's hat.

Rory secured the tug just aft of the *Patrick Henry* on the Mulberry Island wharf, and went aboard with the dispatch, his curiosity aroused. "Sir," he said to Tucker after being admitted to the commodore's cabin, "a courier from the *Virginia* brought this just as we were leaving Gosport."

"Thank you, captain." Tucker looked at Rory with the hint of a smile. "You're just dying to know what's in this, aren't you?"

"Sure, now, commodore, I can't be lyin' to my commander. I'm highly curious." Rory returned the smile.

"Well, have a seat, my young fire-eater, and if I can tell you, I will."

Tucker read the dispatch, and said, "We're going to a party, the day after tomorrow, for the French visitors. A big, day-long *soirée*. Flag Officer Buchanan emphasizes the importance of impressing and entertaining our guests. The government is desperate to gain France's recognition and support for the South. Those are my words, not Buchanan's. He encourages us to bring guests, family and friends, particularly of the female variety. Make the French feel at home, I suppose," he mused.

Tucker continued. "Women would certainly make the occasion more festive! The only problem with that is, not many of us have loved ones at hand. But you, Dunbrody. You've that lovely young miss in Richmond. And her family. Excellent! I'll write them an invitation to be my guests, Mother, Aunt, and Uncle, the more, the merrier. I'll be a proper chaperone, won't I, captain?"

"Aye, aye, sir," Rory responded, resignedly. "How will we get the invitation to them in time, sir?"

"I'll send the steam launch this afternoon. It's for captains only, for the *soiree*, with the exception of the Norfolk crowd, of course. So, it will be you, Barney, Webb, and me. Not a word of this to the other captains, now, until I get the order out. I don't want to show favoritism. You just happened to carry the dispatch."

"Aye, aye, sir. I'm lookin' forward to it, to be sure. And not just because of Carrie Anne. I've not seen the below-decks of *Virginia*. We'll get a proper tour, I'll warrant."

As it turned out, Carrie Anne Eastman's aunt and uncle, the Farwells, her cousin Natalie, and her mother were delighted to be a part of the festivities, and the commodore's guests, to boot! The Farwells had close friends in Norfolk, with a spacious mansion and guest rooms galore. They had ample time to entrain for Norfolk the next day. Aunt Harriet wrote a thank-you note to the commodore, and another note to Rory expressing the family's pleasure at being able to see him. She sent both by the steam launch on its return.

Citizens of the Confederacy had thus far spent a dismal winter, with the losses of coastal territory in the Carolinas and Georgia, and threats of more along the Mississippi. The prospect of a victory with a new weapon, unmatched by the North, was a lift to their spirits. A festival to anticipate that victory, with foreign guests, was just the tonic they needed.

The festival day dawned sunny, and the commanding officers of the James River Squadron joined their commander aboard the flagship, thoroughly enjoying their cruise downstream and into the Elizabeth River. They steamed up its broad expanse, past the Portsmouth Naval Hospital to starboard and secured to the Gosport quay. The officers approached a series of tents set up in an open space in the shipyard surrounded by large, slant-sided buildings. Pennants, streamers, and ribbons of red, white, and blue adorned every tent, and the large awnings covered the temporary seating, which faced a podium and lectern.

An Army band played military airs on a makeshift bandstand to one side of the podium. Two linen-covered tables on either side of the seating area served as bars, and the visitors kept the white-jacketed Negro bartenders busy. French officers mingled with their counterparts in the Confederate Army and Navy, and Buchanan had arranged for several translators to be present. Rory found Carrie Anne's family enjoying the company of John Taylor Wood, Bob Minor, and two French officers.

"The Captain of the Confederate States Ship *Old Dominion*," announced Minor, with a great grin upon his face. Rory stopped and bowed to all, joining the group. Wood and the two officers finished a technical conversation with the aid of a translator, while Rory kissed the hands of Carrie Anne, Natalie, and the two older ladies, and shook hands with Mr. Farwell.

"Pardon me, Mr. Farwell," said Bob, "I must spirit Rory away for a moment to meet our visitors."

"By all means, lieutenant."

"Sure and I don't even have a drink, yet," Rory exclaimed.

"Duty first, even for an Irishman." said Bob. "*Capitaine, lieutenant,* may I present Rory Dunbrody, lieutenant commanding CSS *Old Dominion.* Captain Dunbrody, *Capitaine de Vaisseau* Jean Gilbert

Duquesne, commanding the sloop of war *Cuirassier,* and *Lieutenant de Vaisseau* Jean-Phillippe-Ernest de Fauque de Jonquireres of the sloop of war *Gassendi.*" Minor took a deep breath.

"*Je vous en prie, capitaine, lieutenant,*" said Rory, using his grandfather's marginal but understandable French.

"*Splendide,* you have *les Francais,*" said Duquesne, in passable English. "We communicate!" The French captain, about forty-five years of age, was tall, barrel-chested, with a broad and friendly face, blond hair worn somewhat long, and the look of a weathered and competent sailor. "Have you brought your ship with you?"

"She's but a little tug boat, *capitaine,* with one gun. I left her upstream, where she'll stay out of trouble."

"He's modest, captain," said Bob. "He's been in command two weeks and has already damaged a bigger Federal cruiser."

"Ah, you Confederates," smiled Duquesne, "you do so much with so little. *Tres courageux!*"

"You're very kind, captain," said Wood, "and you've come so far to observe our efforts."

"What you're doing is well worth looking at, lieutenant," said Duquesne. "And we were, how do you say, in the neighborhood. Our squadron has been on station in the North Atlantic for three years, commissioned to inquire on disputes surrounding the French fisheries off *Terre-Neuve* , Newfoundland. Tell me, *Capitaine* Dunbrody, how a young Irishman comes to the Confederate Navy."

Rory explained his origins, noting his grandfather's service in the French army, and the fact that he had lost his friend Tobias to the Union Navy, and no longer had anyone with whom to practice French. "This Tobias," Duquesne asked, "he is an Antiguan black, and a sailing master? He must have overcome much to rise so far!"

Bob, Taylor Wood, and Lieutenant de Fauque de Jonquieres had gone off for a look at the exterior rolled armor plates of the *Virginia,* nearby. While Rory and Duquesne strolled to the bar for a drink, they discussed the technological changes that surrounded the *Virginia's* imminent introduction to battle. "Did you know we're talkin' of coatin' the armor plate with animal fat, to increase the chances of shot glancin' off the sides?" Rory asked.

"*Incroyable!* We are very interested in how your ram will work, my friend," said Duquesne. "Our naval architects have reintroduced the weapon in our new ironclads, but we've had no battles in which we can test it."

"Sure, you have several ironclads, now, but all in Europe, are they?"

"*Mais oui*, they stay close to home. Our rival, England, is their focus. And they are not good deep-sea ships. Very crank, I think you say. This war of yours may force improvements in ironclad sea keeping, out of necessity."

"Here in America, we've studied and admired your scientific efforts, your *Genie Maritime*, that have given us exploding shells and armor plate. Mr. Wood was my instructor at the Naval Academy. He talked about your research all the time."

"Yet, we still struggle to stay ahead of the English and their resources," said Duquesne. "The new tactic of combined sea-land operations that your cousins across the bay have used so well in the Carolinas, that, my friend, may be the most significant change to come from this war."

"I read that your troops in Mexico, with the Spanish and British, have moved inland, sir," said Rory. "Is your fleet still a presence on the coast of Mexico?"

"Indeed they are, *Capitaine* Dunbrody. That is our squadron's next stop. The troops are inland to avoid the season of malaria and yellow fever in the coastal areas. The debt repayment to the European nations is still being negotiated."

"To a lighter subject, *capitaine*," said Rory. "Come meet my beautiful friend." Rory introduced Duquesne to Carrie and her family. The French captain charmed them all immediately. As they were explaining that they were all guests of Rory's commander, Jack Tucker appeared, and it was clear that he and Duquesne were kindred maritime spirits, practical, bluff, hearty, and experienced, and each loving a well-told story. The stories flew until the program at last began.

Commodore French Forrest, commandant of the Norfolk Navy

Yard, introduced the French squadron commander, who thanked his hosts with Gallic charm and gave way to Flag Officer Franklin 'Old Buck' Buchanan, somewhat lower on the charm index, but just as earnest in his delight at a chance to enlist the respect of the French.

The speeches over, all went aboard *Virginia* for a tour. Rory walked with Duquesne.

"*Formidable!* It will be a daunting sight to those in wooden hulls who understand the shift in the balance of protection."

"Sure, *capitaine*, I'm thinking none of us have the true picture of what this ship's armor can do to an old fashioned fleet."

"It will not take long for that true picture to emerge, my friend."

The French veteran and the young Confederate examined the casemate's interior. "*Mon dieu*, this was a big *fregate!* The casemate alone must be fifty meters long." The eight guns in broadside fired through ports fitted with sliding shutters that closed after the guns fired and were run in. The shutters were still being fitted, and the parts were not on hand. The two pivots fore and aft, seven-inch Brooke rifles, fired through one of three ports each at bow and stern of the casemate, depending on the bearing of the target. A pilothouse was elevated at the forward end of the casemate, at the 'spar deck' or 'shield deck' level, and a ladder from the gun deck led up to it. The foredeck and after deck, outside the casemate, were designed to be awash under two feet of water when the ship was under way with all her ammunition and stores aboard.

"How are the engines?" The big Frenchman looked down the grating in the main deck into the engine room.

"Adequate, when she was a steam frigate," replied Taylor Wood, "but slow with all the weight of armor. And the steering! It takes a mile to turn!"

"*Oui*, lieutenant, but still, more powerful than anything anchored across the Roads, yes?"

"Right you are, captain, but we hear rumors that the Yankees are frantically building their own armored ship."

As they left the ironclad, Carrie Anne and her family greeted them. Captain," said Fred Farwell, "we've enjoyed meeting you, and thank you for your interest in our new ship."

"*M'sieur*, it has been my pleasure to meet your beautiful family and your fine naval officers. *A'Dieu*, and *bon chance*. And you, my young *Irlandais*. You will do well in the Hampton Roads. *Prudente, mon ami.*"

"*Oui, mon capitaine, merci et au revoir.*"

As the French officers boarded their launches for the return journey to their squadron, Carrie Anne and Rory waved goodbye and walked for a time along the quay, watching them row away.

"Do you think the French would ever recognize us and come to our aid, Rory?"

"Not unless we no longer needed their help, love. It's the way of nations. Everyone wants a sure thing. But they're a pleasant folk, all the same."

"Rory, promise me you'll be careful when the *Virginia* attacks the Federal fleet."

"As careful as a lad can be, with shot and shell flyin' all about, love. I've a steel plate mounted at the front of the pilothouse, did you know?" Rory said, in an effort to reassure her.

"It won't stop a cannon ball, though, will it?" She smiled ruefully at Rory. "Just don't do anything foolish, please."

"Y'have my word I won't dive in the bay to rescue anyone." Rory threw back his head and laughed. "I've tried that before. It's not a workable approach, sure, and it isn't. And without Tobias t'pull me out, I'd be sunk, is the way of it." Tobias had saved Rory from drowning in their days aboard USS *Active* in Puget's Sound. "But, love; no one knows when we'll attack. That ironclad needs lots of shakedown and fixin', t'be sure."

As they walked, Rory could not take his eyes from her beautiful face and figure and her blonde hair burnished by the winter sun. He felt a palpable tug at his heart. *I'm falling deeper in love with her daily*, he mused. *I hope I'm stationed on the James forever!*

As they rejoined the others, Rory promised, "I'll send word I'm all right, as soon as action ends."

CHAPTER 5
THE BROAD RIVER CAMPAIGN
FEBRUARY 1862

The captains of four gunboats sat in the cabin of Flag Officer Du Pont, with Charles Davis, captain of the fleet, the sailing master of his flagship, Tobias St. John, Brigadier General Fitzsimmons, his chief of staff and Captain Smithson of the *Wabash* Marine contingent. "Gentlemen," said Du Pont, "we have a great opportunity to cripple a major transportation facility and command post of the enemy! The town of Coosawhatchie is a hub of the Charleston and Savannah Rail Road and was, until we secured Port Royal, a trans-shipment hub for cargoes down the Coosawhatchie River through the Broad River to Port Royal and the ocean. It is also the headquarters for the Confederate Army's district command under General Robert Lee. Here, look at this chart! You can see that Coosawhatchie's egress to the Atlantic now is our opportunity to cut the rail road in two, and disrupt their district army operations!"

Du Pont leaned back in his chair with a rueful expression on his face. "I'm a bit out on a limb with this operation, gentlemen. I've been entreating our commanders in Washington to increase our forces here in the South Atlantic Blockade. With more troops, we could make our way inland and cut the eastern Confederacy in half. But so far my requests have been unanswered. We've occupied so many ports along the coast that we're spread dangerously thin. General Fitzsimmons can let us have one regiment, but for only two weeks. Still, it's my judgment that this effort is worth a try."

"Sir," said Smithson of the Marines as he examined the chart, "these two batteries near the confluence of the Broad and the

Coosawhatchie appear to be well-placed and formidable."

"Precisely, captain. We'll have to reduce them before we can bring armed ships' boats further up the Coosawhatchie in support of the Army's attack on the railhead. Silencing and capturing those batteries will be our first task!".

"Sir, the Coosawhatchie's a shallow stream," said Tobias, leaning forward to point to the river on the big chart. "Cargoes have to be transferred from seagoing vessels to shallow draft lighters to reach the rail head."

"I appreciate the cautionary note, sailing master," said Du Pont with a warm smile. Over the last few months, the flag officer had developed a fatherly affection for the black navigator. "You'll note the gunboats of these four commanders are the shallowest drafts in the fleet."

"Yes, sir," said Tobias, realizing that Du Pont had planned thoroughly, as usual, and was a few steps ahead of his sailing master.

"Excellent point, 'though, Mr. St. John, about the lighters," Du Pont pondered for a moment, brushing his hand across his brow and the "Roman consul" cut of his hair. "You've given me an idea. In addition to putting six pounders in our ship's boats, we can arm several lighters with heavier ordnance. Lighters will make more stable gun platforms. That will strengthen phase two of the operation, after we capture the batteries."

Du Pont turned to General Fitzsimmons. "General, we can bring our gunboats within easy range of both batteries. We'll have to make an assault from the boats by our Marines on the Hall Island battery, but the battery above Boyd's Neck should be open to attack from your troops advancing up the south bank of the Broad."

"The terrain below the Boyd's Neck battery is my biggest concern, flag officer," Fitzsimmons replied. "That's low ground, and swampy. We'll have to be careful of our timing, as our progress afoot could be slow."

"We'll bear that in mind, general. Gentlemen, other concerns?" The discussion turned to quantities of shot needed and other logistical questions. Planning completed, the officers left the great cabin. Tobias and Smithson went topside to the quarterdeck. The two had led a landing party ashore two months before to secure the captured Fort Walker, on

Hilton Head Island, guarding the entrance to Port Royal Sound.

"I wish I were going with you, captain," said Tobias.

"You'll be back in action soon enough, Mr. St. John," replied the Marine with a smile. "Maybe in this operation. It's my experience in land-sea actions, anything that can go wrong will go wrong!"

"That's the voice of experience, without a doubt, Captain Smithson. Good luck to you."

The next day, *Wabash* moved up the Broad River as far as her 23-foot draft would allow, and anchored. Tobias could see the "90-day" class gunboats, led by *Seneca,* bombarding the two rebel batteries on either side of the Broad, and hoisting out boats preparatory to the Marines' assault on the Hall Island battery. The "90 days" referred to the length of construction time, very fast, indeed. To his left, he could see, through the pines, live oaks and magnolias lining the river, occasional glimpses of Fitzsimmon's blue-clad Union troops advancing along the river bank about a mile east of the Boyd's Neck battery. Captain Rodgers, commanding the *Wabash,* stood beside Tobias on the quarterdeck. "Do you have your glass on Smithson?"

"Yes, sir, his men are mustered on deck aboard *Ottawa,* and ready to land as soon as the bombardment concludes." Tobias could see the shells from the *Ottawa's* muzzle-loading rifle tearing great chunks of the Hall Island battery's earthen parapet and hurling them into the air.

"Captain," called Du Pont from further aft on the quarterdeck, "Look at Humphreys. He appears to be adrift and closing on the Boyd's Neck battery." Rodgers and Tobias swung their glasses in unison toward the bank on the port side. Sure enough, the USS *Chingatchgook,* commanded by Lieutenant Humphreys, was dangerously close to the Boyd's Neck battery with no discernable way on her.

"Signal from Ch, Ch, *Chingatchgook,* sir," called the young signal midshipman, stumbling over the name of Cooper's hero. "'Am adrift, engine disabled,' sir."

"She's just gone aground, bow on, sir," cried Tobias. "Her stern's swinging in to the bank and she's masking the battery, sir."

"Well, that's half a blessing," said Rodgers. "The battery's firing into her, but can't reach *Seneca* and *Huron* because she's masking their fire!"

"Yes, sir," said Tobias, with his glass still trained on the battery, an easy task at anchor on the placid waters of the Broad. "The battery has two 32 pounders commanding the lowland approach that the troops will use. And they've shifted their other guns' fire to the *Chingatchgook*. Her longboat's been smashed to smithereens, sir."

"Captain Davis, Captain Rodgers," called Du Pont to his fleet captain and flagship commander, "those men will have no way of abandoning the gunboat under point blank fire. We've got to get them off!"

"I agree, sir," said Rodgers, "she can only bring three guns to bear on the battery and her gun crews are completely exposed."

The three senior officers conferred near the port rail. In the distance, the Confederate battery was mounting an intense fire upon the stranded gunboat. "Sir," said Rodgers to Du Pont, "I'm inclined to send the two launches. They'll carry the entire gunboat crew." The launches were each 42 feet long, and each could carry more than 100 men in moderate weather.

"Who will command?" asked Davis.

"I'm thinking to send St. John, with Lamson in the second launch," Rodgers responded. As ship captain, it was his responsibility to handle the details of the flag officer's order. He leaned closer to the other two senior officers and continued in a murmur. "St. John is by far the most experienced junior officer aboard, and highly competent as well. But he's a Negro, and some of our acting masters would not be comfortable with him in command. Lamson will be. He's accepting of St. John's skills, regardless of race." Du Pont and Davis nodded in agreement.

"Gentlemen, let's repair to my cabin," said Du Pont. "Captain Rodgers, please have St. John and Lamson report to us for orders."

February sunshine streamed through the stern windows of Du Pont's cabin as Roswell Lamson and Tobias sat across from the flag officer, flanked by Rodgers and Davis. Tobias listened as first Du Pont and then Rodgers detailed their orders. As they concluded, Du Pont asked Tobias how he intended to approach the stranded gunboat, Tobias leaned forward, his hands clasped in front of him on the big mahogany table belonging to the wealthy flag officer. "Sir, it strikes me that the gunboat will shield us from view as we approach. The battery troops won't see us in any detail. What if we took a one hundred-man detail in the boats and had them lie down on the bottom-boards? We could attack the battery by sprinting around each end of *Chingatchgook*. She's only ten yards off the bank. We could attack through the embrasures! If we towed two cutters aft, the gunboat crew who are still fit could evacuate the wounded. We'd clearly outnumber the Rebels, and we may surprise them."

The two captains looked guardedly at one another, and then at Du Pont, who fixed Tobias with an intense gaze as he pondered. Lamson's eyes were as big as saucers as he turned to stare at Tobias. A smile came to Du Pont's face. "I've been hammering the Navy Department for weeks for resources to let me be more aggressive. If this isn't aggressive, I don't know what is. I'm betting you'll make it work, St. John! Carry on! Captain Rodgers, please detail the men he needs."

"Aye, aye, flag officer." Rodgers' approval of the decision registered clearly on his face. "Mr. St. John, if Mr. Humphreys or some other officer senior to you is still alive, you must tell him that you're acting on the express orders of the flag officer."

"Aye, aye, sir." Tobias, who had been tense as he faced the prospect of his idea being rejected with disapproval or even scorn, took a deep breath of relief as he and Roswell, dismissed, left the cabin.

"Tobias," said Roswell, laughing in relief, "even if I'd thought of such a plan, I don't think I'd have the nerve to present it. Well done! What a great opportunity!"

"Let's wait 'til we see the end of action before we make such pronouncements, my friend. Let's adopt 'cautious optimism' as our approach."

A small steam launch took the two four-ton launches and the cutters in tow, keeping the hull of the *Chingatchgook* between it and the battery. Each rowing launch carried fifty men easily, included a midshipman second-in-command and three boatswain's mates. The *Wabash* lay a mile below the Boyd's Neck battery. Her 8-inch Parrott rifle pivot was at its extreme range, and moreover, unable to fire on the battery for fear of hitting the Union gunboat. At a 500-yard distance from *Chingatchgook,* the steam launch cast off her tows, and the two launches pulled steadily toward the gunboat, towing the empty cutters. Closing on the battered hull of the gunboat, Tobias hailed. "Ahoy, the *Chingatchgook!*"

A head with a bloody bandage wrapped around it appeared over the gunboat's starboard rail. "Ahoy, the launches. Can you take us aboard?"

"Aye, aye," Tobias responded as the launches drew alongside. "Who's in command?"

"The officers is all dead," The wounded man hesitated, seeing Tobias' skin color, and then discipline reasserted itself. "Sir", he added.

"Hansen," Tobias called to one of his boatswain's mates in the stern, "bring that cutter alongside the gunboat." Roswell followed suit in the other launch. No need to whisper, with the racket of the battery's guns masking the sound of the Union sailors' voices. "You, there, aboard the gunboat, get all the men that you can into these boats, we're sending men aboard to help. Boarders, get everyone alive into the cutters as quick as you can." Ten men from each launch scrambled over the gunwale and soon were passing wounded to the cutters and assisting the unhurt crew, using pilot's ladders they'd brought for the purpose.

"Quiet, you men," Tobias ordered as the last of the gunboat's crew boarded the cutters. "Pull toward that steam launch with your able-bodied men. Senior petty officer in each boat is in command. The steam launch will tow you to *Wabash.* We're going to take the battery!" and with that, Tobias and Roswell gave their orders to "give way all" and the 20 oarsmen in each launch pulled quickly around the gunboat and grounded on the bank below the guns of the battery.

Each man of the assault party carried a cutlass and a Navy six shot Colt revolver. Boatswain's Mate David Hansen's cutlass and Colt were in his waistband, and he carried a double bit axe in his hand. Tobias looked, and looked again at the big Norwegian. Hansen smiled back. "Ya, sure, Mr. St. John, it vill come in handy, you vill see." The battle-lust shone in his eyes.

The battery had three embrasures in the north parapet, set on a low rampart and facing the gunboat, as well as two in the east parapet, trained downstream. "Mr. Lamson, take the right embrasure," Tobias called. Mr. Casey", he said to his midshipman, "take the starbowlines and attack the far left embrasure. Port-side men, follow me!"

They scrambled through the shallows and the sand of the riverbank. As they ran toward the battery, their heads were level with the sills of the embrasures. Startled Confederate gunners began to pop their heads out of the embrasures and quickly withdrew them in a hail of gunfire from the Colt revolvers. Tobias fired his Colt as his men boosted him up to the middle embrasure sill. He tumbled into the battery, his cutlass in his right hand, his Colt in his left. A gunner had dropped his ramrod and reached for a musket. Tobias cut him down with a cutlass stroke to his neck and was pushed aside by a rush of *Wabashes* firing and swinging. He could hear the cries of the Rebel officers as they tried to rally their men. "Gunners, form on me," he heard one call, the "me" ending in a scream as a cutlass provided punctuation.

The 100 sailors, with surprise on their side, soon overwhelmed the 75 men of the battery, most of whom had no time to grab a weapon. As he organized the disarming of the Confederates on his side of the battery, Tobias saw, out of the corner of his eye, the motion of the powder magazine door being closed by a gray-clad arm with the gold insignia of a Confederate Army captain.

"Bo'sun's Mate Hansen," he called. "I need your axe."

The Norwegian appeared from behind a 32 pounder smoothbore cannon now in the possession of the U.S. Navy. Tobias pointed at the magazine door. "That's locked from the inside, Mr. Hansen. Can you get me in?"

"Ya, sure, Mr. St. John, You yoost give me a little room, and ve vill have kindling in a yiffy!" He swung the axe, again and again. After six blows, it slipped from his sweaty hands. "Helvete ogsa!" he swore. Hansen picked up the axe and with a dozen more blows, the remnants of the door swung open. The large room was almost dark, lit only by a hooded lantern on the far back wall. Large canisters of powder were stacked in rows, with narrow passages between them.

A great place for an armed man to hide, thought Tobias. *If he chooses, he can blow us all up in a moment.* "Mr. Hansen, stand by. He's undoubtedly armed, and there's no sense risking more than one sailor. I'm going in to convince him to surrender. Report to Mr. Lamson, and convey my order to move all our men out of the battery as soon as possible." Tobias paused for a moment, thinking. "Tell him I want all the prisoners in formation next to the magazine. Train a thirty-two on them and load it with grape."

"Aye, aye, sir," said Hansen, a doubtful expression on his face. "Yones, Yacobsen, train that thirty-two on the prisoners. You heard Mr. St. John. Where's Mr. Lamson?" Off he strode to find the acting master.

Tobias eased into the magazine and stood in the deep shadow of the first tower of stacked powder canisters. He listened for a time but heard no sound. "Captain," he called to his unknown adversary, I'm Sailing Master St. John of the USS *Wabash,* commanding the attacking force. The battery is in our hands and your men are prisoners of war. You've fought as bravely as anyone could. You can honorably surrender your sword. I beg you, don't force us to bring men in to take you by force."

"Yankee, ah can tell by your accent y'all are from Massachusetts. I thought y'all were smart enough to know that if I fire a well-placed round in this here magazine, you and all your Yankee shipmates will be blown to hell!"

"Captain, I've moved my men out of the battery, except for the gun crew with grapeshot trained on your men, just outside the magazine door. If you fire the magazine, you'll kill all your men, and only a few of mine. You're obviously a resourceful and courageous officer. Don't you owe it to your cause to live to fight another day? Officer exchanges of prisoners are occurring every day!"

"Damn you, Yankee!" A pause ensued, and then, Tobias heard a sigh. "All right, Yankee, I'm coming out, pistol butt first and sword, pommel first."

The Rebel captain came toward Tobias, silhouetted against the dim light of the hooded lantern. The captain's jaw dropped as he came close enough to see Tobias' face. "God damn you, you're a nigra! I'll never surrender to a nigra, you black bastard!" and the captain dropped the pistol from his right hand, then suddenly reached to the top of a stack of powder canisters and toppled it. The cascading cans of powder knocked Tobias down. The Rebel flipped his sword, grasping the pommel he'd offered Tobias moments before, and swung at the prostrate Antiguan. Tobias rolled away just in time. His pistol and cutlass were gone, and the Confederate captain was rushing after him with great saber strokes.

Tobias dodged around the end of a canister row, and ran toward the back of the magazine. His hunter was screaming, "I was a slave trader, you dog. I bought and sold hundreds of you. I hope I sold your mother!"

Tobias paused at the end of the row, struggling to control his breathing. *I'm going to take this slave-mongering son of a bitch!* He thought. He peered through the gloom of the dimly-lit magazine and listened to the footsteps of the approaching Rebel. As the artillery captain reached the end of the row, Tobias sprang in front of him, bending double to escape a saber stroke, and still with his head close to the floor, back to the Rebel, moved to a side-to-side "ginga" motion, placed his hands and forehead on the floor, and extended his right leg in a graceful, powerful Capoeira sweep-kick, striking the captain at the base of the skull and knocking him, dazed and nearly unconscious, to the floor. Tobias rolled the Rebel on to his stomach, yanked his coat halfway off, and tied his sleeves in a square knot. Then he seized the artilleryman by his shirt collar, and dragged him to the magazine door.

"Hansen, move the prisoners away from the door. I have their commander!" Tobias heard the shuffle of the prisoners as his men backed them away from the front of the magazine. After a moment, he opened the door with its shattered hasp, and dragged the still-groggy battery commander out between two ranks of Confederate artillerymen. *What a curious group of sideboys*, Tobias thought, fashioning a nautical simile in his mind and giggling to himself. A mutter of disbelief and dismay rose from the captured gunners as they saw their commander dragged out of the magazine by a Negro in a naval officer's uniform. *Nice touch*, thought Tobias. "*The murmuring chorus.*" Tobias was startled as the murmurs were suddenly drowned out by a burst of cheering from the *Wabash* gun crew and men of the *Wabash* landing force peering in through the embrasures at their commanding officer and his prisoner.

As the cheering continued, Union sailors rushed forward to take the Confederate commander in hand. Hansen turned to Midshipman Casey, standing beside him. "Ya, sure, that Master St. John, he's a pistol, you betcha!"

A day later, the *Wabash* was on patrol off the coast of South Carolina near Charleston. Tobias and Roswell Lamson were off watch in the wardroom.

"The Flag Officer was certainly pleased when we gave our report," said Roswell.

"It was good news, my friend," said Tobias. "Ninety gunboat sailors rescued, 100 prisoners taken, the two batteries secured without army help, and the hull of the *Chingatchgook* towed for repairs!"

"Yes, and we got to return aboard, and leave the clean-up of the batteries to the army! This navy life is not all bad!" Roswell chuckled. "Your heroics were a bit on the risky side, my friend," Roswell added, turning serious. "The prudent course would have been to exit everyone and let that fool blow himself up. "

I'm afraid I let my anger rule my judgment, Roswell. When I found out he'd been a slave trader, good sense left me."

"Well, your actions, however engendered, should mark you for promotion," said Roswell.

"Oh, Roswell," said Tobias, ruefully, "Look at my face. You must know that I'm as high as I will ever go in the navy. I know of no other black commissioned officers, and I doubt there ever will be. I'll not rise to lieutenant."

Roswell thought for a moment. "Perhaps you're right, but it shouldn't be that way. Why, the Negroes in my division are hard workers, and many are good seamen, as good as any aboard. And you, you're the best navigator aboard, and a terror in combat!"

"I'll settle for the respect of my shipmates, Roswell, but unrealistic expectations will serve no purpose. Life is what it is. I agree with you about our 'black jacks'. The army is missing a bet by not enlisting them as the navy has. I know hundreds of well-educated freemen from New England who'd make fine soldiers."

"Judging from what I've seen of this war, its duration will soon force the army to use Negro soldiers," Roswell responded. "Where did you get your education, Tobias?"

"At a Quaker academy in New Bedford. Then I went a-whaling like my father. There's a big community of black whalers in New Bedford. After a few cruises, a navy-officer neighbor in New Bedford, my mentor, if you will, convinced me to try the navy, and found me a billet aboard a friend's frigate as an able seaman, and then I worked my way 'aloft '."

"I'm glad you did, shipmate," said the Oregonian.

"I appreciate that, Roswell, thank you."

"How did you subdue the Reb artillery officer? We heard no clash of arms from outside the magazine."

Tobias explained the encounter in the dark, and the use of Capoeira.

"I never heard the like," said Roswell in amazement. "And you say this 'kapoweera' comes from Brazilian slaves who disguised it as a dance form?"

"Yes, they'd always practice to music and quickly change from martial confrontation to an intricate dance as soon as the slave masters appeared. So its technique uses primarily legs and feet as offensive weapons. It's worked its way up into the Caribbean from Brazil. My father taught me.

"You're full of surprises, Tobias."

Ten days later, the squadron flagship found herself once again in Port Royal Sound. Du Pont and Davis sat in the flag officer's cabin, as Du Pont read just-delivered dispatches from the Navy Department. "Damn and blast!" Du Pont spun the three-page dispatch down the table to where his fleet captain sat. "Strategic misguidance at its worst! Look at that! They deny me any more ships and men on one hand, and call on me to secure northern Florida on the other. We'll have to abandon any hopes of advancing against Lee and closing the railroad from Savannah to Charleston." Du Pont's lips were drawn into a pencil-thin line as he and Davis exchanged a glance of exasperation. "Well, orders are orders. We'll have to minimize any loss of ground we've already seized. What are your thoughts, Charles?"

Davis thought for a moment. "We lose all but one company of General Fitzsimmons' men at the end of the week. They'll have to garrison the batteries. We've already re-emplaced the guns so they bear landward and upstream. Then, we'll have to withdraw all but one gunboat for the Florida expedition. The remaining gunboat will have to extend its patrol route to include the batteries at the Coosawhatchie mouth, sir."

"Very well, Charles, carry on. Another opportunity lost. We'll have to make the most of the next one."

CHAPTER 6
THE FALL OF FERNANDINA, FLORIDA
MARCH 1, 1862

The March sun rose red and swollen over the Atlantic shore of Georgia. Acting Master Roswell Lamson and Sailing Master Tobias St. John stood at the rail of the *Wabash*, gazing into the mouth of St. Andrews Sound south of Jekyll Island before descending into their armed howitzer boats for the attack on Fernandina, Florida. The twenty-four-foot howitzer boats each mounted a small four-pounder field gun in the bows, which could be fired from the ship's boat, or later used as field artillery in any land engagements. The boats would be towed by several shallow-draft light gunboats into St. Andrews Sound and through the inside passage south up Cumberland Sound to Florida's St. Mary's River estuary, near the town of Fernandina. Fernandina was guarded by Fort Clinch, a Federal coast fort taken by the Rebels at the beginning of the war.

"We'll probably spend our first day here taking soundings past Cumberland Island on the way down to the St. Mary's River and Fernandina," said Tobias. "I told Flag Officer Du Pont that my pilots' network sent word the Rebs have abandoned Fort Clinch, but I guess he has to be cautious. It would save a lot of time if we just sailed south to St. Mary's."

"I know you set great store by your informants, Tobias, but I remain skeptical, at least about this bit of information," said Roswell. "Why wouldn't the Rebels fight to maintain a port for their blockade-runners? We've already captured Port Royal and Roanoke Island, and we threaten Coosawhatchie. Fernandina is the southernmost rail port in the South, and Fort Clinch guards it. They need to hold on to all they can.

No, I think your boys may be wrong on this one."

"Oh, ye of little faith. You're just thirsting for more action, my piratical friend." Tobias laughed. "I can see you now, cutlass a-waving."

Roswell grinned self-consciously. He and Tobias had become friends aboard *Wabash,* and the recent action on the Broad River had deepened that relationship. Roswell quickly steered the conversation back to the topic. "Who did Du Pont appoint to collect your intelligence while we're gone?"

"The *Sabine* stayed at Port Royal, and her first officer will meet each week with my pilot. He wasn't too happy, but I explained to him that his findings still go directly to the flag officer."

They entered their boats and were taken in tow by one of the small gunboats, the *Ottawa.* The deeper-draft ships departed for the St Mary's River. After a day of sounding and groundings, the *Ottawa* towed her train of boats through to Fort Clinch on Amelia Island to find that the Confederates had, in fact, to everyone's surprise (except Tobias), evacuated it, as well as a battery nearer to Fernandina.

Roswell and Tobias led their men to seize the railroad bridge between Amelia Island and the mainland, and stationed videttes, or pickets, on the mainland side until morning. At daybreak, their men secured Fernandina, and the *Ottawa* went upriver to seize the town of St. Mary's.

Tobias and Roswell established quarters in Fort Clinch, as *Wabash* and the army transports had finally arrived off St Mary's. The fleet landed troops, who took over garrison responsibilities in the two towns. They gazed over the parapet and across the broad blue expanse of Cumberland Sound at the mouth of the St. Mary's River. Even in winter, the weight of the humidity was palpable.

"The conduct of our men was exemplary, Tobias," said Roswell. "The civilians in the towns remarked on it. I wish we could say the same of the army."

"Poor discipline always leads to pillaging, Roswell. You're right about our men. They're a well-disciplined crew. And you are right about Fort Clinch. Why would anyone abandon it? Nine guns, some rifled. True, the curtain wall's not complete, but there're substantial ramparts and parapets, and several bastions in good repair. The Rebs could have mounted a spirited defense. I'd have been doubtful about the intelligence, too, if I hadn't had the track record of my pilots' network to go on. It's a mystery."

CHAPTER 7
THE BATTLE OF HAMPTON ROADS
MARCH 8, 1862

The day dawned bright, the sky a brilliant blue. Rory watched as white, fluffy clouds moved slowly under a light breeze out of the northwest. The past two days had been blustery, with a cold rain. Flag Officer Buchanan had hoped to attack the day before, but the weather had made it impossible. Tucker had received a Buchanan dispatch that read:

It is my intention to appear before the enemy off Newport News tomorrow. You will, with your squadron, be prepared to join us. My object is first to destroy the frigates Congress and Cumberland and turn my attention to the batteries ashore and the gunboats. You will use your best exertions to destroy the enemy. Sink before you surrender.

- Buchanan

Upon receipt of the dispatch, Tucker had readied his squadron, and the evening previous, had anchored off Day's Neck, downstream from Mulberry Island and just out of range of the Newport News batteries.

"So much for a sea trial to work out the little problems aboard the *Virginia*," said Rory, when Tucker had read the order to his squadron officers.

"The sea trial will be from Gosport to Craney's Island at the mouth of the Elizabeth," said Captain Webb of the *Teaser*.

"Gentlemen, from the rigging, we can see the mouth of the Elizabeth." Tucker rose from his cabin table, where he had convened his officers. "I'll want the midshipman with the sharpest vision, and any of the rest of you who are drawn to the mastheads, to watch for the *Virginia* after daybreak. It will take her ninety minutes to clear the river, at least."

The morning following, officers of the squadron festooned the rigging, watching for a sign of smoke toward Gosport, which would herald the sally of the world's newest ironclad.

At noon, a call from the masthead of the *Patrick Henry* identified smoke from more than one Confederate steamer approaching the channel at Wise's Point, near Craney Island. It had to be *Virginia, Beaufort* and *Raleigh*.

"Beat to quarters!"

The command, given by commanders of English and American warships for at least two hundred years when action was imminent, sent the drummer aboard the flagship to his drum, and sailors to their battle-stations.

As *Virginia* and her consorts traversed the distance between Craney Island and Newport News, their Confederate sister-ships, *Patrick Henry*, followed by *Jamestown, Teaser* and *Old Dominion,* stood down-river at full steam, gun crews at the ready. Tucker surmised that the Yankee gunners in the Newport News batteries would expect him to come down-channel at the most extreme range possible. Instead, he led his squadron as close to the Newport News shore as he could, and the first two batteries were unable to adjust their elevations in time. Their salvos went over the squadron entirely. The third battery depressed their muzzles, and damaged the *Patrick Henry*, wounding several members of one gun crew.

Meanwhile, Buchanan was making good on his intent to engage the sloop of war USS *Cumberland*. *Cumberland* formerly was a frigate, bigger than a sloop of war. Her upper works had been cut down, and her armament decreased from 44 to 24 guns, making her a "razee", a ship "razed" or torn down. *Cumberland* and the sailing frigate *Congress* were moored under the guns of the Newport News batteries, and within rifle shot of Union infantry troops on the shore edge, as well as field artillery batteries. Rory stared at *Cumberland* through his glass, remembering his successful engagement with her while he served aboard *Rose of Clifden* in the early days of the war. Further east, near Fort Monroe, the Union frigates *Roanoke, Minnesota*, and *St. Lawrence* had begun to move toward Newport News, but they were still well out of range.

Virginia closed the range to the *Cumberland*. The forward pivot sent shell after shell into the wooden sloop of war, smashing, exploding, splintering, killing. *Cumberland's* twelve-gun broadsides were striking *Virginia's* side time after time, shaking and vibrating the huge armored casemate, but doing no damage to her crew or fighting capability. *Virginia* came under fire from the *Congress*, enduring 25-gun broadsides from the big Union frigate with no apparent effect.

Raleigh and *Beaufort* opened fire on USS *Congress*, to counter her pounding of *Virginia*. The Rebel ironclad was at full speed, nine knots, and four hundred yards from *Cumberland*, her bow aimed amidships at the wooden sloop. The iron ram at *Virginia's* bow crashed into *Cumberland* below the waterline, tearing a huge hole in her hull.

The *Cumberland* began to founder, water pouring in through the hole in her hull. The weight of the sinking sloop bore down on the *Virginia's* ram, still imbedded in *Cumberland's* side, as the Rebel steamer, engine at full astern, tried to pull away from the sloop that now threatened to take her under.

As *Cumberland* settled in the water, the surgeon and his mates on the lowest deck did their best to bring the wounded to the upper decks. *Cumberland* still fired broadsides as rapidly as ever, even though her gun deck was awash. With a lurch, *Virginia* pulled free of the sinking Yankee. *Cumberland* finally went under, her ensign still flying. Taylor Wood thought, *no ship was ever fought more gallantly.*

Virginia's stern pivot had thus far been the only gun the ironclad could bring to bear on *Congress*. Buchanan knew he must turn *Virginia* around to bring her broadside to bear on the Union frigate, a long slow process of moving upriver and then back, all the while under fire from *Congress*, the shore batteries, and *Minnesota*, which had moved within range.

It was at that moment when the James River squadron passed the Newport News batteries and entered the arena. They were still under fire from shore, and now from *Minnesota* and *Congress*. *Patrick Henry* and *Jamestown* returned the fire from *Congress*, and were joined by *Virginia*, now positioned for maximum effect.

Teaser and *Old Dominion* were engaging the shore batteries and the Yankee field artillery with their shell-firing pivots. They were under a hail of return fire. "Hot work, Mr. Glendenning," Rory shouted through the smoke of battle.

"No doubt, sir," said the executive officer, ducking as a huge column of water from a Yankee 32-pound ball crashed down on the pilothouse.

"Sir," said Midshipman Ormsby, "The *Minnesota*, she's gone aground, sir." Ormsby handed Rory his glass. The big deep-draft forty-gun frigate, being towed into shoal water to avoid *Virginia*'s ram, had grounded at the three-fathom curve.

"Keep an eye on *Virginia*, midshipman, as if she could fly a signal in this hell storm." Rory gave Ormsby his telescope back.

"*Congress* aground, sir. She's surrendering." The Yankee frigate had raised a white flag. "*Beaufort* alongside to remove the prisoners and burn the ship, sir. *Virginia*'s signal."

"Look," said Glendenning, "the shore batteries and infantry are firing on our ships while we're taking the wounded off under flag of truce!"

"Sure, Buchanan's going to be one pissed-off sailor, at that breach of the rules of war!" Rory shook his head grimly. "Those damn Yankee soldiers don't realize they're causin' the deaths of their own sailors."

"*Patrick Henry*'s number, sir." Ormsby read the flagship's signal to Tucker. "Burn the *Congress*."

Glendenning trained a glass on the *Patrick Henry*. "She's launching boats. It must be too shoal for her to come alongside *Congress*. Whoa! She's hit. Looks to be a boiler explosion. Paddle wheels stopped, sir."

"Hard a-starboard, helmsman. All ahead full, Mr. Glendenning. Mr. Edwards," Rory shouted to the boatswain on the deckhouse. "Get a detail ready with a hawser for towing. We're taking *Patrick Henry* under tow." Tucker's ship was drifting toward the north shore, and under intense fire from the Union troops there.

"At least *Old Dominion* will be doing something she's actually designed for - towing!" Rory clapped Glendenning on the shoulder. "Make sure we maintain fire on the shore. We're both getting to short range. We need to keep those Yanks busy."

As the tug slowed and came to a parallel course with the steamer, the deck crew on the tug's fantail tossed a heaving line to the seamen on the bow of the *Patrick Henry*. Attached to the towing hawser, the line was quickly hauled aboard the paddle wheeler and when the hawser followed, it was secured to her fore bitts. The tug slowly took up the strain on the hawser. "All ahead one third," said Rory to Glendenning, who relayed the order to MacKenzie in the engine room.

"*Teaser* and *Jamestown* closing on us from astern, sir," said Ormsby.

"Very good, midshipman," Rory replied. "We can use all the help we can get."

The tug was rocked by a tremendous jolt from amidships, followed by a cloud of scalding steam. "Boiler's hit, sir," cried Glendenning.

"Sure, you've the right of it, Mr. Glendenning. Get those men out of the engine room. Mr. Ormsby, signal to flag, 'boiler disabled, in need of tow', if you please."

"Aye, aye, sir." Ormsby, and everyone else in the wheelhouse, seemed to be reassured by Rory's calm demeanor. *If they only knew how I'm shakin' inside,* Rory thought. *I've met the divil and he's afloat on Hampton Roads!*

Old Dominion's towline was transferred to *Jamestown*, and she towed *Patrick Henry* out of range of the batteries. *Teaser* did the same for *Old Dominion*. As they headed for Sewell's Point, Ormsby made another report. "*Congress* on fire, sir. *Virginia* has discontinued the action and is headed our way.

"Not a moment too soon, Mr. Ormsby; night is falling. Ask Mr. MacKenzie to report to the wheelhouse, if you please. I'll want reports from all division officers on what it will take to have this ship in action tomorrow morning. Lots to do, gentlemen!"

Rory reached for the waist-level brass rail that ringed the pilothouse, and clutched it with both hands. *I'm exhausted, without a doubt,* he thought. *The action ended just in time. I'll not expect everyone to be razor-sharp tonight as we continue the work, not judging from the way I feel.*

The Confederate fleet anchored under the protection of the batteries on Sewell's Point, on the south shore of the Roads. This anchorage would afford the Confederates more time for rest, and give quick access to the remainder of the Federal squadron in the morning, absent the necessity of a long and tortuously slow procession down the Elizabeth River from Norfolk and the Navy Yard. The disadvantage of this anchorage was its distance from the Naval Hospital and from the repair facilities of the yard. Rory's ship needed both.

When the round shot had pierced the boiler, hot steam had seriously scalded several firemen in *Old Dominion's* engine room. The boiler itself would need to be patched if the tug was to take part in the next day's battle.

"It's a simple thing, really, sir," said Chief Engineer MacKenzie. We just require a patch and the artisans to weld it."

As they anchored, Rory and Chief MacKenzie were rowed to the *Patrick Henry*, where Rory received permission to have his injured crewmen transported to Portsmouth Hospital, and to seek help for his boiler from the Navy Yard. He also decided to visit the *Virginia* briefly to check on how his friends had weathered the battle.

"Quick, Chief, to the cutter." The six strongest oars aboard the tug drove the cutter to the side of CSS *Virginia*, coxswained by Midshipman Ormsby. "Wait here, gentlemen," said Rory as he boarded the ironclad through an entry-port. "I'll be right back."

Rory found Taylor, smoke-blackened, grimy, and exhausted, having just concluded an inspection of the outside of the casemate. "How are you, Taylor, are you wounded?"

"No, Rory, just a bit battered. But Bob was wounded trying to burn the *Congress*. He was shot in the gut, but I think he'll be all right. He and Flag Officer Buchanan are being transferred to the naval hospital. I think he'll recover, too. How were your casualties, Rory?"

"I had three firemen scalded when the boiler was hit, and one gun crewman took a minie ball in the arm from the Indiana regiment ashore," Rory replied. "None dead. What's the overall butcher-bill?"

Taylor looked grim. "Eight dead, six of those from *Patrick Henry*.

Nineteen wounded, plus yours. Buchanan was so mad when the troops fired on our men taking off *Congress'* wounded under flag of truce, he went on deck firing a rifle, and took a minie ball in his hip. I counted ninety-eight indentations in our casemate from shot." He brightened a bit. "What a testimony to the armor! And we destroyed two Union ships and killed hundreds of Yankees!"

"The enemy, our friends," Rory sighed. "And tomorrow, another day. Good-bye, Taylor! I'm off to the Yard to get my boiler repaired." And with that Rory reboarded his cutter, and up the Elizabeth they went to seek out welders and mechanics.

The Yard was ablaze with lights, and MacKenzie, the veteran engineer, quickly found the help he needed. As men and boiler plate were being loaded, Rory looked up to find the Yard commandant, himself.

"Commodore Forrest! *Old Dominion* is in your debt for the boiler repair these fine lads are about to effect!"

"Captain Dunbrody, my congratulations on your part in the action. Several of us from the Yard were aboard the tug CSS *Harmony* today as observers. You were bold to take Tucker in tow right under the Yankee guns!"

"Thank you, sir. We'll be back at it in the morning if your lads here are successful." The artisans beamed under the gaze of their commander. *That can't hurt,* thought Rory.

By eleven o'clock, the cutter had reached Sewell's Point, and the Yard's workmen were aboard *Old Dominion.* Work commenced immediately. Rory hoped the boiler patch shaping, hammering, and welding would be completed in time for his crew to snatch a few hours of sleep before the new day's action began.

As Rory dozed in the captain's chair in the wheelhouse, he would occasionally awaken to see the *Congress* still afire. The flames would periodically reach a shotted gun, and the boom of the report would startle Rory into wakefulness. Officers and crew of the *Virginia* and the other ships, too excited to sleep, could be seen on their upper decks looking at the frigate aflame.

At one point, Rory saw a low craft, her deck almost awash, with an odd-looking superstructure like a cheese-box, cross in front of

Minnesota, silhouetted in the glare from *Congress.* Just after midnight, the fires burning on the Union frigate reached the magazine and she exploded, sending great bulks of fiery materials blazing hundreds of feet into the air, as the timbers of the hull, hissing, crackling, sank beneath the surface of the Roads.

CHAPTER 8
HAMPTON ROADS, THE SECOND DAY
MARCH 9TH, 1862

Dawn was breaking. Thanks to the hard work of the Yard crews, the *Old Dominion*'s boiler had been patched and tested. Fortunately, it had been struck by round shot, not an exploding shell, and the impact had been at the top of the boiler, which was easier to access. MacKenzie had steam up in the engine room, and the welds were holding. At 6:00 a.m., the *Virginia*, followed by the other Confederate ships, weighed anchor and bore down upon the still-grounded *Minnesota*, firing a shot at the frigate as soon as she came within range.

A question in many minds during the night had been: who will command? Franklin Buchanan was in Portsmouth Hospital. His command pennant still flew from the jack staff of the *Virginia*. Did this mean that the time-honored tradition of next in rank succeeding to command had been abandoned? Most officers assumed that in the absence of Buchanan, the command would devolve to Jack Tucker, the next most senior officer. But with Buchanan's flag still flying that morning, Tucker simply continued to command *Patrick Henry*, and *Virginia* approached *Minnesota* under the command of her first lieutenant, Catesby ap R. Jones.

James Rochelle, executive officer of *Patrick Henry*, and Lieutenant Carson, second lieutenant, puzzled over the command question as they looked out over the waters of Hampton Roads at the *Minnesota*, aground.

"The command ought to have been formally transferred to Captain Tucker in conformance with navy custom," said Rochelle, "but here we are, following Lieutenant Jones."

"It must rankle Captain Tucker, sir," said Carson, "but Jones is a good man and we must do with what we have."

"Well put, Mr. Carson. Look, alongside *Minnesota!* It looks like a shingle on the water with a cheese box rising from the center! No paddle wheels, no sails, no stack. What could it be?"

"Whatever it is, sir, it's firing on *Virginia*." Carson pointed to two puffs of smoke from the turret of the USS *Monitor*, the Union ironclad Rory had noticed in the glow from the burning *Congress* the night before. Designed by John Ericsson, and constructed in Brooklyn in less time than it took to reconstruct the *Merrimack*, it had arrived during the night to take part in the battle, and, in so doing, had transformed the battle into the first clash of armored ships in history.

The *Monitor* fired its two eleven-inch Dahlgrens from a revolving turret, supported by a single, vertical iron shaft set in the center of the turret deck. Two single-piston engines within the turret itself controlled its rotation. The *Monitor's* armored deck was 172 feet long, longer than the hull beneath. The deck was only seven inches above the water, making it an improbable target. The turret was a more promising target, but it was protected by nine inches of layered, one-inch iron plate. The *Monitor* was much more maneuverable than *Virginia*, and drew roughly half as much water, thirteen feet versus twenty-two.

Because of shoal water extending from *Minnesota*, the deep-draft *Virginia* brought her broadside to bear on the Union frigate at a range of one mile. The *Monitor* quickly left the *Minnesota's* side, closing the range on the Rebel ironclad. Each time *Monitor* fired, her turret would rotate so that the guns no longer faced her target, and could be run in to the turret and reloaded without fear of being struck by *Virginia's* return fire.

Rory stood in his wheelhouse, his telescope fixed on the two ironclads. Quentin Glendenning, his able first lieutenant, stood beside him. "Look, Mr. Glendenning, they're circlin' each other like a pair of lads in a boxing ring."

Glendenning had his own telescope. "And those guns in the Yankee's turret are eleven-inch Dahlgrens, by the look of 'em, captain. They throw a 180-pound bolt. One of those hits us, we're kindling!"

"Fortunately for us and the rest of the squadron, *Virginia* has the

Yankee's full attention." Rory could see the other Rebel gunboats; all at a respectful range from the *Monitor*, just in case. Keeping their distance from the *Monitor* had the effect of placing the *Minnesota* at long to extreme range, but Rory concentrated the fire on the frigate, realizing that the gun they carried would not harm the *Monitor* in the slightest.

"Saints preserve us, Mr. Glendenning, it must be like the fires of hell in those two ships." Rory shook his head in awe. "Concussion, wood frames splinterin', temperatures risin', smoke collectin'; look, *Virginia's* lost her stack, blown away. That'll reduce her power and fill the ship with smoke! Ah, the poor divils."

The two ironclads had pounded one another for over an hour when Glendenning cried out, "Sir, *Virginia's* aground, on the edge of the North Channel." He pointed to the casemated ironclad, to port of *Old Dominion* and three-quarters of a mile away.

"Helmsman, hard a-port! Steady up on *Virginia*. Glendenning, tell MacKenzie full speed ahead. Everything she's got! Faith, and see the damned Yankee. She's taking position at two hundred yards where none of *Virginia's* guns will bear!" The tug increased speed, throwing a huge bow wave as her blunt bow surged through the water.

"Mr. Edwards!" Rory shouted out the wheelhouse window to the boatswain on the afterdeck. "We'll be gettin' a towing hawser on *Virginia*! Same drill as yesterday with *Patrick Henry*. Different result, I hope to heaven!"

Edwards marshaled the afterguard, readying the heaving line with its heavy monkey fist, and flaking the thick towing hawser down along the after deck. Two burly deckhands secured one end of the hawser to the after bitt, a sturdy, six-inch by six-inch post with its lower end set in frames belowdeck, and a one-and-a-half inch diameter rod extending from each side of its upper end on the afterdeck.

"Mr. Edwards," Rory shouted once again. "I'd be obliged if you'd have a detail check the readiness of the cutter and the dory. I suspect we may be using them." The tug's larger boat, the cutter, was in chocks on the deckhouse roof, itself a deck. A small, six-man dory was secured, upside down, on top of the wheelhouse.

"Mr. Glendenning, if we take a hit from *Monitor*, and you're still standing when I am not, do not hesitate to get the men off if we can no longer carry out the tow. Sure, and those are hellish big guns!"

Virginia had gone aground with her bow toward the shore between Newport News and Fort Monroe. *Monitor* was two hundred yards off her starboard bow, positioned so that the bow pivot could not bear on her, neither from the bow port nor from the starboard "corner" port. Rory brought *Old Dominion* in to *Virginia* from astern, swinging her stern around to *Virginia's* stern.

Rory could see sand and mud being churned up by *Virginia's* huge screw, as her Chief Engineer, H. Ashton Ramsey, tied the safety valves down, and threw pitch, oily cotton waste, and every other quick-burning combustible he could think of into the boiler fires to raise steam enough to pull the ironclad off the shoal. *Sure, maybe with a little pull from Old Dominion, we'll tip the balance,* Rory thought.

Sailors emerged from *Virginia's* after gunport as the tug's heaving-line monkey fist landed on the after deck. Sailors splashed through the six inches of water covering the after deck and seized the heaving line and the hawser at its end. They made it fast to a towing bitt. Taylor Wood appeared on *Virginia's* after deck.

"Taylor, I'm going to take up slack slowly," Rory shouted through his speaking trumpet. "When we're taut, ask Mr. Ramsey to give her all she's got. We'll do the same."

Taylor gave a wave, and ducked through the gunport, followed by the crewmen of the *Virginia's* afterguard. Rory noted that the *Virginia* had used up so much coal and ammunition that the after deck, which was designed to be submerged under two feet of water, was now barely awash. Then, from the corner of his eye, he saw *Monitor* shifting position toward *Old Dominion.*

"Brace yourselves, men! I believe we're about to receive an introduction to the world's most modern warship!" Rory watched as the hawser tightened. *For the love of Mary, hurry up, hurry up,* he prayed. *Sure, and I'm not the most devout man, but this is a moment when it seems fully appropriate,* he thought.

Rory stared at the *Monitor's* turret as it slowly and steadily revolved. He could see the two gunports rotate into view, and then found himself looking down the muzzles of the two eleven-inch guns. "Hawser taut, sir," called Edwards from the afterdeck.

"Mackenzie, all ahead full!" Rory shouted the order himself down the speaking tube, unwilling to take time for Glendenning to relay the command as protocol dictated. The *Old Dominion* surged ahead.

Rory thought he saw *Virginia* move slightly as the tug's big screw propeller churned. The first lieutenant repeated the order by ringing 'full ahead' on the engine room telegraph. The telegraph bell was the last thing Rory heard before he was deafened by a huge roar, and he was knocked flat on the wheelhouse deck.

Rory and Glendenning, each semi-conscious, staggered to their feet, supporting themselves by grasping the railing running inside the wheelhouse. Rory looked at Quentin Glendenning who was bleeding from the ears. *I suppose I am too, I've no doubt,* he mused, dazedly.

They looked aft, together. "Holy Mother of God! Quentin, Jasus, the bastards have gone and blown the stern away." *Old Dominion* was settling slowly by the stern. Two 180-pound bolts from *Monitor* had blown the frame aft of the deckhouse into splinters. The after bitts were no more. The hawser trailed from the stern of the *Virginia*, no longer attached to the tug.

A few of the afterguard had managed to reach the deckhouse. Boatswain Edwards' mangled body was half submerged, as the port side of the tug was sinking lower into the water, now lapping at the gunwale.

Engineer MacKenzie appeared in the wheelhouse. "Sir, I've cleared the men from the engine room. The boiler fire's out and we're taking water fast. The shaft is bent all to blazes, sir."

"Very good, Mr. MacKenzie. You did well. Ormsby, are you alive?"

"So far, sir!"

"Get aft and get the cutter into the water. Get the wounded and the crew aboard." Rory took a deep breath and tried to shake off his not-un-rational fear of going in the water. *I wish Tobias were here. I could use a strong swimmer close by*, he thought, shivering in the heat of battle. Tobias had rescued Rory from drowning in Puget's Sound, an entire war ago.

Rory forced himself into action, distracting himself from the specter of going overboard. "Mr. Glendenning, muster the gun crew forward. Then take charge of getting the dory in the water at the bow. I'm going to maintain fire on *Monitor* 'til we go under, and get the gunners off in the dory. Get a detail to bring up every shell we've got left for the Parrott. Then take command of the cutter and make for the *Virginia*. She's closest."

"Aye, aye, sir. Look, sir. The *Virginia*. I think she's starting to move off the shoal!"

"Heaven save us, you're right, Quentin. Get a move on. We've only minutes 'til she's free, and moving away."

Rory moved to the foredeck, and directed the gun crew, now reassembled, to train on *Monitor*. "Come, lads, maybe we'll get lucky, and put one through her gunport." Just then, Rory could swear he felt the ancient battle spirit of Ireland's kernes and gallowglasses surge through his veins.

Virginia was now backing off the shoal, and with her rudder to port, was turning her bow to starboard, bringing her bow pivot and eventually her port broadside to bear on *Monitor*.

The cutter, with Glendenning, Ormsby, MacKenzie, and the crew, whole and wounded, had reached the *Virginia*. They were quickly taken aboard through the stern gunport, as the ironclad swung its bow toward *Monitor*.

The *Virginia*, in backing her stern to port, cleared a field of fire for the eight-inch Parrott on the bow of the *Old Dominion*. The tug was settling by the stern but on a keel even enough to enable the Parrott to fire. "Serve vent and sponge! Load. Prime." Rory peered over the barrel of the pivot gun. "Train left." The gun was aimed directly at *Monitor's* turret. "Fire!" The round exploded against the turret's armored side, doing no discernible damage. "Serve vent, and sponge."

Monitor, having effectively destroyed the tug, was wasting no more shots on her as she slowly settled beneath the surface of Hampton Roads. Rory managed three more rounds before he ordered the gun crew into the dory. Before Rory joined them, he rushed into the wheelhouse and grabbed his beloved Irish flag from the signal locker. Stuffing it inside his shirt, he tumbled into the dory as they cast off. The water had just reached the gun truck. They pulled mightily for the *Virginia,* clambered aboard the shallowly-submerged after deck, and splashed for the gunport, casting the dory adrift.

"Welcome aboard, Mr. Dunbrody!" Taylor Wood stood near the seven-inch Brooke pivot rifle he commanded. "I've already allocated your men to duty stations," he said. "It's a great boon for some of our men to be relieved for a time. I'll take your gun crew here at the stern pivot, if you please."

"Aye, aye, Mr. Wood," said Rory. "An isn't it a relief to be inside armor after facin' those Dahlgrens with naught between us but air? I'd best be reportin' to Lieutenant Jones."

"Sir," said Rory's gun captain, Blakely, standing at the stern gunport, "she's going down."

Rory rushed to the gunport. *Old Dominion's* bow was almost beneath the surface. "Sure, that was a short-lived command," he said to Taylor and the tug's gun crew, "but she was a good old bucket, right, lads?"

"Aye, sir, she was," said Blakely.

"She'll be a fine menace to navigation, sinkin' at the edge of the North Channel, I'm thinkin', Taylor," said Rory.

"May many a Yankee hull find her bones, then," Taylor turned to his gun crew, and Rory made his way to the pilothouse, to find Catesby ap Roger Jones, Lieutenant Commanding.

As Rory walked forward along the gun deck, the rush of battle excitement subsided for a moment. He suddenly realized that he had lost a command. Like any commander whose ship has sunk, he would face a court of inquiry, and, possibly, a court martial. *Ah, well,* he thought, *first, to live through the day!*

Rory noted the condition of the casemate interior after two days of intense battle. The armor outside had sustained hundreds of hits. Inside, the wood backing for the armor was splintered in a number of places. Where the backing had been damaged, dents were visible in the rolled iron plating. Soot covered every surface, as the stack, now restored, had been shot away the day before to the extent that the boilers had lost draft.

Rory noted that two of the broadside guns had been hit in the barrels, and were damaged and truncated. Now, after each shot, the gun crew had to pour water on the muzzle to cool it and extinguish the fires set by the muzzle flash igniting the wood backing around the gun ports.

Rory found Jones near the forward pivot, in earnest conversation with Lieutenant Eggleston, commanding the starboard broadside guns. When they had concluded, he reported. "Lieutenant Dunbrody, late of the *Old Dominion,* with crew, reporting, sir."

"Oh, yes, Dunbrody," said Jones, distractedly, and then brightened. "Dunbrody, we're very grateful for your attempt to pull us off the shoal. Your effort may have been the difference. Sorry about you losing the tug. A mighty spirited response, you firing at the Yankee practically 'til your deck was under water. I'm recommending recognition for you, if I survive."

"Very kind of you, sir. Commodore Buchanan did instruct us to sink before surrendering," Rory said dryly. He brushed his hands together expectantly and looked around. "How can I serve, now that I'm aboard? Mr. Wood has assigned my men to duty stations."

Jones thought for a moment. "I'll ask you to serve as flag lieutenant, for the rest of the day, Mr. Dunbrody, the same role Mr. Minor played yesterday. Just keep station on me. I'll give you various duties."

"Aye, aye, sir. Nice to see you again, Mr. Eggleston," he said to the starboard battery commander.

"It seems a long time since New Orleans, Mr. Dunbrody."

The two ironclads were once again pounding away at one another. Jones peered out a gun port at the *Monitor.* "Mr. Dunbrody."

"Sir."

"Go aloft to the pilothouse on the spar deck. Send my runners, Midshipman Marmaduke and my clerk, Mr. Sinclair, to report to me aft on the gun deck. Assume the watch, and tell the helmsman to port his helm until the bow bears on the Yankee. We're going to ram her."

Jones strode aft to find Taylor Wood. "Mr. Wood, muster a boarding party at the forward gunports. We'll ram and then board."

"Aye, aye, sir. Lieutenant Butt, Bo'sun Hasker, your assistance, if you please. Call for volunteers among the crew for a boarding party.

Organize them into sections. We'll need men with sledgehammers and spikes, to wedge that damn revolving turret, and a group to light and throw oakum grenades down pipes, and cover vents with wet blankets. We'll want armed men to give the other sections cover. Understood?"

"Aye, aye," Wally Butt and the boatswain responded.

Rory had introduced himself to Marmaduke and Sinclair, and took command in the pilothouse as they exited. The *Virginia* turned slowly to present her bow to the *Monitor.* Jones returned to the spar deck and called for 'all ahead full' as the *Virginia* bore down on the *Monitor.* At the moment before impact, *Monitor* turned aside, and *Virginia* was able only to strike a glancing blow, and then sheered off, making boarding the *Monitor* impossible.

As the ships collided, *Monitor* fired a salvo at point-blank range. The shield where the rounds struck was pushed in three inches. If a second salvo had struck the same spot, Lieutenant Wood was convinced it would have penetrated the shield.

"Sir, the Yankee is drawing off into shoal water," Rory reported as he looked through the slits in the pilothouse bulkhead.

"I wonder what he's up to?" Jones was not confident that he'd driven *Monitor* off.

"He could be replenishing ammunition in the turret, sir," Rory ventured. "They must have a complicated system of sending up shells and charges from below, with that rotating turret. You'd have to line up the apertures in the gun deck and the turret deck precisely."

"Then we'll take this opportunity to deal with *Minnesota,*" said Jones. "Mr. Sinclair, ask the gun division commanders to shift target to *Minnesota.*" The gunners soon were rearranging the interior of the Union frigate, flagship of the South Atlantic Blockading Squadron when Flag Officer Goldsborough was present. Fortunately for Goldsborough, he was down the Carolina coast directing an amphibious operation against New Berne, North Carolina; and his empty quarters aboard *Minnesota,* rather than he, suffered the *Virginia's* shelling.

The USS *Dragon,* a tug alongside *Minnesota,* exploded in a cloud of steam during the Rebel bombardment. "Not a good day for tugs, Mr. Dunbrody," observed Jones. "Speaking of which, I was surprised not to see

Teaser alongside you when we were aground."

"I believe she was at the other end of our line, sir. I did note *Patrick Henry* and *Jamestown* coming your way, but they were too far distant to arrive in time." *Sure, I'm not about to throw mud at sister ships,* thought Rory.

"The Yankee's returning, sir," Sinclair reported.

"Very well, Mr. Sinclair, please ask the gun division commanders to fire at the little pilothouse box at the bow. We'll see if we can blind her." Sure enough, as *Monitor* returned to extremely close range, the *Virginia's* shells struck the pilothouse and exploded, temporarily blinding her commander. The *Monitor* once again retired to shoal water, and the *Virginia* was unable now to follow or to close with *Minnesota* because of falling tide and serious leakage caused by the grounding. Her stocks of ammunition were low, and Jones decided to retire from the battle scene. The day's end found the Confederate squadron at the Navy Yard.

CHAPTER 9
REPORT TO PRESIDENT DAVIS

Once the *Virginia* had been placed in drydock, the crew was released from duty. The officers went aboard *Patrick Henry,* the flag vessel now afloat. While aboard, Wood received an order to report to Buchanan in the hospital. Upon his return, he entered the wardroom, where Rory was packing a small sea bag.

"Rory, you look like a man about to travel." Wood sat down at the table, and placed a large, folded United States flag on the chair next to him.

"And aren't I the lad with one ship sunk out from under, and the next in drydock? So I went to our fine commodore, and I says 'Your Worship, could I be easin' up the line to Richmond to see a fair-haired lady, me being without a ship, and all?' And Commodore Tucker saw the right of it, and I'm off for three days."

"You are brazen and outrageous, my friend," said Wood with an appreciative chuckle.

"And who was my instructor at the Academy where I learned my behavior, now?"

"*Touché.* As for me, Flag Officer Buchanan has asked me to carry a dispatch to President Davis, and the flag of the *Congress,* and report to the President on the battle."

"Be sure and give my regards to your Uncle Jefferson." Wood was President Davis' nephew. "Seriously, now, there's no better man to tell the tale than you, Taylor. Will y'be takin' the train in the morning?"

"That's my plan, Rory."

"We'll be on the same train, then."

"Good, Rory. I'll come by for you as I leave, and we can travel together."

On the train trip to Petersburg, and then on to Richmond, Wood found himself cast in a hero's role. At each stop, he was called upon to recount the details of the battle, and the reaction of the crowds was uplifting. On one occasion, as Rory looked on in mixed admiration and amusement at Wood's obvious discomfort as being seen as a celebrity, Wood turned the tables on the laughing Irishman by introducing him as the captain whose ship was sunk under him as he tried to rescue the *Virginia*. The crowd loved the story, and roared its approval.

As they pulled into the Richmond station, Wood said, "Rory, I must report to Mallory, and then he'll take me to the President. Come along with me. You're every bit the participant that I was and it will be instructional to them to see how we functioned as a squadron."

"No, Taylor, you've the order from the flag officer. I'm just on leave, and I'm a commander who lost his ship. I'm thinkin' they'd as soon not acknowledge me, what with a court martial hangin' over me."

"Nonsense. This will help the Cause. And remember, I'm senior. This is an order."

"Aye, aye, sir. I confess it's a thrill to think of meeting the President. And I do seem to get along with Secretary Mallory." Mallory had given Rory his lieutenant's commission, and had personally expressed his pleasure at Rory's conduct in action off Cape Hatteras against USS *Cumberland* and more recently, on Virginia's eastern shore.

Rory and Taylor reported to Secretary Mallory at the Mechanics Institute Building. Mallory did not raise the question of a court of inquiry. The three then walked across the square to President Davis' office, the one in the old court building. The President also had an office upstairs in the White House, several blocks away on Clay Street. Davis greeted his nephew warmly. Mallory introduced Rory to the president, and Taylor explained Rory's part in the battle.

"You young gentlemen and your comrades have given the cause of the South a great lift," exclaimed Davis, who then summoned several other cabinet members, including Secretary of War Benjamin. Taylor presented the flag of the *Congress* to the President, and the men present were startled, upon unrolling it, to find several spots saturated with blood. In the ensuing meeting, Taylor presented a candid appraisal of the battle and its portents.

"The battle was a draw," said Taylor, "so far as the two vessels engaged were concerned. "But in its general results, the advantage was with the *Monitor*."

"The *Monitor* was well handled," Taylor continued, "and saved the *Minnesota* and the remainder of the fleet at Fort Monroe. We met our equal, and I could not predict the outcome of a second engagement."

Adjutant-General Cooper turned to Rory and asked, "Mr. Dunbrody, is your thinking along similar lines?"

"It is, to be sure, sir. My father is a Southern shipbuilder; and knowing what I've learned from him, I found myself asking: 'if these ships are equals, which side can build more, faster?' Sure, I believe every man here knows the answer."

The room was silent for a moment, as each man considered the comments of the young officers. The discussion resumed and turned to the specifics; draft, speed, capabilities and repairs.

Finally, Davis said, "Gentlemen, I urge rapid completion of repairs and alterations. We still have opportunity. And you, and your comrades, have the undying gratitude of the Confederacy."

Wood spent the night at his uncle's residence in the White House of the Confederacy. He returned to Norfolk the next day. Mallory walked Rory back to his office, where he arranged for a coach to take Rory to the Farwell's home.

"Please realize, Mr. Dunbrody, what a service you all have done the navy by your action at Hampton Roads." The Secretary shook Rory's hand firmly. "Your report was candid, and accurate, but you must understand that the navy will now be looked upon as an effective service, and we shall be able to go forward without nay-sayers in Congress nibbling at our limited resources because we've failed to prove ourselves. Because of Hampton Roads, we'll be seen for the first time as a robust fighting force to be reckoned with!"

"Sure, I'm the grateful one, for the opportunity you gave me to be a part of it, Mr. Secretary."

"You've earned it, lieutenant! On the subject of ironclads, I've heard from your father and some others regarding a contract to construct an ironclad in North Carolina," said Mallory. "Please tell him I hope to respond by late spring. We will soon have some changes in the cabinet, and I must wait to seek new commitments to this project. This will take some time. I'm afraid everything seems to take more time than we have."

The Secretary's coach deposited Rory at the Farwell mansion on Church Hill, where his stamina was stretched by the need to recount the battle once again to an awakened and welcoming Carrie Anne and the entire household, including the servants. He sat next to Carrie Anne on the davenport, and held them spellbound until his eyes could no longer remain open. He fell contentedly asleep in Carrie Anne's arms. Carrie Anne's Uncle Fred and their butler Cicero helped him upstairs to a guest room, and he fell back into a sleep which lasted past mid-day.

CHAPTER 10
FLIGHT FROM NEW BERNE
MARCH 11, 1862

The war was going splendidly for General Ambrose Burnside, United States Army. He had taken and garrisoned Roanoke Island, cleared Albemarle Sound of Confederate ships, established his Fort Monroe supply lines, controlled the North Carolina coast from the Virginia line to Ocracoke Inlet, and held sway over virtually all of Pamlico Sound. It was time for the next prize: New Berne and the mouth of the Neuse River.

Eleven thousand men embarked from Roanoke Island, and Burnside's fleet anchored off Slocum Creek, near the mouth of the Neuse after sundown on March 12, 1862. New Berne lay seventeen miles up the south bank of the river. Patrick and Siobhan Dunbrody could read the handwriting on the wall. New Berne would fall to the Union forces, and a Confederate shipbuilder had best be moving on. A week later, Rory received this letter.

> *My Dear Rory:*
>
> *I hope this letter finds you well. Your sister and I have this night packed all we could into one of the big yard wagons, together with a shallow-draft dory, and set out for Scotland Neck and my friend, Peter Smith, via Williamston. Near Williamston, we will find the Roanoke River, launch the boat and proceed to Edwards Ferry, where Peter will meet us. Our yard foreman is driving us to the Roanoke, and will return to New Berne. He will live in our home and try to maintain the yard in the face of certain Yankee occupation.*
>
> *I say 'certain', as I have had many conversations recently*

with my friend, General O'B. Branch, who commands the New Berne district. O'B. is a political appointee, and no soldier, but he is energetic and determined, and has begged Richmond for more men. None have been forthcoming, and he has four thousand men to face almost three times that number, by all estimates. He is desperate.

Some of his five regiments are well-trained, and one has an interesting team of leaders. The Twenty-Sixth North Carolina is commanded by Colonel Zebulon Vance; like O'B., a political appointment, and a charismatic character if ever there was, a 'good-ol' mountain man.' His lieutenant colonel, Harry Burgwyn, is young and Virginia Military Institute-trained, a good, professional soldier. Together, they do well, and some other regiments match them, but they'll be overwhelmed, and they have no navy support. We can hear the gunboats bombarding our fortifications, even now.

We will continue to be ship builders, but in Peter's cornfield on the bank of the Roanoke. I'm hopeful that your sister's good health will continue as we move inland. As you recall, she tends to avoid illness better near the coast. So, in haste, we depart. I'll mail this from Williamston, and write with our new address soon.

With great affection,

your Da'

CHAPTER 11
THE FEDERAL ASCENT OF THE JAMES,
MARCH - MAY 1862

John Randolph Tucker received his due as "Senior Officer Present" at the second day of Hampton Roads as he appeared before the Confederate Congress to receive its Congressional Resolution to all officers who were engaged for their "unsurpassed gallantry." It was a high moment in his career, and his officers, aware of his disappointment at not commanding on the second day, were immensely pleased that he was chosen to stand in for the recovering Buchanan before Congress.

Rory and the other officers of the squadron were seated in the visitors' gallery of the Hall of Congress. The Hall of Congress had been located on the southwest corner of the second or main floor in the stately classical-revival-style Virginia capitol. The state capitol had seen double duty as the Confederate capitol building since Richmond had become the capital of the Confederacy. The south wall of the chamber featured floor-to-ceiling windows. The officers could view the handsome columns of the two-story portico. It was not uncommon for members of Congress to access the portico by stepping over the low windowsills. Tucker accepted the 'Thanks of Congress' on the officers' behalf before a joint session of the Confederate House and Senate. Navy Secretary Mallory was seated with other cabinet members in the front row. At the end of the ceremony, among the crowd in the hall outside the chambers, he motioned to Rory.

"A very satisfactory session, wouldn't you say, lieutenant?"

"Indeed, sir. Commodore Tucker is a fine commander, and very well respected by his men."

"As I said earlier, the navy is very proud of your part in the battle. But a court of inquiry is required because of the loss of your tug, and I want to apprise you of some unusual circumstances in that regard." Mallory looked solemnly at Rory.

"What's wrong, Mr. Secretary?"

"The Department of the Army has notified me of a concern from their intelligence arm, General Winder's 'Safety Committee.' Their concern regards your loyalty, given your brother's service with the Union. They also raised the question of diminished degree of loyalty to the South because you were raised in Ireland, and not North Carolina. It's nonsense, of course, but these allegations could be raised at the court of inquiry. When it's held, I'd advise you to retain your own counsel."

"Aye, aye, Mr. Secretary. I'll do that, but where could this be coming from?"

"I'm looking into that, myself, lieutenant, and very discreetly," said Mallory. "I'll let you know what I discover."

"I appreciate that, sir," said Rory, as they parted company.

Two weeks later, the men of the James River Squadron were drawn up in a hollow square on the grounds of the Gosport Navy Yard. Their officers, within the square, read them sections of the congressional resolution praising their valor. Captain Josiah Tattnall, CSN, ("Old Tat") would assume the duties of Squadron Flag Officer and commander of CSS *Virginia,* replacing "Old Buck" Buchanan, soon to be the Confederacy's first admiral. Rory had been assigned as second lieutenant aboard Tucker's *Patrick Henry*, replacing Lieutenant Carson, who, with Lieutenant Glendenning, had been reassigned to ironclads being built in Charleston, South Carolina.

Rory stood next to the *Patrick Henry's* acting master, Thomas Dornin, during the Gosport ceremony. "Well, now, Tom, have y'served with 'Old Tat' before, at all?"

"No, Rory, but I know those who have. They say he's a real fire-eater."

"Sure, he looks it, doesn't he?" The two officers smiled as they carefully glanced at their new squadron commander. Tattnall was a sixty-seven year old veteran, with deep eyes set under prominent eyebrows, and a square jaw. His white shoulder-length hair and white beard accentuated the strength of his determined appearance.

"Grizzled, I would call him, Rory," said Tom. "Definitely grizzled."

The squadron did not have long to wait to test the degree of Tattnall's resolve. In early April, the squadron officers met with Tattnall to hear his plan for destroying or capturing the *Monitor*. "Gentlemen," said Tattnall, "the Yankees under General McClellan are landing in force, and moving up the York-James peninsula. General Magruder is preparing a defensive position from Yorktown, and extending along the Warwick River. We must help our defense by taking the offensive on our battlefield here on the James!"

Tattnall shook his fist. "We will take the *Monitor!* We will attack the U.S. Army transports anchored at Hampton Creek, and when *Monitor* steams to defend them, *Virginia* will engage and the other ships of the squadron will board her, stop her vents and ports, and wedge her turret, compelling her surrender. We will take her if Hell's on the other side of her!"

Cries of "Aye, aye!" and "Hear, hear!" resounded from the spar deck of *Virginia* where the officers met.

At 6:00 a.m., April 11th, *Virginia, Patrick Henry, Jamestown, Beaufort,* and *Raleigh* sailed from the Gosport Yard, leaving Portsmouth, the Naval Hospital, Lovett Point, and Craney Island to port as they exited the Elizabeth River and bore directly for Hampton Creek, dead ahead across the Roads.

Patrick Henry was immediately astern of the flagship. Rory stood at the forward pivot with his gun crew. Midshipman Ormsby, who had also been assigned from *Old Dominion*, was Rory's runner for communications with Captain Tucker, who was stationed on the bridge above the paddle wheels. "Look, now, Mr. Ormsby," said Rory, pointing ahead, "the Commodore's assembled the crew for a bit o' prayer." On the exposed section of *Virginia's* spar deck, aft of the pilot house, a sizeable number of the crew knelt with bowed heads while Tattnall asked for blessing. "It must be Taylor's influence. He's a devout lad."

"Is that Lieutenant Wood, sir?" Ormsby asked.

"Oh, aye," replied Rory. "All the cursin' and swearin' of the crew bother him somethin' fierce. I'm afraid he's set his expectations too high, bein' they're sailors, and all. But we can use all the help we can get to bring the *Monitor* out. I know you're Jewish, but a prayer's a prayer."

"To be sure, sir, as you might say on the Emerald Isle," Ormsby commented, impishly.

"Very ecumenical of you, Ormsby. I'm confident your South Carolinian Jewish community would agree," returned Rory in kind. Returnin' t' the question of the *Monitor*, just keepin' the status quo is their best gambit, until more ships and more troops arrive. I'm wagerin' they won't budge."

"There's a huge side wheeler off Fort Monroe, sir."

"The *Vanderbilt*, I'm thinkin'. She won't budge, either."

Rory gazed across the water. "Mr. Ormsby," said Rory, "help a lad raised in Galway to understand the complexities of the South. How is it that we North Carolinians pronounce the name of our city, Beaufort, with a 'Bo', yet you, a South Carolinian, lament the loss of your Port Royal Sound city, Beaufort, pronounced with a 'Bew'?"

"States' Rights, sir, the very thing we're fighting for!"

"You're very quick, midshipman." Rory smiled. "You'll be a lieutenant in no time!"

"Aye, aye, sir, if you say so, sir." Ormsby laughed. "It's quite an experience, sir, serving with an Irish North Carolinian."

"T'be sure, Mr. Ormsby. Look, you can see *Monitor*, now, under the guns of Fort Monroe." Rory pointed to starboard, where the *Monitor* was raising steam. "Maybe she'll come out when we take these transports, but I've my doubts."

Virginia bore away to starboard, directly for *Monitor*, and began steaming in circles just outside the range of the Fort's guns. *Jamestown* and *Raleigh* bore down on the transports, three brigs at the mouth of Hampton Creek, while *Beaufort* and *Patrick Henry* fired on the shore batteries to cover their approach. *Monitor* did not move. "Careful and steady does it, men," called Rory to his gun crew as they continued to lay down fire on the shore batteries.

Jamestown had the three transports under tow, U.S. ensigns flying upside-down from their gaff peaks. The prizes were towed right in front of

Monitor, just out of range of the guns of Fort Monroe. The Federal ships made no response. In exasperation, Tattnall fired a gun to windward, hoisted the captured flags aboard *Virginia* under the Stars and Bars, and led his squadron back toward Sewell's Point. Tattnall tried again, but nothing would induce the Federals to engage the Rebel ironclad.

McClellan's army slowly advanced up the peninsula toward Richmond. On April 20, Tucker assembled his officers and the captains of the other squadron vessels, except the *Virginia*.

"Gentlemen, we've received orders from Richmond," Tucker said. "Flag Officer Tattnall is to remain in Norfolk, to guard Norfolk and our rear while I take the rest of the squadron, you all, upstream to coordinate with General Joe Johnston's defense of the capital. Of course, Norfolk must be the flag officer's first concern, so our rear will be unprotected."

Tucker sighed in resignation. "I wish the Navy Department could spend some time in these waters, to see what we're up against. I'm meeting with General Joe Johnston tomorrow, to coordinate our activities with his in defense of the capital. I suspect we'll be transports and artillery support for infantry over the next weeks."

Tucker's prediction was correct. For the next two weeks, the James River Squadron ferried troops, fired on Union artillery batteries, and operated as an extension of Johnston's cavalry in the stretch of the river between City Point and Chapin's Bluff. Meanwhile, Tattnall fumed at the removal of much of his command, and its placement "under the authority of a landsman who can know nothing of the nature of the naval service." It became apparent that Johnston's forces were unable to hold back McClellan's advancing army, and the Confederates began a withdrawal toward Richmond.

Rory sat in *Patrick Henry*'s wardroom. It was crowded with the ship's officers, relaxing while the ship was at anchor off Deep Bottom; halfway between City Point and Drewry's Bluff, and across the James from Bermuda Hundred. They had just landed a battalion of infantry at Deep Bottom. In the hubbub around him, Rory carefully and surreptitiously read a letter from Tobias, sent through Rory's Uncle Liam in Ireland. When the civil war had separated Rory and Tobias, they arranged to write through Liam, cautiously, to avoid being charged with communicating

with the enemy. This letter had been written five weeks earlier, in late
March.

> *Dear Rory:*
>
> > *May this find you well, and in line for promotion. I am
> > well, and in Florida, where, as you will know by the time this
> > reaches you, we have recently taken Fort Clinch and St. Mary's,
> > eighteen miles north of the mouth of the St. Johns River (no relation,
> > ha, ha!)*
> >
> > *As someone who loves a pull of the British Lion's tail, you'll
> > appreciate our most recent adventure. We ascended the St. Johns
> > River to a point in the cypress swamps at Dunn's Creek, more than
> > 85 miles from the mouth. A local slave pilot had informed me that
> > the famed schooner America, the 1851 winner of the cup from Great
> > Britain that bears her name, had been scuttled by the Rebels (no
> > offense!) to preclude our capture of her.*
> >
> > *She's a beautiful sailer, mounting three small guns. I was
> > put in charge, and with the able help of a shipmate, a young acting
> > master from Oregon, we put our crew to the task. After a week of
> > labor, under most unpleasant conditions (although I could argue
> > that they were just right for an Antiguan), we stopped her cocks,
> > pumped her hold, and raised her. The surroundings and humidity
> > reminded me of our days together in the Brazil Squadron, searching
> > for William Walker the filibuster upon the rivers of Central America,
> > before our transfer to USS Active.*
> >
> > *The schooner America is now with the Blockading
> > Squadron as the USS America. We hope she'll intercept one of
> > those British-built blockade-runners with a haughty upper-class
> > Englishman as captain, (most of the fastest runners seem to be
> > commanded by the British) and let the Saxons (as you call them)
> > know we Americans still build the faster ships.*
> >
> > *Let me hear from you.*
> > *I remain your good friend,*
> > *Tobias*

"Orders, gentlemen," said First Lieutenant Rochelle as he entered
the wardroom. "We're bound for Norfolk with *Jamestown* tonight, and

we'll tow two vessels each upriver to Richmond the next night."

"Is this the end of us in Norfolk, then, sir?" asked Rory.

"So it would seem, Mr. Dunbrody. My sense is that the army believes it will be impossible to defend Norfolk, if McClellan's advance continues. We'll be sending down our masts to lower our silhouettes, and loading with enough anthracite to get us through without smoke."

That night, an hour past midnight, the two ships slipped into the Elizabeth River, undetected by Union gunboats patrolling the Newport News bank of the James.

The two steamers lay at the Gosport Yard during the following day, and Rory took the opportunity to visit friends aboard *Virginia.* Rory sought out John Taylor Wood in the wardroom.

"Taylor, we're here to tow the *Richmond* upriver. D'ye think *Virginia* will be joinin' us?"

"Rory, all we do is sail to Sewell's Point and dare the cowardly Yankees to come out," Taylor replied. "We're covering the army's withdrawal. I have my doubts that we'll get upriver, with our deep draft. It will be a near thing. I hate this absence of a daring stroke. I keep thinking there must be something we can do."

"Sure, it'll be a long war, Taylor. We'll think of something. D'ye know how Bob Minor is recoverin'?"

"He's mending well, and has all our prayers."

"Well, then, I've no doubts he'll be up and about before long. Keep yourself safe. I'll see you in Richmond."

As darkness fell the following night, the *Patrick Henry* took under tow a brig loaded with ammunition and the half-finished hull of the river ironclad CSS *Richmond. Jamestown* towed two more half-completed gunboat hulls. The *Richmond* was a miniature version of the *Virginia,* drawing only ten feet, one hundred fifty feet long, designed to carry pivots fore and aft, and four guns in broadside.

"She'll be effective in river defense, Mr. Ormsby, when they finish her."

"Aye, aye, sir. Will we tow her to Rockett's Wharf?"

"That's the plan, Mr. Ormsby." Rory watched as the towing hawser rose out of the water behind *Patrick Henry.* He was in charge of the towing detail on the afterdeck. "Hawser taut, sir," he called to Tucker and Rochelle on the bridge. "Damn, I miss old Bo'sun Edwards," he said to Ormsby. "Sure, and he was a rare old sailor!"

"Yes, sir. He was a great help to me, as a raw midshipman."

"I wrote his widow a letter about his life and death in battle," said Rory. "Far and away the least enjoyable part of command."

The two steamers eased away from the Gosport dock and crept down the Elizabeth and up the James, not a light showing. The evening of the following day, having passed through the hundred-foot gap in the obstructions placed in the river below Drewry's Bluff, they delivered their charges to Rockett's Wharf, just below Richmond. It had greatly expanded as a shipyard since the day in December 1861, when Rory had first gone aboard *Old Dominion*, and now occupied both banks of the James.

Two days later, May 8th, the *Patrick Henry* was anchored alone off Mulberry Island, when three Union steamers approached from Newport News. "Beat to quarters, Mr. Rochelle," said Tucker as the Union ships were identified. "I believe the lead ship is a new ironclad."

The ship leading the Union squadron was USS *Galena*, an ironclad more conventionally designed than was the *Monitor*. Mr. Rochelle had his glass trained on her. "She looks to have some sort of iron strake cladding, sir," he said to Tucker. "She's pierced for two broadside guns to the side, and has two massive pivots, fore and aft. My guess is they're rifles. But the hull looks just like a sailing ship with lots of tumble-home. No casemate like *Virginia*, and no turrets. One mast forward, and no yards crossed."

"They're more than a match for this wooden steamer, Mr. Rochelle," said Tucker. "Weigh anchor, if you please. We'll precede them upstream, and see what they're about."

The three Union ships hove-to off Day's Neck. Rory and the crew of *Patrick Henry* watched in some dismay as the *Galena* and her consorts silenced the Confederate battery at Day's Neck in one hour, then leisurely steamed upriver once again.

"Mr. Rochelle, I believe our only course is to make for Drewry's Bluff, and strive to make those obstructions impassable," said Tucker.

"There is no Confederate vessel on the river that can stop the Yankee ironclad, except *Virginia,* and she'll likely never make it upstream. We must protect the capital."

"Aye, aye, sir. Quartermaster, steer for City Point. Half ahead," Rochelle called down the speaking tube to the engine room.

Patrick Henry was finally out of sight of the Union squadron, which had stopped at Harden's Bluff to bombard the battery there. "*Beaufort* in sight, sir," said Lieutenant Rochelle. "She's headed down stream. Signaling interrogatory: 'are Yankees downstream?'"

"Reply: 'affirmative', Mr. Rochelle, and slow to one third."

Rory, standing with his gun crew on the foredeck, could see the tiny *Beaufort's* new commander, Lieutenant William Sharp, who had replaced Parker, standing with a speaking trumpet on his bridge wing. *Beaufort*, a forty-foot long, one-gun former swamp canal tug with a crew of ten, reversed her course and came abeam of the flagship. Lieutenant Sharp raised the speaking trumpet.

"Sir," called Sharp, "Secretary Mallory dispatched us to help stop the Yankees."

Tucker, Rory and everyone else within earshot worked hard to suppress grins. Tucker raised his own speaking trumpet. "Well, I hope you can do it," he called. "I'm getting out of their way."

"I'll fall in astern of you, commodore," Sharp responded after a short pause, and the two ships made their way up the James.

"Sound command decision, I'd say," said Rory to Ormsby.

"Aye, aye, sir," the midshipman replied with a smile.

The two ships threaded their way through the gap in the obstructions below Drewry's Bluff, and anchored in the stream. For the next week, the squadron complement and the men of an army artillery battery labored feverishly to improve the obstructions. Rory's attention was elsewhere, for he received notice of his court of inquiry date, eight days hence, and a directive from Mallory's office to report there immediately.

CHAPTER 12
MISS FORTEN, MEET MR. ST. JOHN
APRIL AND MAY 1862

The *Wabash* had returned to her station off Charleston as the flagship of the South Atlantic Blockade Squadron, leaving Tobias ashore at Beaufort, South Carolina, on detached duty assisting Edward Pierce, the federal agent in charge, with the Port Royal Negro education program. Only weeks before, an initial group of teachers had set sail from New York to teach the freed slaves of the Sea Islands around Port Royal.

"Gideon's Band", Pierce called them. They set up quarters in the abandoned stately houses of the slave owners, in towns and on plantations, and began to teach in makeshift schoolhouses; tents, farm outbuildings, churches and cotton barns. Tobias' quarters were aboard *USS Ottawa*, but he had a room ashore in the Education Project Superintendent's office, in a two-story home on Bay Street in Beaufort. The Army's headquarters were being established across Port Royal Sound on Hilton Head Island, and it was there, in late April, that Tobias waited with Pierce on the low and desolate shore for a steamer from New England with another contingent of northern teachers, men and women, white and black, to join the Port Royal Experiment.

"This side wheeler looks promising," said Tobias with his glass trained on a steamer entering the Sound.

"They're supposed to be aboard the *Bosworth*," said Pierce.

"That's the name on the bow, I can just now make it out."

"Excellent! I'm eager to have you meet several of the men and women aboard." Pierce had developed a strong respect for Tobias' educational background in the three months they'd been associated.

"One young woman in particular, Charlotte Forten, may have much in common with you. She, too, has ties to Massachusetts. She studied at the Higginson School and the Normal School in Salem, and then taught at Salem's Epes Grammar School. She's quite well thought of as a poet, too."

"She sounds formidable, Edward."

"And you are shy and retiring?" Pierce smiled. "She's from a strong abolitionist family in Philadelphia, and wealthy."

"White abolitionists?"

"No, a Negro abolitionist family, Tobias."

Tobias cocked his head and looked at Pierce, as the steamer came along the wharf. "Are you match-making, Edward?"

"You could do worse, sailing master. Wait 'til you see her."

The two men had been taking advantage of the wait to stretch their legs ashore. The *Ottawa* was secured at the new Army wharf.

As they returned to the gunboat, the *Bosworth* was transferring the 50-teacher contingent directly to Ottawa.

The 158-foot screw gunboat cast off lines and backed slowly away from the wharf. Pierce and Tobias stood on the foredeck with an attractive, raven-haired woman with soft, dark eyes. Charlotte Forten was further south than she had ever been.

"I'm not used to temperature like this in April," she said with a smile.

"You'll get used to it, Miss Forten. Meet Mr. St. John, our outstanding navigator and spy-master."

"Spymaster? How intriguing!"

"Edward is exaggerating, Miss Forten, I'm a sailor on assignment to help with the Port Royal education project."

"And not a spy?"

"I can't tell you about that." They both burst out laughing.

"Tobias made the earliest contact with our abandoned freedmen here, Miss Forten. He's been a huge help to me in contacts with them."

"And there are many fine watermen among them, Miss Forten," said Tobias. "I've been able to help my Service by gathering information on the local waters from my new piloting friends."

"Quite resourceful, Mr. 'Sinjin,' is it?"

"Yes, miss, it's the British pronunciation of 'Saint John'. I was born into slavery in Antigua. But please, call me Tobias."

He smiled what he hoped was his most charming smile.

"I must seek out the superintendent," said Pierce. "Please excuse me, you two." Pierce moved aft toward a group on the quarterdeck.

"He's nice, but needs work on his subtlety," said Charlotte, smiling demurely.

Tobias laughed. "He's my friend, and means well, Miss Forten."

"Call me Charlotte, please, Tobias. It's quite startling to find a commissioned officer of color. I was unaware the Navy allowed them."

"I've been quite lucky, but the navy has no outright prohibitions against black officers. Just quotas, and unwritten custom. I believe we'll have more black officers by war's end, judging from the talent of the slave pilots I'm meeting. The navy is woefully short of experienced officers with its expansion, and the freedman pilots I've met can stand a watch in any man's navy!"

"How gratifying to hear that"

"You're very brave to come so far to help these people. You'll find them very grateful, and keen to learn."

"I couldn't just stay in Philadelphia, with so many people in need."

"Why did you leave Salem?"

"I contracted tuberculosis and I needed to go home. Do you have friends in Salem? Mr. Pierce said you grew up in New Bedford."

"I studied with the Quakers, and then went a-whaling. I know that the Folgers of Nantucket and New Bedford have family in Salem. You studied there?"

"Yes and later taught. The Quakers provide fine education. Do you read the classics?"

"Some, although mathematics was my strength. What will you teach these people who've been forbidden to learn?"

"Reading, writing, spelling, geography and arithmetic. A bit distant from my schooling, but we must start slowly. Perhaps someday some will learn cartography."

"You are a student of my craft, then?"

"Yes, navigator, but without your application. I don't risk running aground if I made a mistake in class."

They glanced over the rail, having been absorbed with one another for the entire width of Port Royal Sound, and found themselves in the broad expanse of the Beaufort River, approaching Beaufort. The *Ottawa* bore up and secured to the town wharf, much improved and strengthened since the Union capture.

The teachers disembarked and were given a half hour to wander about Bay Street before boarding rowing boats manned by freedmen rowers who had, until recently, plied these waters as slaves. Freedmen thronged the waterfront area.

Tobias, Pierce and Charlotte strolled eastward along Bay Street, passing as they did so, several groups of U.S. Army officers likewise taking their ease, and staring at the many freedmen with ill-disguised contempt.

"Can you believe the number of these shiftless niggers," said one young lieutenant, with a sneer. And now these abolitionist do-gooders are here to try and teach the un-teachable! Amazing! And look, there's one of those baboons in a navy officer's uniform!"

"Excuse me," said Pierce who then retraced his steps and stood before the lieutenant.

"My name is Pierce", he said to the officer whose sneer remained in place. "I am General Hunter's personal representative in this effort to 'teach the un-teachables'. I'm concerned that we not lose capable officers like you, and so I must warn you the officer you've insulted is the most dangerous hand-to-hand combat expert in the U.S. service, with dozens of kills to his credit." He gestured toward Tobias. "He's remorseless. Have a care, I implore you. He hates white officers. I'll try to control him!"

The lieutenant stared at Pierce, open mouthed, and then shrugged. "R-Ridiculous", he stuttered, as his companions took him by the elbows and urged him away, looking over their shoulders.

Tobias and Charlotte turned away and laughed as Pierce rejoined them. "You must forgive Edward," said Tobias, "he tends toward hyperbole."

"Is any of that true?"

"Only remotely," smiled Tobias, taking her arm. "Let's find these boats of yours."

"You seem unsurprised and unconcerned by their disdain," she said, puzzled.

"Well, you and I encounter that every day. For me, it's much less intense and obvious in the navy. There are actually a few of my fellow officers who respect me for my skills, and don't dwell on my race. The rest are, in the main, circumspect about their biases. And those officers back there? They're army. And probably have never seen combat. I have. Their insults seem less important, as a result. My! I did go on, didn't I?"

"Not at all," Charlotte assured him. "I found that fascinating."

They found the boats awaiting them in a cove near the massive Joseph Johnson house on Craven Street. As the teachers were helped into the boats, the stroke oar of the one Tobias and Charlotte boarded spoke to Tobias.

"You de officer landed at Fort Clinch an' drove de rebs out of Fernandina. I 'member you!"

"You're right, I was there," said Tobias. "How did you come here?"

"Oh, dey move us up from Fernandina to be nex' to de schools here. We all be livin' in de ol' public libery, an' goin' to school. I'se an ol' boatman so they lets me row, too."

"Then, take us where we must go, Mr. Stroke Oar."

The large flatboats easily carried the teachers across the broad Beaufort to Ladies Island, with the deep voices of the oarsmen keeping rhythm with their traditional rowing songs. They boarded horse-drawn wagons for the ride to adjoining St. Helena's Island. Tobias sat on a bench beside Charlotte who marveled at the passing scene along the dirt track. "This island is absolutely flat," she said, "and the moss hanging from those live oaks! The pendants are more than four feet long! And those stiff, defiant-looking plants, they must be palmettos."

They presently reached a small plantation, the Oaklands, where they were greeted by the school project general superintendent. As they were settling in, Pierce and Tobias said their goodbyes and returned on the wagon to the boat.

A week later, Tobias and Charlotte met by chance in Beaufort, as she was in town with a few other teachers for supplies. "How was your first week with your students?" Tobias asked as they found a seat on the veranda of the cotton exchange, overlooking the water.

"They are so eager to learn, both children and the grown ones," she replied. "There are very few stupid ones. We use a Baptist church for a school house, and when all 140 are reciting at once, it is bedlam, truly."

"I should like to see that, once, before I return to the *Wabash*," said Tobias.

"When must you go?"

"In a week."

Charlotte's face registered a fleeting look of disappointment. "Well, then we must arrange a visit, where I can show them one of their race who is a leader. I've been teaching them of other leaders, like Toussaint l'Overture."

"I'm hardly the caliber of the great Toussaint," said Tobias with a laugh, "but I suppose you must make do with what's available."

"False modesty, Tobias. Mr. Pierce has told me of your exploits in Louisiana and on the Broad River. Can you come this week?"

"Indeed, Tuesday would be possible."

"And one more appointment, this weekend, before you go. We teachers are being taken by the artillery to Barnwell Plantation on Port Royal Island, to see if the Rebels appear across the river. They wish to show us that we are safe under their care."

"Then not all army officers are scornful of your efforts."

"Apparently not, Tobias. I confess we are encouraged by the gesture."

"General Hunter's influence, I'll warrant," said Tobias. "David Hunter is a supporter of the experiment." Tobias reached out, taking Charlotte's hand. "I'm grateful for the invitation, Charlotte, and for the opportunity for another day with you."

She flushed, and then smiled. "Saturday, here at nine, then. Wear riding clothes. We'll be on horseback."

"Oh, my," groaned Tobias. "Not one of my favorite activities, but for you, dear Charlotte, I'll do it!" He smiled bravely as they said goodbye.

The following Saturday, they met again at the cotton exchange. "Thank you again, Charlotte, for letting me watch you teach last Tuesday. You were right, it was bedlam," said Tobias, "but of a most encouraging kind!"

"It was kind of you to come, Tobias. When I introduced you, I could see in the students rekindled hope and pride."

"I should get on my horse before it becomes too high," quipped Tobias.

Charlotte laughed out loud. "It's not as if we people of color have all that many opportunities for pride in this country. Take it while you can, dear Tobias. But, it is time to mount our horses, come along."

A small group of ten teachers rode with the battery commander, keeping out of the dust of the battery train behind them. Glancing back, Tobias could see teams of horses pulling caissons and 12-pounder howitzers up the road and out of town west toward the Broad River and their destination, the Barnwell Plantation. Charlotte and Tobias talked as they rode in the early May sunshine. "Is this not beautiful, Tobias? See the colors, the yellow Jessamine, the deep pink of the azaleas, the violets all purple and white. And the fragrances! Such a lovely Springtime."

"Not to sound unappreciative of beauty, but the lovely colors and the white of the Cherokee rose are accompanied by the rising of the fleas in the Carolina Spring."

"Enough of your grumpiness! You must be reacting to your seat on that horse!" Charlotte said, teasingly.

"It's true, I am a most indifferent rider, dear Charlotte. And I'm always astounded at how high one is when seated on one of these beasts. At times like this, I think of my good friend, Rory, a sailor who also rides like the wind. I wish you could see him ride, he looks as comfortable as you on horseback."

"Where is your friend, Tobias? On another ship?"

"In another navy, unfortunately. We correspond very carefully, and to my knowledge, he is well, and the last I heard, in New Orleans. He's about your age, I would guess, and like you, willing to meet challenge head-on!" Charlotte nodded at the compliment. "We exchange letters through his uncle in Ireland. I should not be telling you this. It's a court martial offense to communicate with the enemy."

"I'll keep your secret, Tobias, rest easy. But how can you stay friends with one who fights to maintain slavery?"

"Rory holds no case for slavery, just the opposite. He grew up in Ireland amid the subjugation of his race by the English. But his family is in the South, and he felt he could not leave them. There are many like him in the Confederate forces, just as there are many on our side for whom slavery is unimportant, or even acceptable."

Charlotte was silent for a time. "It is sad that you are away from him," she said, at length.

"I miss his humor and his intellect," said Tobias. "And his irreverence. You have re-supplied me in two of those respects, thank you, Charlotte."

The banks of the Broad River had appeared in the distance while they talked. They had entered the expansive confines of the Barnwell Plantation. "I'm glad we're almost there, Tobias. I was growing concerned about your continued seat on your horse." She smiled. "I wish we had a carriage for the ride back."

"You can drive a carriage? You are a horsewoman!"

They pulled to the side to let the limbers and caissons of the battery surge ahead. They were now close to the bank of the Broad River, at Laurel Bay. Across the river, amid the live oaks and magnolias, they could catch glimpses of a Confederate cavalry patrol. The battery unlimbered, and soon the howitzers were lobbing shots in the cavalry's direction.

"It is nice to see them far across the water," said Charlotte. "We live in fear that they will raid our plantation and carry us and our students away."

"It would take a far stronger force than they can muster to do that, Charlotte. We are at a stalemate here, with neither force strong enough to change the status quo. They can ride around the batteries we captured, but cannot retake them."

"Nonetheless, I take comfort in my revolver."

"Revolver! You ride, you shoot? You are one surprise after another," cried Tobias, with real astonishment.

"We believe the Rebels are incensed by Lincoln's latest action, emancipating the slaves in the District of Columbia. The slave owners who have fled may be moved to desperation."

"Oh, Charlotte, the navy increases its presence here daily. Port Royal Sound is the hub of the South Blockading Squadron. The Rebels can't spare the men they'd need to retake it."

"Well, that's almost as comforting as my revolver." The battery had limbered up, and they were riding back toward Beaufort now, amid pines and brilliant trumpet flowers. "This week, I'm going to share Shakespeare's poetry with my class. And my friend John Whittier has sent me a song. I'll teach it to them."

"Are they up to encountering Shakespeare?"

"Oh, yes, Tobias. They love rhyme, and sing verses constantly. We have several freedmen from Edisto Island, where Gullah, a patois, is spoken. It sounds unintelligible at first, but it's really a form of Elizabethan English, from Shakespeare's Day."

"I wish I could be here to see it. I'm sorry to have to leave here, and you, Charlotte."

"We each have our responsibilities, Tobias. Another time, another place, perhaps," she said, wistfully.

"I will hope for that most fervently, dear Charlotte!" They rode beside one another in silence, to the sounds of the horses' hooves and the clink and jingle of the battery behind them. Tobias was deep in thought. *I love Monique dearly and deeply, but this woman fascinates me in a different way. It's probably well that our paths are unlikely to cross again.*

CHAPTER 13
CSN COURT OF INQUIRY.
MAY 1862

Rory was ushered into Mallory's office to find the Secretary and a young officer awaiting him. "Mr. Dunbrody, meet Lieutenant Richard Burroughs. The Navy Department has assigned him as counsel. Like Captain Semmes, Mr. Burroughs is a line officer and a member of the Bar." Burroughs stood and offered his hand. He was swarthy and black-haired, wearing his hair at almost-shoulder length. "I'm pleased to meet a hero of Hampton Roads," he said in an Acadian or "Cajun" accent.

"I'm happy that the Secretary has involved himself in your assignment, lieutenant," Rory replied, gratified and somewhat surprised that Mallory would pay this much attention to a mere lieutenant's case.

"By the way," said Mallory, "Mr. Farwell of Richmond sought me out and begged to be allowed to contribute to any legal costs beyond the Department's capacities." Mallory smiled. "Said it was his patriotic duty."

"Sure, and did he, now? What a grand fellow!" Things were happening faster than Rory could keep up.

"I have more good news," said Mallory. My sources in the Army Department," he paused and beamed. "I do have them, you know. They tell me that the source of the allegation that you're disloyal is the intelligence section of General Winder's Safety Committee, commanded by a Major Grenville Donovan. You recall him, I'm sure."

"Yes, sir," Rory addressed Burroughs. "I killed his brother in a duel," he explained.

"So I understand," said Burroughs. "Over the affection of his fiancée, I believe. Motive enough for these accusations, I'm sure. We'll deal with this in court, Mr. Dunbrody, have no fear."

"Let me offer this," said Mallory. "I have bad news as well. One of the members of the court, Commander Cawood, is from Louisiana, and his family has connections with the Donovans. Further, General Winder purports that his organization's role is 'spy catching.' He's notoriously inept at it, but also has a reputation of being very corrupt. Frankly, we don't have much in the way of an intelligence operation organized here in the Confederacy. It would not do for me to interfere with the selection of the court. So, you'll have to convince the unbiased members that no court martial is called for. I'll leave you two to confer. Please take all the time you need," said Mallory as he rose to leave the room. The two officers rose as well, and Rory called out his thanks to the retreating figure of the Navy Secretary.

"Let's get to work, Mr. Dunbrody," drawled Burroughs. "I'm going to enjoy this case."

The Court of Inquiry regarding the loss of the CSS *Old Dominion* convened eight days later. The captain's cabin of the *Patrick Henry* served as the courtroom. It was all the way aft, as far from the engine as possible, and spanned the width of the ship. The stern windows let in considerable light from the bright May day outside. The three members of the court sat with their backs to the stern windows, with the president of the court, Commodore William F. Lynch, in the center, flanked by Lieutenant Benjamin Loyall and Commander J.W. Cawood. Judge Advocate Willard Presnell sat at a table to the court's right. The members of the court had been selected from among officers who had not served with Rory. All of these officers had seen action at the Battle of Roanoke Island.

Rory and Burroughs sat at a table facing the court. Witnesses waited outside the cabin to be called, most of them on deck. Rory could see the banks of the James River through the stern windows. The ship was anchored a mile upstream of Drewry's Bluff. The weighty humidity on the James settled between the high bluffs lining the river like warm meal pouring into a silo. Rory felt as if he were drowning in sweat, and nervously tapped a pencil on the note pad in front of him, until Burroughs reached over and gently grasped his hand. "Nothing to worry about, lieutenant. We have enough character witnesses to assure your canonization."

"Sure, beatification would suffice, counselor," Rory replied with a forced smile, and took a deep breath.

Commodore Lynch called the court to order. The judge advocate rose. "Mr. President and members of the court, the purpose of these proceedings is to determine if a court martial is warranted in the case of the sinking of the Confederate States Ship *Old Dominion*, Lieutenant Rory Cormac Dunbrody, commanding. The sinking in question occurred March 9, 1862, during the Battle of Hampton Roads."

He continued. "Defense counsel has provided a witness list. Those witnesses can corroborate the facts in this case, which are: The CSS *Virginia* ran aground on a shoal while engaging the USS *Monitor* on the day in question. The *Old Dominion* took the *Virginia* under tow and attempted to pull her off the shoal. Shells from the *Monitor* struck the *Old Dominion*. The *Old Dominion* maintained fire on the *Monitor* while sinking. The only *Old Dominion* casualties were as a result of the *Monitor's* gunfire. Surviving crewmembers of the tug boarded *Virginia* and joined her crew in continuing to engage the *Monitor*."

Rory shivered involuntarily, at the memory. For a moment, he thought he could smell the gun smoke.

Commodore Lynch, the president of the court, glanced at Burroughs, who rose and announced, "The defense will stipulate to these facts, Mr. President."

"Thank you, counselor. Please proceed, Mr. Judge Advocate."

Presnell continued. "As part of my responsibility to ensure all facts in this case are examined, I call Captain R. A. Simmons of General Winder's Safety Committee to the stand."

Presnell administered the oath to a balding, round-shouldered army captain, who swore in a very soft voice to tell the truth and the whole truth.

"Captain, your intelligence section has brought to the court's attention the allegation of a confidential source that Lieutenant Dunbrody is in frequent contact with his brother, Timothy Dunbrody, a Union Army captain, and further that Lieutenant Dunbrody's sympathies are with the

Union and further, that he purposely and recklessly exposed the tug under his command to certain destruction. Is that correct?"

"Yes, it is."

"Your Section further quotes its source as alleging that Mr. Dunbrody's Union sympathies also are owing to the large numbers of Irish immigrants to be found in the Union Army, and his proclivity to support the interests of men who, like him, grew up in Ireland. Is this correct?"

"Yes, it is."

"Have you any evidence, documents, letters from brother to brother, anything which you have presented to this court to support these allegations?"

"No, sir."

"Have you identified any witness this court could call to substantiate this allegation?"

"No, sir. The confidentiality of our source precludes exposure as a witness."

"Have you evidence that any of the thousands of Irish immigrants in the armies of the South are secretly supporting the Union cause because greater numbers of Irish serve in the Federal service?"

"No, sir, but we all know of the appalling lack of intelligence and enterprise among the recent Irish immigrants."

Burroughs sprang to his feet. "Mr. President, move to strike!"

"Granted," said Lynch. "The court will disregard that last unconscionable utterance."

Rory whispered to Burroughs. "Sure, with a Court President named Lynch, he'd do well t' think twice about utterin' that remark!"

Burroughs smiled in response.

"I have no further questions of this witness," said Presnell.

"Mr. Burroughs?" said Commodore Lynch.

Burroughs rose. "Captain Simmons, is your Section commander Major Grenville Donovan?"

"Yes," Simmons replied with a frown.

"And are you aware that Mr. Dunbrody killed Major Donovan's brother, Thomas, in a duel?"

"Mr. President!" Presnell was on his feet. "I must object! Major

Donovan is not here to respond to the implication defense counsel is advancing."

"I withdraw the question," said Burroughs, satisfied that the implication was clear.

"No more of that, Mr. Burroughs," admonished Lynch.

"Aye, aye, Mr. President," said Burroughs. "Captain Simmons, I show you defense exhibit one, a partial list of Confederate officers with brothers fighting for the Union. This list was just compiled by our Department of War and Department of the Navy, and contains more than one hundred and fifty names. Are you aware of any of these officers, whose circumstances match those of Mr. Dunbrody, being under investigation by your section?"

Simmons took a moment to review the list, and said, "I'm unaware of any such investigation."

"No further questions," said Burroughs.

"Has the court any questions of this witness?" Lynch asked.

Commander Cawood leaned forward. "Captain Simmons, has your section investigated allegations of some officers of the *Virginia* that tugboat assistance at Hampton Roads was less than prompt?" Rory's fists clenched and Burroughs place a restraining had on his arm.

"No, sir," replied Simmons enthusiastically, "but I'll certainly bring it to Major Donovan's attention!"

Rory whispered to Burroughs, "they've orchestrated their testimony, the spalpeens, and that's a fact!"

"Worry not, my client. Cawood obviously has not looked at your witness list. We will call the one man who can convincingly refute the implication. And he doesn't know it!" Burroughs smiled in anticipation.

"Any further questions from the court?" Lynch looked to Lieutenant Loyall.

"Yes, Mr. President," said Loyall. "Captain Simmons, from the accounts of the Hampton Roads action you've read, would you say that the *Virginia* was central to our navy's success?"

"Yes, sir, from what little I know."

Loyall continued. "Let me pose a hypothetical question,

Captain. If an army unit was central to a battle's success, say, one of our artillery regiments, and it was in danger of being overrun by superior Union infantry forces, would it not be the duty of a Confederate infantry unit commander who could aid the artillery to do so, even if it meant destruction of his infantry command?"

As Simmons gave the obvious "yes" answer, Burroughs leaned over to Rory and whispered, "I think we're home free."

Simmons was dismissed, and the judge advocate announced he had no further witnesses.

"Mr. President," said Burroughs to Lynch, "the defense calls Lieutenant Alexander Warley, former commander of the CSS *Manassas.*"

Burroughs presented a parade of Rory's former shipmates, commanders, and subordinates, all who testified to his courage under fire and his command presence and skills. Thomas of the *Rose of Clifden,* Wood of the *Virginia,* Tucker of the *Patrick Henry,* and Ormsby of the *Old Dominion* were followed, at last, by Catesby ap Jones of the *Virginia.*

"Lieutenant Jones, in your opinion as commander of *Virginia,* was Mr. Dunbrody's decision to attempt towing your ship off the shoal a reckless endangerment of his vessel?"

"Far from it, sir, it was his duty and he did it without hesitation. I am convinced that his efforts enabled us to continue the action."

"Thank you, sir. A member of this court asked a previous witness if Army Intelligence had investigated allegations by the *Virginia's* officers that tug assistance was not timely. Are you aware of such allegations?"

"I can remember wondering about the proximity of other tugboats, as we were aground, but I had no doubts as to *Old Dominion.* Mr. Dunbrody and his crew had us under tow in an amazingly short time, and as I said a moment ago, I'm certain his aid brought us back into action."

"Thank you, sir. No further questions. Mr. President, may we offer the defense?" Burroughs referred to what would be known in a civil court as the closing statement.

"Proceed, Mr. Burroughs, if there are no further questions from the court. I see none," said Lynch. Cawood looked exasperated, scowling in his chair.

Burroughs launched into his closing. "There has been no evidence presented to this court which suggests that Mr. Dunbrody's conduct in commanding his ship on March 9, 1862, was anything other than the courageous and skillful actions of a man performing his duty to his country. I urge the judge advocate to recommend that no court martial is warranted in this case, and pray the court to concur."

It was late in the day, and Lynch adjourned until the morning. Rory spent a restless night, notwithstanding his defense counsel's expressed confidence that all would be well in the morning. As the court reconvened the next day, Rory noted that Presnell, at least, had a pleasant expression on his face.

"Mr. President and members of the court, as judge advocate in this case, it is my duty to ensure that all facts in this case are thoroughly examined, and, based on those facts, recommend to you whether a court martial is warranted. I recommend that no court martial is warranted, based on the evidence presented."

"Thank you, Mr. Judge Advocate," said Commodore Lynch. The court will recess for deliberations."

As Rory and Burroughs stood, watching the court file into the captain's day cabin to deliberate, Presnell approached and whispered, "Don't go far, this should be quick."

Within fifteen minutes, the court had returned and Lynch, the president of the court, intoned their finding: "This court finds no grounds which would warrant a court martial in this case, and declares it finds every evidence of courageous conduct and exemplary leadership on the part of Lieutenant Dunbrody."

On deck afterwards, amid the congratulations of his fellow officers, Burroughs had a final word for Rory. "You've made an implacable enemy of this Donovan fellow, without a doubt. He's in a place where he's able to cause all kinds of mischief. Be vigilant!"

"Thanks, counselor, I surely will. You're one of nature's noblemen, entirely! Yet, I don't doubt that the mere accusation of disloyalty will tar me with the brush of suspicion. In that, Donovan's succeeded, damn his soul!"

CHAPTER 14
DASH AND DARING:
ROBERT SMALLS TAKES THE CSS PLANTER,
CHARLESTON
MAY 13, 1862

As the mist over the waters off Charleston was dissipating just after daybreak, the lookout at the fore topgallant crosstrees of the USS *Wabash* called out, "Steamer two points off the port bow, six hundred yards, under a white flag. The *Onward's* abeam of her, sir. Looks to be escorting her."

The officer of the deck ordered 'beat to quarters', sent a midshipman to call the captain, and rushed to the port rail with his speaking trumpet. "Steamer ahoy! What steamer is that?" he called.

"Steamer *Planter* from Charleston," came the reply, and so began the unfolding of a most surprising tale. Tobias was summoned to the quarterdeck as the all-Negro crew of the *Planter* began to come on board.

Captain Rodgers and Flag Officer Du Pont stood together on the quarterdeck. Fleet Captain Davis was ascending the companionway. "Ah, good," said Rodgers, "St. John's here. I think it'll be a comfort to these blacks, sailing master, as they first come aboard, if they can talk to one of their own, particularly an officer. Would you ascertain the details of their situation, please?"

Tobias resisted the temptation to reply 'yassuh'. "Aye, aye, sir," he responded. He turned to a handsome, stocky black man in his early twenties, with a well-trimmed mustache and goatee. "I'm Tobias St. John, the sailing master. You've brought us a smart-looking steamer, thank you very much. Can you tell us how you did it?" Tobias extended his hand

and smiled.

"Robert Smalls, sir, pilot of the *Planter*. I told the gunboat, sir, we brought you some of the old U.S. guns." He began to laugh. "I'm a happy sailor, sir. We thought the *Planter* might be of some use to Uncle Abe."

"Indeed it will, pilot," said Tobias, glancing at the side-wheel steamer. It had a high pilothouse and a high-sided main cabin built right up from the gunwales. A pivot 32-pounder was mounted on the foredeck, and a six-inch howitzer aft.

"I'd like to arrange for your crew to be comfortable, fed, and have a place to rest. Let me see if the gunroom's available, and then you and I and the captain and commodore can sit together in the great cabin while I write all this down."

"Yes, sir, that's very kind. These are my family, and my brother and his family, and some friends and crewmen. My brother John was assistant engineer. There're fifteen of us, and a cargo of heavy guns for Fort Ripley, over to the harbor's middle ground."

"Excellent, pilot. Wait here, please, while I make arrangements."

Soon, the *Wabash's* great cabin held its tenant, Du Pont, Captains Davis and Rodgers, Robert Smalls, and Tobias, all seated around the flag officer's table. Du Pont had dispatched Roswell Lamson to take command of the *Planter*. The crew and families were comfortably settled in the gunroom, attended to by the captain's clerk, and a veritable squadron of curious stewards and seamen. The resourceful coup was the talk of the ship.

"Mr. Smalls, congratulations on a daring action," said Du Pont. "Please give us the details of how you carried this out."

"Yes, sir. The white officers often sleep ashore when we have no night deliveries scheduled. And we often do sail at night, so's the sentries and guards around the harbor are used to that. I knows all the passwords, signals and challenges. We waited for a night when the officers slept ashore, and left slowly, giving all the right whistles and signals as if we was on a routine run. I wore a straw hat, the same kind as our captain wears. When we fooled the sentries at Fort Sumter, I knew we'd make it, if you all didn't sink us as a Rebel ram. I told the folks, 'We're all free niggers, now.' We hoisted a white bed sheet and the sun come up just as the gunboat spotted us through the morning mist. We have on board a number of cannons, the Confederate code book, and troop locations."

"Well done, Mr. Smalls," said Du Pont. "Thank Heaven *Onward* had a good lookout. Gentlemen, I'm going to take *Planter* into the service as a blockade gunboat, and recommend to the secretary of the navy and President Lincoln that we award half the prize money to Mr. Smalls and his entire party. I'd also like to recruit you, Mr. Smalls, as a pilot in the U.S. Navy. You can ask Mr. St. John, here, how he feels about his service as a Negro officer, as you consider my offer."

"Yes sir, Commodore, that's mighty kindly of you. I'd like to think that over, right quick." Smalls, understandably, looked a bit dazed at how fast and how well events were moving.

"Flag officer," said Tobias, "perhaps Mr. Smalls and I could take a turn around the deck, and I could answer questions as they come to him."

"Splendid idea, St. John. Mr. Smalls, we'll give you some time to reflect. Let us know if we can provide you any information you need to decide."

Tobias and Smalls left the cabin, and climbed to the quarterdeck, walking slowly around it, aft, then athwartships, then forward to the main deck, and then retracing their steps as they talked.

"So, Mr. St. John, how is it in your Yankee navy for black folks?"

Tobias was impressed with the candor and confidence of Smalls' question. "Maybe just a bit better than you'd expect, but not so much better that you'll shout 'hallelujah.' Some officers and men judge you on your seamanship. A few, a very few, even look at you as an equal. But many are sure you're inferior, and they make sure you live up to their expectations."

"Well," Smalls replied, scratching his chin, "at least they can't sell you. I reckon I'll give it a try. I know the pay's good, and I got a family."

"True enough, Mr. Smalls. Now, I have some questions for you. You know some slave pilots, up and down the coast?"

"'Deed I do, Mr. St. John."

"Are any as bold as you? Willing to try to take another ship?"

"They might be a couple. I knows one up to Wilmington. He's

got a whole shipload o' wildness in him. I could see him tryin'."

"I have an idea, Mr. Smalls. We've been using the slave grapevine, the Black Dispatch, to get sailing times for blockade-runners. I'm working with a spymaster who might be able to set me up with a white agent in place, connected with the shipping industry. I'd be placed as a slave pilot. If some other slave pilots, real ones I could trust, knew I was coming, they could protect my identity, and we could plan a ship-taking from inside Wilmington. What do you think?"

"Hmmm. I could get word to my fren'. The rest be on you. You know, Mr. St. John, they catch you and don't know you is U.S. Navy, they take you, whip you, and you ain't free no more. They do know you is U.S. Navy, they hang you nex' thing from a big oak branch. No more drinks in d' wardroom for you. Just another nigger wid' a stretched neck."

"Very graphic, Mr. Smalls. No wonder you're a great pilot. You have an eye for detail." Tobias smiled broadly. "Let's go set our plans before the flag officer, quickly, before I change my mind." Smalls laughed in response.

Du Pont was in his cabin. Tobias and Smalls waited in the companionway. *Life was simpler and more pleasant in Antigua,* thought Tobias. *What is it that draws me to this maelstrom?* He had seen the actual Maelstrom on his whaling voyages. It was an apt analogy. *Drawing the unwary mariner in, deeper and deeper.*

"The Flag Officer will see you!" Tobias was jerked from his reverie by the flag lieutenant. Tobias and Robert Smalls entered the cabin. Smalls announced his acceptance of the offer to join the naval service.

"Splendid," said Du Pont. "I've asked Mr. Lamson, now in command of *Planter,* to take your family and crew to Beaufort, South Carolina, to make sure they're well-settled and provided for. I'm hopeful you'll have some prize money soon. You may spend some time with them before sailing, and then we'll assign you a ship."

"Mr. Smalls, there is a pilot in Beaufort, a former slave, Isaac Tatnall. He is a friend. Please have your brother, John, make his acquaintance, and mention my name."

"Flag officer, Mr. Smalls and I have talked more about extending the effort Mr. Pinkerton and I have been embarked upon, the collecting of information regarding ships running the blockade, and placement of an agent in a blockade port."

"Yes, sailing master?"

"We'd like more than ever to collect the ships themselves, sir."

"Like the *Planter,* you mean?"

"Precisely, sir. Mr. Smalls just confirmed that our earlier, untested plan could actually be carried out! We could mount an effort by which we arrange for defections, as it were. I'm sure the Rebels will call it 'theft.' Whatever the label, sir, we'll be a ship to the good, and they, one poorer, each time we succeed. And they can ill-afford to lose ships, or any other resource."

"The details of this system, Mr. St. John?" Du Pont leaned forward.

"Mr. Pinkerton was coming to support in-place agents, rather than implanted ones, when last we talked. If he could identify a Wilmington agent who had access to the shipping industry, with need for a slave pilot, I could play that role, arrange to meet other slave pilots connected with me through the Black Dispatch, and we could plan to sail the targeted blockade-runners to our inshore picket lines."

"How many are you thinking would be possible, Mr. St. John?"

"Two, maybe three. Certainly one, sir. Even if it's only one, sir, the morale value, positive for us, negative for them, is tremendous!"

"Quite true, sailing master. I'm sure you're aware of how dangerous, how fatal, this scheme could be for you."

"Yes, sir. I'm willing to take the risk, sir. Not to say I'm not frightened when I think of all that could go wrong. But I'd like your permission to pursue it with Mr. Pinkerton."

"Permission granted, Mr. St. John. You'll leave for Washington City on the next dispatch schooner. What do you think of our rash sailing master, Mr. Smalls?"

"I think he know why he's doing this, Commodore," said Smalls, quietly.

"I suspect you do, pilot. You're dismissed, gentlemen, with my profound thanks and admiration."

Tobias and Smalls left the cabin and made their way on deck.

"I don't b'lieve I've ever been talked to like that by a white man before," Smalls said.

"The nicest part, my friend, and the most unusual, is that Du Pont means it."

CHAPTER 15
THE ASSAULT ON DREWRY'S BLUFF
MAY 1862

Rory was exhausted. Since the James River Squadron had brought its ships upriver of the Drewry's Bluff obstructions on May 9th, the men of the squadron and those from an artillery battery emplaced on the bluffs had worked to improve the obstructions in the river. Several hulks had been sunk to obstruct the river bed, and the CSS *Jamestown* had been sacrificed as well, seeking to ensure that the only possible passage open was the hundred-foot gap at mid-stream, upon which every gun on the bluff was trained. The guns had been augmented by pieces from the squadron, their highest caliber cannon.

The artillerymen and the squadron personnel built two emplacement positions, one at an elevation of 110 feet, and the other at eighty feet. They also dug pits, and Rory was set to work building platforms in back of the log and earth parapets, a labor he'd most recently carried out on San Juan Island, Washington Territory.

I wonder where the war has taken Henry Robert? Rory mused, as his crew completed a platform for a Brooke rifle, and Rory began to set the blocks for the training and preventer tackle, just as any broadside naval gun would use to control aim and recoil. Henry Robert, U.S. Army engineer, and later the author of *Robert's Rules of Order*, had worked side-by-side with Rory to construct a redoubt for artillery confronting the Royal Navy in a Pacific Northwest border dispute just prior to the Civil War.

Lieutenant Rochelle oversaw a crew who were building a log wall on the bluff in back of the gun emplacements. The wall would prevent cave-ins from Union shells landing higher up the bluff above the guns.

"No point in being buried alive, men," called Rochelle, as ten men lifted another log into place, lashed it to the one under it, and spiked it to a vertical support post.

The ships were moored upstream of the bluff. An anchor watch was left aboard, but most of the crews lived in tents on the crest above the bluff and its gun batteries. The men were in high spirits, as the weather had been gentle. Most sailors saw tent living as a lark, a kind of "camping-out."

The high spirits were tempered by the arrival, on May 13th, of the crew of the *Virginia,* by train from Norfolk. Taylor Wood told the story to the squadron officers in the big officers' mess tent.

"On May 9th, the flag officer was told by General Huger in Norfolk to remain at our Sewell's Point buoy to cover the withdrawal of the army from Norfolk and the Navy Yard," said Taylor. "In the morning, we noticed there was no flag flying at our batteries on Sewell's Point. They'd been abandoned during the night, unbeknownst to us, and when we sent Catesby ap Jones up the Elizabeth, Norfolk was in chaos, with army units in flight and the Gosport yard in flames. General Huger and Commodore Lee, the Yard commandant, had fled. The Federals had landed at Ocean View, and were advancing. We'd been left to our fate by the army."

"No instructions from Richmond?" Rochelle asked.

"None that night," said Taylor. "But the week before, Richmond had precluded us from trying to run out to the Chesapeake. So, we anchored *Virginia* off Craney Island and began to lighten ship, to reduce the draft to eighteen feet, which our river pilots told us would get us over the bar and up the James. We had it down to nineteen feet, in the middle of that night, when the pilots told Commodore Tattnall that it would have to be sixteen feet, because the west winds had lowered the water over the bar. We couldn't do it. So we blew her up, marched twenty-two miles to Suffolk, and took the last train to Petersburg."

Stunned silence greeted the tale. Catesby ap Jones entered the tent. "Officers of the *Virginia,*" he said. "Flag Officer Tattnall wishes us to fall out the men in the morning and turn to with the squadron detail to get the gun pits ready. This evening, we'll receive army tents from General Johnston's command."

Morning brought another addition to the sailors ashore.

Midshipman James Morris Morgan arrived, via Norfolk and Richmond.

"Jimmie, me lad," cried Rory, as Morgan entered the mess tent. "You're a sight for sore eyes!"

"Hullo, Rory, sir. I guess I'm home at last."

"You've a tale to tell, I've no doubt," said Rory. "Gentlemen," he said to the other officers in the tent, "allow me to introduce Midshipman Jimmie Morgan, late of New Orleans and the CSS *McRae*, and my second in an affair of honor in that fine city. Jimmie, meet First Lieutenant James Rochelle of the *Patrick Henry*, Lieutenant John Taylor Wood, late of the *Virginia,* and Midshipman Archibald Ormsby, late of the *Old Dominion*. We're all artillerists, now. Tell us how you came here."

"A pleasure to meet you all, gentlemen," said the diminutive midshipman. "I left New Orleans after Farragut took the city, April 25th. I've been on trains, mostly, until I arrived at Norfolk to see my friends Mr. Eggleston and Mr. Marmaduke, aboard *Merrimack*. We were shipmates on *McRae*."

"Mr. Eggleston told me to report to Commodore Lee, the Yard commandant, for orders. He told me to get the first train to Richmond, as they were evacuating Norfolk and burning the Yard. Here I am. I confess to being hungry. No food on the trains, not for someone my size trying to compete at the stations, when they had food."

"Come with me, Jimmie, and we'll set you to rights," said Rory, leading Morgan to the galley end of the tent. "How did Savez Read come through the battle?" Lieutenant Charles "Savez" Read had been Rory's other second in the duel with Zouave Colonel Thomas Donovan in New Orleans.

"He sank with colors flying, sir, or darned near. Captain Huger was mortally wounded during the battle. Savez took command and promised Captain Huger he wouldn't strike the colors. *McRae* sank, and as she was going under, some damnyankee boat crew rowed up and made off with the colors, sir."

"Sure, and that's a tragic story, Jimmie. Where is Savez?"

"Making his way to Memphis to join the CSS *Tennessee,* last I heard, Rory. We all made hurried exits, before the Yankees came ashore in force."

By mid-day, the gun emplacements were complete. Taylor Wood had armed a number of the *Virginia's* crew with Enfield rifles provided by Johnston's command. These were army veterans from Magruder's command he'd recruited in January as seamen for the *Virginia.* Quite a few of them were sharpshooters. The Enfields were the best weapon available, although their stocks tended to swell in very wet weather, making it impossible to withdraw the ramrod from the stock housing for loading after firing. The veterans knew to stick the ramrods in the dirt between volleys during heavy rain.

In mid-afternoon, word came from troops down river on the north bank that five Union warships, including *Monitor* and *Galena*, were approaching Drewry's Bluff. Wood received permission from Tattnall to take his riflemen across the river to Chapin's Bluff, slightly downstream, and harass the Yankees when they appeared.

"Gentlemen," said Tattnall to his officers that evening, "if the Yankees force the river here, they'll be shelling Richmond by mid-day tomorrow. We're the only obstacle to destruction of the capital."

Rory and his gun crew were at their big eight-inch Brooke rifle at 7:30 the next morning, as *Galena* calmly anchored four hundred yards from the bluff. Rory's gun weighed eight tons and fired a projectile weighing 120 pounds. The artillery unit and a gun crew from *Jamestown* served the guns in the smaller emplacement, lower down the bluff. *Monitor* and the three other ships were downstream, out of range, but being peppered by Wood's riflemen. *Galena's* commander bent a spring line from his anchor cable to his quarterdeck, hauled in, and thus swung his broadside to bear on the Rebel gun emplacements. Neither side had fired a shot, and all waited expectantly, impressed by *Galena's* purposeful maneuvering.

"He's cool as a cucumber, sir," said Ormsby as he, Rory, and Morgan looked down on the Union ships.

Galena fired a round, and the gunnery began. *Monitor* and *Galena* were unable to elevate their guns sufficiently to damage the

Confederate works, high on the bluff.

Casualties were light, thirteen to the side. *Galena* fired over two hundred rounds, but her topsides were a wreck, as she took over fifty hits, half of them penetrating her three-and-a-half-inch armor.

As the Union ships withdrew, Tucker observed, "Plunging fire is very effective against armor. The height of the bluffs saved us today."

The next day at breakfast, the mess tent was crowded. One table held Wood, Morgan, Ormsby, Rochelle, and Rory. Conversation was spirited, and the table was abuzz with talk of President Davis' visit to the site the evening before. General Robert E. Lee, younger brother of Gosport's commandant, had accompanied the president. Lee was principal military advisor to President Davis, and his duties in that role had included commanding the South Carolina district at Coosawhatchie, but he had not, as yet, had an actual field command. Davis, himself, remembering Rory from his visit with Taylor to the Capitol at Richmond, had introduced Rory to the courtly General Lee. The best part of the visit had been the wagonloads of pies, turkeys, beef, and fresh bread sent by the ladies of Richmond, a gift from Heaven for sailors used to hardtack or weevily biscuits.

When meeting Lee, Rory had searched the general's face and demeanor for any signs that he'd heard of Grenville Donovan's accusations of disloyalty. He'd seen none, but worried about it, just the same. *Sure, the bastard Donovan will have me flinchin' every time I meet an army man. Sometimes I think the services are nothing more than incubators for gossip*, Rory thought.

"Gentlemen," said Taylor, raising his coffee cup, "I give you the men of the *Merrimack*, who saved Richmond."

"To the most effective gun on the bluff," countered Rochelle, "the *Patrick Henry's* eight-inch!"

"And whose colors flew above our redoubts? The *Virginia's*, that's whose," said Wood, answering his own question.

"Might that be, lieutenant, because the *Virginia's* colors had nowhere else to fly, she being in a million pieces, whereas the *Patrick Henry's* still fly at her masthead as she floats, floats, sir, upon the river she yet defends!" Rochelle concluded, and smugly crossed his arms.

"My esteemed superiors," said Rory, "your horses are so high, y'can't reach your breakfast. Surely, there's enough glory to go around. Don't forget, our artillery comrades fired their cannon in the battle, too, and they, last I heard, are on our side as well. Shouldn't the question be 'how do we win the war,' rather than 'who won the battle'?"

"We will prevail, Rory," said Taylor, passionately. "How can we not, over so venal and cowardly a collection of opponents?"

"My brother and Morgan's brother excepted, I'm sure," said Rory, "and your father, too, Taylor, for that matter. But as you told your uncle, our president, the *Monitor* and the *Merrimack* fought to a draw and would again. And I heard you last night say that the *Galena* was very skillfully handled."

"Granted, I did say that," Taylor admitted.

"Here we are, gentlemen, displaying the utmost valor and skill at arms, and we're retreating!" Rory leaned forward, over the table. "We face a nation as dedicated to its cause as we are to ours, but, sure, they've twice the resources. If we can't take the war and the pain of it, to them, and force the weak among them to pressure their leadership to sue for peace, we'll lose a war of stalemate, defense, and attrition, see if we don't!"

Rory looked sheepishly at his comrades. "It's sorry I am. I got a wee excited, I did, sure and all."

"And summed up the situation quite well, I thought," said Taylor. "We need to take the war to them."

"We'll find a way, Taylor," said Rory.

As Rory and Ormsby walked back to the tents housing *Patrick Henry*'s crew, the midshipman said, "Mr. Wood was a bit full of himself this morning, wasn't he, sir?"

"Ah, sure, Archie, Taylor can be pompous, self-righteous and sanctimonious at times, but he's a grand lad in a fight!"

Late that night, in a nearly-deserted mess tent, Rory read a rare letter from his brother Tim, forwarded him by their father, Patrick.

My dear brother, Tim began,

Father has told me of your part in the Hampton Roads battle. I am relieved that you were unhurt, and that your dash showed through. I frequently regret we are on opposite sides of this war. I know we each had the best of reasons, but I wish it were different. And over, also. I'm very proud of you, little brother. And I miss your cheerful outlook. The Western Theater is a discouraging engagement. The men in my unit frequently argue over our reasons for fighting this war, preserve the Union, or abolish slavery. Knowing your loathing of subjugation, I'm sure the same questions, slightly rephrased, must wear on you. You're in my thoughts, Rory. Stay safe!

Affectionately, Timothy

God save you, Tim. I wish it were over, too, Rory thought, his spirits on the ebb.

CHAPTER 16
TOBIAS MEETS THE PRESIDENT,
JUNE 1862

President Lincoln, in carpet slippers and a shawl, sat with his
Navy Secretary, Gideon Welles, and the Assistant Secretary of the Navy,
Gustavus Fox, in Welles' office. Lincoln frequently popped next door
to the gray brick Navy building just west of the White House, when an
important event or issue was before him. The Washington bureaucracy in
1862 was small, miniscule by 21st century standards. Gideon Welles was
a moderate, thoughtful man, a bit dour, but a competent administrator
with a wide range of experience: Connecticut legislator, editor-publisher,
Navy procurement bureau chief, and advisor to Andrew Jackson. Lincoln
found him an excellent sounding board for ideas and policy. Welles' beard
was longer than Lincoln's, and whiter, too.

Many a naval officer sported a beard in these times, and Fox had
worn his while spending eighteen years afloat. His position now could be
described as the Chief of Naval Operations of the 1860s. He had intimate
and detailed knowledge of every aspect of navy life. He was decisive, and
provided a perfect balance to Welles' more-generalized experience.

The three hirsute officials were discussing a dilemma facing the
president: balancing the demands of abolitionists and those who favored
leaving the slavery issue alone. Lincoln had concluded that retaining the
institution of slavery would not serve to hold the Union together, and
that it should be abolished, but the North was divided on that issue. The
astute politician knew that he must move carefully, and wait for just the
right moment to issue the emancipation proclamation already in draft
form in a locked drawer of his office. Issued at the wrong moment, the

proclamation could engender a controversy that would detract from the war effort, if not halt it entirely in the midst of political chaos.

"Gentlemen, I need a signal victory in the land war to give me the platform for the Emancipation Proclamation!" Lincoln sat back in the comfortable easy chair that was always his during these sessions. "With my cautious commanding general, I have my doubts such a victory will be given us soon." Lincoln's opinion of McClellan had been fashioned by a series of disappointments.

"I sent Congress a message last March recommending compensation to any state adopting gradual abolition. They're still debating. In April, I abolished slavery in the District of Columbia, to the cheers of the Abolitionists. In May, when General Hunter unilaterally, and without authorization, abolished slavery in South Carolina, Georgia, and Florida, I revoked his action, fearful of losing Kentucky and Missouri support, and the cheers of the Abolitionists turned to vituperation. Editorials castigated me, gentlemen! Frederick Douglass is still savaging me in every speech. I tell you, it's two steps forward, and one back. Or worse, the reverse!"

"I sense you came here for a purpose beyond finding sympathetic ears, Mr. President," said Fox with a smile.

"Very astute of you, Gus, as usual. I need a gesture that will find favor with the Abolitionists, without inciting the Copperheads and the pro-slavery people in the border states to riot. I was hoping we might have a Negro candidate among those recommended to you for the Medal of Honor that Congress authorized last December. There will be none from the army, obviously, thanks to Jim Crow, but the navy has thousands of black sailors."

"It so happens, sir, that I was reviewing the list last week," said Fox.

"We might have known," said Welles, "given your thirst for detail. Mr. President, I applaud this idea, but Secretary of War Stanton told me he was not anticipating awards of the Medal of Honor until next year."

The President smiled in resignation. "Well, Gideon, Secretary Stanton may have to cease running the country by himself for a little while, at least until we make this gesture. Gustavus, have we any candidates?"

"Yes, sir. Farragut recommended a young sailor aboard *Hartford* at New Orleans, and before that, Commander French of the *Preble* brought a black sailing master to my attention. This man went aboard *Vincennes* while the fuse to the magazine was burning, lit by poor Captain Handy, and cut it at great risk to himself. Saved the ship, for certain."

"I'd like to see those files," said Lincoln.

"Aye, aye, Mr. President. It happens that the master, Mr. St. John, is in town, meeting with Pinkerton, sir, as we speak. He's been active in information-gathering for the Blockading Squadron from the black grapevine, to find sailing dates for blockade-runners." Fox spoke to Welles. "I think this would be a helpful circumstance for the navy, Mr. Secretary."

"Indeed, it would, Gus, and for a number of reasons, a helpful circumstance for the country. Mr. President, selection of a black hero for this honor will undoubtedly help with your short-term need for more time until the right moment to issue the proclamation. The navy's pride in its accomplishments will be increased during a difficult period. But more importantly, your ability to convince the public and the recalcitrants in army leadership that Negroes will make effective soldiers will be enhanced. Sir, you know, I'm sure, it's not far off that we will need the manpower in the army that blacks represent. Selecting a black among the first Medal of Honor winners will make that manpower more politically available."

"Sound advice, as usual, Gideon," said Lincoln. "I believe I would be safe to assume that you have a suggestion as to which of these candidates might best serve the national interest?"

"Since you ask, Mr. President," said Welles, without the hint of a smile, "Mr. St. John seems the most beneficial choice to the war effort. To reinforce the knowledge in the military and in the country that a black can attain commissioned status, and then exhibit bravery and leadership worthy of the nation's highest honor, will be of inestimable value to people's eventual acceptance of Negro infantry units."

"Gideon, Gus, thank you once again for helping this beleaguered old president out of another briar patch. I will read these files and get back to you within a day. I'd be grateful if you'd arrange for Mr. St. John to visit me this afternoon. Through the back entrance, please. I'd like to keep the press ignorant until I can surprise them. More ignorant than usual, if that is possible."

"As you wish, Mr. President," said Welles.

"Mr. President," said Fox, "as you will be talking to St. John, let me share with you more detail on the nature of his next enterprise, which will be quite dangerous, and in the heart of the Confederacy. Flag Officer Du Pont has endorsed this effort." Fox quickly outlined the essentials of Tobias' plan.

After leaving the Navy Department, Lincoln walked back to the White House next door, a tall figure on the path, alone with his thoughts. His confidence in the judgment of his navy secretariat had risen immensely after the navy had managed to focus the industrial power of the machinery manufacturing community, build the *Monitor* in ninety days, and bring her from the Brooklyn Yard to the Chesapeake in time to thwart the actions of the *Virginia* on the second day of the Battle of Hampton Roads. Conferring with Welles and Fox today had not lessened his high opinion of their counsel.

* * *

"Nice to see you again, sir." Tobias was seated in Pinkerton's office, a leather portfolio next to his chair. Pinkerton was reading the plan Tobias had outlined to Flag Officer Du Pont aboard *Wabash*, and the report of the flag officer regarding the acquisition of the steamer *Planter.*

"You state here that I had reevaluated the effectiveness of inserting agents as compared tae developing agents in place."

"Yes, Chief Pinkerton, that was my recollection of our conversation."

"Och, quite accurate, Mr. St. John, I mind it weel. I've continued that reevaluation since our last meeting. My conclusion is that I've wasted much time attempting to implant agents, who are often found out, when I could have been collectin' information on southern Unionists who were already in place and harder to uncover. I've only just begun to assemble a stable of potential agents."

"Have you identified any in Wilmington, sir, who might serve our purpose as owner of a slave pilot?"

"Just one, Mr. St. John, a widow, a Mrs. Devereaux, whose late husband owned a modest shipping line, which she has continued, operating it under the direction of a hired manager. We discovered, through the Black Dispatch and through my interviews with 'contrabands,' that she has been centrally involved with the Underground Railroad."

"Have you contacted her, Mr. Pinkerton?"

"Aye, we've sent her word that we'll send an agent to act as a courier, and ask her for selected information as we identify our needs. I'm thinking that we could send you, Mr. St. John, and that, instead of her courier, you could become her co-agent, to accomplish your goal of capturing more blockade-runners and other Confederate vessels."

"I'm willing to undertake this, Chief Pinkerton."

"I was sure you would be, Mr. St. John. May I call you Tobias? We are going to be close colleagues. My name is Allan."

"Of course you may, Chief. . .Allan. I must work to change my appearance. There are many in the southern maritime establishment who know me on sight."

"And even beyond that, Tobias, a change of your stride and your speech. I've found that these also are keys, which men use to recognize others. Y' willnae be kent, even by those close t' ye, if ye can change your walk and your talk."

"Oh, yes, mon, and when my beard is grown, and my hair is longer, and you hear the sway and lilt of the Islands in my speech, and see the same in my walk, you may be sure not many will find Sailing Master St. John, oh, yes!"

"Convincing, indeed, Tobias. You'll no' be recognized by many."

The two men were deep in a discussion of forged documents, passwords, courier routes, and escape plans when Pinkerton's secretary knocked. "Sir, President Lincoln has sent an aide to request the presence of Mr. St. John, at your convenience."

"Tobias, I believe we can conclude this later. My convenience is precisely that of Abe Lincoln's. Any idea what this is concerning?"

"None in the world, Allan. I'm on pins and needles, as my

Quaker teachers might say."

The aide, a young infantry lieutenant, waited beside a carriage, and Tobias was soon rolling up Pennsylvania Avenue.

Tobias was ushered into the oval office of the president who rose from his chair to greet him. Tobias announced himself. "Tobias St. John, Mr. President, an honor to meet you, sir."

"Mr. St. John, the honor is mine, sir. When I meet a man of your courage and accomplishment, I am the one who is, frankly, in awe. Please tell me of your upbringing and service to your country. I'm curious to learn the ingredients of a hero's make-up."

"Sir, I'm scarcely a hero. A well-trained naval officer and seaman, yes. I confess I feel a certain obligation to make the most of my opportunities. Perhaps that leads me to occasional recklessness, by the standards of others."

"I should say so, judging from this record," said Lincoln, holding Tobias' file. "And I understand from my staff that, with Pinkerton's help, you're once again to go in harm's way."

"So it seems, Mr. President. The more southern Negroes we can induce to flee the Confederate south and come to us, the quicker the war will end. The six million southern whites depend heavily on the labor of the three million southern blacks."

Tobias then explained his Antiguan background, his New Bedford upbringing and Quaker education and his whaling and navy voyaging.

Lincoln said, "You've seen a good part of this world, and have managed not to be diminished by misfortune. An enviable state, I'd say."

"I'd count myself a fortunate man, Mr. President."

"We often carve our own good fortune, sailing master. Your valor has moved me to confer on you your country's highest honor, the Medal of Honor. We'll photograph the ceremony here. We'll make it a small gathering, and restrict attendance, then widely publicize and announce it after you've returned to your station, and begun your transformation for your role behind enemy lines. The fewer people who see you in person now, the safer you'll be on your clandestine assignment."

"Agreed, Mr. President. Sir, I'm moved beyond words by this

recognition. Thank you for this honor and your confidence."

"Both richly deserved, young man. God bless you."

As Tobias walked back to Pinkerton's office to tell him the news, he was close to overcome with emotion. *I feel my value so suddenly recognized,* he thought. *I've never experienced this before.*

As Tobias left, Lincoln mused, *I hope this proves a blessing for him, rather than a curse. The latter is often the way with honors. It will certainly help the nation.*

CHAPTER 17
ONE OF TAYLOR WOOD'S RAIDERS
JUNE 1862

Rory and Taylor Wood sat in the mess tent after the bugler assigned to the gun batteries of Drewry's Bluff had sounded retreat. Bugle calls in the two opposing armies, like their respective Articles of War, were virtually identical. Rain had fallen for days during and after the battle of Fair Oaks, in which General Joe Johnston had been wounded, and had been replaced by Robert E. Lee as commander of the Army of Northern Virginia.

"Will this rain never end?" Wood looked out at the rain-filled dusk beneath the tent flap. It was quiet now, but during the recent battle, the sound of guns had been continuous.

"It's holdin' back McClellan, on either side of the Chickahominy," said Rory. "I was in Richmond today. Sure, the whole city's a hospital, with men lyin' on pallets in the streets. The Farwell's mansion's a hospital of its own, with men in every room." The battle of Fair Oaks had cost the Confederacy six thousand casualties, and the Union five thousand. McClellan's three corps were still in place, but the rains had made the peninsula impassable, and Lee had time to regroup.

"Did you see your young lady, Rory?" Wood had just moved his wife and children from Petersburg to a safer location in Greensboro, North Carolina.

"Didn't I just, and aren't they what keeps us clingin' t'sanity in this chaos, our loved ones?"

"Yes they are, and it will enable us to persevere! I've been thinking of our talk, about taking the battle to the Yankees. I believe I have a plan worth taking to Mallory, one that will cause the Union pain, and certainly alleviate the boredom of manning this battery against an opponent too reluctant to try forcing the James."

"Faith, now, you're a man of action, and that's a fact. What's on your mind, Taylor?"

"At war's beginning, when I was at Aquia Creek battery on the Potomac, I'd see gunboats and merchant ships anchor out at night, just begging to be cut out, like Decatur in Tripoli! We could do that now, on the Potomac, the Rappahannock, the York. We'd have to become 'naval cavalry', wagons pulled by horses with whaleboats aboard in chocks, the sailors mounted, mobile, amphibious, able to launch at night, take a vessel, burn it, and ride off again before any reprisal!"

"And all we need are sailors who are horsemen. You're one, I'm one, there must be others!" Rory was grinning in anticipation.

"I've permission to take this to Mallory. You triggered the idea. Come with me. He obviously likes you and your record. We'll persuade him together."

"Sure, I'd be proud t'be part of your command, oh, great captain of naval cavalry. Let's leave in the morning."

The next morning, the two naval officers rode the seven miles into Richmond. The wounded had been cleared from the streets, and taken to better, if not adequate, facilities. The rain had stopped. They rode up the hill to the old gray stone Mechanics Institute on the west side of Capitol Square, housing the Navy Department. They had not long to wait at Secretary Mallory's office.

Mallory listened while Wood outlined his proposal. "I like this, lieutenant. It's dramatic. It has flair. And, it can be done quickly. It's not like waiting for Tredegar Iron Works to roll the armor for an ironclad. And it's cheap!"

"Sure, Mr. Secretary, just two or three boats and wagons, teamsters, a doctor and an ambulance, ten men the boat, and their horses, and three weeks to train. We'll be ready in no time!" Rory's enthusiasm was contagious.

"Excellent. I'm going to approve this proposal, but you must realize I'll be unable to release you to carry out the actual raids until the threat of a naval assault up the James on Richmond has been removed. I have every confidence that this will take place. Robert E. Lee will seize the initiative from McClellan, without a doubt, and I predict that the front will shift from York peninsula back to the Shenandoah Valley, and the area south of Washington City. This will take some time, as does everything in this damn war. So, you may proceed with preparations; wagon and boat construction, recruiting, determining areas to attack. But you must wait for my release, based on the situation at Drewry's Bluff, before setting the raids in motion. Is that clear?"

"Aye, aye, Mr. Secretary," they responded.

"You're in command, Mr. Wood. Mr. Dunbrody is assigned to your command, and you may select a third officer. Thirty warrants, seamen and petty officers, eight teamsters, a doctor and assistant, and the requisite horses, wagons, boats, and weapons. You may devote half of your duty time to this, and the other half to your defenses at the Bluff. I'll have the orders cut today. Good hunting, gentlemen!"

"Thank you, Mr. Secretary," they chorused. They exited the building, bubbling with eagerness.

A note from Carrie Anne arrived the next day.

My dearest Rory,

My friends, the Van Lews, mother and daughter, will entertain a selection of prominent Confederate leaders in their home next Saturday, at seven in the evening. I have been invited with instructions to bring 'that fine young naval officer from New Berne,' as my guest.

The Van Lews believe that we Richmond civilians must help to cheer our brave men at the battlefront in the aftermath of the carnage of Fair Oaks. I will do my part by lifting your spirits! Please tell me that you can attend, and that I will see you at the Farwell's any time after five in the afternoon. We can walk to the Van Lews' from there. The 'theme' of the affair is to honor the Richmond Howitzers Regiment.

With much affection,
your Carrie Anne

That Saturday, Rory and Captain Tucker rode into Richmond.

"Handsome Jack" Tucker's status as one of the highest-ranking naval officers defending Richmond, and as a widower, qualified him as a "prominent Confederate leader" for purposes of the festivities.

"Perhaps you'll meet some cavalrymen tonight, Mr. Dunbrody. You can discuss the world of the horse-borne, in preparation for your new enterprise with Lieutenant Wood."

"Ah, sure, that's a grand idea, sir. A damn' sight more attractive it is, talkin' about 'em, rather than ridin' 'em. I'm one sore sailor, after my first week of getting used to bein' back in the saddle!"

Tucker chuckled. "I'm sure you'll survive the transition, my young friend. Better you than me, at over fifty. Mr. Wood tells me you're an accomplished horseman."

It's comin' back to me fast, sir, after all those hours in the saddle when I was young in County Meath, at my uncle's stables. Grand summers they were, sir, rollin' green hills and valleys, until the potato blight."

"You'll soon be riding through another beautiful green countryside with its own special blight, Mr. Dunbrody."

"No doubt, captain. No doubt, at all, at all. Here we are, sir, at the Farwell's. They'll think it grand t'meet the famous Captain Tucker, sir. Please come in with me."

After a delightful hour of conversation among the Farwells, the Eastmans, Tucker, and Rory, and being fortified with a cooling libation in the newly-returned warm weather of early June, the entire party strolled the short distance to the Van Lew Mansion.

Uniforms and beautiful summer gowns were in abundance. Many officers wore their dress uniforms with the gleaming gold insignia prominent on the sleeve. The Army of Northern Virginia was slowly learning not to wear the dress uniforms in combat, as the gold insignia of the officers made excellent targets for the Union sharpshooters. The incidence of Confederate infantry officers with their arms in slings was lessening, and by war's end, small, matte' stars to denote rank would be the very practical norm.

A small orchestra played, the inlaid wood floor of the great hall was filled with dancing couples, and Rory and Carrie Anne made the most of their rare moment together. Carrie Anne and cousin Natalie were much sought after by unattached officers, and Rory had frequent interludes to talk to brother officers of the other services. Natalie had confided to Carrie Anne that she intended to diminish considerably her duties as a chaperone in order to leave more time for seeking her own social encounters. Her cousin did not protest.

At one point, while on his own, Rory was startled to see George Pickett, in the uniform of a brigadier general, not two feet from him.

"General Pickett, sir! A long way from San Juan Island."

Pickett turned, and smiled as he recognized Rory. "Mr. Dunbrody, I do declare! And a lieutenant now. Congratulations to us both!"

"Indeed, general. Is your brigade close by?"

"I'm with my old friend, General Longstreet, and his division, sir, and my Virginia boys are lookin' forward to a rematch with the Yankees after Fair Oaks. Your old fencing partner, von Klopfenstein, is still my aide. Here he is now. Major, look who has turned up."

"Ach, ja. The Irish sailor. *Guten abend*, lieutenant." The Prussian's condescending manner had not diminished. He and Rory had developed a mutual antipathy when they were on station together during the "Pig War," several years before, in Washington Territory.

"And a good evening to you, major," Rory replied.

"I haf heard you've gone to war with Louisiana infantry colonels, Irish. Your swordsmanship must have improved."

"Ah, sure, major, it's just the luck of the Irish."

"Dunbrody," said Pickett, "I heard you've seen some interestin' action, right here in Virginia."

"Well, general, me first command was sunk from under me by the *Monitor* while tryin' t'pull the *Merrimack* off a sand bar in Hampton Roads. But before she went, she caused the Yankees a bit of hurt. And one ship we tangled with, the *Cumberland,* is on the bottom of Hampton Roads."

Rory suddenly realized that he was trying to impress the Prussian with his record. *Sure, I don't need any more wary enemies*, he thought. *I'd best downplay my successes.*

"Excuse me, gentlemen. I see a young woman in need of a dance partner." Pickett and von Klopfenstein nodded, and Rory started in Carrie Anne's direction, but an infantry staff officer asked her to dance before he could reach her. Disappointed, he noticed he was abeam of the bar and the punch bowl. A cavalryman, in an officer's uniform with no insignia of rank, stood nearby. Clean-shaven, not handsome, yet compelling, slender, with a firm jaw and keen blue eyes at once amused and defiant, he smiled at Rory.

"There's a major who doesn't like you much, lieutenant."

"You've the right of it there, sir. You're very observant, and all. I can see you're a dashin' man of the horse cavalry. What I can't tell is should I be salutin' ye, and calling you 'Sir'? Let me pour you a drink, and you can enlighten me."

"The name is John Mosby, and I've been a captain and adjutant of cavalry, and a lieutenant. At the moment, I'm a private, and scout for the man over there." Mosby pointed to a flamboyant, luxuriously-bearded cavalry general, who Rory recognized at once as J.E.B. Stuart, leader of the Virginia cavalry. "And just a cup of that fine coffee yonder, if you please."

"We'll make it a coffee for 'Captain' Mosby, then. I've no doubt it should be, by all rights. Rory Dunbrody is my name, and I'm a lieutenant on detached shore duty to John Taylor Wood."

"Well, we're a pair, Mr. Dunbrody of the Emerald Isle. A captain with no rank, and a sailor with no ship! Let's sit us down and unfold this mystery."

"Sure, I never could resist the challenge of a conundrum, Captain Mosby. You first, sir."

"Well, I served as adjutant and captain in the First Virginia Cavalry, under Colonel 'Grumble' Jones, when Congress changed the law regarding selection of officers, and made all ranks under general subject to election by the men of the unit. Jones was voted out, and Fitzhugh Lee, no fan of mine, voted in."

"I lost my commission, but fortunately, General Stuart thinks I'm an able scout, and I'm now acting as his personal chief scout. In fact, I've just discovered a gap in the Union lines that will accommodate a brigade of cavalry, and if J.E.B. Stuart has his way, soon will. What an adventure that will be!"

"Sure, my story's not the equal of yours, but it may reach the same conclusion." Rory outlined his set of experiences in the CSN, with special emphasis on his upcoming 'naval cavalry' endeavor. "So, as you can see, Captain Mosby, although I may be somewhat accomplished as a horseman, I'm very rusty at the craft, and moreover, I've a need for expert advice on the most recent techniques and tactics. Sure, you're just the lad I'm lookin' for!"

"You're quite a performer, lieutenant, with the brogue. I'm a great fan of stage presence. You see, I'm a lawyer in civilian life. I think we can advance the Southern Cause by a short 'seminar in the saddle,' if you will. Let me frame a proposal. Your commander, Mr. Wood, detaches you for a two or three day cavalry ride behind enemy lines, during which you observe technique and tactics which will be useful in your 'cutting-out' expeditions. Everyone benefits, and we have a fine ride!"

"Sure, and it's a grand plan, Your Worship," said Rory with a grin in his best stage-Irish accent.

"We'll take it directly to General Stuart! Who could resist his endorsement?" And so they did, and with the approval of the broad-shouldered cavalry commander in hand, they mentioned to Captain Tucker that they'd lay it before Lieutenant Wood in the morning, and walked away with the endorsement of Tucker, too.

Rory timed his approach to Carrie Anne perfectly, as a crimson-sashed artillery officer finished a dance, and Rory adroitly stepped in front of a red-pantalooned Alabama Zouave, to reach her side first.

"Where have you been, sailor-boy?" Carrie Anne arched an eyebrow.

"Sure, I've been courtin' another," said Rory, smugly. He laughed. "In this case, a lawyer-turned-cavalry-scout who's takin' me on a ride with him day after tomorrow."

Rory was enlivened by the prospect of action, and grew even more heady as he danced in Carrie Anne's arms. As they waltzed, they spun near the edge of the dance floor next to the veranda doors, which were open in the warm June night. They danced on to the darkened veranda, and to its end, past couples in each other's arms, and paying no attention to one more. They stopped near a stair to the upstairs deck, and kissed, an opportunity which had been absent for most of the year. *My God, I love this woman so,* he thought.

"The subtle chaperoning that your living conditions impose has been difficult to overcome, love. I feel as if we're out of prison tonight," said Rory.

Carrie Anne threw her arms around his neck and rested her head on his shoulder. "I've the same feeling, Rory. You're here so seldom, and when I see all the wounded, and the carts of corpses in the streets after a battle, I'm so frightened for you, for us."

"I think I'm more at risk from that spalpeen, Grenville Donovan, spreadin' lies as he did at my court of inquiry, than from cannon fire."

"But, love, you were exonerated, vindicated!"

"That time, sure, but won't he be tryin' it over and over?"

The evening had worn on, and most of the older guests, including Mrs. Eastman, the Farwells, and Tucker, had departed. The orchestra still played and the bar still served. "This is a large mansion, is it not?" Rory asked.

"With many rooms, my darling."

"And cousin Natalie is no where to be found?"

"Vanished!"

"Up these stairs, then?" He sought her gaze anxiously.

"Oh, yes!"

They found their way to the deserted third floor, into a bedroom facing south to the river.

"I want this, Rory. I want you." Her breathing was rapid, her face already flushed.

"I'll not refuse, my love."

In a matter of moments, gown, uniform, stays, smallclothes, lay scattered on the floor. Rory and Carrie Anne joined as lovers; hungry, quite impatient lovers, oblivious to the music below in deference to the music of their pulses pounding. On a finely-made Virginia four-poster, their skin glistening in the streetlights' dim glow through the open window, the midnight breeze off the river cooled them as they made love at last.

"Oh, love," sighed Rory, "to see your beautiful body, caress you, to bring you to that joyous moment; I've dreamed of it since New Orleans."

Later, as Rory walked Carrie Anne back to the Farwell residence, they paused beneath the elms to talk and embrace again. "You were so good to me, love. I shall treasure the memory."

"Rory, you must contact me the minute you return from your cavalry outing."

"Upon my word as a Dunbrody, I shall," he said. "Tell me, love, are the Van Lew ladies in some danger from the authorities? There was talk of it tonight, the kind of party gossip one often hears at these affairs. People love to see themselves as in the midst of calamity, as long as they're not in danger from it, themselves."

"Elizabeth tells me they've been reported several times, accused of improper attention to the Union prisoners. I think gatherings like this one help to diffuse the criticism. But Elizabeth has also hinted that she helps slaves escape to the North. There are many Unionists in Richmond, particularly families of German descent. I think the Van Lews maintain a network that passes messages and contraband slaves to the North." She raised her chin and looked Rory in the eye. "I agree with Elizabeth. That is a Christian endeavor."

"And so it is, my love. But you must be careful how closely your friendship grows. The Confederacy has its own spy-catchers, and they watch carefully. These are men not above inventing facts to suit their fiction. Our friend Grenville's a good example."

"And if I were accused," Carrie gasped, "you might be caught in the same net of suspicion."

"Sure, I was raised in a nation where informers are rife, and the rights of the accused amount to the end of a rope. The same will happen here, in wartime. Be very cautious, love."

"And the same to you, Rory Cormac Dunbrody, as you ride with Jeb Stuart. That's not going to be an evening in the rocking chair before the fire."

CHAPTER 18
MOSBY'S RIDE,
JUNE 12-14

John Taylor Wood was quick to approve Rory's proposed adventure with the Virginia cavalry, and two days later, Rory rode to meet Mosby at Stuart's headquarters, just north of Richmond. James Ewell Brown ("JEB") Stuart had resigned from the Union Army at the war's beginning as a cavalry captain, and had become a lieutenant colonel commanding the First Virginia Cavalry Regiment. Now, as a brigadier general, he commanded the cavalry brigade that included the First Virginia.

During a scout for Stuart, Mosby had discovered a lightly defended gap in McClellan's line at the north side of Richmond, where Totopotomoy Creek flows into the Pamunkey River, beyond Bethesda Church. Rory spent the night in the cavalry encampment, and at daybreak, the brigade, twelve hundred strong, rode to Hanover Court House, west of the Pamunkey, where they bivouacked for the night. Rory brushed, curried and fed his horse, a strong bay. He and Mosby shared a tent.

"Tomorrow, you'll ride along with me as we scout ahead of the main body of troops," said Mosby. "I see you've a holster for your Navy Six."

"Aye, it's a fine weapon. I've brought my saber, too," Rory replied.

"In my time with the First Virginia, I discovered that the Colt six-shot was a weapon far better suited for the horseman than the carbine, or even the saber. I've taken to carrying two, holstered at my belt, and two more holstered either side of my horse's neck, just in front of the saddle."

"Sure, and I can see that. Easy to handle, with twenty-four shots loaded and close at hand."

"I've taken the liberty of acquiring three more Colts, for you," said Mosby, "if you're inclined to experiment."

"Very kind of Your Worship, lookin' out for this sailor out of water."

"Oh, you'll do fine, lieutenant. I've seen you ride. But, I think you'll be better prepared for the unexpected with four Navy Sixes."

"Never a doubt, Captain Mosby."

The next morning, they rode out with a squad of troopers from the Ninth Virginia Cavalry. As they approached the Totopotomoy, they came upon a small force of blue-coated cavalry that scattered in to a copse of woods along the bank as they rode down slope toward the creek. Mosby sent a man back to report to Stuart. He soon returned, leading a troop of the Ninth Virginia.

Closer to the Pamunkey, at Linney's corner, they surprised a troop of the Fifth U.S. Cavalry, and Mosby led the saber-swinging Confederates as they smashed into the Union force. Mosby rode with a Colt six-shot revolver in either hand. Rory followed, his left hand on the reins and his Navy Six in his right. "Sure, it seems quicker than my saber," Rory thought, as he fired at a blue-coated sergeant who was about to swing his saber. The sergeant left an empty saddle, and Rory fired again, at a trooper who had clubbed his carbine, but could not swing it in time. Suddenly, the little clearing was free of Union riders, and Mosby dismounted, followed by the Ninth's troop commander and his men.

"Lieutenant, may we send back to General Stuart, and ask that we have permission to ride through to the Pamunkey? We'll find good hunting there," said Mosby.

Stuart cast his lot with a full encirclement of the Union forces, and Mosby led the troop of the Ninth in an advance to the river and downstream. They pulled up on a rise and saw the Pamunkey below them. A small wharf on the southwest bank held two supply schooners unloading. As the troopers charged down the slope, the stevedores scattered and the crew raised their hands in surrender.

"Mr. Dunbrody, would you take a detail and burn the schooners, please," called Mosby. "It seems it would be your specialty."

"Aye, aye, Captain Mosby," Rory responded. He gathered six cavalry troopers, explained where to find the lantern kerosene stores, and told them to break kindling from the cabin furniture to start the blaze. Another squad of troopers, guns held on the crewmembers, were ushering them off the schooners.

"Corporal," said Rory to the senior trooper in his band of six, "Take two men and fire the smaller schooner. You others come aboard this one with me." Rory pointed to the larger of the two. As the four Confederates went aboard, they saw a trooper with a carbine gesturing to an angry-faced older man wearing an officer's cap, apparently the schooner's captain.

"Sir, this 'un won't move," the trooper said, pointing his weapon at the captain.

"Very well, trooper," said Rory, "I'll reason with him. Have you seen what's in the hold?"

"Horse fodder and small arms ammunition, it 'ppears to me, sir."

Rory turned to the captain. "Captain, we're firing your vessel. Move ashore, please."

"Go to hell, you rebel," the captain said, cholerically. Then, in an abrupt change of tone, he wailed, "She's all I have, my livelihood, and my wife and daughter are aboard." A round-faced woman of the captain's age and a comely young girl came up through the companionway from below at that moment.

"Yes, sir, I quite understand, but you should have thought of that before you shipped a cargo of contraband."

"I told you it would come to this," scolded the captain's wife.

"God damn you sir," the captain exclaimed. "Just what I'd expect of a Rebel and a damned Irish one, at that!"

The wife was scolding, the daughter was weeping, and the captain was haranguing when Rory roared, "at ease! You, sir! Take your wife below and take what personal items you wish. You have three minutes. Trooper, keep an eye on this young woman, please." Rory watched the Union couple descend the companionway out of the corner of his eye, and saw an expression on the captain's face that sent him bounding down the companionway two stairs at a time. He burst through the door of the cabin. The wife's face froze in alarm. The captain's hand was under the mattress. He withdrew it clutching a revolver, just as Rory seized his wrist with a grip of iron. Rory wrenched the weapon from the Yankee's grasp. "Gather your things and leave the cabin ahead of me, ma'am," he said to the woman as he shoved her husband through the cabin door. "And when you next hear the Irish disdained, remember the Irishman who spared your husband's life. I could shoot him where he stands!"

The Union family was hurried off the schooner at gunpoint, much shaken. "Ready to light, trooper?" Rory asked.

"Yes, sir," the cavalry trooper responded, match in hand.

"Light her off, then, and be damned to the ungrateful blatherskites!" Rory signaled to the corporal on the smaller schooner, who put his match to a pile of debris stacked around the mast in the open hold. The Rebels ran quickly down the gangways.

The flames leapt to the mastheads. Pillars of fire shot up from the holds, and birds in the nearby trees were startled into flight. The troopers held their mounts, enjoying the conflagration, like children with fireworks.

"Mount," called Mosby, who had been watching the unfolding drama from a distance. The troop swung into their saddles and clattered off. "I thought those women were fixin' t' outflank you, there, lieutenant, for a moment," Mosby said with a chuckle.

"Sure, I was fair flummoxed, is the truth of it, Your Worship. Women in a battle area, not a good thing, at all, at all!"

Crossing a road paralleling the Pamunkey, they followed it down stream and overtook a convoy of wagons. They stopped the convoy, overturned the wagons, and then burned the contents and the wagons themselves. That road intersected another, with telegraph lines strung along it. Mosby directed two troopers to climb the poles and cut the wires.

Toward evening, Mosby halted the troopers in the vicinity of Tunstall Station. "Very quiet," he said. "Lieutenant, please hold the troop here. I'm going on ahead for a look around. I have a feeling."

The riders dismounted as Mosby disappeared over a rise. Spirits were high. The supply wagons had yielded better rations than the Confederates were used to, including a wagonload of wine cases. Suddenly, Stuart's advance guard rode into the clearing, and as the lieutenant was reporting to the colonel commanding the advance squadron, they heard a shot, and the voice of Mosby shouting orders.

When they galloped over the rise, a squadron of the Eleventh Pennsylvania was withdrawing. Mosby explained to the colonel, "I drew my saber and gave orders as if I had a squadron just over yonder, sir. Sure enough I did. When they heard you all, they withdrew. A good thing for me. This horse is too tired to outrun anyone."

Sure, the horse isn't the only tired member of this troop, thought Rory. *I'm damn' glad Mosby gave me two water canteens along with my four pistols. I'm near to done with thirst.*

Into the evening, and all through the night, Stuart pressed forward, burning and looting supply depots and wagons. Along the York River Railroad, they attacked a supply train. Fires burned in their wake like beacons. By mid morning of the next day, they had returned to Richmond, exhausted, exhilarated, and the toast of the town.

As Rory prepared to rejoin Wood's unit, he stood by Mosby's tent while he and the scout, still invigorated by the ride, talked of lessons learned. "Well, now, captain, you taught me that surprise and a bold front will win through almost always."

"What about mobility and living off the land?"

"Those, too, Captain Mosby!"

"The next time you see me, Mr. Dunbrody, I hope to be a real captain again. I'll be asking Stuart to give me a unit under the Partisan Ranger Act that Congress passed, and let me range behind enemy lines. I want to discombobulate that pompous bastard, General Pope, and his new Union Army in Northern Virginia."

"Sure, how could Stuart refuse you, now, after what you've done these last three days? Lee praised you, himself, in his congratulatory dispatches. Good luck to you, Jack, and thank you."

"And the same to you, Rory. Keep your head down."

CHAPTER 19
BUILDING THE CSS ALBEMARLE

Rockett's Wharf was a beehive of activity, befitting its recently attained status as Virginia's preeminent Navy Yard. After the burning and evacuation of Gosport, the Confederate Navy had nowhere else to turn for ship construction in the Old Dominion. Now referred to as 'Rockett's Yard,' about to expand to both banks of the river, and just downstream from Richmond proper, it was the genesis of Confederate vessels ranging from the ironclads *Richmond* and *Virginia II* to the twenty-one-foot double-ender whaleboats being constructed for Taylor Wood's latest project, the raids on the Chesapeake's western shore. Even the wagons to carry the boats were being modified at Rockett's, and fitted with chocks to keep the boats steady in the wagons across the many miles of bad country and riverfront roads they would travel.

Rory and Taylor sat in the superintendent's office at Rockett's, going over details of their raiding plans.

"I'm bringing on Sidney Lee as the third officer of our raider contingent, Rory. He's senior to you, so he'll be my nominal second in command, but there'll be many opportunities for independent operation, so chain of command will not be central to our efforts."

"It suits me fine, Taylor." Rory smiled. "I've been followin' you since you were a 'Firstie' at the Academy, and I was a fifteen-year-old 'Youngster.' I've no complaints with your command decisions."

"True, Rory, we've been a long way together."

"Lieutenant Lee is General Fitzhugh Lee's younger brother, is he not, Taylor?"

"He is, and a fine officer, like his brother."

I'll not be braggin' about my learning from Mosby, thought Rory, *not if Sidney Lee dislikes John Mosby as much as his brother does.*

Taylor Wood lowered his voice, and leaned closer to Rory. "Tell me, Rory. I know the men are skeptical, perhaps amused, by my reliance on our Lord for guidance and sustenance during combat. Do you find it troublesome or uncomfortable?"

"Sure, now, Taylor, there's nothing wrong with a prayer before battle. Many find it comforting. I'm less devout than you — than many, to be sure — but we need to find strength where we can. You just need to remember that those across the line from us may be as devout as you, and have the strengths of your beliefs, as well. I won't argue that there is none of the oppressor nor the odious among the Federals, but, remember, many of them were comrades, and brave and true at that. This isn't a war with evil only on one side, and good only on the other."

"True, true, but their leaders do vex me so."

"And ours, them, I'll wager. Let's talk about how we might vex them, Taylor. Where shall we strike first?"

"Why, on the Potomac, Rory. Close to their capital. Let them know that nowhere are they beyond our reach!"

And so, as the weeks passed, the raiders came closer and closer to readiness; and McClellan's forces, closer to withdrawal. The 25th of June saw the beginning of the Battle of the Seven Days, seven engagements as the Union Army withdrew across the peninsula from Yorktown on the York River to Harrison's Landing on the James. The battles of Oak Grove, Gaines' Mills, Garnett's and Golding's Farms, White House Landing, Savage's Station, White Oak Swamp, and Malvern Hill cost the South twenty thousand casualties, and the North, sixteen thousand.

In early July, McClellan informed Lincoln that his army was 'safe' in Harrison's Landing, and favored the President with a letter pointing out ways in which McClellan believed the president could improve his military and political strategies. Lincoln's dissatisfaction with McClellan was not diminished.

General Pope's Northern Army of Virginia was in the Shenandoah Valley, and Lee moved north to confront him at the Rapidan River and Culpeper. McClellan would not attack Richmond without reinforcement from Pope, which Lincoln would not condone. Opportunity fell victim to indecision and caution.

In late July, as Rory was reading a copy of the *Richmond Examiner* in the mess tent, he noticed an article on the capture of "a well-known scout for General J.E.B. Stuart," one John Singleton Mosby, by elements of the New York Cavalry. "Our dashing cavalry lad has encountered some bad luck," Rory thought.

The very same day, Rory received a letter from his father.

> *My Dear Rory,*
>
> *You may have read that the Yankee General Burnside, with a large portion of his troops, has been withdrawn from this part of North Carolina. Burnside was a competent, careful and successful general officer, so his leaving may help the Confederate cause in North Carolina. His replacement, General John Gray Foster, may or may not possess the same qualities, but one of his first actions was unsuccessful. He moved against some of our cavalry just miles down river from us, at Hamilton.*
>
> *Several weeks ago, he sent three gunboats up from Plymouth, and of course our "partisan telegraph" got word to us long before the gunboats did. Company B of the First North Carolina Cavalry was patrolling around Hamilton. Alex Andrews, a friend of ours, was in command. He had his men line the bank in the brush, just above a big bend in the river. His men opened fire on his signal, and riddled the gunboats with minie balls.*
>
> *A number of Yankee sailors were shot, and the boats turned tail, after blasting the riverbank with cannon fire. By then, Alex's boys had "skeddadled," as they say in these parts. Alex followed them a long way downriver. The cavalry would snipe, and the Yankee cannons would roar. Pretty soon, the Yankees would fire at the bank before the cavalry opened up. The Yankees couldn't see anything, of course, so Alex made it a guessing game. It was quite a play, in several acts.*
>
> *It may have saved our little shipyard here in Edwards Ferry, as most folks think the gunboats were on their way to destroy the railroad bridges at Weldon, upstream from us. They'd have*

blown our "cornfield enterprise" to bits, sure as I'm a Dunbrody.
We have just heard from Mr. Secretary Mallory, awarding
us a contract to build an ironclad. The Navy Department wants
to name her the Albemarle. We've been practicing on schooners
while waiting to hear. We've built a ways for launching, and
have constructed a blacksmith shop to turn out the iron fittings.
Collecting the iron for the armor plating will be a great challenge.
If we're desperate, you may hear of several railroad derailments in
North Carolina. (Just my little joke!)
Siobhan sends her love. She has thus far avoided the fevers
that in the past have seemed to plague her this far inland. Stay safe,
and wend your way through Edwards Ferry if you can.
your Da'

Taylor Wood joined Rory in the mess tent. The twitter of the birds softly rose above the hum of insects in the Virginia afternoon. It was a comforting sound. Rory had to remind himself that, among the insects common to the bluff, was the tick. The troops and sailors of the Drewry's garrison were often reminded to stay on the trails, or wear high cavalry boots to avoid the pesky arachnids. "What are you reading, Rory?" asked Taylor.

"A letter from my Da', Taylor. He's setting up a make-shift shipyard at Edwards Ferry, with his partners, and getting to work on a new ironclad."

"Any news of that Yankee brother of yours?"

"Not in this letter. In his last one, he was a bit down on us being on opposite sides. Timothy finds ways to get the occasional letter to our family, but it's random, at best. Tim loves to correspond, 'though. I remember when I was a tiny lad at Uncle Liam's in County Galway, Tim would write from the western frontier, about Indian raids, and all. He'd print big letters, and use short words, suitable for a four-year-old, and then he'd illustrate them. He'd paste cut-out pictures from magazines, or snipped photographs of his battalion mates, right beside his printed text. Just the thing to capture a wee lad's attention."

"He sounds like a caring brother," said Taylor, reflectively. "I'll include him in my prayers, for your sake, Rory."

"Ah, sure, you're a fine shipmate, Taylor. When I came to the Naval Academy, Tim was stationed in New York, for a time. He'd make a point of visitin' his baby brother several times a year. He'd be grateful for your prayers, and I am too, sure, and I am."

CHAPTER 20
PRELUDE TO ESPIONAGE,
ANTIGUA AND ILES DES SAINTES
JULY 1862

Back aboard *Wabash*, Tobias was feted for his receipt of the Medal of Honor. His first Sunday back aboard, at the morning 'rig for church' formation, Captain Rodgers called the ship's company to attention, and Flag Officer Du Pont read the citation which President Lincoln had read at the small, more private ceremony in Washington, D.C. Du Pont then hung the medal, with its bronze, five-pointed star, around Tobias' neck on its red and blue ribbon. Three cheers were rendered by the ship's company, after which, Captain Rodgers returned to the traditional Sunday service, a short reading from the Scriptures, followed by his reading of the entire Articles of War.

Later, Tobias' messmates in the wardroom admired the small, framed photograph of the award ceremony, which the president himself had presented to Tobias before he had left the capital.

The following week, at the beginning of July, Tobias received orders for temporary duty in St John's, Antigua. He was to allow his hair to grow in order to prepare his disguise for his forthcoming assignment in enemy territory, at Wilmington, North Carolina.

As his schooner entered the beautiful Harbor of St. John's, he felt a pang of homesickness and nostalgia, remembering his days as a child on this island. The twin turrets and the bulk of the Cathedral rose halfway up the hill to his left as the schooner anchored. He made his way ashore, and up the hill to the old family residence at Number Four, High Street, at the corner of High and Temple streets, where his cousin Mitchell now lived. Mitchell's son Daniel answered Tobias' knock as he stood on the veranda. "Dad, dad," called little Daniel. "Cousin Toby's here!" Daniel, uniquely, had Tobias' permission to call him "Toby." Tobias lifted the twelve-year-old in one arm, and threw the other around the shoulders of his cousin, Mitch.

"So good to see you bot', an' be home again," said Tobias, falling gently into the patois of the island. "You're gettin' too big to lift, Daniel."

"Are you home on leave, mon?" Mitch asked.

"No, cousin, I need to board here for a month, and let my beard grow and hair lengthen. I need to change my look, just a bit, you see."

"You about to do somet'ing dangerous, mon!" Mitch declared.

"Oh, yes, cousin, I open my mout' once too often," Tobias laughed. "Now, I pay d' price."

"You'll be seeing Monique, in Terre-de-Haut?"

"You may be sure of dat," said Tobias, "but I need to think about us first. It is hard to be apart for so long, but I can't figure how to be together."

"I hear you, cousin," said Mitch.

Monique Duvalliere, Tobias' childhood friend, and now his cherished lover, lived south of Antigua in the town of Bourg des Saintes, on the island of Terre-de-Haut, most populous of les Iles des Saintes. Monique lived independently, owning her own fabric shop, but providing companionship and support for her widowed father, Pierre, a semi-retired fisherman of Breton descent, like most of the residents of Terre-de-Haut. She had several brothers, all fishermen and married, and the family was close. Her late mother, a beautiful former slave from the neighbor island of Terre-de-Bas, long ago had saved her father from his wrecked fishing boat. Her beauty caught his eye. He had paid for her freedom and married her.

"Mitch, my dear cousin," said Tobias after a week in St. John's, "you're a most accommodating host, you may be sure."

"What is it you want, Cousin?' asked Mitch, laughing. "When you start out like dat, I know there is a request to follow, oh yes!"

"Not that I'm tired of playing with Daniel, but I want to visit Monique. Can you get me there, or find out when one of her brothers will sail to English Harbour?"

"Oh, yes, Tobias, we can do dat. We can't have you pining away, so close to your lovely fren'."

Three days later, Tobias rode a donkey across the island, through the cane fields and past the sugar mills, to English Harbour at the island's south shore. There, he met Monique's brother, Etienne, and his schooner. They crossed the forty-mile wide Guadeloupe Passage and sailed south past the leeward side of Guadeloupe. As always, the volcanic canyons or "chutes" on the slopes of Mt. Soufriere funneled violent gusts of wind down the mountain and into the waters off Basse Terre, threatening "knock-downs" to surprise the unwary mariner. Etienne, as much at home in these waters as in his own living room, sailed nonchalantly past Pointe de Vieux Fort to les Iles des Saintes, and the principal city, Bourg, on the island of Terre-de-Haut.

"You're on your own, *mon ami*," said Etienne. "I need to unload cargo. I think you know the way to Monique's."

"*Merci*, Etienne." Tobias climbed the streets leading up from the harbor side to Monique's little fabric shop. He pushed the door open and entered the shop. "Monique?" He called softly.

"*Cherie.*" The lovely, blue-eyed woman ran from the back of the shop, embraced him fondly, and held him at arms length. I heard you were at home. The island grapevine, *oui?* I'm so glad to see you!"

"And I, you, my love, my dear. I have been thinking so much of you, of us. It is most perplexing, truly!"

"Oh," she said in mock pique, "now I'm perplexing?"

"No, our situation, not you!" Tobias laughed, in spite of himself. "I'm trying to be serious, to be analytical, and you won't let me."

"Part of my charm, *cherie*. And you tend strongly to be analytical. You're a navigator, after all. Let us go upstairs and you can tell me, of your thoughts, and our 'situation.'" Monique's apartment was over her shop, up an outside flight of stairs leading from her small courtyard.

Tobias gazed out her front window, overlooking the harbor, before he spoke. "Oh, love, you are here, place bound, caring for your father, secure in the separate and isolated world of the Saintes, and my life takes me away, for months or years at a time, and yet we long to be together. I could never ask you to go to New Bedford. I am never there, myself. We are complete together, but our lives are contradictions, incompatibles."

"Our world is not perfect, true, but we see each other as often as fate allows. You have your other love, the sea. I care for my father, and I am at peace here among my family and childhood friends, in these beautiful islands. It could be worse!"

"Would you ever want to travel, to see the rest of the world?"

"With you as my guide, if our situations ever allowed such a journey. But you tell me much about far lands, in your letters, in your visits. Then, too, I know this world can often be unpleasant and dangerous for people of color. I am, for now, content. You have my proxy, to take risks. But, not too many!"

"I'm somehow comforted, but I'm not sure why, my love."

She laughed. "You're comforted because I'm undemanding, but I can fix that! Are you hungry, Tobias? I'll cook dinner, but you must go to the market for me. I have a list."

Tobias walked down the cobblestone street to the bustling marketplace with his list in his hand. With his arms full of groceries for their dinner he returned from the market, climbing the narrow street to Monique's apartment past the brilliant Bougainvillea covering the walls along the side of the street. The front door was ajar, and he called as he entered. "Monique?"

"In here," she called from the bedroom. "Put down the groceries and come to me." Tobias pushed open the bedroom door. She lay, naked, reading one of his letters, her breasts brushing the coverlet. The afternoon sun shone through the louvers shading her window, lighting the beautiful curve of her back and buttocks, and she then rolled to face him, a warm smile on her face, her arms lifting. "You must be tired from shopping. Come lie down with me." Tobias felt her hand at his belt, and stepped out of his white duck trousers. "I am so glad to see you, my love," she said, "and I see you are very glad to see me."

The sun was setting by the time they finally descended to the courtyard. Monique poured two glasses of sauvignon blanc and placed them on the table beneath the bougainvillea. As Tobias raised his, he noted his shaking hand.

"You're trembling, dear," said Monique, smiling.

"It is nothing, love. Perhaps it is Mount Soufriere or Pele. Oh, yes!"

"Oh, my sweet, I felt the earth move, and there were eruptions, but not, I think, from the volcanoes."

CHAPTER 21
ORDERS COME TO ST JOHN'S, ANTIGUA
SEPTEMBER 1, 1862

Tobias sat in Mitchell's dining room, reading intently.

"What is the letter, cousin Toby?" Daniel sat across from Tobias. Daniel considered Tobias his own big playmate, and was a constant companion when Tobias came to visit.

"These are my instructions for my next assignment, Daniel. I have to memorize them, because I can't carry them to remind me. If someone were to read them over my shoulder, it would be very dangerous."

Master Tobias St. John, USN
September, 1862
Dear Mr. St. John:

> *On the 11th, instant, you will take ship aboard the schooner Santa Victoria, at St. John's, Crown Colony of Antigua, bound for St. George, Bermuda. You will pose as a newly-acquired slave pilot, property of Mrs. Amanda Devereaux, the widow of a wealthy Wilmington ship-owner. Mrs. Devereaux is, in fact, such a widow, but in addition, she is an agent of our Secret Service, dedicated to the defeat of the Confederacy and the abolition of slavery, and since her husband's death has been working toward those ends.*

> *Many masters give their slaves names from the Greek and*

Roman classics. I have constructed and enclosed your forged papers, bill of sale and passes, under the name "Marcus Aurelius", "Marcus" for short.

Mrs. Devereaux's pilot, Cato, a freedman posing as a slave (all of Mrs. Devereaux's servants are freedmen, and all aid her efforts as our agent), will meet you at the office of her shipping agent in St. George, Mr. Callender, on the late afternoon of the 13th, instant. Mr. Callender will arrange for your lodging while you wait in St. George. You will go aboard the Carolina Princess, the Devereaux blockade-runner, commanded by Captain Waylon, for her run to Wilmington. Captain Waylon and Mr. Callender, as you no doubt have surmised, are unaware of the work Mrs. Devereaux and her black servants do for the Union.

At Wilmington, you will "apprentice" under the tutelage of Cato, and devise a plan with Mrs. Devereaux and her associates to deliver at least one blockade-runner into Union hands. You will also observe, to the best of your ability, the nature of the defenses at Federal Point (now called Confederate Point by the Rebels).

I have enclosed information concerning sailing times, coordinates off New Inlet, and shore bearings at which a collection of blockade vessels will entrap the ship or ships you arrange to capture. Memorize and destroy these, along with the rest of this communication. Upon the night twenty-four hours prior to the trap, signal the blockading squadron by means of a bonfire at New Topsail Inlet, twenty miles north of Cape Fear.

Time is of the essence. My other North Carolina sources inform me that Confederate Secret Service agents are newly suspicious of Mrs. Devereaux, not for our plot, but for her activities providing sanctuary for runaway slaves on the Underground Railroad.

This may be one of my last enterprises as Secret Service Chief of the Army of the Potomac. I am closely connected with General McClellan. Rumors are rife in the capital regarding the near-certainty of his dismissal by Mr. Lincoln as commander of the Army of the Potomac. I am sure to be replaced as well, if he *is dismissed. As one of my duties has been the personal security of President Lincoln, it is possible I may continue to serve the president directly.*

I wish you the best of good fortune in this endeavor. It has been my pleasure and honor to work with an individual of your courage and determination.

I remain your humble and obedient servant,

Allan Pinkerton,

Chief of the Secret Service

of the Army of the Potomac

"Do you have to leave soon?" Daniel asked.

"In ten days, Daniel," Tobias replied. "Still lots of time for sailing and swimming with you."

"I will miss you, Cousin Toby," said Daniel.

"And I you, little cousin," said Tobias. But anytime you want to see me, get your dad to take you to Auntie Monique's. I left the photograph with her that President Lincoln gave me."

"Oh, splendid, mon," cried Mitchell, in mock anguish. "Now, he'll be after me daily for a sail to Terre-de-Haut!"

"Do you good, Mitch! Get you out more, cousin."

Amid the ensuing laughter, Mitch pointed his finger at Tobias. "You just be careful, mon," he said. "This island would not be the same without you."

CHAPTER 22
BLOCKADE RUNNERS IN BERMUDA
SEPTEMBER 1862

St. George, capital of Her Britannic Majesty's Colony of
Bermuda, was a wild and wanton place in the autumn of 1862. Six
hundred-plus miles from Charleston, and a bit less from Wilmington,
it was one of two preferred stops for cargoes shipped from Great Britain
to be transferred to swift blockade-runners for the Carolina leg of their
journey. Nassau, in the Bahamas, shared Bermuda's distinction as a
blockade transfer point, and shared also her reputation as a town whose
visitors recognized no tomorrow.

Captains and crews of blockade-runners made thousands
of dollars per voyage, if they could run the gauntlet of the Union
blockade. Wealth, or death. For those who survived, it was a heady brew.
Champagne, women, song, and all-night carousing, were the norm for the
crews that returned from their runs.

Tobias St. John, Master, United States Navy, sat in a bar near the
St. George harborside. He would not have been picked from a crowd as
a commissioned American naval officer, with his Antiguan accent, long
braided black hair, and full beard, grown out over the last two months.
He had arrived aboard a Cuban freight schooner, which Pinkerton had
used on occasion to transport agents when he needed to avoid using a
Union ship.

The bar's clientele was a rich mix of blockade-running crews,
freemen and slave, Irish, English, Hispanic, Southern, all drinking heavily
and recounting story after story of the delights and downfalls of their
dangerous trade. Tobias could tell by the sun that his rendezvous hour

was upon him. He left the bar and walked up the quay to Callender's Shipping Company, housed in a one-story whitewashed and red-roofed building facing the Roads of St. George.

Mr. Callender proved to be a chatty and loquacious companion while Tobias waited for Cato. "You could do worse than serve Mrs. Devereaux, I'll be bound," said Callender, white-haired and wizened. His years at sea before his present shore job had left his face weathered and wrinkled. "She's a kind mistress, and her sea-going servants are well-rewarded for hard work. Quite a bit of freedom, no beatings, good treatment, well-kept, that's what I've seen. What's your name, boy?"

"Oh, yes, sah, dey calls me Marcus," replied Tobias in the lilting tones of the British Caribbean. "My owner in the Florida Keys, he sold me to her for a good price. Said, wid de war, he did not have enough work for me."

"Well, Marcus, there's lots of work in these islands for a good pilot. Here's Mrs. Devereaux's pilot, now. Cato, this is Marcus, waiting for you this last half-hour."

"Thank you, Mister Callender, sah." Cato was a burly man of forty, hair beginning to gray, in a threadbare old merchant officer's coat and a peaked cap with no insignia. "Let's us walk to the quay, and row to the *Princess*, Marcus. You can stow your gear."

They walked to the harbor side amid great stacked rows of cotton bales to be loaded aboard trans-Atlantic packets to the British Isles. A small dinghy was secured to a bollard on the St. George harbor quay. Cato and Tobias rowed to the *Carolina Princess,* anchored in the Roads. Captain Waylon was aboard.

"Captain, this is Marcus. The pilot Miz Devereaux just bought from de man in the Keys? She tol' me she wants fo' us to train him, so's he can fill in fo' me, or take a second runner."

"Welcome, Marcus," Captain Waylon said with a smile and a pronounced upper-class English accent. Like many blockade-runner captains, Waylon was a furloughed Royal Navy commander, about to amass a fortune in the burgeoning blockade-running trade. "We'll entrust your education to Cato, a superb instructor."

Cato showed Tobias below, to a small stateroom in the extended deck house aft of the bridge. She was a ship among the first of a new breed of blockade-runners. The first wave of runners had been ships of whatever type was available; large, slow freighters, even sailing vessels. As the Union was able to add more ships to the blockade that were quicker, more maneuverable, and of shallower draft, the runners kept pace by buying similar ships. They began to burn only anthracite coal, producing minimal smoke. British blockade-running companies had turned to the so-called "Clyde Steamers," (steamers of average size from Scotland's River Clyde) with shallow drafts and good speed, many of them side wheelers. Their drawback as blockade runners was their limited cargo capacity. The British builders next turned to craft built for the purpose of running the blockade, long, with large cargo space and screw propellers. They were narrow of beam, with powerful engines and iron hulls. The *Carolina Princess* was among the first of this type, painted in a mottled camouflage pattern of two shades of light gray. When viewed in a mist, or in the dark of night, she tended to blend in with the background of wave and sky.

Tobias knew that the captains of the successful Clyde Steamers often cleared five thousand U.S. dollars per voyage. The blockade, even at its most severe, could be described as porous. At the height of the Union's strength, only fifteen percent of inbound blockade-runners were seized, and, outbound; ten percent.

If I'm successful, thought Tobias, *I'll make a visible and statistically noticeable impact. And, I'll free a number of souls from bondage.*

"When your gear is stowed, let us make our way back to de bar," said Cato. "We can talk, an' you can meet some other pilots, an get d'lay of d'land." Their return trip to the quay took them by an anchored blockade-runner owned by the Confederate Navy, the CSS *Okracoke*, a Clyde steamer. The navy had entered the blockade running business, in a serious way.

Back on the bar veranda, as the sun set, and the torches were lit, the two pilots exchanged experiences at a secluded table. Cato had been all his life working for the Devereauxs.

"Mr. Devereaux was a good massa, never mean, but strict. I learned fast the sands of the Cape, and dat was good enough for him. I was worth keepin', and treatin' well, 'cause his ships was his life, and I kept 'em safe.

"Miz Devereaux, now, she su'prise us all. She jus' read, and thought, and ran de house, kindly, y'know, and we never thought she was goin' free us, or dat she thought it right. When Massa Devereaux die, we learn quick." Cato laughed out loud at the memory. "She hold a meetin'. We all goin' be 'conspirators', and help the Undergroun' Railroad. Den de war come, an' we all 'agents'. Dat woman, she free a passel o' black folks, wid her eye on freein' more."

Tobias recounted his whaling and navy navigation experience, never abandoning his Antiguan accent. He thought it prudent to stay "in role" at all times. He shared his misgivings about his lack of espionage experience.

Cato listened and declared, "You do fine. I show you the old an' new inlets, and gives you marks and bearings, and you'll fool anybody except a twenny-year pilot. You got the 'front,' man, the bearin'. An' de experience! I heard 'bout dat U.S. Coast Survey. Only de best pilots work for dem. You can carry this off!"

A tall, very thin black man with a scarred right cheek stood smiling down at Cato. "I hear tell dis be a fren' of Smalls and Tatnall," he said, pointing at Tobias.

"Cassius, sit you down," said Cato. "This be Marcus, goin' t'work for Miz Devereaux."

Cassius shook hands warmly. "Smalls and Tatnall, they say 'look for you,' Marcus. Only, they didn't say your name. Jus' you was an officer. You mus' be good, be an officer in a white man's navy. You be careful of dis ol' man, Cato, he a wild one."

"Oh, mon, I hear the same of you from Smalls."

The pilots sat and drank until late in the evening, exchanging stories and information on the shifting sands of the mouth of the Cape Fear River, and the ships that plied those waters.

"The fast, new ships like *Princess,* dey will be the future," Cassius told Tobias, "but dere's always a place for the older and slower, for some of dose are just plain lucky. "An' luck, my fren', is the most important of all the t'ings dat go into piloting!"

"Cassius pilots an 'old-an-slow,' Marcus," said Cato. "*Fair Maid of Roanoke* make eight knots on a good day, wid a followin' wind, but she's made twenny trips this year."

"De owner, he an ambitious fellow, he is," said Cassius.

"He also de most pompous man in Wilmington, maybe in de world." Cato began to giggle so hard he had to stop for a moment to catch his breath.

"I think his son, my captain, give him a run for de title," said Cassius. "Barrymore Beauchamp Godfrey, the Third. He pretty much as arrogant as de Second, an' only just a little better sailor."

"Mr. Godfrey, II, is your owner, then, mon?" Tobias asked of Cassius.

"Oh, yes, and a very rich one too. But as de Yankees bring more and more ships, it could be harder to run."

"But for now, it safe enough dat women and children still book passage," said Cato. "It be hard to blockade the Cape Fear River. Frying Pan Shoals go seventeen miles south from the Old Inlet mouth by Fort Caswell, and New Inlet come out east and north of the shoals, above Smith Island and Bald Head, so you need two fleets, one for each inlet. That take forty, fifty ships."

"The Yankees will have them, bye an' bye," said Tobias, staying in patois. "The Rebel ports are closing, one-by-one. Morehead City, Fernandina, Port Royal, Norfolk and Richmond, New Orleans, all closed. Mobile and Galveston are so far away from the Virginia fightin', de supplies dey land in dose ports are always too late. The Yankees can concentrate on Charleston and Wilmington."

"Well, we better keep our eyes open for them damn Yankees, then," said Cato with a wink. "Let's go for a stroll along Water Street, and talk strategy."

Leaving the bar near Bridge Street, they crossed the square and turned toward St. George's Harbour along Water Street. Half a dozen blockade-runners were anchored in the harbor. The warehouses along the wharves were crammed with arms, ammunition and anthracite coal, all awaiting transport to Wilmington and Charleston.

"Are we all agreed to try this grand theft?" Tobias asked the question on all their minds, and looked at his companions for a reply.

"Cato is only half-free as long as he's in the South, and can be grabbed and sold. I'se ready for freedom, and some Yankee Navy pay as a pilot. It's workin' for Robert Smalls," said Cassius.

"And Miz Devereaux is noticin' lots mo' folks watchin' her house and her," said Cato. "The Rebels, they're suspicious, wid all the contrabands we sending north along the Undergroun' Railroad. It's time to go, an take our families wid us while we can."

"And three ships in the bargain, as we go," said Tobias. "I have coordinates where the navy will meet us."

"How do we signal when we're comin' out?" In response to Cato's question, Tobias shared the detail of Pinkerton's instructions.

"It sounds like it could work," said Cassius. "But first, we need three weeks to teach you the run."

"We' got the trips planned," said Cato. "We should be ready the first of October."

The pilots retired, each to his own ship, having resolved to meet again clandestinely in Wilmington or in Smithville, the small town close to Forts Caswell and Johnson and to both inlets, where many of the pilots lived. Wilmington lay twenty miles upriver from Smithville, which in the next century would be called Southport. They needed to meet in secret, as it would not do for Cassius to be seen with servants of Mrs. Devereaux, if she were under suspicion of Confederate intelligence officers.

Cassius went aboard Godfrey's *Fair Maid of Roanoke*, a steamer of shallow draft, a bit shorter and broader of beam than the Clyde Steamers, and with less powerful engines. Nonetheless, she was well-piloted and hard to spot in the mists and surf on a dark night, and was among the most successful blockade-runners in September of 1862, before the great two-year heyday of swifter blockade-runners began in earnest. It would take her three days to reach Wilmington, at eight knots. A 250-foot steamer like *Carolina Princess* could make the trip in forty hours, at sixteen knots.

The next morning, the Devereaux side wheeler negotiated the narrow and twisting channel out of St. George's Harbour, turning north and then west, with the length of the Bermudas to port. They passed the broad mouth of Great Sound, within which lay the Royal Navy Dockyard and the town of Hamilton, and saw several Royal Navy ships at anchor. Tobias stood next to Cato on the bridge, looking aft. He could see Cassius' ship, the *Fair Maid*, now falling astern, and the low silhouette of the Navy's steamer, *Ocracoke,* almost keeping pace with *Princess.*

CHAPTER 23
BEHIND THE LINES, CAPE FEAR RIVER
SEPTEMBER, 1862

Tobias and the *Carolina Princess* approached the Carolina coast thirty-eight hours later, two hours past midnight. Their landfall was some twenty miles north of Cape Fear, as they had run around the north end of the Union blockade line. The coast near New Topsail Inlet was low and flat, and the first inkling of its proximity was often the white line of surf on its shore. Woe be-tide the ship hoping for a landfall in a mist or heavy rain which obscured the breakers. No rain fell this night.

"Land ho!" called the lookout in the foremast crosstrees. "Deck, there! I see the surf line!" Captain Waylon turned the ship over to Cato, who turned to port to run inshore of the blockading squadron until they reached New Inlet. At this point, a mist or fog would have helped. No lights showed, and the sound of the engines and paddle wheels was muffled and lost in the crash of the surf. They paused periodically to take soundings.

"Bo'sun," called Cato, "relieve the leadsman and his crew with the 'dipsea' lead." The deep-sea lead was at the end of a two hundred-foot line, and so required a line of several men spaced along the rail holding the line and letting go from bow to stern in turn so that the line became perpendicular just as the last man aft dropped his section and the leadsman, furthest aft, could move the line up and down, as it was perpendicular, in a search for the bottom.

Captain Waylon had used the deep-sea lead to warn of the impending shoal waters off the coast. When the call "twenty fathoms with this line" had come to the bridge, Waylon had known he was close to the coast.

Tobias stood on the bridge, his eyes alternating between an examination of the coast, to starboard, and a watch for blockaders, to port.

The new leadsman moved forward along the rail, and used the hand or shallow water lead line. The *Princess* paused periodically to cast the lead as the ship made her way south along the coast. "By the mark, five," came the whispered call, passed up to the bridge by a line of sailors, whispering in turn.

"That's the North Breakers shoal, just north of Big Hill," said Cato to Tobias. "We'll skirt it and stay right along the surfline from here. Mostly five fathoms all the way."

"Steamer to port," came the whispered warning. A blockade gunboat loomed in the darkness, 220 yards ahead and to port. They ghosted by at half-ahead, unnoticed by the Yankee ship. They crept on, still stopping periodically for a cast of the lead.

Suddenly, a whispered call: "The Big Hill to starboard!" A hillock, even one not exceeding seventy feet, was a significant landmark on this table-like coast. Soon they began to pass batteries being erected along the shore, batteries which next year would be connected by a great earthwork, to be known as Fort Fisher, after a North Carolinian killed at First Manassas. It would be an L-shaped emplacement one mile long on the Atlantic shore, and six hundred yards wide from the Atlantic to the Cape Fear River. The Confederate Army's Colonel Lamb was just now starting to shape it.

Next, they saw the silhouette of Colonel Lamb's pride and joy, Mound Battery, which would become Fort Fisher's southern end. Its sixty-foot height made it stand out along the shore, even in the pitch black of pre-dawn.

"Mound Battery's always a welcome sight, Brother Marcus," said Cato as they left the guns atop the hill to their starboard side. "When we be in range of those guns, the Yankees bear off right quick! And we can signal her to have the range lights lit near Burke signal station on the west riverbank. We lines 'em up, and sails right up the Inlet. Helmsman, ease her to starboard, if you please."

They bore to starboard as did the Atlantic shore, ending a mile

further in old Federal Point, now Confederate Point, currently defended
by a battery that would soon be mounted in a raised mini-fort known as
Battery Buchanan. They brought the just-lit range lights into alignment,
and were over the bar, rounding Confederate Point, and headed up the
Cape Fear River to Wilmington to unload.

She would take on a new outbound cargo of cotton in a
few days. All but the slave members of the crew would go ashore in
Wilmington, and take pleasure in its many seductive opportunities for
leisure and recuperation. Cato, Tobias, and the assistant engineer, Uzal,
another Devereaux servant, would drop down-river in the meantime to
Smithville, and home, in the spacious haven of the Devereaux mansion.

"Watch for a real circus when we docks," said Cato to Tobias as
they eased upriver. "The consumer goods we carry inbound gets auctioned
off to speculators, crowds of 'em, an' den dey sells 'em to de rest ob de
white folks, at real high prices." As they pulled into the wharf, Tobias saw
hordes of speculators, pushing and shoving to be in the most advantageous
spot as the ship unloaded.

Cato, having piloted the *Carolina Princess* upstream to
Wilmington, now piloted the Devereaux cat-rigged gig downstream.
Tobias and Uzal tended the sheets of the big gaff-headed mainsail. They
passed Beery shipyard and the turpentine shipping docks on the west side
of the river and sailed the eighteen miles to Smithville, landing at the town
wharf past Bonnett's Creek and the new earthworks at Fort Johnson. The
three secured the gig and made their way to the mansion on Nash Street.
The servants' entrance at the side of the house was framed by windows
through which several servants could be seen in a large room functioning
as a dining room, kitchen pantry, and general gathering place for the
household staff.

"Home is de sailors!" Cato called as they entered. Joy and
relief were evident on the faces of the Devereaux staff, to see two of
their number return from the vagaries of the sea. A butler, two maids,
a coachman, and the cook, with Cato and Uzal and their families,
completed the Devereaux household. Cato introduced Tobias as Marcus
Aurelius, and Tobias felt instantly at home.

"Miz Devereaux has no secrets from us, Marcus," said Jacob, the

butler, "and we supports all you is tryin' to do. Welcome to 'belowstairs.'
Miz Devereaux wants to greet you as soon as you've had a chance to catch
your breath."

Tobias arranged his braids, combed his beard, slipped into
a clean sailor's shirt and trousers, and went to seek out Jacob. Mrs.
Devereaux's personal maid, Gabrielle Turner, was in the hallway.

"Have you seen Jacob, Miss?" He asked, noticing Gabrielle's
sweet face and smile, and her classic figure, which her maid's uniform did
little to disguise.

"Oh, Marcus Aurelius, I am not 'Miss' in this household. We are
all friends. I am Gabrielle. Please call me that."

"I will, then, thank you, Gabrielle."

"And I am sure Marcus is not your name, not with your mission.
Perhaps you can tell me your real name, someday," she said with a wink.
"Jacob is in de scullery. I'll take you." She led him through the kitchen
and to the scullery.

"Follow me, Marcus," said Jacob, and they walked up the
back stair and through the dining room to the large front parlor, where
Mrs. Devereaux sat reading. "Marcus is here, Miz Devereaux," Jacob
announced.

Amanda Devereaux rose from her chair and extended her hand.
She was an inch or two above five feet in height, with dark brown hair, a
firm chin, and wide-set eyes in an attractive face. Her smile was warm,
and she had a determined air about her. "Welcome to Smithville, Marcus.
I'm glad you're here, for we have much to do in a short time."

"Oh, thank you, ma'am," replied Tobias. He waited for her to be
seated before he lowered himself onto the chair opposite her. "Why do
you say our time is short?"

"I have noticed increased surveillance from men I can only
assume are Confederate Secret Service agents. They are not particularly
subtle, whether by design or ineptitude, I cannot tell. But I have
received a coded message from Mr. Pinkerton telling me he has learned
independently that my behavior with regard to the Underground Railroad
has attracted Confederate attention. He urges me to end my affairs here
and flee."

"Oh, no, ma'am, what a hard thing that must be to contemplate!"

"Perhaps not as hard as you think, Marcus. I'm quite well-off, and my money is all in British banks. I've brought nothing but luxuries through the blockade, so I've made exorbitant profits, and haven't helped the war effort a bit. I treasure my employees and their families, and fleeing with them would make them safe, for I would take them to England and continue their employ there. Even though I've freed them all, they masquerade as slaves. If something happened to me, they would be back in bondage."

"Timing, it seems, is everything in espionage, Miz Devereaux. May we talk of making your exit a safe one?"

"Let us do so, Marcus. I know that is not your name, but you're safer my not knowing your real one. Are you comfortable using that Caribbean accent?"

"Oh, yes, ma'am, you may be sure of dat. I learned it the first ten years of my life." He smiled. "Cato tells me he can have me trained in three weeks. Will that fit your new schedule, Miz Devereaux?"

"Perfectly. It will bring us to the next new moon. I'm confident the *Ocracoke* and *Fair Maid* will sail on the first day of the new moon. I will inform them that *Princess* will sail the next night, citing too much traffic out the Inlet as the reason for delay."

"Is not the presence of the *Princess* necessary to trigger the trap?"

"Indeed. We must fire the flare to illuminate the runners, and ensure that the lead ship heads to the bearings we've given the Federal fleet. We'll send our white crewmembers home for the night thinking we're not sailing. Then, we'll gather our blacks, families and all, Cassius' too, and quietly cast off in the wake of *Fair Maid* and *Ocracoke*. That's where you come in!"

"How so, ma'am?"

"You will waylay the *Ocracoke* pilot, Campbell, the day before. We'll imprison him here. He has a reputation as a heavy drinker, and frequently misses sailings. I will seek out Captain Stirling, and offer you, my spare pilot, as a replacement. He is a naval officer, as *Ocracoke* is a navy blockade runner. Do you know him?"

"No, ma'am, I suspect he's not from the old navy. He won't recognize me."

"Good! You will lead the *Ocracoke* to the trap. Cassius will ensure that *Fair Maid* joins us. We'll follow, undetected, we hope, and fire the flares to alert the blockaders. Four Union ships will be waiting. *Ocracoke* may try to run, and will risk sinking. Of course, as a navy ship, she carries a gun. Her crew won't be tried as pirates if they resist, unlike the other, private ships. You must prepare yourself, with flare and flotation aid, to survive."

Tobias whistled softly. "Miz Devereaux, what a coup, if we bring it together. Three ships, counting *Princess*."

"The Union will buy *Princess*, and make her a blockader. She'd be most useful inshore, with her speed, shallow draft, and low silhouette."

"You're a woman who knows her ships, oh, yes, indeed!"

She smiled modestly. "Thank you, Marcus. I've been paying attention. All I will lose is the house. But, Marcus, our plan, like most, ignores the unexpected. Anything can go wrong and something probably will. We must be ready to improvise. From what Mr. Pinkerton hints at, you're quite good at that."

"He's very kind. I'll do my best. And hope you and I will someday reminisce with pleasant memories."

And so the wheels of the plan were set in motion. Tobias made two runs through the blockade under Cato's guidance. On one run, instead of approaching along the surfline, they made the entrance to Wilmington straight on, passing within a hundred yards of two blockaders who never saw them. He noted carefully the bearings from the New Inlet to Mound Battery, Battery Buchanan, Zeek's Island to the south of the inlet, and Target, on the north end of Smith's Island's Buzzard Bay.

On weekends, he and Gabrielle posed as a couple in love, crossing the river and picnicking quietly amid the pine woods, the sand dunes, and the swampland along the shore of New Inlet and the Atlantic shore where Fort Fisher was taking shape. Tobias made careful mental notes, and enjoyed the company of the comely Gabrielle, who took to her role in this espionage with relish.

"I'm glad we didn't have to do this in the summer," said

Gabrielle. "The wind sometimes blows from the northwest, and the smell from the turpentine distilleries is awful."

As Tobias and Gabrielle made their way in and out of the mansion, they frequently noticed men watching from a distance. "Amanda is right," thought Tobias. "They are not subtle." He hoped his disguise would be sufficient. It had not yet been tested, but the blockade-runners and Confederate Navy ships that crowded the Cape Fear River and the Harbor at St. George were full of officers who might have known him in the U.S. Navy before the war.

Prior to Tobias' last training run, the *Carolina Princess* had dropped downriver to Smithville, where Cato and Captain Waylon could assess which pass or inlet was less well-guarded, and which provided the best chance of a successful blockade run. The next morning, Tobias saw the *Ocracoke* secured to the Smithville wharf, just aft of *Princess*, on a similar mission.

Tobias was walking down the wharf on his way to the mansion, when Pilot Campbell of the *Ocracoke*, obviously in his cups, called to him. "Here, you, boy! Pick up this sea bag an' take it to mah quarters!"

Campbell's large sea bag lay on the wharf, and he was obviously in no condition to carry it. Tobias paused, and stared at the pilot, speechless for a moment. Campbell grasped his belt-buckle, and in one motion, whipped his belt free of his trousers. "Goddamn you, you shif'less nigger, when I speak, you say 'yassuh,' or I'll beat the hell out o' you."

Campbell raised the belt, the buckle at the swinging end, and struck Tobias repeatedly over the head, as Tobias, his wits now about him, knelt with his arms protecting his head, groveling audibly. His thoughts were far from groveling, however. "I'll repay thee for this, thou bastard spawn of Satan," he thought, reverting to Quaker cadences and Old-Testament epithets.

Campbell ceased, exhausted by his efforts. "Next time, I won't treat you this kindly, boy. Now get that bag aboard." Tobias ran quickly to the bag, holding it in front of his face to hide the hatred in his eyes, and ran up the gangway and to the pilot's stateroom, off the small deckhouse wardroom of the *Ocracoke*. Campbell followed, weaving and still shouting as his breath permitted.

A lieutenant sat at the wardroom table. He looked up, startled as Tobias entered, followed on his heels by Campbell. "I say, pilot, a bit of decorum in the wardroom, if you please," the lieutenant said in a distinct upper-class British accent.

Another furloughed RN officer, Tobias thought. There was something familiar about this one.

"Campbell, my good man, have you been beating this black?" The lieutenant turned to Tobias, who was edging toward the companionway to the deck. "Run along now, boy, like a good fellow," he said, condescension dripping from every pore.

Tobias seized the moment and ran through the door to the deck. As he exited, he heard Campbell say, "I'll beat whatever Colored I like, Mr. Ludlow!"

Damn, thought Tobias. *Ludlow, that lieutenant in the Admiralty pub at Nelson's Dockyard. Of all the bad luck.* A full year before, Tobias had stopped at Antigua for leave on his way back from the Pacific Northwest, and had encountered the very same officer. They had argued over Tobias' presence in what Ludlow considered a white man's public house.

By the time Tobias reached the mansion, the welts Campbell had inflicted were throbbing noticeably. Gabrielle was in the great room inside the servant's entrance.

"Marcus, what happened? Sit here, let me look." Tobias half collapsed into a chair as Gabrielle expertly examined his head and arms. The buckle had drawn blood in several places.

"Campbell from the *Ocracoke* beat me when I didn't pick up his bag fast enough to suit him," he told Gabrielle, lapsing inadvertently into his normal New Bedford accent.

"So that's what you sound like," she said, laughing. "Very Yankee, my fren' Marcus. Best be careful. Now, hol' still while I puts this salve on these cuts."

"I can't tell you how good your fingers feel," he said, his eyes closed.

"Oh, Marcus, we bes' both be careful. You' skin feel good to me, too." Gabrielle stepped back, smiled wistfully at the tall Antiguan, and put her hands on her hips. "Let's get to business. Miz Devereaux say we need to get ready this week to leave. We also gonna need to tell our Undergroun' Railroad folks up an' down de line we shuttin' down. We need to start packing. When is yo' nex' run?"

"Day after tomorrow. I need to stay out of sight until *Ocracoke* leaves. There's a British officer aboard who met me in English Harbor, as the war was starting. The less he sees of me, the better."

"Well, then, we'll spend a day inside, and let you heal. I know you want to kill that Campbell, but it good you didn't. We'd all be in for it, then. Jus' another ten days."

The Devereaux mansion had been an effective stop on the Underground Railroad. Runaway slaves who were headed north toward the Federal forces at New Berne on the Neuse could stop and replenish their stock of turpentine and onions that they used to throw off the bloodhounds sniffing for their scent. Jacob was an excellent forger of day passes. The Devereaux household would map the route to a series of abandoned barns for the runaways, fill their bags with food, and send them on their way up the plank road toward Wilmington. The fortunes of war would soon cause this stop on the Railroad to close.

CHAPTER 24
THE LAST RUN OF THE CAROLINA PRINCESS, OCTOBER 1862

Carolina Princess completed her penultimate run without incident, and docked at Wilmington for a quick turnaround. All of the blockade-runners liked to take advantage of a new moon and high night tides for their outbound runs, and there were only four days until that optimum hour. Two miles below Wilmington, where the Brunswick River joins the Cape Fear, they had reduced their speed to pause abeam of an ancient cypress festooned with Spanish moss. There, the crew toasted their successful run at the "Dram Tree," as many safely arrived blockade-runners had before.

A new steam-driven cotton press had begun operation near Beery's Shipyard across the river from Wilmington. Cotton bales were being tightly compressed, and the runners could accommodate double their normal cargos. Once loaded, *Princess* dropped down-river to Smithville, joining several others, including *Fair Maid* and *Ocracoke*.

Through the Black Dispatch, Gabrielle and Jacob arranged for their slave conspirators to lay a large bonfire in a remote field at New Topsail Inlet. The bonfire builders had been provided a slow match from the stores of *Carolina Princess*, so they'd be far away from the fire when it caught.

The Wilmington slave intelligence network had provided Tobias and Gabrielle with the name of Campbell's favorite watering hole. They had waited outside the tavern two nights in a row, following discreetly as Campbell wove his way from the tavern to the ship. He always used the same route, which included a dark alley off Bay Street.

Monday morning, before their Tuesday night departure, Gabrielle sent word through the "telegraph" to light the fire Monday night.

That night in Smithville, Gabrielle and Tobias waited in the dark alley with a cart and horse close by. Tobias carried a sap made from a leather bag filled with minie balls from the ship's armory. As Campbell passed a particularly dark doorway in the alley, Tobias stepped behind him and knocked him unconscious with one blow. He and Gabrielle quickly gagged and bound the pilot.

"Gabrielle, get the cart," whispered Tobias. When she drove into the alley, Tobias tossed the pilot into the cart like so many turnips in a sack. They chained Campbell in a basement room of the mansion. "Much as I'd like to rid the world of you, you maggot," said Tobias to the helpless but now-conscious pilot, "we'll leave you alive to suffer the ignominy of being part of our escape."

Outside the room, they found themselves alone. "Marcus, everything depend on whether the Rebel captain take you as pilot," said Gabrielle.

"Not everything, dear Gabrielle," said Tobias, taking her by the hand. "If he doesn't take the bait, I'll come with you all in *Princess,* and we'll follow him out just the same. I just won't be aboard to make sure he's taken."

"It all scare me, Marcus." She threw her arms about his neck and kissed him. "I want you to live, Marcus Aurelius Yankee. I want to see you in Englan', without your beard and long locks, and kiss you then."

"You are impish, woman," he said, holding her tightly as she clung to him, aroused in spite of himself.

"You got no idea, honey," she said.

On Tuesday afternoon, several runners dropped downriver from Wilmington and anchored in the channel. *Fair Maid of Roanoke* left the Smithville wharf and joined them.

Ocracoke and *Princess* remained secured to the wharf. Captain Stirling paced agitatedly up and down the wharf, in front of his ship's gangway. Mrs. Devereaux's coachman pulled up at the Bay Street curb, and Mrs. Devereaux alighted, nodding cordially at Stirling.

"Going tonight, Captain Stirling?" Amanda asked, innocently.

"Not unless that worthless scoundrel of a pilot appears, dear lady," he replied.

"Oh my, captain, Campbell's at it again, is he? What a shame to miss the new moon."

"I'll have no choice, unless my pilot graces me with his presence."

"My dear captain, why don't you take my new pilot, Marcus? Cato says he's fully accomplished and competent for New Inlet. And he could follow Cassius in *Fair Maid*, if your confidence doesn't match mine. No cost to the government. Look on it as my patriotic contribution for the Cause."

"Damn!" Stirling reddened. "Excuse my language, Mrs. Devereaux. I'm so angry with that sot, I'm ready to take extreme measures. This cargo must go through, and I must pick up a critical load of arms in Bermuda." Stirling paused for a moment, and then smacked his fist in his palm. "I'll do it! Have him report aboard in an hour. We'll all go out together. And thank you, dear lady."

"Not at all, captain. It's my duty. But *Princess* won't be joining you this evening. A bit crowded in the channel. I think we'll go tomorrow. I'm sure Captain Waylon will see you in Bermuda." Amanda smiled sweetly, and went aboard her ship.

Captain Waylon was in the charthouse. "Captain," said Amanda, "I should tell you that I've loaned Marcus to *Ocracoke* and Captain Stirling for his run. Campbell's missing, again."

"Aye, aye, ma'am. It will be a good experience for him. We're all ready for departure Wednesday night. The weather may be better for us. Looks like a storm is likely."

"Very well, captain. I'll have Cato and Uzal sleep aboard, tonight, so you can spend your evening at home."

"Thank you, Mrs. Devereaux."

As midnight approached, the pieces of the elaborate plot seemed to be falling into place. Campbell was locked securely in the mansion. The Devereaux household was aboard *Princess,* as well as Cassius' family. The white crewmembers were home, asleep. Uzal had raised steam, but the smoke from the anthracite coal used to heat the boilers was virtually unnoticeable in the dark. The ship's stack emissions gave no hint of her readiness. Cato stood by at the helm, mentally reviewing the course he would follow. Not a light was showing aboard, to maintain the fiction that they would not leave until tomorrow night. The bonfire had burned bright at New Topsail Inlet the night before, and a blockade ship had reported the signal to the Northern Blockade Squadron flagship, USS *Minnesota.* Four blockade vessels patrolled in tight formation near the pre-arranged bearings, ready to open fire at the sight of red rockets to be fired by *Carolina Princess.* Their crews realized that assembling at an agreed-upon spot was a rare chance to succeed in stopping the elusive blockade-runners.

On the bridge of the CSS *Ocracoke,* Tobias stood beside the helmsman, and spoke to Captain Stirling. "Oh, captain, Cassius tell me Cap'n Godfrey of *Fair Maid* say he carry a hooded stern light until he come abeam of da' Mound. We can use it for bearings."

"Very well, Marcus. Carry on. We'll cast off in fifteen minutes, and you will take us out behind *Fair Maid.* We'll pass her as soon as we leave the Mound astern."

"Aye, aye, captain." Lieutenant Ludlow was on the main deck, checking the lashings of the compressed cotton bales. Tobias prayed fervently that he would stay off the bridge until they were under way, and the press of running the blockade would distract him from a close scrutiny of his substitute pilot. When he had told Amanda of his fears, her response had been, "You could fool your mother, dear, if she'd never seen you this way."

Nonetheless, Tobias had raised his comfort level by carrying a Colt Navy Six in his belt, in the small of his back, and had noted the location of a fire axe with a four-foot shaft on the bulkhead of the chartroom abaft the bridge.

At midnight, Cassius was guiding *Fair Maid of Roanoke* north, northeast through New Inlet, a hooded light at her stern. Tobias gave his helm orders to the grizzled quartermaster at the wheel of the *Ocracoke,* following dead astern of Cassius' ship. Behind *Ocracoke,* unseen, the *Carolina Princess* had cast off from the wharf, and Cato steered in *Ocracoke's* wake.

The *Ocracoke,* a Clyde steamer, carried two small cutters in davits aft, above the after cargo hold, and two large longboats in davits just abaft the bridge on either side of the ship. Tobias could see the cutters as he looked aft through his night glass for his bearings.

Outward-bound through New Inlet, the channel took a "dog-leg" to the right just before reaching the Mound Battery, and *Ocracoke* was now heading southeast by east. The Mound was visible on the port quarter, falling rapidly astern, and Zeek's Island, at the north end of Smith's Island, was visible on the starboard quarter. They must be fifteen hundred to two thousand yards from the Mound before Cato, astern, could safely fire the flares. The 6.4-inch rifle and the ten-inch smoothbore Columbiad on the Mound would then be at extreme range, and would have to risk hitting friendly Rebel craft if they fired at the blockaders.

"Southeast by east, a half south," Tobias said to the quartermaster at the helm, who repeated the command. The ship altered course to starboard, coming right by two degrees of the thirty-two point compass rose.

"Captain, the Mound is a thousand yards astern. We can ease her to a due-east bearing in five minutes. Shall I leave *Fair Maid* to port as we pass her?"

"Very well, pilot." Captain Stirling turned as Lieutenant Ludlow entered from the bridge wing.

"Cotton bales all battened down, sir," Ludlow reported.

"Ease her two points to starboard, quartermaster," Tobias ordered. "Coming up on fifteen hundred yards from Mound Battery, sir." This was the point at which the blockading squadron usually felt safe in stationing small gunboats as an early-warning line at long range from the Mound's guns. The ship began to pitch as it headed into a moderate east wind.

"Fair Maid has doused her glim, sir." Tobias was risking speech in front of Ludlow, but the captain would certainly notice if he failed to do his duty in a normal manner. He could feel Ludlow's eyes on him.

"Captain," said Ludlow, "a word with you in private, sir, by your leave?"

"Very well, lieutenant." The two officers exited to the starboard bridge wing. From the corner of his eye, Tobias saw Ludlow point at him. At that moment the sky astern turned crimson as *Carolina Princess* fired three red rockets, illuminating herself and *Ocracoke*. A moment later, gun muzzle flashes from at least four large ships lit up a 180-degree arc ahead of the three blockade-runners, as the steam-powered sloops of war and gunboats of the Northern Blockade Squadron opened fire.

"Starboard two points," said Tobias to the helmsman, consciously running *Ocracoke* toward the edge of seaward shoal east by southeast from New Inlet, toward Sheep Head Rocks. The bridge wing door burst open, as Stirling and Ludlow rushed through it.

"What're those big Yankees doing in this close?" Stirling demanded of Tobias. "They never risk their big ships this close in! And what's your mistress' ship doing behind us firing flares, you conspiring knave?"

"I told you I knew him, sir," shouted Ludlow. "That damned Blackamoor is a Yankee Navy sailing master!"

"Master-at-arms, quartermaster, anyone, secure that pilot. Shoot him if necessary!" Stirling took the helm as Ludlow and the quartermaster lunged at Tobias, who bounded, inches from their grasp, to the door leading to the chartroom. Snatching the fire axe from its mount on the bulkhead, he ran out the after door to the main deck. Ludlow fired at Tobias from the spar deck abaft the charthouse, but the motion of the ship as she pitched precluded accuracy at anything more than point-blank range.

As Tobias made his way aft, hidden behind the cotton bales, *Ocracoke* grounded gently but firmly on the shoal at the outer south edge of New Inlet. *Carolina Princess,* her lights blazing to show the Yankee blockading boarding parties the way, passed *Ocracoke* to port flying a white flag. *Fair Maid of Roanoke,* too slow to outrun the blockaders, and with big Union sloops of war to port and to starboard, had lowered her colors, and raised a white flag. The Mound Battery had fired only three rounds at long range before its commander realized that friends were as thick as foes in the target area.

The action level aboard *Ocracoke,* however, was still high. It was, after all, a navy vessel. A gun crew was firing the ship's only armament, a twelve-pounder pivot, forward. The hull groaned in the clutch of the shoal. The engineer had the paddle wheels at full throttle, all astern, attempting to pull the ship off the sand. Ludlow, at the head of the master-at-arms detail, was searching the ship for Tobias. And four Union ships with broadsides totaling thirty guns were firing methodically into the steamer.

Tobias was on the cargo deck just below the main deck. The Yankees were firing roundshot, to avoid setting the steamer afire. Their broadsides were shaking the ship every minute, sending splinters flying as they punched holes in the bulwarks. Tobias moved aft, working his way toward the after cargo hold. He saw Ludlow and two men descend the 'midships companionway and begin to come aft. Ludlow carried a sword in one hand and a revolver in the other. The men were similarly armed. One carried a lantern.

The hold was crammed with cotton bales and a few crates of other commodities. Tobias peered around a crate at the approaching men. Should he fire, exposing his position, or wait as they came closer, making his escape less probable?

Through the after hatch above him, Tobias could hear the chief engineer and the firemen and stokers from the engine room. The chief engineer called out to Ludlow and his men. "There's two feet of water in the engine room. My fires are doused. I'm going to find the captain and tell him I think we should abandon."

"I'm going to find the damned pilot if it's the last thing I do," declared Ludlow. "If you two want to go topside, go ahead."

The master-at-arms' men needed no more encouragement. They turned and ran toward the companionway to the main deck, taking the lantern with them before Ludlow could protest.

"They're pounding us to pieces, men. Abandon ship!" Stirling's voice shouted down the main hatch. "Get the boats in the water. Man the falls, there. I'm not eager to spend time in some Yankee prison. Let's save ourselves, and fight another day!"

In the dimness, Tobias could see Ludlow hesitate. "That's right, you ignorant Limey. Stay here with me, and let your mates leave. You'll do well here in the 'tween decks. We Coloreds can see in the dark, you know!" Then Tobias laughed, maniacally, and dropped flat to the deck.

Ludlow fired a fusillade of shots at the sound of Tobias' voice. None came near Tobias, who held his fire. "I hope you die here, you black bastard!" Ludlow shouted into the darkness. He ran to the companionway and climbed to the main deck.

Seeing him go, Tobias rushed to the starboard side of the cargo hold, gun in his belt and axe in hand. He stepped onto a pile of crates in front of the after cargo door, an iron hatch in the ship's side tightly secured by metal turn-screws or "dogs." He grabbed his axe and used the head to pound each "dog" until it loosened. He then wrenched the cargo door open on its hinges, and could see the water below him. Several crewmembers were lowering the starboard cutter from its davits, directly above him. Tobias saw it reach the water, still secured to the davit above him by the davit ropes, or "falls" that had lowered it, with two seamen already in the boat. He stepped to the cargo hatch ledge, leaned out, and grasped the ropes of the after fall.

He slid down, hand over hand, to the cutter below as it floated on the swell. He surprised the two sailors already aboard, who had not seen him descend. "Climb back up those falls or die here," snarled Tobias. "I'll shoot you where you stand!" The two sailors saw a fierce black countenance with a pistol and an axe. They wasted no time in struggling back up the falls to the deck. Their shipmates above, lowering the cutter, cursed him, but had no pistols to shoot him.

Tobias cast off the two fall blocks, freeing the cutter from *Ocracoke.* He sat amidships, and fitted two sweeps into their oarlocks. With his long reach and muscled upper body, he sculled easily toward the closest Union sloop of war, a grin of victory on his face.

* * *

Three days later, Tobias sat in the flag cabin of USS *Wabash,* as Frank Du Pont read the report of the espionage operation from Rear Admiral S. P. Lee, Du Pont's counterpart commanding the North Atlantic Blockading Squadron. Congress had created the permanent ranks of rear admiral and commodore in July, replacing the previous temporary honorifics of flag officer and commodore.

"Congratulations on your new rank, Admiral," said Tobias.

"Thank you, Mr. St. John. I'm still getting used to it. Admiral Lee says if you didn't already have the Medal of Honor, he'd recommend you for one."

"Kind of him, sir."

"Deserved, I'd say. Three good blockade-runners denied to the Rebels. Arms and ammunition shipments made more difficult. And shortly, we'll have three new blockade vessels. We bought *Carolina Princess* for a fair price from Mrs. Devereaux, that fine patriot. *Fair Maid* has been brought into the navy. And we have floated *Ocracoke* off the shoal. When she's repaired, she'll join the fleet."

"What of those courageous pilots who risked their lives, sir?"

"Yes, yes, they're well settled. Cato and Cassius, as well as the engineer, Uzal, were brought into the navy. Their families have been settled with Isaac Tatnall, who has moved back to Great Tybee Island. Mrs. Devereaux took her domestic staff with her to Great Britain, as freedmen *de facto*, as well as *de jure*."

"That's wonderful, sir. Mrs. Devereaux is a brave and gracious woman. Mr. Pinkerton must be pleased."

"Indeed he is, although he is certain he'll be reverting to private detective status if General McClellan is relieved as commander of the Army of the Potomac. As he points out, we learned valuable lessons regarding entry to Wilmington, the capabilities of the Federal Point Batteries, and the current workings of the Underground Railroad. This is invaluable intelligence information!"

Tobias relaxed his posture. "Yes, sir. I'm glad the pilots have been recognized."

"Speaking of deserving pilots, your friend, Mr. Smalls is still aboard the USS *Planter*, supporting troop landings in the islands around Charleston."

"I'm glad he's working out, sir. Perhaps I'll have a chance to see him while I'm aboard."

The admiral smiled. "You haven't asked about prize money, Mr. St. John. Or should I say," he grinned, "Marcus Aurelius?"

"I really hadn't thought of it, admiral."

"Well, you need to think about it, as you are now quite

financially comfortable. Four floating ships shared in the prizes, but you were the fifth 'ship' share, and you were both the officers and lower deck of your 'ship.' You reap a fifth of the inter-ship profit, Mr. St. John, close to six figures."

Tobias' jaw dropped in astonishment. "My God, I never dreamed of this," he thought. "My, my thanks go to you, sir," he stammered, "for giving me this opportunity."

"Congratulations, St. John, and welcome back to the South Atlantic Blockading Squadron. Captain Rodgers will be glad to have you back in your old billet aboard *Wabash*."

CHAPTER 25
TAYLOR WOOD'S CHESAPEAKE RAIDS
SEPTEMBER AND OCTOBER 1862

In mid-August, Rory received a letter from Mosby.

Dear Rory

I've had an adventure or two since last we met. Been captured, exchanged, commended by Lee himself, and still not promoted from private to captain! After I saw you, I asked Stuart for a command of rangers under the Partisan Ranger Act to harass Pope and his forces in Farquier and Louden counties, in Northern Virginia. I'm perplexed he didn't approve. Maybe he couldn't spare the men. Instead, he recommended me to Stonewall Jackson as a scout. After consideration, I thought this a splendid idea, because I know Jackson likes partisan operations.

I was on my way to join General Jackson, and waiting for a train at Beaver Dam station on the Virginia Central RR, when I was captured by a New York cavalry troop. I was carrying papers from Stuart to Jackson that described me as a 'captain without commission.' The Federals treated me as an officer, and the exchange commissioners arranged for my exchange in ten days. I spent four days in transit, mostly in a transport anchored off Newport News.

I saw lots of McClellan's and Burnside's troops leaving the port. The steamer captain, (a Southern sympathizer), told me the Federal troops were on their way to join Pope outside Washington City. I concluded that the Yankee campaign up the James River was over. When I landed in Richmond, I got an audience with Lee, and told him my findings. He agreed, commended me, and told Jackson, who attacked at Cedar Mountain before Burnside could reinforce Pope.

 I'm on my way to Jackson now, at Manassas, so I must close. May your war be as exciting as mine,

Your friend,
Jack Mosby

Early to mid August saw McClellan abandon Malvern Hill and Harrison's Landing, and, marching the Army of the Potomac down the peninsula to Newport News, embark and move north by ship to Washington to join forces with Pope and the Union's Army of Virginia. The Union Navy disbanded their James River Flotilla at the end of August, and Mallory sent word to Wood that he was free to initiate his Chesapeake raids.

 It was a day in early autumn when thirty mounted men, three boat-laden wagons, and a horse-drawn ambulance slipped out of Richmond at dawn, and made their way, on back roads of indifferent quality, northeastwards toward Westmoreland County on the Virginia side of the Potomac. Lieutenant Lee was not available to accompany this first raid. Rory had persuaded Wood to add Midshipman Ormsby in his stead. He had already recruited Chief Engineer Mackenzie, and Blakely, the gun captain, recently promoted on Rory's recommendation to gunner's mate. Rory felt confidence in his boat crew, supported as he was by three "Old Dominions." The sailors in the detachment had been training on horseback two days a week for the past six weeks. They had achieved a modest degree of comfort in the saddle. Blakely, in particular, had proven to be a natural rider.

 The wagons carried the boats, securely lashed down, on chocks. Each wagon also carried basic dry rations, oars, masts, slow match, ammunition, and a small powder keg, suitable for demolition of a variety of targets. Wood was determined to be prepared for every eventuality.

 They were riding behind the second wagon on a road outside Miller's Tavern when the bank collapsed and the wagon and boat slid slowly toward a gully alongside the road.

 "Avast driving! Way enough! She's capsizing!" Rory shouted warnings and commands clearly understood by the mounted sailors alongside the wagon, but unintelligible to the teamsters driving the wagon.

"Whoa! Unhitch the team!" Rory shifted into teamster language, and the wagon and boat, free of the horse team, slowly rolled on its side in the gully. They used the limb of a stout oak and two sets of block and tackle to heave the whaleboat back into the chocks of the re-righted wagon. An hour's effort had the boat firmly in the chocks. But there was no chance of crossing the Rappahannock and leaving Essex County that day.

The next day found the raiders in Westmoreland County along the south bank of the Potomac. With their center of activity in Oak Grove, Wood divided the force to cover as much of the river as possible, looking for targets. Wood went upstream, while Ormsby took the area near Montrose, and Rory's men kept watch in Northumberland County, south of Sandy Point. Across and down river from Rory's position on the bank, he could make out the distant Point Lookout, at the mouth of the Potomac on the Maryland side. It was the site of a lighthouse, and a battery guarding a Yankee prison complex for captive Confederates.

They watched for several days from the bank for targets. The men grew restless, and the officers became concerned about being too long in one place, in an area harboring Union sentiment as well as Confederate, with Union picket boats patrolling the far bank. Rory's men had established contact with a family living close to the riverbank. Rory's men maintained a rough bivouac in the woods nearby, but Blakely or Rory would regularly visit the home of Bethany Scott, mother of two young boys, whose husband was away serving in a Virginia infantry regiment. Biscuits and other warm dishes would be transported back from the riverbank house to the encampment tucked away in the woods.

On the third night of their scout, Rory sat in Bethany's kitchen, as a bucket of stew neared readiness. "Sure, it's more than kind of you to feed the lads like this, ma'am. It's keeping morale up, in the absence of any ships to board."

"Oh, lieutenant, it keeps my morale up, too, to do something for the cause while my Jarod is away with the army. My heart goes out to all those poor boys the Yankees have in prison down to Point Lookout. Why, you can almost see them from here. I have friends on the other side of the river and I hear things. They're starving those poor boys."

"Faith, now, wouldn't it be grand if we could give the Yankees something to stew about, so to speak, and give our imprisoned comrades a little lift of spirit, to boot? You've given me an idea, Mrs. Bethany Scott!"

The next morning, right at daybreak, Rory trained his telescope on the lighthouse at Point Lookout, and then moved it to his left, upstream, so he looked at the battery above the riverbank, and the cleared woods and fencing a half mile beyond, where the Point Lookout prison lay. "Blakely," he called.

"Sir," replied the gunner's mate.

"Ride upstream to Montrose and find Mr. Ormsby. Give him my compliments, and tell him I require that he bring his boat and crew here at his very best speed with his powder and ammunition. The surgeon is with him. We'll need him as well. Tell Mr. Ormsby we have a target."

"Aye, aye, sir," Blakely replied, and ran for his horse.

Ormsby's whaleboat and wagon arrived late that afternoon. They were concealed in the woods near a little cove out of the line of sight from the Point Lookout battery some five miles distant across the river. Blakely had returned with the boat, as Ormsby's guide.

"You made good time, midshipman. Bring your men up to the tents and I'll explain our course of action to all at once. Am I correct in assumin' you found no targets in your sector?"

"Nothing at all, sir. The river was empty."

"Carry on then, assemble your crew. Good work, now, Blakely!"

"Thank you, sir," the gunner's mate replied.

"Good afternoon to ye all," Rory began, as twenty men sat cross-legged in the sand amid the riverbank trees. "We'll hope that wind which has been blowing downstream will hold through the night, for we'll be needin' it after sundown. Here's what I hope we can do. My boat will ghost past that battery yonder." Rory turned, and pointed to the three thirty-two pounders emplaced by the shore across the river. "We'll land just above the lighthouse on the point. After we break in and disarm the lighthouse keepers, we'll build a bonfire from the lighthouse's combustibles. We'll set off our powder with a slow match, hopin' it

will make as much noise as Saxons on Guy Fawkes Day, and shatterin'
the great lens of the light. I'm thinkin' the conflagration will draw the
attention of the gunners from the battery. Are y' with me, so far?"

"Sir, what about my boat?" Ormsby asked.

"You, Mister, will have grounded your boat on the bank just
upstream of the battery and out of sight. You'll take positions overlookin'
the battery and wait till we join you after the explosion. I'm guessin' it's a
five minute, hard row. When the twenty of us are together, we'll surprise
the battery, who'll be watchin' the lighthouse burn, I'm hopin'."

Blakely spoke up. "How many guns in the battery, sir?"

"Three, as best I can tell. That means we'll be twenty to their
thirty, but they'll be away from their side arms and muskets. We'll get
the drop on 'em. We'll carry lanyards to bind their hands, and send them
runnin' toward the prison while we spike the guns and blow the magazine.
Then, it's a dash for the caissons and horses on the Northumberland
County shore. If the wind's blowin' upstream or down, it should be a
broad reach."

"Questions, gentlemen?" Rory took a deep breath and stood
back, arms crossed with a great, self-satisfied grin on his face and a twinkle
in his eye. "Well, now, Mr. Ormsby. Mr. MacKenzie, the least you could
say would be, 'audacious!'"

"Will we go if the wind alters or dies, sir?" Mackenzie asked.

"Sure, it will be a long row, Engineer, but I'm guessin' it will
hold after sundown, as it has for the past two days. If we're successful,
we'll force the Yankees to bring more troops from the front lines to guard
against raids like ours. We might even give a few lads the chance to escape
in the confusion. And the ones that don't, may it lift their spirits! I'm
thinkin' their conditions can't get much worse, no matter what!"

The men sat in a stunned silence for a time, and then began to
cast sidelong glances at one another. Only the rustle of the wind through
the pines was audible.

Rory laughed, hoping for a spark among the men. "He's daft,
you're thinkin'. Over the edge. You could be right, you know. But,
we've no other targets, and you're all picked men, a bit daft yourselves, I
wouldn't wonder. Are y' with me?"

A chorus of "aye, aye, sirs" rippled through the ranks of the men sitting on the sand, and then they were standing, shouting, those with side arms waving them aloft. Rory could feel his Celtic battle frenzy begin to surge.

"Carry on, then. We'll muster by the boats as soon as it's dark. Doctor, I'd be obliged if you'd accompany the teamsters and the wagons downstream. Brunell," Rory said to the chief teamster, "take the wagons a mile down stream. With luck, we'll be back across about six bells. That's three in the morning. About two, light this green-glass lantern and show it at the shore. We'll respond in kind when we see it, so you'll know it's us, and not some boatload of Yankees."

Rory rode the short distance to Mrs. Scott's house. "We'll be leavin' as soon as it's dark, ma'am. The men send their thanks. Y' might look for fireworks at the point after midnight. God save ye, kindly, now." She waved, smiled and stood speechless as he rode away.

Darkness settled over the mouth of the broad Potomac. The crews of the two 26 foot whaleboats stepped their masts in the square depression or "step" carved in to the keelson, and shaped to the bottom or "heel" of the mast. The mast was fitted with shrouds, a forestay, running backstays and a dipping lug mainsail, loose-footed and mounted on a spar suspended from, or "bent," to the masthead by a halyard running through a block, and then secured to a cleat on the mast near the step. The wind blew downstream, from the northwest.

The eight sweep oars were laid amidships on the thwarts, parallel to the keel. With the wind behind them, they turned their bows toward the light on Point Lookout. After an hour, the wind began to die. "Can you whistle up a wind, Mr. Blakely?" Rory referred to the mariner's superstition that whistling at sea would bring a storm from a calm.

"I can try, sir," replied the gunner's mate.

"Ah, well, now, wouldn't we be better employed striking the sail? Ease off the halyards, lads, and grab the dip." A long lanyard was attached to the forward end of the main yard, which extended a third of its length beyond the mast. When the boat tacked, a sailor would pull downward on the lanyard, thus "dipping" the yard and allowing it to move free of the mast on the opposite tack. A sailor now grasped the lanyard to keep the main yard fore and aft as it was lowered, to rest on the thwarts while the men prepared to use their sweep oars.

"Toss oars," Rory commanded. Each of the eight oarsmen seized a ten-foot oar, set its handle on the bottom boards, and held it so it was vertical. "Out oars." Each rower lowered his sweep and set it in his oarlock. "Stand by to give way together. Give way all." Eight blades caught the river surface simultaneously, were pulled through an arc ending at each rower's chest, and were released from the water to reach and take another stroke.

Forty-five minutes later, Rory whispered "way enough," and both boats glided to a stop beside one another. Rory pointed toward a cove just upstream of the battery, and Ormsby waved in acknowledgement as his boat headed toward the shore. "Easy, now, lads, no splashing," said Rory quietly to his crew, as they passed the battery, dimly silhouetted against the distant lights of the prison. Five minutes later, they drew the boat up on the bank of the Potomac just upstream of the Point Lookout light, and ran toward the lighthouse. Two men carried a powder keg in a sling. Others carried axes in addition to their weapons.

A small cottage stood near the lighthouse, and three of Rory's men battered down the door, surprising the lighthouse keeper and his wife at dinner. They were soon bound and made as comfortable as possible under the circumstances. The axe-wielding sailors had already broken down the lighthouse door, and were piling combustibles from its ground floor and the keeper's cottage into a bonfire stack, complete with small powder charge and ready to light. Others had led a slow fuse up the circular stairs to a charge packed at the base of the huge, multi-faceted lens. Next, a long slow fuse was led out the door, a charge of a length that would allow a seven-minute burn. Rory lit the fuse, and in moments they had pushed the boat into the Potomac, and were silently rowing upstream past the battery, aided somewhat by a breeze just springing up from the southeast.

They quietly grounded their boat in the cove next to Ormsby's whaleboat, and were approaching his position overlooking the battery when the powder went up with a roar, igniting the bonfire combustibles, but not scattering them. Rory called to Ormsby and his men, the sound of his voice not carrying to the battery because of the noise from the burning lighthouse.

"Glad to see you, sir," said the midshipman, as the reunited twenty men of the raider force watched the activity unfold before them. The artillerymen in the battery were shouting and pointing to the lighthouse, their attention focused downstream. A second explosion, louder this time, shattered the lens and extinguished the light. Flames were licking out the windows of the lighthouse along its circular staircase.

"Now's our moment, sure and it is, Ormsby," said Rory as he clutched the midshipman by the shoulder. "Now, men," he called, waving them forward. "Remember, don't fire your pistols until close range." They ran forward, crossing the thirty yards to the rear of the battery quickly, each armed with two 1851 Navy Six Colt revolvers.

Rory was first through the entry port at the rear of the battery. He collided with an officer emerging from his quarters against the battery's rear wall, while struggling to draw his sword. The collision knocked one pistol from Rory's left hand, but he fired the other, wounding the Union lieutenant. Many of the Union gunners were unaware of the danger to their rear as they still stood along their parapet looking at the lighthouse fire. Rory's shot startled them and they turned to see twenty armed men, some firing Colt revolvers at them.

"Drop your weapons and surrender or we'll drop you," Rory shouted in his best masthead voice. Hands quickly shot into the air. Most of the gunners were away from their weapons, and their officer was bleeding from a shoulder wound, and in no shape to rally them. "Ormsby, take charge. Mr. MacKenzie, Blakely, with me to the magazine!"

The three men opened the door to the powder magazine, and soon had torn apart a number of canisters and scattered the powder charges where they were sure to ignite the entire stock of explosives. With a practiced eye, Gunner's Mate Blakely measured a length of slow fuse and led it out into the battery. Ormsby's men had bound the hands of the gunners behind them with the lanyards they carried for the purpose and were marching them out of the battery in two files, with revolvers still trained on them. "No one like a sailor to be able to truss up a prisoner with a secure knot," Rory remarked to MacKenzie as they watched.

Meanwhile, Blakely and a small detail were driving spikes into the touchholes of the 32-pounder cannon, rendering them unusable for the foreseeable future. Rory climbed to the platform along the rear parapet. He saw a platoon of guards from the prison running toward the lighthouse. Behind them, a brace of horses pulled a hand pumper with a fire hose. He climbed down from the platform and exited the battery. The Union gunners were in a column of twos, at pistol-point. Four of them, their hands freed, held a stretcher bearing their wounded lieutenant.

Rory addressed the thirty men. "Gentlemen, we're about to ignite your magazine. Obviously, it's in your interest to make your best speed toward the prison and away from the explosion. I'm paroling you. If you have a shred of honor, you'll not fight until exchanged." Rory laughed, outright. "At the double, march!" As the Union gunners stumbled toward the prison over the rough ground, Rory called to Blakely. "Gunner, light the match. Men, to the boats at the double."

The breeze still blew gently from the southeast as the boats pointed their bows to the Northumberland County shore. "Set your sail, Mr. Ormsby," Rory called to the whaleboat abeam. "Let's see what we can do on a reach!"

They were a cable's length from shore when the battery magazine exploded, battering the whaleboats with the shock wave. Rory looked aft, to see debris blown skyward against the backdrop of flame.

Rory found himself drenched in sweat. *Faith, I was too busy to notice how frightened I was*, he thought. "Mr. Blakely, can you sail this man o' war?"

"Aye, sir, I can do that," the gunner replied.

"Carry on then. And wake me when it's time to light the signal to shore." Rory leaned back in the sternsheets, his head cushioned on the gunwale, and fell fast asleep.

Thirty-six hours later, he reported his Point Lookout activities to Taylor Wood. The lieutenant commanding was pleased, although he confessed to a certain level of envy. "Outstanding initiative, Rory! And you didn't lose a man! I admit I wish I'd found a likely target here, but such is war. Let's move upstream tomorrow, before we head for

Richmond."

"Thank you sir. Our crews are keen men in a fight, and that's a fact! But I have a feeling, sir, a target will turn up tomorrow."

And sure enough, having moved northwest to King George County, they found a transport schooner, the *Frances Elmore,* anchored at the mouth of Pope's Creek, on the Maryland side.

As night fell, Wood assembled the men and prepared the boats for their assault on the schooner. The men were provided their arms, and Wood gave a prayer before they boarded the boats. Wood took the lead boat, with Rory's and Ormsby's boats following.

Rory grasped the tiller. "Bowmen, shove off, there!" The bow pair of the second whaleboat shoved the bow off the shore and climbed in, joining the alternate pulling and backing of the port and starboard sides as they brought the bow around to bear on the distant schooner.

Presently, they were up to the schooner, looming above them. "Way enough! In bows! Grappling hooks! Toss and ship oars! Boarders away!" Wood's boat crew had preceded them on the deck of the schooner. In short order, the unsuspecting six-man crew of the *Frances Elmore* was bound, and in the boats. Wood's men quickly stripped the vessel of valuables. Mackenzie and a detail laid combustibles in the most effective places, and set her afire. Off they rowed to the Virginia shore, with their prisoners, well before the nearest Federal cruiser reached the burning schooner.

Safe in Richmond, with their prisoners in Libby Prison, the officers of the raider contingent met to assess their next expedition. Sidney Lee had joined them as second in command. "Next time, gentlemen," said Wood, "we'll change direction, and head east to the shores of Mathews County, there to interrupt the enemy's main line of communication and transport, from Fort Monroe to Washington City."

"Sir," said Lee, "I know you were familiar with Potomac waters, and last week the raid was successful. Have we similar knowledge of the waters from New Point Comfort to the Piankatank?"

"Good question, lieutenant. We will 'recruit' a local pilot to aid us," Wood said. "It will be our first task, when we reach the shore."

Two weeks later, three wagons and thirty men set out from

Richmond toward the Chesapeake shore. Crossing the Pamunkey just before it flowed into the York, they headed for New Point Comfort, and Wood "impressed" a pilot to guide them in their quest. Thinly-veiled threats against his family had persuaded the unfortunate pilot to aid the expedition. The raiders ranged along the Chesapeake coast and the banks of the Piankatank and Rappahannock rivers, looking for target ships. Occasional brushes with Union patrols provided enough excitement to keep drowsiness away.

The unit was organized according to boat. Each ten-man boat crew comprised a separate command, with its own search area. Rory's crew now included Ormsby, Mackenzie, and Gunner's Mate Blakely, as well as six seamen formerly of the *Patrick Henry.* Their assigned search area was the south bank of the Rappahannock.

Autumn rains fell frequently and the brush was always wet. Each night they would find shelter in the barn of a Southern sympathizer, the house of a truly brave Rebel patriot, or, in the last extreme, under tents in the woods.

The welfare of the horses came first. They were walked after hard rides, cooled, curried, and fed before the men. Rory's crew was armed according to the recommendations of John Mosby, each man with four Navy Sixes; two holstered in front of the saddle, and two at the hip. Some men carried sabers and carbines, but these were expected to serve as secondary or "last resort" weapons. The Colt revolvers gave each man twenty-four rounds to be fired easily from horseback.

Toward week's end, they moved away from the bank of the Rappahannock to camp at the edge of Dragon Swamp, near the upper Piankatank. The next morning, Rory and two of his men stumbled across a Union cavalry patrol of ten riders. Without a moment's hesitation, Rory drew two pistols, urged his horse forward with his knees, and fired twelve shots at the surprised Yankees. Rory's men followed suit.

Rory called out in the voice he normally used to hail the maintop in a gale, "Troop, by squad, line abreast. Charge!"

This imitation of Mosby's tactics in the "Ride 'Round McClellan" had the identical and desired result. The Union cavalry assumed that a troop-size force of forty men confronted them, and rode for their lives, influenced in no small degree by the fusillade of thirty-six quick rounds the three Rebels had been able to fire.

A week of stormy weather produced no targets. Then, after rowing miles north of New Point Comfort, the raiders saw a full-rigged ship, the *Alleghanian*, of fourteen hundred tons and laden with guano, anchored off Gwynn Island at the mouth of the Piankatank River to ride out the storm. As before, the crews grappled the prize before resistance could be marshaled, and the twenty-five-man crew was soon peacefully subdued. Wood made ready to place the *Alleghanian*'s seamen in the ship's boats and make off with the valuables in the cargo, with the officers as prisoners.

"Sir," said Rory, "Let me remain behind with Mr. Ormsby and Mr. MacKenzie and my boat's crew; and give me five more men from yours. When you fire the ship, I'll hide in her lee. A Yankee cruiser will arrive to extinguish the fire, sure as a gun, sir. We'll board her by surprise."

Wood listened intently, with a determined look in his eye. "I think this could work, Dunbrody. Lieutenant Lee and I will delay our departure 'til we see the Yankee approach, and try to keep attention on us while you surprise him. If you can take her, set her afire and bring your men to our rendezvous point."

As Wood's men took to their boats, Rory smiled ruefully at Ormsby. "Sure, it sounded like a good idea when I thought of it, but now?"

"Not to worry, sir," said Ormsby. "The men are used to you, and know the value of a good officer who's also a lucky one, and a wild Irishman, besides."

It was 2:30 a.m. when the USS *Commodore Truxton,* a converted Hudson River ferryboat, eased alongside the burning *Alleghanian.* Her 32-pounder bow pivot fired at Wood's and Lee's boats as they made for the far Piankatank shore. Hoses were throwing streams of river water on the merchantman, which was on fire aft, and smoldering forward. Her masts had already burned and toppled, bringing more fire to the deck area. The *Commodore Truxton's* boatswain led a boarding party of fifteen over the gunwale of the *Alleghanian* to her deck and into her hold to extinguish the flames. As the *Commodore Truxton* fired on the two fleeing boats, her crew's attention was focused forward, and upriver, where Wood and Lee were drawing close to shore on the Piankatank's southwest bank.

Rory eased his whaleboat around the stern of the *Alleghanian*, where he and his fifteen-man raider crew had been hiding, and grappled the low stern of the *Commodore Truxton*. The crew of the after gun, a rifled howitzer, was also paying avid attention to the drama of the fleeing boats. Five of them surrendered as Rory's men surrounded them, and the others fell to pistol shots or cutlasses as they turned to fight, or fled forward.

As the acting master commanding the howitzer crew turned to face Rory, his face reflected his dismay at realizing his failure to defend his ship against boarders. He was pulling his sword from its scabbard when Rory shot him. The Union officer crumpled and his sword clattered to the deck.

At the moment he fired, Rory recognized his adversary. "Jasus, it's Tom Avery, from my Academy class!" He watched as Avery fell slowly, agonizingly, backward, clutching his chest. He rushed to Avery's side. "Tom, damn, I'm sorry." Avery's head had struck the wheel of the howitzer as he fell, and was cocked at an awkward angle. Rory gently cradled the acting master's head with one hand, and with his other arm under Avery's shoulders, laid the body full length on the deck. Rory reached for his classmate's wrist. "No pulse. I've killed him. Damn all."

Forcing himself to focus on the fate of his boarding party, Rory rose and called out orders. "Mr. MacKenzie, starbowlines, and grapplers, follow me up to the pilothouse deck. Ormsby, Blakely, and port oars, turn this howitzer and fire rounds through the deck house into the forward 32-pounder crew!"

Rory led his men up the starboard stairway to the pilothouse deck. Ormsby's contingent manned the howitzer. They reversed it so that it pointed through the maindeck cabin, a wide-open space that had once carried many passengers, carts and wagons ferried across the Hudson River in the *Commodore Truxton's* ferryboat days. They fired two quick rounds forward, dismounting the bow 32-pounder and killing or wounding most of its crew.

The captain and the executive officer of the *Commodore Truxton*, having heard the commotion, stormed out of the pilothouse, pistols drawn. Rory held his Navy Six in his left hand, and his saber in his right.

He fired at the captain, and missed, but slashed the man's shoulder with his saber. Mackenzie, behind him, laid the flat of his saber across the executive officer's skull, knocking him to the deck. The pistols of both Union officers clattered into the scuppers.

Rory crashed through the pilothouse door. The local pilot stood near the helmsman at the wheel. Both raised their hands quickly after seeing Rory's Navy Six. Ormsby appeared in the pilothouse doorway. "Main deck secure, sir!"

"Good! Secure the prisoners and keep the Stars and Stripes flying. I see running lights downriver. If they're Union gunboats, I want them thinking all's well aboard this ferryboat. Leave the pilot here with me for a moment. Send MacKenzie below to secure the engine room."

"Aye, aye, sir." Ormsby sent two men below with the unhurt prisoners, and set two more to bind the hands of the helmsman and officers.

Rory stared at the civilian pilot, a slight, balding man with a worried expression. Rory hoped he was like many pilots in the border states, more committed to making a living than tied to the patriotic cause of the side who employed him. "Now, then, pilot," said Rory, "I'm going to let you go home to your wife and family, instead of to prison in Richmond, if you simply tell me the names of the two steamers after us."

The man's face reflected his struggle in choosing between the two alternatives. "Oh, sir, I'd be in terrible trouble if I did that."

"If you don't, your wife and children will not see you until after the war, *if* you live. If I know Richmond prisons, you won't. Come now, pilot, you're only under contract to the navy. You're not commissioned. Think of your loved ones."

The pilot swallowed hard and said, "They're the *Crusader,* closest, and the *T.A. Ward.*"

"Who's senior, *Truxton's* commander, or *Crusader's*?"

"*Truxton's*, sir."

"Mr. Ormsby, find a dory and put this man over the side. Then bring me the captain."

"Aye, aye, sir. The Yankee captain's being treated for the saber cut you gave him, sir. One of his men's binding him up, under guard."

"Very well, Mr. Ormsby, I'll go to him. I want to hear him speak. Is he conscious?"

"Yes, sir. First gunboat's closing, sir. Fifteen hundred yards."

"Mr. Blakely," said Rory to the gunner's mate. "Take two men and ready the howitzer for firing. We're going to surprise a Yankee gunboat or two!"

"Aye, aye, sir," replied Blakely, with a will.

Rory turned to Ormsby. "Just before the first gunboat reaches us, we'll cast off, and pursue Mr. Wood and Mr. Lee. I want the first Yankee within hailing range. She's the *Crusader*. I'll request that she follow us, and that the second gunboat, the *T.A. Ward*, extinguish the fires aboard *Alleghanian*. Have MacKenzie and Blakely rig a fuse to a gunpowder barrel, in the hold, aft, starboard side. We'll run this bucket aground, set the fuse, abandon ship, and hope the first gunboat is alongside when the gunpowder goes off!"

"Aye, aye, sir. I'll have the whaleboat alongside our port bow. We'll abandon without the Yankee seeing us."

"Very well, Mr. Ormsby. You'd best put the prisoners, wounded and hale, in the largest boat and trail it after the whaleboat, with a boat's crew of our men aboard."

"Aye, aye, sir."

"Have MacKenzie keep the pumps going to the gunboat detail aboard *Alleghanian*. I want them surprised as well, when we cast off. With the shots this Yankee was firing at our boats, their detail aboard *Alleghanian* must have thought our howitzer rounds through the main deck cabin were more of the same."

Rory hurried to the deck forward of the pilothouse, where the Union captain's wound was being bandaged. "How are you, sir?" Rory asked, courteously.

The captain glared at him. "Well enough, you damned pirate! You've made a charnel house of my ship!"

Rory recognized a Massachusetts accent, similar to one Tobias would affect on occasion. *I believe I can duplicate that*, thought Rory.

"And isn't it fortunate, then, captain, that you're alive to grouse about it, praise the saints?" Rory smiled and returned to the pilothouse.

Rory raised the speaking trumpet to his lips. *"Crusadah,"* he said, striving for the Union captain's accent, "I'd be obliged if you followed me in support. I'm pursuing the raidahs. They're headed upstream."

"Acknowledge, *Commodore Truxton,"* came the reply.

Rory dropped the trumpet and turned to his men. "Ormsby, cut the hoses, and cast off! Blakely, fire regular rounds from the howitzer. Make sure your rounds fall nowhere near our boats."

Ormsby cut the fire hoses extending to the *Alleghanian* with a fire axe. Below decks aboard *Alleghanian*, the water stream diminished to a trickle, the first inkling that *Commodore Truxton's* fire-fighting detail had that their ship had departed in pursuit of the raiders.

The *Commodore Truxton* steamed upriver, after the raiders' first two boats. The *Crusader* followed in her wake. *T.A. Ward* came alongside *Alleghanian* minutes later, and joining with the still-astonished *Commodore Truxton* firefighting detail, renewed the effort to extinguish the fires.

Rory focused his night glass on the first two boats. He could see them ashore, being loaded onto the wagons. "Helmsman! Hard a-port, and steer her for the bank. Lash the wheel, and get for'd to the boat."

"Aye, aye, sir. Good luck, sir." The helmsman put the wheel over, lashed the spokes, and disappeared forward. Rory shouted down the engine room speaking tube. "Mackenzie, get your men into the boat!"

Rory turned to the gunner's mate. "Blakely, train the howitzer to starboard, primed and loaded, and then get you and your men in the boat. Ormsby! Cast off and pull like hell to the wagon at the rendezvous as soon as you have everyone accounted for. I'm staying aboard to make sure the powder blows. Smartly, now!"

"Aye, aye, sir," they responded, a trifle reluctantly, but disciplined to obey, nonetheless.

The *Commodore Truxton* ran upon the sandy and gently sloped riverbank, with a tremendous jolt that separated her strakes at the stem, and caused her to begin leaking from the bow. The *Crusader* came into hailing distance just astern. Rory's whaleboat-load of raiders, towing the *Commodore Truxton's* boat filled with Union prisoners and four guards, pulled toward the rendezvous eight hundred yards upstream. Rory shouted through the speaking trumpet, "I'm aground and require assistance!" Then, he lit the minute fuse leading below to the powder barrel, which Blakely had placed in the hold aft and on the starboard side aboard *Commodore Truxton*. Rory watched the fuse for a moment to make sure it was burning, and then ran to the howitzer. *Crusader* surged alongside the *Commodore Truxton's* starboard rail. *Crusader's* seamen, standing by with heaving lines fore and aft, wondered why the deck detail of *Commodore Truxton* was not at the gunwale to receive the lines.

Rory trained the howitzer on the *Crusader's* pilothouse, yanked the lanyard, and as the shell blew the *Crusader's* pilothouse to splinters, he ran for the *Commodore Truxton's* foredeck. Before he reached 'midships, the powder barrel exploded. The powder barrel destroyed the transom and afterdeck of the *Commodore Truxton*, and blew a hole in the side of *Crusader* below the waterline. Both gunboats began to settle, stern-first, into the placid waters of the Piankatank.

An angry gunnery lieutenant, the ranking officer of *Crusader* left alive, led a boarding party aboard *Commodore Truxton*. They found only Lieutenant Rory Dunbrody, CSN, struggling back to consciousness, outside the starboard door of the pilothouse. They bound his hands and took him aboard *T.A. Ward*, the only Potomac Flotilla ship off the Piankatank still afloat.

Rory regained full consciousness in the morning aboard the flagship of the Potomac Flotilla, USS *Brandywine*. He was soon taken, under Marine guard, to the cabin of the Flotilla Commander, Commodore Andrew A. Harwood. Harwood sat at the cabin table, flanked by a young lieutenant. "Lieutenant Rory Cormac Dunbrody, Confederate States Navy, sir," said Rory, coming to a fully-braced position of attention. He did not salute, of course, as both he and the commodore were not wearing their uniform hats inside the cabin. Naval tradition forbad saluting while "uncovered".

"Good morning, lieutenant," replied Harwood. "I believe you are acquainted with my flag lieutenant?"

Rory looked closely at the flag lieutenant. "Travis Prescott Bates, the third?" Rory laughed. "Sure, Commodore, Lieutenant Bates looks quite a bit different since we were seventeen-year-old middies. 'Tis a pleasure, Travis."

"Good to see you, Rory. Regret the circumstance, of course. Sir," said Bates to Harwood, "as I mentioned, Mr. Dunbrody was always a bit adventuresome."

"He's changed very little, then," said Harwood. "Mr. Dunbrody, you've sunk two of my gunboats, burned a merchantman, and falsely led the captain of the *Crusader* to believe *Commodore Truxton* was still under control of the U.S. Navy. The president has labeled Southern naval commanders 'pirates,' and suggested they be punished accordingly, by swinging them from the yardarm. Why should I not be planning your hanging?"

"Commodore, with respect, sir, you won't hang me because you are an honorable and veteran sailor who recognizes that my actions were those of an officer of a foreign navy, whose country is a belligerent. You recognize that my actions were taken within acknowledged and accepted rules of engagement, including a legitimate *ruse de guerre*, one which you, yourself, would employ should the opportunity arise; and one which, in your extensive and diverse experience, you may already have employed. Sir."

"Thank you, lieutenant. What do you think, Mr. Bates?"

"Sir, I think that Mr. Dunbrody, being profoundly circumspect and politic, forbore to mention that, if we hang him, they will hang at least one of us in retaliation."

"You two young gentlemen give me hope that the naval profession may indeed have a bright future. I will inform the exchange commissioners of your capture, Mr. Dunbrody."

"And I thank you most kindly for that, Commodore. A cavalry friend of mine wrote just the other day of the most courteous treatment he received from members of the Union forces involved in his exchange. Isn't it gratifyin' to see that his treatment mirrors my own?"

"Careful, sir," Bates said with a wry smile. "I know for a fact he's actually kissed the Blarney Stone."

"Your advice is noted, Lieutenant Bates. Please escort Mr. Dunbrody back to his quarters. Dismissed, lieutenant."

"Aye, aye, sir," Rory responded.

Travis Prescott Bates, III, lieutenant, USN, escorted Rory back to his stateroom, with the Marine assigned as Rory's guard following in their wake. As they neared the companionway to the gundeck, Rory turned to his friend. "Travis," said Rory, "I am at the ebb tide of my life. Faith, my friend, I've never been so full of sorrow. The Irish have the Banshee's cry, the world's most lonely and despairing sound. I can hear it through my whole being, sink me if I can't."

"Rory, you'll be exchanged in days. The commodore's a straight-shooter, and I could tell he liked you. What's to be downcast about?"

Rory sighed, and looked across the river to the far Potomac shore. "I killed Tom Avery yesterday. Our classmate. A lad I traded class notes on gunnery with. I didn't know it was he until I'd shot him through the heart."

Bates considered for a moment. "He'd have shot you, if he'd had the chance. It's war. It's a sad war, with friend against friend. But we can't change its nature. Remorse, it seems, comes with the conflict."

"Damned senseless, by my lights," said Rory.

"No doubt, my friend. May you and I survive it." Bates put a reassuring hand on Rory's shoulder.

"God save you, Travis. And His blessing follow you."

"Thank you, Rory. The same to you. Let's go below to your palatial quarters. I'll look in on you, tomorrow. We'll likely be sending you to Old Capitol Prison."

"And thank you kindly, Travis."

CHAPTER 26
RETURN TO RICHMOND, VIRGINIA
NOVEMBER 1862

Washington City's Old Capitol Prison that housed Rory had also incarcerated a host of celebrity prisoners, including the lovely Rebel spies Belle Boyd and Rose Greenhow. Just north of the Capitol Building, the red brick building had served as the temporary capitol after the British burned the city in 1814.

Rory was housed with twenty other prisoners in a room that had served as part of the U.S. Senate chamber. There was room for little else, aside from the three-tiered bunks and one small table in the room's center. The food was just adequate for sustenance, and the blankets were as clean as those used by the infantry, which Rory found was not a high standard. Most of the daylight hours were spent regaling one another with tales of the war, and a new addition to the room was prized, for he would bring with him tales as yet unheard.

The specter of Avery's death still haunted Rory. It led him to examine his place in the war, and it was not a pleasant review. The closer he looked, the clearer it became that he lacked passion for the southern cause. *Perhaps I should resign, offer my sword to the Union,* he pondered. *But then I'd be sinking to the level of the turncoats against Ireland I've always despised. Carrie Anne and my family would be shattered and harassed as well. No, the honorable thing is to stay, to fight for my shipmates and the navy, and to make the best of a difficult choice. May the war be short. There's enough suffering on either side to fill the cup of misery for three wars.*

In ten days, the exchange had been arranged. He was placed
aboard a transport schooner bound for Newport News, where he was
formally and duly exchanged for a Union officer of equal rank. A steam
launch bore him up the familiar bends and reaches of the James River, all
the way to Richmond. His spirits rose as the river took him to the capital,
and he resolved to put doubt behind him. He reported to the Navy
Department, in the Mechanics Institute Building, and was greeted by an
enthusiastic Stephen Mallory, his round face beaming.

"I've read Mr. Wood's account of the last raid. He gives you
great credit, lieutenant! Congratulations! Two Yankee gunboats to your
account, a lighthouse destroyed and an assault on a Yankee prison and its
battery! You've done your country, and the navy, a great service."

"Ah, Mr. Secretary. You're kind to say so, sir. Sure, I'm proud of
what we accomplished, and Taylor was a masterful commander. But what
a sadness I feel, havin' shot one of my Academy classmates. It drains the
joy, sir, truly it does."

"This is indeed the cruelest of wars, Mr. Dunbrody. But your
accomplishments are undiminished by the pathos of brother against
brother."

Mallory brightened as he returned to business. "President Davis
has scheduled a reception in honor of the raider contingent; an afternoon
gathering at the White House. The men and their families, if available,
will meet the president in a receiving line in the dining room, and repair
to the central and west parlors while the President, the Speaker of the
House of Representatives, and the President of the Senate extend their
congratulations and the Thanks of Congress. An informal reception will
follow, inside, and on the grounds. Cabinet members, senior members of
Congress, flag officers and generals, and their ladies, have all been invited."

"Very kind of President Davis, sir, and very kind of you. The
men will be grateful, and take great pleasure in attending and being
recognized."

"They richly deserve it, lieutenant. And now, young man, I must
move to another subject. Lieutenant, I believe you have the 'touch'. I
know of no other way to put it. Everywhere I place you, you bring credit
to the navy, and in the most timely of circumstances. I want to place you

where your penchant for successful enterprise will do the cause the most good. Therefore, I'm acceding to Commander Bulloch's request that you be assigned to his command in Great Britain to help him build, acquire, arm, and launch commerce raiders and ironclads from Europe, so that we might continue to let slip these hounds of war and bring great pain to the enemy."

"Sir, can you tell me any salient particulars of the situation in England?"

Mallory stepped from behind his desk and began to pace, his hands clasped behind him. "In his efforts to put our ships at sea, Commander Bulloch has been severely hampered by Ambassador Charles Francis Adams, and, we think, Henry Shelton Sanford, U.S. Minister to Belgium, who doubles as U.S. Secret Service chief in Europe. We know that Sanford and Adams have built a network of spies who've infiltrated all the ship-building facilities in Great Britain, and all the communication centers that carry news of ship activity. Ports, shipyards, machinery-manufacturing, telegraph offices, the post, no avenue of naval activity is safe from these gentlemen's espionage."

"They seem formidable adversaries, sir."

"And yet, Bulloch has thus far managed to overcome these obstacles. As you may know, Dunbrody, we've built, paid for, and sent to sea two cruisers from England, the *Alabama* and the *Florida,* and we've purchased the blockade runner *Fingal* that brought Commander Bulloch here when you saw him last November. We've also contracted for another cruiser, and three ironclad rams. All this activity has attracted the attention of the Union's European representatives and agents. Our men cannot now move without their knowledge. Surveillance is constant. Commander Bulloch thinks you could move more easily in Britain than any other Confederates, because of your knowledge of the island and its customs, and your accent, particularly if you go unannounced and establish a clandestine connection with our agents there."

Rory gave Mallory a look of disbelief. "I'll be a spy, sir?"

"Think of it more as a low-profile agent."

"Is it possible, sir, with *Alabama's* now burnin' Union ships at sea, and stoppin' neutral ships, that the British government will be under more pressure to prevent our ships bein' built?"

"That is Bulloch's greatest fear, Mr. Dunbrody. We did not fare well at the Battle of Sharpsburg, in Maryland, in September. We think Burnside intends to confront us at Fredericksburg, back in our territory in Virginia. Britain is mindful of our seeming lack of success in the land war. It makes it difficult for their government to resist the Union's diplomatic pressure."

"Has Commander Bulloch no one in Britain to whom he can turn for this kind of help, sir?"

"Oh, we have friends—Mr. Priolieu, Fraser, Trenholm and Company—but these are financiers, not naval men. Bulloch and his men cannot move without being recognized. If they go near one of the ships under construction, it gives Ambassador Adams fuel to complain that these are Confederate warships, and that they contravene British neutrality and their Foreign Enlistment Act of 1819. That Act allows us to construct a ship and send it to sea if there are no guns or any war materials aboard, and if it's under British private ownership and command. Once clear of British waters, we can meet our ships and arm and man them. Any overt interest in the ships by our agents makes that more difficult, and could lead to seizure of the ships by the British."

Rory considered Mallory's explanation. "I can see where I might be useful, sir, under those circumstances."

"Good," replied Mallory with a satisfied smile. "It's settled. You'll be useful as a courier, as well. You'll be carrying one million dollars worth of cotton certificates to aid in paying for the next round of ship construction and acquisition."

"A million dollars worth, sir!" Rory exclaimed, wide eyed. "How much does that weigh?"

"They're large denomination certificates, lieutenant. They all fit nicely into a portfolio."

"Sure, and I won't be sleepin' soundly on the trip, Mr. Secretary."

"You'll do just fine, lieutenant. You'll also likely be aiding Lieutenant Sinclair and Lieutenant North. They're each working independently of Bulloch to secure more raiders. They're having the same difficulty as Commander Bulloch with the Union agents."

Heaven save us, thought Rory, *He's got a divided command, with Confederate officers competing against one another for assets and glory! What a melee it must be!*

"Last month, I sent our famous ocean scientist, Commander Matthew Fontaine Maury, to England," said Mallory. "He'll also act independently to get ships to sea, while continuing his electric torpedo research. I'm hopeful his high reputation as a scientist will allow him to move more easily as an agent."

Yet another division in the European command, thought Rory. Aloud, he said, "Mr. Secretary, I'll go where you wish, and do my best for the Confederacy. But I must tell you, sir, I'd much rather be firing broadsides and calling away boarders."

"I understand your desires, young man. But you are perfect for this assignment. Both Bulloch and I are in complete agreement on that. And, if his worst fears are realized, and Britain precludes us from further activities, France would be our next option, and you speak French. Commander Bulloch intends to have you lay the groundwork for that possibility."

"Aye, aye, Mr. Secretary. Bad French, sir. I speak bad French."

"Be that as it may, as an incentive, Mr. Dunbrody, should you and Commander Bulloch be successful in getting raiders to sea, we have decided that you will serve aboard one as a senior lieutenant. That will get you back to the place you wish to be. And you may visit your family in Edwards Ferry for a day or two on your way to Wilmington and your blockade runner to Europe."

"Aye, aye, Mr. Secretary, and thank you, sir, for your confidence."

"I'll see you at the reception for Mr. Wood and his raiders. Let me add my personal thanks to the 'Thanks of Congress' you'll receive. Your assault on Point Lookout and the sinking of the two gunboats were acts of unparalleled vision and courage."

The reception was held on the main floor of the White House of the Confederacy. The honored guests were admitted to the entry hall and guided to the left, where the short reception line had formed in the dining room. Short speeches took place in the Central and Western Parlors, joined together by opening the pocket doors that separated them. Mirrors on the red brocaded walls made the rooms seem larger. A number of army and navy senior officers were present. A small podium and lectern stood at one end of the Central Parlor. After the President of the Senate and the Speaker of the House of Representatives had offered the "Thanks of Congress" to Taylor Wood, representing the entire contingent, President Davis walked to the lectern. The slender and distinguished-looking chief executive addressed the guests soberly, the weight of his office apparent in the way he bore himself.

"Ladies and gentlemen, in this struggle for independence and for our rights, we face a numerically and materially-superior foe. It is in our spirit and firm conviction that ours is the just cause, that we must find our strength and courage. These men, like our valiant army thrusting its way into the enemy's very own territory, have shown us that courage and audacity can overcome great odds, and they inspire us to continue our struggle for justice and freedom."

"Lieutenant Wood, Lieutenant Lee, Lieutenant Dunbrody, Chief Engineer MacKenzie, Midshipman Ormsby, and the valiant men of Wood's Raiders have underscored a lesson we shall teach our foes again and again; they will not prevail, and we shall prevail! My congratulations to Mr. Secretary Mallory and the Naval Service. Three cheers for these valiant sailors and teamsters!" Cheers resounded through the building.

The senior elected officials and other dignitaries of the Confederacy then mingled with the honorees, many of whom found their way to the White House grounds. Davis smiled at Rory when they encountered one another. "Mr. Dunbrody, you turn up regularly for recognition, it seems. Well-deserved, I must say. My nephew is encouraging me to use the Act Congress passed allowing dual army and navy appointments. He said it would make sense for combined operation liaison. He holds you up as an example of an officer at home afloat and ashore. Himself, too, of course."

"Sure, he's a fine example, Mr. President. I believe I introduced Miss Carrie Anne Eastman, and her mother, Mrs. Eastman to you in the receiving line," said Rory, turning to include the women in the conversation.

"Charmed, ladies. I'm delighted you could join us to honor

these men." Davis bowed and moved to greet others.

Pickett, von Klopfenstein, Mosby and Stuart stood talking together. Mosby was listening to von Klopfenstein, and his face bore a skeptical look. Stuart and Pickett saw Rory at the same moment and motioned him to join them.

"General Pickett, you've been promoted again!" Rory acknowledged the major general's insignia on Pickett's shoulders and collar.

"Mr. Dunbrody, as I live and breathe! Congratulations on your sinkings. Even the army has heard. Please introduce these lovely ladies." Ever the gallant, and clearly enjoying his new status as a major general and division commander, Pickett bowed to the Eastman women, and smiled warmly at Carrie Anne.

"I saw you from afar at the Van Lews' last June, Miss Eastman, but Mr. Dunbrody failed to introduce us. I was terribly disappointed, I sho'ly was. Now that we meet, I just may forgive Lieutenant Dunbrody for his oversight." Carrie Anne smiled demurely from behind her gloved hand, and Rory feigned relief.

"Thank you, General," Rory said. "Good afternoon, General Stuart, Major von Klopfenstein, Captain Mosby. Let me introduce Carrie Anne Eastman, and her mother, Mrs. Eastman." Rory looked hard at von Klopfenstein, mentally daring him to mention Carrie Anne's relationship with Colonel Donovan, and the scandal of the duel. He was certain the Prussian knew of her engagement to the Zouave colonel, as von Klopfenstein had alluded to the duel at the Farwells' mansion the previous June.

"You grow more formidable with each passing moment, Dunbrody," said von Klopfenstein. "Two Yankee gun boats! Soon, you vill run out of room to carve notches on your gun butt." As always with the Prussian, menace seemed to lurk beneath the innocent surface of the banter itself. "Be careful, Fraulein, danger seems to follow our young Irish."

"Sunshine, too, Herr Major." Carrie Anne smiled sweetly and directly at von Klopfenstein.

"Still," said von Klopfenstein, "it must be difficult to throw one's self wholeheartedly into a fight when one's dear brother serves with the other side. I met a Major Donovan of Army Intelligence who said that very question arose in your court of inquiry hearing, *nicht wahr*? Do you find it a blot on the family crest, yes, 'leutnant'?"

"No, Major, for my brother and I each followed our own conscience, and honorably so. Presumably, you followed yours, assuming you have one!"

General Stuart, alert to the escalating animosity, and determined to avoid confrontation, stepped forward and shook Rory's hand warmly. "Mosby tells me you'd promised to test his 'four-pistol' approach to cavalry arms, Lieutenant. Can you share any results?"

Rory was silently grateful for Stuart's intervention, not wanting to embarrass his friends and superior officers. He seized the opportunity to change the subject. "As usual, General, Captain Mosby was disturbingly accurate. My boat crew was armed with the 'Mosby four-Colt set.' Twice, we rode through U.S. cavalry patrols and scattered them before they could effectively use saber or carbine." Stuart nodded approvingly at Mosby, and, artfully including Pickett and von Klopfenstein, engaged Carrie Anne and her mother in conversation.

Mosby and Rory stepped into a nearby alcove formed by a hedge and a tree on the grounds. "You're still encountering your Prussian," said Mosby, "and I've got mine."

Perhaps we can make a trade," said Rory, laughing. "Tell me of yours."

"Baron Heros von Borcke, Major and aide to General Stuart." said Mosby. "Gilds the lily like no other. A true Baron von Munchausen. He embellishes a story better than anyone I've ever met, and I've known many politicians. Every time I lead my men into a melee, by the time I return to headquarters, he's informed the press it was all his doing."

"Mine sounds a shade more sinister, Captain, darlin'."

"No doubt you're right, Rory. I'm glad my Navy Six advice was sound."

"As am I," said Rory. "I remembered your letter on capture and exchange when the same happened to me. It was comforting. Now that you've survived Sharpsburg, I'd venture you've a charmed life."

"I try not to offend the gods of war, Rory."

"Good luck against this next campaign against Burnside, Jack. Mallory's just told me I'm to go to England to arm and acquire raiders."

"England? Congratulations! Maybe you'll get a ship of your own, again. If I make it through this campaign, I think I'm assured of my partisan rangers."

"I'll read the papers in England, Jack. I've no doubt they'll carry your dazzling exploits."

"Stay safe, my friend," said Mosby, as they rejoined the others.

Wood had joined the group, and Pickett and his aide had left. "Sure, it's our great leader," said Rory. "I saw you deep in conversation with Mr. Mallory."

"Yes I was. We've decided to have the raiders lie low for a time. We'll lull the Yankees into slumber, and then pounce again. In the meanwhile, I'm assigned to the CSS *Richmond* here."

"I'll think of you, my friend and commander, when I'm tossin' on the briny. I leave tomorrow for Wilmington, with a two-day stop at Edwards Ferry to see my family."

"Good luck through the blockade, Rory. I hope our paths cross again."

"God save you kindly, Taylor."

Rory and the Eastmans took the Farwell's carriage back to Church Hill. "Mother," said Carrie Anne, "Rory may wait for days or weeks until the tide and moon are right for a run through the blockade. I want to go to Wilmington 'til he leaves. I could stay with Uncle Jeremy." She explained to Rory, "Uncle Fred has a brother in Wilmington."

"Let me write to your Uncle Jeremy," said Mrs. Eastman. "I think it would be all right. I know you two will be separated for a long time. I could accompany you on the train, if your aunt and uncle agree."

"Mother, it will take too long to write, and wait for a response. Rory could be gone by the time we get there. Can't we telegraph Uncle Jeremy?" she pleaded.

"I'm sure your Uncle Fred can arrange a telegram, dear. We'll ask this evening."

Rory had been listening to the discussion with a bemused look.

"And isn't it a fine thing for a lad to listen to his immediate future being planned by two such lovely ladies?"

"And do you object to the plan, lieutenant?" asked Carrie Anne, her eyebrows arched.

"Oh, 'tis a fine plan and all. And completed without meself raisin' as much as a hand to join in the planning effort. Think of the energy I saved by you two doin' all the work!"

"If you behave yourself, sailor, perhaps next time we'll even consult you," said Carrie Anne, quite full of herself, and looking forward to an extension of the time she could spend with Rory. "Mother, I'm a grown woman. I can make the trip without a chaperone, really."

"We'll see, dear."

CHAPTER 27
CARRIE ANNE AND RORY: NORTH CAROLINA
INTERLUDE
NOVEMBER 1862

By the time Rory had reached the railroad bridges across the
Roanoke River at Weldon, N.C., the realization had sunk in that he was
leaving his home of eleven years for an indefinite return to the British
Isles. It was an exciting prospect, true enough. The portfolio of cotton
certificates under his arm added to the drama. As most of his last eleven
years he'd been at sea across the world, rather than in North Carolina
itself, the wrench of uprooting was negligible. He'd ridden the Richmond
and Petersburg Railroad and then the Weldon and Wilmington to the
town of Weldon, where his father and sister met him with a boat crewed
by Patrick Dunbrody's shipyard workers. He was pleased to see that
Siobhan's health was good, and so far unaffected by the change of location
from New Berne.

They rowed and sailed the fifteen miles downstream to Edwards
Ferry. Rory sat in the stern sheets of his father's shipyard cutter as it
followed the meanders of the Roanoke, listening to the creak and thump
of the protective leather sleeves against the tholepins. Patrick's rowing
craft still used the old fashioned wooden pins, two to each oar, instead
of the newer oarlocks or "swivel crutches" as their British inventor called
them. In Patrick's boat, the oar was placed between the two pins and a
lanyard was put over the top to keep the oar from popping out.

"I'm glad Edwards Ferry is on my route, Da'. I've no idea how
long I'll be in Liverpool. It's grand to see you and Siobhan."

"I hope you'll be there long enough to slip across the Irish Sea for
a sit-down with your family in Meath and Galway."

"T'be sure, Da', I've been planning that very trip."

"And it includes a visit to the belle of Clifden, Mary Katherine O'Shaughnessy, I'm thinkin'," said Siobhan with a twinkle in her eye.

"Rude it would be for me to miss my childhood playmate, now," said Rory with a smile, as the cutter, with masts rigged fore and aft, eased around the last bend before Edwards Ferry, the low banks covered with southern pine and box elder. As the river narrowed slightly, with low banks of a natural crossing on either side, Rory saw a number of shacks and sheds framing a cornfield with a gentle slope at bankside.

"Welcome to Tillery's Field, better known as Edwards Ferry. We begin framing CSS *Albemarle* next week," said Patrick. "You can see it's high enough ground not to be flooded in the spring. So far we've set up a sawmill and a forge. We'll build two more sawmills in the woods. What we need most, though, is iron."

"How will y'be findin' that in the South, Da', with hardly any industry t'draw from?"

"Gil Elliott is scroungin' wherever he can. We've written to Governor Vance about the Atlantic and North Carolina Railroad's iron reserve. He's a board member of the railroad."

"We heard in Richmond that he's restarted the Carolina Navy, and built a State-owned blockade runner, the *Ad Vance*."

"Sure, son, he's got fingers in many a pie. I, myself, am in charge of recruitin' our workers. I've persuaded many of our old crew from New Berne, joiners, carpenters, mechanics, to come join us."

"Strange it seems, to be building ships in a cornfield."

"Yet, it's a foremost project for the Navy, son. The Chief Constructor, himself, John Porter, is in overall charge. The owner of the field, my friend, Peter Smith, is workin' on a new type drill for piercin' iron plate. We'll need it. She'll be armored all over, 152 feet long, forty-five foot beam, and an eighteen foot ram forward."

"What armament, Da'?"

"Two eight-inch Brooke Rifles on pivots, firin' through six gunports."

The cutter eased to the riverbank, and the crew shipped their oars. "We're living in a little house just down the road to Scotland Neck," said Siobhan. "We'll have a little supper, and you can regale us wid tales of Union gunboats and such."

Rory relaxed that evening as he rarely could, among the familiar and tantalizing smells of an Irish kitchen, and within a loving family.

Rory had caught the train from Weldon to Wilmington, and after the exhausting journey, slept soundly in his Wilmington hotel. The portfolio containing the cotton certificates was in the hotel safe. He wore his best uniform the next morning as he strolled the three blocks down Princess Street and south along Front Street to the wharf where the *Herald,* an already-famed blockade-runner, lay alongside. She was to be his transport through the blockade and on to Bermuda, where he would catch a packet for England.

Sailing was scheduled four days hence, depending on weather. She had just completed a fifteen-day quarantine imposed on blockade-runners. A yellow fever epidemic in Wilmington from mid-October to mid-November had proved fatal to hundreds of people. Rory could smell the stench of kerosene, which Wilmington residents had burned for weeks in the hope that it would impede the pestilence.

Rory gazed at the sleek lines of the paddle wheeler, painted a camouflage mottled light and dark gray, but his mind was elsewhere; excited about the prospect of seeing England once again, of being close to family in Ireland, and of seeing Carrie Anne when she arrived at her uncle's home in Wilmington. *That should be soon,* he thought, *and it can't be soon enough!*

Rory was careful where he stepped. The water table was high and the drainage poor. Many of the side streets were deep in mud in the rains of November. Mud aside, it was a charming town, with more than its share of theaters, bookstores, and libraries.

When Rory returned to his hotel, he found a note from Carrie Anne waiting for him. She had arrived that afternoon, without Mrs. Eastman, and was settled in with her Uncle Jeremy's family, just a few blocks from the hotel. She included an invitation for dinner that evening.

Still in uniform, and looking every inch the dashing naval officer, Rory walked north from his hotel to the Jeremy Farwell House on Walnut Street. It was a chill evening, and he wore his knee-length gray greatcoat with a white scarf at his neck, and his uniform cap pulled over his eyes. In the twilight, he could look down Walnut to the river and across to the yards and docks on the west bank. The Farwell's butler opened the door, took his coat, hat, and scarf, and seated him in a drawing room off the parlor.

"Miz Eastman will be down directly, sir. The Farwells have been delayed on their return from Wrightsville, but I expects them soon. May I get you something, sir?"

"Not just yet, thank you. Perhaps when Miss Eastman joins me." Rory smiled his thanks at the butler.

"Very good, sir."

Rory rose as Carrie Anne entered the room, a broad smile of welcome on her face.

"Aren't you the vision, woman, with your golden hair and blue-green eyes and your altogether ravishin' figure, and all?"

Carrie Anne rushed across the room to Rory. "I am so glad to be here, Rory, and so glad to be in your arms," she said as she threw her arms around his neck and kissed him passionately.

"No more than I, my dear, and aren't we the surprised ones, now, to be alone in the middle of the day?"

"My aunt and uncle may be a bit late, dear. We can sit and talk by ourselves. What a luxury! Let me ring for Bronson, and we'll have a 'drop of the creature,' as you say."

"You'll be an Irishwoman, yet, without a doubt!"

Drinks in hand, they sat close in the drawing room, and stared at each other for a time without speaking.

"I could spend my days just this way, sure, and I could, love," said Rory. "I feel as if I've fallen from the maintop when I think of being away for months or more."

"We have been lucky, Rory, you being stationed so close to me, in Louisiana and in Richmond."

"'Tis time we talked of the long-term, girl, for I can't envision my life without you in it. Yet I've been avoidin' the thought, what with the uncertainty of war. But it's time, now."

"Rory, I never expected a swift proposal. I'm twenty years old, a woman whose lover killed her fiancé, and whose reputation was suspect, and who sees injustice in her beloved homeland daily. I don't expect Utopia. But I love you, and you have loved me, and my hope is that you'll return."

"How could I not return, with your blessed hold on my heart? Pay attention, woman, I'm slyly hintin' marriage!" They both collapsed in giggles, as the door opened and her aunt and uncle entered.

Dinner was a delight, with stories, and tales of the war's lighter side, and Carrie Anne's relatives subsumed in the obvious glow of the devotion between their niece and her beau. Rory and Carrie Anne agreed to meet for lunch at his hotel the next day.

Upon leaving the Farwell's, Rory walked toward the waterfront, euphoric after the evening, and the experience of actually having stated his feelings for Carrie Anne, and hearing her reciprocate that deep caring.

His state of wellbeing left him totally unprepared for the remainder of his evening. He chanced on a public house, bright lights and spirited conversation within, and stopped to enjoy. At the bar, he fell into conversation with one of the many sea officers present, a Savannah-born mate on a successful blockade-runner. The mate regaled him with tales of the passage through the inlets to Nassau and Bermuda, and, at length, launched into the strange tale of the black Caribbean pilot and the October demise of three fine Rebel steamers at his hands.

"Conspiring and consorting with traitors, yes, but you have to admire the nerve of the black bastard, to jump into the middle of a ship full of sworn enemies, with no one to back him, and bring the whole damned outrageous affair to a glorious conclusion, at least from a Yankee viewpoint. The Brit, Ludlow, swears he's a master in the Yankee navy. Says he met him in Antigua. Claims he's a bare-handed, cold-blooded killer who made his name in the Northwest Indian wars. Makes a great story. I think the nigra scared the Hell out of old Ludlow!"

"Sounds as if, my friend," said Rory. "The man will be a legend, with only a few more tellin's of the tale!" Rory smiled to himself. *Now I know what Tobias has been up to,* he thought.

"It seems to me," said Rory to the mate, "that pilots, as a group, are as brave as any — braver, in fact! Every eye on them in the dark of night, no lights nor landmarks easily seen, guns all around, shoals everywhere, the worse the storm, the more likely they are t'be out in it, sure, aren't they keepin' the Confederacy afloat, now?"

"I couldn't have put it better, myself," said the mate.

Easing his way out of the bar, he was jostled by a burly man who then turned and cursed him in a clearly Cockney accent. Rory recognized him, instantly, affront-recollection being a Celtic trait.

"Well, now, if it isn't that Saxon muddlehead journalist, Broderick? From the Crown Colony of British Columbia, interviewin' me on San Juan Island. Y'wanted t' pick a fight with me there, and here you are, tryin' again."

"Gor'blimey, if it isn't the mick from Puget's Sound. Let's go outside and see how big you talk in a fight with a Briton, you bloody teague!"

"Come on then, y'stupid limey," said Rory, handing his uniform tunic to the bartender with a nod, and walking out the door. A crowd followed the two belligerents into the alley next to the tavern. The alley was strewn with loose cobblestones, a pile of lumber along the side of the tavern, and pallets that had borne produce for the kitchen stacked haphazardly next to the delivery door. Rory was carrying neither sidearm nor sword, and turned, expecting a fistfight. Broderick, with a sly grin, reached into his boot and drew out a six-inch knife.

"Isn't it kind of you to fight with my weapon of choice, now?" Rory said, and a momentary look of confusion crossed Broderick's face. Rory bent over the pallets, seizing one three-feet square, and picked a four-foot long two-by-two board out of the lumber stack.

Rory held the pallet in his left hand, grasping the cross piece furthest from him and resting the pallet on his left fore arm, like a shield. His right hand held the two-by-two like a club. He ran its end down the row of crosspieces on the pallet rhythmically, several times over, producing a thrumming sound. *Just like sword and buckler practice in County Meath with Grandpa Fearghus,* he thought.

Broderick stood, nonplussed. Unsettled as he now faced a foe who had armed himself, however strangely, he simply waited, the knife in his right hand. It was the wrong strategy.

"Remember that sound, y'stupid Sassanach," said Rory and feinted to his left. Broderick leaned to his right in response, and Rory swung the two-by-two against Broderick's left knee. Broderick howled with pain and lunged at Rory's left side. Rory parried with a lift of his left arm, and his pallet easily turned the blade aside.

"*Faugh-a-ballagh!*" Rory cried. He raised his arm and, with a circular motion, swung the two-by-two against Broderick's neck and skull. The Cockney tried to ward off the blow with his left arm, but Rory's strength smashed through his guard and he crumpled to the ground, unconscious, his knife clattering on the cobblestones. Applause and cries of "bravo!" came from the crowd of onlookers, half-drunk as they were. Rory dropped his weapons, picked up the knife, and marched back into the tavern. Reclaiming his tunic, he took a seat at the bar, where onlookers vied to stand him a drink.

"A toast to the Rebel navy," cried a man in the crowd, and the tavern crowd roared its approval. Rory's earlier conversation companion, the mate from the blockade-runner, sat next to him at the bar. "What was that drumming business with your cudgel on your shield?" He asked.

"Well now," said Rory, "that's the sound of 'swashbuckling,' don't y'know. The Celtic legions would run their swords up and down their buckler shields, 'swash their bucklers,' to terrify the enemy. Me grandfather Fearghus taught me that, just as he taught me that last fine whack alongside the Saxon's head. A perfect *moulinet*, it was!"

"And your war cry there at the end? Celtic too?"

"Sure, 'clear the way' in Gaelic. Has a fine ring to it, doesn't it, now?"

"That Limey journalist will sure enough remember it!" Rory's companion laughed. "The British seem to have a lot of their reporters in the South. I can think of one who'll be eager to leave." The Savannah officer smiled, and bought Rory a drink.

Rory slept late the next morning, but made his way to the Farwells' to meet Carrie Anne for luncheon. He had time to spare, and was feeling none the worse for his encounter the evening before. "What more diversion could a lad desire," he found himself humming, the words of "Jug of Punch" seeming highly appropriate in his current mood. *A woman who makes me wish to sing, a string of victories, and a good meal and a drop of the creature before me (paraphrasin' now, a bit outside the meter),* he thought.

Carrie Anne and Rory walked arm-in-arm from her uncle's to the hotel, immersed in the moment. The sun shone, barely warming the chilly autumn air. "The hotel chef is known far and wide, so they tell me," said Rory. "And the hotel has other interestin' features."

"Such as, lieutenant?"

"As befits a modern and tall, four-story building, it has a freight elevator, which I, myself, with the help of a well-placed and generous tip, have learned to operate! And it has an Otis gripper mechanism on the cables, for safety."

"And the significance of this?"

"We can take a postprandial stroll, nip around to the back, unseen, and take the elevator to my fourth-floor room, without compromisin' your reputation in the slightest!"

"Are you proposing a tryst, Lieutenant?"

"Without a doubt, Miss."

She threaded her arm into his and squeezed, smiling at him with a sparkle in her eyes. "Propose away, then."

The meal was everything they'd been led to expect. The freight elevator was both clandestine and efficient. They were alone in the dim light of the room, its curtains drawn against the bright sunlight, enough of which filtered through the curtains to create a surreal and romantic twilight. They could make love unencumbered by time and the possibility of discovery.

They lay together on the cool sheets afterwards, tracing the contours of each other's bodies, talking, treasuring last moments together.

"Is this scar from your duel with Thomas?" Carrie Anne traced a long, diagonal scar on Rory's chest.

"It is that, and proudly borne, for your sake, love."

"You need not add more, then, for my sake. Just come back to me whole."

He kissed her gently on her brow. "I will then, upon my word as a Dunbrody!"

CHAPTER 28
ABOARD THE BLOCKADE RUNNER HERALD

The late-November wind blew blustery and chill across the course of the blockade-runner *Herald* from Cape Fear to Bermuda. The *Herald* maintained a small dining salon for the few passengers aboard during each voyage. As a result of the weather, the only passengers in the dining salon were the seasoned sailors who were untroubled by the inner-ear instability of *mal-de-mer*. At the mid-day meal of the two-day run, two passengers were seated at table; Rory, and an attractive, dark-haired woman, about forty years old, with the air of a gentlewoman.

"How do you do, ma'am," said Rory, politely minimizing his brogue. "May I introduce myself? I'm Lieutenant Dunbrody of the Confederate States Navy. It's kind of you to share the dining salon with me."

"What a gracious introduction that was, lieutenant!" his companion said, offering a hand in genteel greeting. I am the Baroness St. Regis, and I am pleased to meet one of the South's naval officers. Your service has certainly gained fame, even notoriety." She spoke with a smile, to ease any edge to her words.

Rory smiled in return. "Only half of what you hear is true, Milady, and isn't it a shame?"

"How unusual to hear an American use our nation's form of address. Is that the hint of an Irish accent I hear?"

"American-born, Milady, but raised in County Galway and County Meath."

"How extraordinary! What takes you to Bermuda, lieutenant?"

Rory decided to be candid about his mission with the baroness, as she seemed sympathetic to the Confederacy. "I take ship from there to Liverpool, Milady, to become part of our Confederate Mission to Great Britain, under Commander Bulloch."

"How exciting for you. My husband, the baron, has a number of shipping interests. We are familiar with Commander Bulloch. He has a splendid reputation. You must be quite accomplished to be assigned to his command."

"Kind of you to say, Milady. I met the commander at the beginning of the war, and he has requested my assignment. I visited England while a midshipman, and encountered many a Royal Navy ship in Europe, and later, on the Pacific North Coast, in the Crown Colony of Vancouver. But I'm told it will be my goal to avoid being readily identified as a Confederate naval officer. Not in disguise, just not highly visible."

"I'm sure you'll be of great value, Mr. Dunbrody. There are many of us in Britain who sympathize with your Cause. And who tolerate at least some of the Irish. I'd like you to visit us while you're in England. My husband would be interested to meet you."

"Sure, it's a pleasure to meet those who tolerate the Irish, after us makin' such an effort t'ease the burdens of the Crown, what with starvation and coffin ships and transportation puttin' so many of us in our place, and all."

She sniffed. "I'm sure your sarcasm cloaks a passion for your people, lieutenant. Are you equally as passionate about your current cause?"

"Milady, I'll always do my duty, and maintain my honor."

"I'm sure of it, Mr. Dunbrody. I hope to see you in England."

"I'd be honored to visit, Milady. It's been a pleasure dining with you."

On his way to his cabin, Rory thought, *What a fine figure of a woman she is! And the baron and baroness could be a great help in putting ships to sea, I wouldn't doubt.*

CHAPTER 29
ON LEAVE IN NEW BEDFORD

Tobias gazed in amazement at the nautical activity swarming on the waters of the Hudson and the East Rivers as the steam dispatch boat carried him toward the Brooklyn Navy Yard, among the busiest in the world, in the midst of the American Civil War. He was under orders transferring him from *Wabash* to USS *Wilkes-Barre*, a gunboat fitting out at the Brooklyn Yard for blockade duty off Cape Fear. The Navy Department had been unable to resist using Tobias' detailed knowledge of Cape Fear waters to enhance the blockade capabilities of a new ship under the command of an inexperienced officer. Tobias was vaguely apprehensive about his role as a veteran navigational advisor to a novice commander.

Tobias had been allowed a seven-day leave between assignments, enabling him to visit his father in New Bedford. He quickly boarded a local packet that took him through Hell Gate into Long Island Sound and ultimately to the Acushnet River and the harbor of New Bedford, Massachusetts, where he had lived from the age of ten until he shipped on a whaler at sixteen.

His father, Carlyle St. John, slave, fisherman, whaler and now faculty member at a prestigious Quaker academy in the city, greeted him as the packet docked. Heads turned along the quay as two tall and strikingly handsome black men greeted one another. The fact that one was in the uniform of a Union Navy officer attracted a high degree of attention, and those onlookers who recognized the new Medal of Honor Tobias wore were more attentive still.

"Hello, father, I've missed you," said Tobias as they embraced.

"And I, you, son. At least we're good correspondents. That keeps our bridges in good repair." The elder St. John smiled warmly, paternally.

They walked, arm-in-arm, up the hill from the harbor, past red-brick warehouses, Greek-Revival banks and ship chandleries, past the stately houses and beautiful gardens that bordered the streets of the city as they rose gradually from the harbor side to the hills above. The sun shone on the houses of Fairhaven, across the river. "You cut a fine figure in your uniform, son. Does the medal weigh heavily?"

"How metaphorical of you, father." Tobias smiled. "About as heavy as my little sea bag. Of course, being the first black to receive the medal, I'm conscious of the weight of expectation. But I'm confident that I deserve it, as well."

"Doubly so, I'd say, given what little I know of your subsequent exploits. Enlighten me."

Tobias described his cutting out of the three blockade-runners as they climbed the hill. His father was amazed. "Tobias, it seems to me you have a talent for this, this knife's edge endeavor," Carlyle concluded.

"Perhaps, father. I should probably limit the number of these adventures. The law of averages is still in effect. But my next assignment seems mundane enough." Tobias outlined the situation aboard the *Wilkes-Barre*, as he understood it. They had ascended the cobblestones of Williams street, leaving behind the imposing edifices of the waterfront. Carlyle lived near where he taught, on School Street, looking down on New Bedford's fine harbor. It was still the preeminent whaling port of the Northeast.

They sat that afternoon in the parlor of Carlyle's modest house, catching up with each other. They talked of Tobias' prize money, carefully invested by Carlyle. Several friends of the senior St. John were participating in the Port Royal teaching experiment, and Tobias brought word of them. Conversation drifted to Antigua, and Tobias talked of cousin Mitch, and friends from Carlyle's younger days. They avoided mention of Tobias' mother, who had been sold shortly after his birth, and died tragically on the island of Nevis.

"Is Commander Cavendish well?" Tobias asked with a smile. Cavendish, a retired navy commander, had been Tobias' mentor when he studied at the Quaker academy. When Tobias returned after six years as a whaler, Cavendish had persuaded him to join the navy as an ordinary seaman, and had arranged a billet on the ship of an old friend. Tobias' mathematical skills and navigation experience aboard whale ships soon warranted a promotion to master's mate.

"He's active and flourishing, and would love to see you, I'm sure."

"Then I'll surely drop in to visit him, father."

They ate their evening meal together, and over dessert, Carlyle looked at his son quizzically.

"I sense you've the urge to visit your former whaling haunts on the waterfront. I'd guess you'll turn up an old shipmate or two!"

"You know me too well, father mine. Would you be disappointed if I disappeared this evening?"

"Not at all. You are here for six more days, and I've a full class day tomorrow to prepare for. Enjoy yourself."

Tobias hung his uniforms in the closet of his old room under the eaves, and dressed in simple seaman's garb. He made his way to a sailor's tavern on Bethel Street. *It looks just the same as it did ten years ago,* he thought. For many decades, the majority of New Bedford whale men had been drawn from African-Americans, Caribbean islanders, Cape Verdeans, and Polynesians. The tavern customers reflected that balance. Tobias surveyed the bar as he edged slowly through the crowd. The spaces between tables were clogged with seafarers of every hue.

"Tobias!" He heard a voice call. He turned toward the bar, and a familiar black face.

"Isaiah Osterhouse! Hello, shipmate." A stocky black man with a wide smile stood at the bar, and waved. Beside him, looking on, was a golden-skinned Hawai'ian in his twenties, with black curly hair to the nape of his neck, a strong nose and chin, broad forehead, and huge shoulders. Tobias made his way to join them.

"Tobias, you still in de navy? Meet my shipmate, Kekoa. Kekoa, dis is Tobias St. John."

"Aloha, Kekoa. Yes, Isaiah, I'm still in the navy."

"We talking about you just dis week," said Isaiah. "Kekoa a navigator, too, and he can do it widout chart an' compass."

"Are you a *kahuna kilo hoku,* Kekoa?" Tobias saw the startled look on Kekoa's face as Tobias used a Hawai'ian term for navigator, literally, "wise one who gazes at the stars."

Kekoa smiled. "I am studying, but not yet a *kahuna.* You know about wayfaring, then, Tobias?"

"I heard of it as a whaler in the Pacific, and I met a man in Puget's Sound, a *Kanaka* like you, Kele Kalama, who told me of it. He had a son, also Kekoa."

"He is my father," Kekoa said, simply. " He has written me of you, Tobias." They shook hands warmly.

"Big ocean, small world," said Isaiah.

"Your father was well when I left him, eighteen months ago."

"He is still so. Sheep herding, except for the Haida raids, is not as dangerous as whaling."

"You're far from home, Kekoa." The bartender brought ale glasses for the three, and Tobias bought the round.

"He tol' me he wanted to see the Atlantic," said Isaiah. "An' we needed him. We were short-handed coming back around Cape Horn. We lost a boat crew to a sperm whale."

"They seem to become more aggressive as the years go by, Tobias," said Kekoa. "Did they attack whaleboats when you were whaling?"

"A few," Tobias replied. "A whaleboat doesn't have a chance against an enraged sperm if he sets his mind to it. I've heard of them crushing the boat in their jaws, and even ramming a whale ship."

"Well, I admit da one that sank our shipmates helped me. The boatsteerer drowned, and I was made his replacement. The captain said he liked the idea of a boatsteerer who could navigate, even if I was Kanaka." The boatsteerer or harpooner aboard a whaler was second in command of a whaleboat and its six-man crew, and ranked below the mates, but above the sailors.

"Oh, yes, I found that, too," said Tobias. "You almost never see blacks or Pacific islanders as boatsteerers. You know, we can always use experienced navigators in the navy. Have you ever thought of that?

" Tobias laughed. "We frequently have vacancies, and the chance of advancement."

"I t'ink about dis many times, Tobias," said Kekoa. "But I hear Kanaka and blacks are never officers, just like whaling. You must be 'most da only one."

"It's true, but it's also wartime, and the navy adds ships to the blockade every day. I could show you the Brooklyn Navy Yard. You wouldn't believe the number of ships. And they all need crews."

"If you t'nk dere's a chance? Uderwise, I have to find another ship, as a focs'l hand. My boatsteerer days were just temporary."

"I tell you what. The man who brought me into the navy lives here. I see him tomorrow. If he thinks it's a good idea, I'll tell you. Let's meet here tomorrow at noon." Tobias saw that Kekoa was clearly interested.

"You always did have a plan, Tobias," said Isaiah. "I want to show Kekoa de Seaman's Bethel. Maybe Reverend Butler say a prayer for Kekoa."

Kekoa joined in the laughter. "I need all da help I can get!" The Seaman's Bethel, on nearby Johnny Cake Hill, was a sailor's chapel, for whale men, and its chaplains were very popular among the whaling crews and their families.

Morning found Tobias walking toward the home of Commander Cavendish. The white-haired old navy man greeted Tobias warmly, and led him into the parlor. "My boy, I'm so pleased and proud to see you, and feast my eyes on the tangible evidence of your success. The decoration and the uniform suit you well!"

They talked of Tobias' experiences over the last several years, since the last time they had visited. Cavendish often nodded, approvingly, as the tale unfolded. When Tobias raised the question of recruiting Kekoa, Cavendish responded with great enthusiasm. "I've had several Hawai'ians under my command. Fine sailors! This one sounds as if he's gone out of his way to improve his navigating skills. My old friend, De Witt Oakley, commands the USS *Woonsocket*. *Wyoming* class sloop o' war, 1500 tons, draws fourteen feet, does eleven knots. We'll collect this young Kanaka and journey to the Brooklyn Yard! You have to report to *Wilkes-Barre* there, do you not? It will do me good to get out of the house!" Cavendish's eagerness was palpable.

And so it was that several days later, when Tobias' leave had ended, the packet to the Brooklyn Yard bore Tobias, Kekoa and Cavendish down the Acushnett and out Buzzard's Bay to the Long Island Sound and Hell Gate once more. Carlyle had said a Quaker good bye to his son with a "take good care of thyself."

"How did you find this Tahitian navigator you studied under, Kekoa?" Cavendish asked as they sailed down the East River.

"I was in the Carolines, on Polowat, and met a *palu*, a navigator there, who told me of the details of star navigation. I was interested, but wishing to return to Polynesia. He told me of Tainoa, grandson of the great Tupaia who sailed with James Cook. Tahiti was closer to Hawai'i. We still sailed double hulled canoes in the Hawai'ian Islands, of course, but only inter-island, so we had lost the art of voyaging thousands of miles across open ocean. Tainoa has taught me much. And I know to use compass, chart,' ded' reckoning and the Massey log, as well."

Kekoa paused, and then asked the old commander a question. "Is your city more accepting of men of color than elsewhere in your country? The blacks I serve with seem most numerous here. Other ports have fewer black sailors."

"I think the Quaker influence makes New Bedford a bit more accepting of the Negro seaman, wouldn't you say, Tobias?"

"I agree, sir, but when a Quaker whaling skipper sets foot on his quarterdeck, all Quaker kindness goes overboard in a trice. They are hard men, in command!"

"An interesting religion," said Kekoa.

"I remember religious discussions with your father, Kele," said Tobias. "He said he owed his good education to the missionary school, but he was somewhat skeptical of their altruism."

"We have a saying in Hawai'i about the missionaries," said Kekoa. "They came to do good, and they did very well. But, since Alexander Liholiho, Kamehameha IV, has been king, the Protestant influence seems to be lessening, and the Anglican, Mormon and Catholic, increasing. It's hard for Hawai'ians to tell if this is blessing, or curse."

Tobias laughed. "I sense you are your father's son."

The packet docked within walking distance of the Navy Yard. *Woonsocket* lay at a wharf close to Tobias' ship, *Wilkes-Barre*. Cavendish had telegraphed his old friend Oakley and the commander of *Woonsocket* was expecting the three men as they requested permission to board. Oakley greeted them at the gangway. "Grand to see you, Thomas," he said to Cavendish. "Sailing master, your reputation precedes you. Welcome aboard."

"Thank you, sir, " Tobias replied. "May I introduce Kekoa Kalama, late a boatsteerer and harpooner aboard the *Janine*." Kekoa had come to a position of attention, and bought his fist to his forehead in salute.

"Excellent," Oakley responded. "The navy can always use another experienced hand. Follow me to my cabin, gentlemen."

De Witt Oakley was a barrel-chested man in his late forties, known as a good sailor, a fair and decisive commander, and highly respected by his men. His interview of Kekoa was calm and direct, and he was obviously impressed with Kekoa's experience in a variety of navigational approaches, including the complicated lunar distance calculations, as well as with his evident desire to learn.

"Young man, I've a vacant billet for a master's mate. I'll make you acting, and if you do as well as I suspect, we'll make you a petty officer in six months. Now, gentlemen, let's talk tactics and strategy." The conversation continued with a lively discussion of overcoming the difficulties of effective blockade maintenance.

Kekoa had brought his sea bag in hopes of acceptance, and was to stay aboard and be mustered in. Cavendish and Tobias bid him smooth sailing. "I'll write to you, Kekoa. You may find that blockade affords long periods of inactivity, suitable for correspondence, when you're not in danger of sinking, of course."

"Thank you for your help, Tobias. I'll write my father with word of our encounter."

Missionary education has its strong points. He can switch from pidgin to erudite English with great facility, Tobias thought. He wished Cavendish well, and walked down the waterfront to the *Wilkes-Barre*.

CHAPTER 30
THE WRECK OF THE USS WILKES-BARRE
NOVEMBER 1862

Tobias sat in the wardroom of USS *Wilkes-Barre,* a fast side-wheel double-ender gunboat of the *Octorara* class. Over two hundred feet long, and drawing only seven feet, she was armed with large pivot guns fore and aft, and four guns in broadside. The most unusual feature of the class was a rudder at each end, making the ships most suitable for narrow-river maneuvering.

Tobias was discussing his recent assignment as master of the *Wilkes-Barre* with two of the ship's officers, First Lieutenant McDonald Fredericks and Midshipman John Jones. Fredericks was an old shipmate of Tobias' from USS *Preble,* as was Jones' brother, Evan. It was while aboard *Preble* at the mouth of the Mississippi that Tobias had saved the *Vincennes* from destruction and earned his Medal of Honor.

"My brother Evan speaks most highly of you, sir," Jones said to Tobias. "He thinks your adventure together when you went aboard *Vincennes* and cut the fuse was the highlight of his naval career."

"Mr. Fredericks will tell you, we had some interesting times aboard the old *Preble.* Where is the other Midshipman Jones?"

"Off Savannah, sir, aboard the *Pawnee.*"

"My old friend Roswell Lamson was sailing master on the *Pawnee,*" said Tobias. "He was just promoted to lieutenant."

"Well, sir, I wish Evan was the only 'other' Mr. Jones. There're about twenty Joneses as officers in the navy, and eight of us named *John* Jones. It's like the old Welsh regiments in the British Army, they give us a number. I think I'm John Jones number three."

"You have my sympathy, Mr. Jones. Please give my best to your brother." Tobias turned to his old shipmate. "I'm glad to be here, Mr. Fredericks. I agree with Admiral Lee. It seems a waste not to use my recently-gained knowledge of Cape Fear."

"I don't imagine Captain Rodgers was happy to relinquish you," said Fredericks.

"Admiral Du Pont said the same, but the transfer made sense to him as well."

"Captain Oldham was glad to have you, I know," said Fredericks.

"Yes, he mentioned that," said Tobias. Oldham, the *Wilkes-Barre's* captain, had said many things in his interview with Tobias, not all of which made Tobias comfortable. Jeremiah Oldham was the scion of an old New England family, a volunteer who had never been to sea save at the helm of his father's yacht. Handsome, seemingly forthright, and espousing the cause of abolition, he'd been in his state's Senate when he resigned at the beginning of the war and received a commission as a navy lieutenant. In his fifteen-minute welcoming talk with Tobias, he'd mentioned his family's strong ties to five U.S. Senators and President Lincoln. *Well-connected, facile, even glib,* thought Tobias. *Caution is the watchword, here.*

"Before last September," said Fredericks, "we'd have welcomed you with a glass to your health. But, as our teetotal Navy Secretary has abolished grog, we'll welcome you with water."

"Most kind of you, sir, even with water." Tobias laughed. "Have you heard what Du Pont's reaction was to the 'dry' navy?"

"Tell us, please, sailing master."

"The South Atlantic Blockading Squadron now receives many barrels a week from the army containing 'medicinal whiskey.' The crews are a healthy lot."

"No hope for our North Atlantic Squadron in that regard, I'm afraid," said Fredericks. "They don't call Admiral S.P. Lee 'Old Triplicate' for nothing. By the book on every detail, and no impulsive actions!"

The *Wilkes-Barre* tossed in the steep chop of the waves six miles south of Cape Fear, half way down the dreaded Frying Pan Shoals, where a line of blockaders hoped to encounter blockade-runners exiting Old Inlet, the least-frequently-used of the channels leading to sea from Wilmington. The wind was blowing thirty knots, and the relatively shallow depth of Long Bay caused the waves to steepen noticeably. It was dusk, and the weak November sun had set.

Wilkes-Barre was the ship furthest east in the blockade line at the six-mile station, and thus closest to Frying Pan Shoals. This was the ship's first time at the end of the blockade line, and the first for the captain, too. Heretofore, *Wilkes-Barre* had been at the center of the line. It was Oldham's responsibility to preclude any blockade-runner from passing "in-shoal," as it were, and one he took very seriously. It was obvious to Tobias that Oldham tended to station his ship closer to the shoal than either necessity or prudence would require, and, as Oldham's chief navigational advisor, he presented his observations, as his duty demanded.

"Pilot," said Oldham in response, "no Rebel will run past me shoalward of my ship, your faintness of heart notwithstanding. We draw only seven feet, and we're at least a hundred yards off the three-fathom line. That gives us eleven feet plus our depth here, to spare."

Tobias knew that ears on the bridge were attuned to the debate. Every man on the bridge had more experience at sea than Oldham, and all were deservedly concerned about his risking the ship. Fredericks was watch officer. Jones was the junior officer of the watch. The quartermaster at the helm was a twenty-year veteran named Macgillycuddy.

"Sir," said Tobias, "visibility is two hundred yards here, and our last cast of the lead showed three fathoms, no more. I beg you, ease to the west. The sands of the Frying Pan shift daily, sir. The ship is too far east for her safety."

"Thank you for your counsel, St. John," said Oldham, testily. "We'll maintain station for the present."

"Aye, aye, sir. Your permission to go forward to the leadsman in the chains, sir?"

"Very well. Carry on, Mr. St. John."

Tobias stood next to Able Seaman O'Mahony, the ship's best leadsman. "And a half two!" O'Mahony sang out, and the call was passed on by a line of men extending to the bridge.

"And a half two, aye, aye," came the reply, passed back down the line. The wind would blow away O'Mahony's calls unless amplified by the line of repeaters. They passed the response back down the line in the naval tradition of repetition as a confirmation that the information had been correctly heard.

"Jasus, Mr. St. John, sir, we're too damn shoal here, we need to ease west, beggin' your pardon, sir." O'Mahony paused in his coiling of the lead line for another throw. He was wet to the skin, of course, but inured to the discomfort after years at sea.

Tobias looked him in the eye. "I'll pass that word, O'Mahony. Again. Carry on."

O'Mahony nodded knowingly. A look of understanding passed between them. No insubordination, but two old hands in complete accord.

"Aye, aye, sir." He whirled the lead around and around with his right hand, preparing for his next cast.

Tobias returned to the bridge. "Captain, the last cast showed fifteen feet. That's eight feet under the keel, and no guarantee that the shoals haven't shifted westward. The swell itself is six feet, sir."

"Very well, very well, Mr. St. John," the captain said, in obvious exasperation. "You've made your point, *ad nauseum*, I might add."

"Helmsman," Oldham said, giving what was clearly a preparatory command. Before he could utter his command of execution, the ship struck hard, grinding over a pronounced shoal, the creak and groan of hogging timbers and straining machinery audible over the clamor of the storm. Oldham stood, transfixed, motionless, speechless.

"We're hard aground, sir," said Tobias. The captain did not respond. "Mr. Fredericks, sir. Permission to fire flares? May I go below to the main deck and assess the extent we're aground, sir?"

"Carry on, St. John," said Fredericks. "Mr. Jones, the red flares, if you please." He shouted down to the foredeck. "Bo'sun, prepare the boats for launching."

Fredericks stepped to the engine room speaking tube. "Chief," he shouted down the tube to the engine room. "Give me a damage report. What's the water level in the engine room?"

Tobias, meanwhile, had found O'Mahony in the chaos, and the two were methodically sounding along the entire length of the gunboat, on both sides. That completed, Tobias returned to the bridge.

The captain, a bewildered look on his face, was receiving a report from Fredericks. "Four feet of water in the hold, sir. Fires are out, and the engine room crew has come on deck. We've fired the flares for assistance. Boats are standing by, ready if we need to abandon. Green water over the starboard quarter, sir. Ten degree list to port, sir." Fredericks stopped, waiting for a response. Tobias, waiting as well, and hearing none, stepped forward.

"Captain, I've just sounded all around. We're grounded starboard side all the way aft to the paddle wheel. Aft, we've got two fathoms under the counter, sir, and the tide is just slack, after flood. We're starting to ebb, sir, and the next high tide is eleven hours out, and a foot lower, sir. I don't think she'll hold together that long."

"Captain," reported Midshipman Jones, "two ships approaching off the port beam showing the night recognition signal."

"Captain," said Fredericks, "we've ships within a short row from us, and we can put the ship's boats in the lee of the wreck," said Fredericks. "I recommend we abandon, sir. We'll not lose anyone. If she survives the storm, we can try to re-float her."

"Carry on, Mr. Fredericks."

The port side boats were launched, and the men clambered down the falls until each was full, at which time each set out for the waiting ships of the squadron, 150 yards distant. Then, the longboat far aft on the starboard side was launched. O'Mahony was the coxswain at the tiller. Fredericks and Jones went down the falls, hand over hand. Tobias and the captain were the last men on board.

"Sir, go down the falls," shouted Tobias, into the wind. "I'll follow you into the boat."

"No, you go on, St. John," the captain replied. "I've lost my ship. I might as well go down with her."

"Captain, come along please. The wind is pounding the longboat against the hull. It's time!"

"Tell them to cast off, and you get aboard," Oldham shouted, adamantly, almost hysterically.

"Mr. Fredericks," Tobias shouted down to the boat. "He won't come. Work around the stern and lay in the lee. I'll bring him down myself."

The boat crew worked the longboat around the stern and into the lee on the port or west side of the gunboat, and pulled alongside, bow and stroke oars grasping the trailing falls from the first longboat. Meanwhile, Tobias took the captain by the elbow and led him to the port gunwale. Oldham moved as if in a daze, and offered little resistance.

"Sir, go down the ladder. I'll follow."

"You go ahead, St. John. I'm staying."

Even in the lee, the swell lifted and then dropped the longboat, each time crashing the longboat's side into the ship's hull with a grinding crunch. Fredericks yelled from the boat. "We can't wait much longer. The swell is pounding us against the hull."

Tobias yelled back, "Pull out into the lee, and wait, Mr. Fredericks. I'll bring him overside, myself!" As the boat pulled about twenty feet away from the hull, its stern to the gunboat, Tobias seized the despondent Oldham, lifted his body to his shoulder, stepped to the gunwale, and jumped, feet-first, into the waves ten feet below. Crooking one arm beneath the captain's chin, he swam toward the boat, twenty feet away, with a powerful scissor kick and pulling with his free arm.

O'Mahony and Jones pulled Oldham aboard the longboat. Tobias grasped the gunwale and hauled himself over it. The captain, lying in the bilges, wailed, "I wanted to go down with her!"

"Well done, Tobias, you saved him in spite of himself," said Fredericks under his breath, as they rowed toward a waiting gunboat.

"Aye, lieutenant, but I've a feeling it's not the end of the story. We got off just in time, though. Her back is broken. I could feel the keel hogging in the swell."

CHAPTER 31
WELCOME TO LIVERPOOL,
LATE DECEMBER 1862

Rory had just settled into his rooms in a boarding house
near the Mersey River in Liverpool. A clerk from the firm of Fraser,
Trenholm, financial advisers to the Confederacy in England, had met
the Bermuda packet, and relieved him of one million dollars worth of
cotton certificates. The clerk gave him the boarding house address and
instructions to meet Commander Bulloch, CSN, at the financial offices
after the weekend. *They're certainly being careful not to have me be seen on
the streets with a known Confederate,* Rory mused.

Rory's mail connection with Tobias, through his Uncle Liam
in Connemara, was still working. When Rory was assigned to Bulloch's
command, he'd written immediately to Liam with Bulloch's Liverpool
address. The clerk had handed him an envelope from Liam, which had
contained a letter from Tobias. Rory, relaxed in a reading chair, a glass of
Irish whiskey on the table beside him. He reached for the letter, opened
it, and read.

> *My Dear Rory,*
>
> *May this find you well and prospering. I have a strange
> tale to recount, the end of which is not yet known to me. It is no
> military secret that my last ship, USS Wilkes-Barre, was lost on
> Frying Pan Shoals in November. The papers were full of tales of the
> shipwreck.*
>
> *It was a bizarre shipwreck. I had repeatedly warned the
> captain, Jeremiah Oldham, that we were too close to the Shoals.
> He ignored me. I have several witnesses to my admonitions to ease*

away from the danger, including the first luff, the midshipman of the watch, and the quartermaster. In the end, I saved his life by taking him into the water and to a waiting boat. He wanted to 'go down with the ship,' of all things.

The ship being wreckage on the Frying Pan, the crew was all reassigned, and scattered to the four winds. I returned to USS Wabash, where I am today. Oldham was brought up for court martial, for loss of his ship.

Now for the bizarre part of my tale. I heard scuttlebutt, just this morning, that Oldham intends to bring charges against me under the Articles of War, for dereliction of duty and malfeasance. A ludicrous accusation, under the circumstances, but as a black man in a white man's navy, I never rest easy. This seems to be prejudice not as blatant as Mr. Fell's of the Preble, but it's a distinction without a difference. I will keep you posted, and hope to hear from you soon.

I remain,

Your friend, Tobias St. John

P.S., Merry Christmas and Happy New Year!

Rory placed the letter on the table beside his chair, and raised his glass. "The same to you, my friend," he said out loud. "May it be, indeed, a happy new year for us both!"

Lieutenant Rory Cormac Dunbrody, Confederate States Navy, awoke in his nondescript Liverpool lodgings on the bleak January Monday following his weekend arrival, and prepared for his meeting at the office of Mr. Charles Prioleau, Liverpool branch manager for the Carolina financial firm of Fraser, Trenholm, the preeminent financial agent for the Confederacy in the British Isles. He had taken a horse-pulled hack to the address of his lodgings, the address given him by the nameless clerk. He'd met none of the principals of the Confederate presence in England.

Rory dressed in civilian attire, that of a young Irish business clerk in a ship chandler's firm, for that was the role he was to project while in Great Britain, according to his instructions from Confederate Secretary of the Navy Stephen Mallory. He wore a brown suit of trousers, vest and long jacket, completed by a soft white dress shirt, black bow tie and a square-crowned bowler hat. He arrived at number ten Rumford Place and after a short wait, was shown into Mr. Prioleau's office. Prioleau and Commander James Dunwoody Bulloch, Confederate States Navy, were already seated at a conference table. Bulloch, like Rory, was in civilian clothes.

Bulloch rose with a smile. "Good to see you again, Mr. Dunbrody," he said as he offered his hand. "Let me introduce our good friend, Charles Prioleau, the manager here." He turned to Prioleau. "This is the young man who I believe will enable us to avoid the Yankee spies, find a vessel, and put it to sea."

Affable and well-dressed, Prioleau immediately put Rory at ease. "Oh, Mr. Dunbrody, your exploits are well known to those of us at Fraser, Trenholm. Mr. Trenholm himself, when he heard you were assigned here, wrote to me with the details of your career, rescuing the 'lost company' from East Virginia, towing the *Virginia* under the *Monitor's* guns, and destroying the Yankee gunboats on the Piankatank!"

Rory blushed in spite of himself at Prioleau's enthusiasm. *Sure, if I listen to this boyo, I'll be taken' on the whole Yankee fleet in no time at all, at all,* he thought. "Ah, you're more than kind sir," Rory said with a smile, "but I'm thinkin' me record's become a bit embellished."

"We'll hold you to a high standard, nonetheless, lieutenant," said Bulloch. "We need all the help we can get, and we've little time to spare. Let me bring you up to date." Bulloch leaned forward, elbows on the table, and began to tick off the elements of his command responsibilities, one-by-one on his fingers. "We've been able to acquire, arm and commission three ships since 1861, *Alabama, Fingal,* and *Florida.* That's the good news. Two ironclad rams are paid for and being completed right across the Mersey River by Laird shipyards. But, the government here is tightening its application of its neutrality laws under intense pressure from Charles Francis Adams, the U.S. Minister to Great Britain. The rams are scheduled to be ready in October, but I'm not sanguine about our ability to avoid seizure by the British in the meantime."

"Are there other types, sir, commerce cruisers, that might be found more quickly, before the door shuts on us?" Rory began to wonder what his duties would entail in the general ship-acquisition scheme.

"We can find them, but Adams has spies everywhere, and as

soon as he sees a likely ship, and sees one of us Southerners dealing with
the builders or the financing, he screams to Lord Russell that Britain is
allowing the completion or purchase of a belligerent ship."

"Where do I come in, sir?"

"Rory, you look and sound like an Irishman. No one has seen
you with me or with Charles here. You can move about without attracting
attention from your accent or appearance. If we can figure out how to
connect you with a banking source unrelated to our operations heretofore,
you could scout out a ship to buy, and arrange payment."

"And get back to sea, sir? You haven't forgotten the 'incentive'
you and Secretary Mallory offered, have you? With all due respect, sir,
just a reminder."

"Yes, yes, if you find a ship, you'll be one of its officers," Bulloch
said with a rather exasperated laugh. "I know how it feels to want a ship
under you, and not have one, believe me, young Dunbrody!"

"Yes, sir, point taken, sir," said Rory, deferentially. "But in the
secretary's defense, sir, only you could carry out your challenging duties,
while ship officers like me are a dime a dozen."

"Kind of you to say, Rory, but slightly inaccurate as far as officers
available in England go. Let me outline the rest of the situation. Charles,
please help me with the details. I'm sure to miss something."

Prioleau smiled. "I've not seen that happen yet in our two year
association, thank you, James."

"Available sea officers come and go in this command. And they're
very few. As I'm sure you know, I'm not in complete command of the
European operation. Lieutenant North is not under me, and competes
for resources, including sea officers. North has an ironclad being built in
Glasgow. I call her the 'Scottish Sea Monster.' She's huge, far bigger than
necessary. Of course, Adams complains to Lord Russell about her every
day. I doubt she'll ever leave England."

Bulloch leaned forward, intense. "I recommended smaller
ships to the Secretary, months ago. Shallow draft, turret ironclads,
framed in the South, with the armor plate rolled here and shipped to the
Confederacy. Pre-fabricated, if you will. That process would not have
contravened British law on belligerent ships, and the British insurers

nervous about commerce raiders would have seen coastal defense vessels, not the high-seas cruisers they're concerned about. But, other opinions prevailed. So, here we are."

Bulloch sighed, folded his hands over his slight paunch in resignation as he leaned back in his chair, and went on. "Then, there's Lieutenant George Sinclair. He's taking the *Georgiana* to Charleston this month. With officers I could use, I might add. And he's outfitting the *Canton* in Glasgow." He glanced over at Prioleau. "Charles has built and paid for the *Alexandra* at Miller's yard here in Liverpool. But, because of his association with the Confederacy, the Union consul here, Dudley, has persuaded the British government to investigate her. And Charles is a British subject. It's discouraging!"

"It sounds so, sir," agreed Rory.

"Finally," Bulloch continued, "the internationally esteemed nautical scientist, Commander Matthew Fontaine Maury, CSN, arrived here last October at Mallory's behest, to conduct further research on torpedoes and mines, but also to acquire and arm ships. His reputation as a scientist makes it easy for him to move around. If he could just figure out how to pay for the hulls I'm sure he's finding, we'd be competing with him, too."

"Well, now, sir," said Rory, trying to lift the mood, "at least you have a million dollars to spend that you didn't have before."

"It's not as easy as all that, Rory," said Prioleau, perking up as the subject finally moved to his area of expertise. "The Confederate Commissioner in Paris, John Slidell, is currently negotiating a loan from Emile Erlanger, a French banker, for $15,000,000. Slidell's counterpart in England, James Mason, has to sign those cotton certificates you brought before they're usable. He's worried about the effect on the Erlanger loan if he signs now. He's refused to sign."

"Sir, do we need both ironclad rams and ocean cruisers? Should we make one a priority over another?"

"A most perceptive question, lieutenant," said Bulloch. Prioleau nodded in agreement. "My feeling is that the rams, delivered quickly, will do more to win the war than the cruisers. Unfortunately, the rams are more easily identifiable as warships, and therefore more vulnerable to Union complaints about neutrality law. The cruisers are easier to find already built, harder to convincingly identify as warships, and therefore easier to acquire and commission. We try to get both, but we get more of what circumstance gives us."

Rory had listened intently to the situation description. "Sure, now gentlemen, it's true I'll be less likely to be identified as a Southerner than an officer southern-grown. I should be able to find prospects. But how to buy them without attracting notice?" Rory brightened visibly. "Sir, I have a strong urge to go to Dublin tomorrow!" Rory smiled at the puzzled looks his comment evoked.

"A homecoming, Rory?" Prioleau asked.

"Of sorts, sir. I long to see my Dublin banker cousin, Richard Branch Dillon Fitzhugh. When we were lads, Dillon and I would visit our Uncle Francis, the horse trainer, at his stables on the Blackwater River near Downpatrick every summer, and we'd spend every day on horseback. He was a wild rider then, and I'm guessing now a man given to risk-taking in the banking business. I wonder if he might offer a solution to our dilemma?"

"It's worth a try, James," said Prioleau.

"I could telegraph him now, and take the packet to Dublin tomorrow," said Rory, his enthusiasm mounting at the prospect of action, even clandestine fiscal action.

"I agree with you, Charles," said Bulloch, "we need to explore this possibility. When you return, lieutenant, we'll provide you with a list of prospective ships, their locations and a travel itinerary for inspecting them. We've also devised a cover story for your travels."

"Of course, there's no necessity to deny you're a Confederate officer if you're confronted with the question, or recognized," said Prioleau. "But there's no need to advertise it, either."

"You'll pose as a clerk for a local ship chandler's firm," Prioleau continued. "As Liverpool has the fourth largest Irish population in the world, after Dublin, New York and Boston, your Liverpool address will raise no eyebrows. We do business with this firm, O'Rourke's."

"If you're asked by someone who recognizes you as a navy officer, tell them you're on furlough," said Bulloch. "Hundreds of Royal

Navy officers are furloughed now and serving on blockade-runners. The concept of furloughs is familiar to many here in Britain."

"Aye, aye, sir," Rory replied. "On the subject of officers, sir, I have two thoughts."

"Go ahead, lieutenant."

"The uncle who raised me in County Galway, Uncle Liam, is in the maritime freight business and has many contacts throughout Ireland with seamen and merchant officers. It could be an answer to our officer and crew shortage. I could ask him while I'm in Ireland."

"Good suggestion, lieutenant," Bulloch replied. "Your other thought?"

"I have some contacts with Royal Navy officers from my Puget Sound days and my Mediterranean service. They might give us names of officers willing to take furloughs and earn prize money. Britain's at peace and there are no prizes during peace time, t' be sure."

"Give us a list and I'll have our sources see if they are in the country," said Bulloch.

"Let me draft the telegram and draw up my list, sir. Then I'll go by the packet office for my ticket." The three men rose, energized by the prospect of finding another ship for the South.

"I'll wait for a while after you leave, Dunbrody," said Bulloch. "We'll let you exit out a side door. They watch the front."

* * *

The packet entered Dublin Bay at the mouth of the River Liffey, the center of Ireland's largest city, after a stormy crossing of the Irish Sea. Memories of Rory's visits in his youth rose up before him, the quay along the Liffey, Dublin Castle, Temple Bar, the narrow cobbled streets perpetually being widened by order of the Wide Streets Commissioners. His cousin Dillon Fitzhugh was waiting at the dock, and hustled Rory into a carriage that took them up Sackville Mall to an office of the Hibernian Bank near Rutland Square.

"Grand to see you, cousin Rory," said Dillon, whose family resemblance was strong. Like Rory, he was six feet in height, broad of shoulder, with dark hair and a strong Irish jaw. "Uncle Francis is in the city on business, and is joinin' us after work at the Harp and

Ha'penny. I'm glad your packet came into the Liffey, instead of the new Dun Laoghaire harbor. That's a long train ride into the city. What's so important to the Confederacy now, that its most dauntless sailor comes to Dublin?"

"Sure, what a fine lad you are, meetin' and transportin' me like royalty and all, Dillon Fitzhugh! I need a banker of great courage to advise the Confederate States. I'm here to buy ships. My commander has access to a million dollars worth of cotton certificates, but there's a bit of a tie-up with the funds."

"Cotton certificates should be good as gold these days, Rory," said Dillon, "what with the cotton reserves depleted and the high unemployment. What's the tie-up?"

"Our government's commissioners are negotiatin' a big cotton bond issue with France, and our lads don't want to issue any bonds in England until the deal is closed in Paris," said Rory. "If we can find ships, we need to be able to pay for them before the Yankees get on to us."

"Are the Yankees watchin' you, then?"

"Sure, Dillon, they've hired spies everywhere. My commander, Mr. Bulloch, thinks they may have infiltrated our own finance house, Fraser, Trenholm. It's as bad as the informers and the Fenians, over here."

"I have an idea, Rory," said Dillon. "If the French deal is in progress, why not have your commissioners sign the certificates with a time delay, say, ninety days? That makes them available for collateral, but gives the French negotiations time to conclude before the certificates themselves are on the market."

"Brilliant, cousin, I think." Rory struggled to follow the financial intricacies. "Could Fraser, Trenholm arrange to sell bonds on the certificates, then?"

"Indeed they could, and the proceeds would be available for purchasin' a ship," said Dillon. "But I'd suggest that Hibernian Bank do the issue, and keep the known Confederate house out of the foreground. The British have been easin' restrictions on Irish bankin' of late, and we're able to issue notes now, d'ye see? We could handle the arrangements here and remove it from prying eyes in England, at least long enough to get your ship to sea. Easier t'hide from any informers inside Fraser, Trenholm.

And, the bank does business with an Irish ship chandlery in Liverpool. We could arrange with them for arms, supplies, and ask them to find a victualer."

"Is it O'Rourke's, now?"

"It is!"

"It's the very firm I'm supposed to be workin' for in my cover story. Fraser, Trenholm does business with them, too."

"Most convenient," said Dillon. "Cover-story continuity! You'll find your ship in no time, at all."

"Sure, and I'll be assigned to her when we do, cousin," said Rory, with gleeful anticipation. "Purchasin' and paperwork is not my favorite part of seafarin'!"

"Let me broach this to me vice president, and make sure the bank can agree to the transaction, Rory," said Dillon. "Then we'll stroll down to the Harp and Ha'penny, near the Ha'penny Bridge, and wait for Uncle."

Dillon had returned with a letter offering the services of the Hibernian Bank to Fraser, Trenholm, should they be required in a bond offer or a nautical transaction. Later, they strolled toward the pub near the Liffey footbridge connecting Bachelor's Walk with the Temple Bar area on the south bank. The toll on the bridge, formally 'Wellington Bridge', had been a half penny. Dubliners referred to the bridge by its toll amount, 'Ha'penny Bridge.'

Francis Xavier Dillon, Rory's maternal uncle, had left his home and horse pastures on the Blackwater River the day before and caught the Dublin train in Drogheda. He smiled a greeting and rose to embrace his two nephews as they entered the crowded Harp and Ha'penny. Uncle Francis and his nephews sat at a corner of the varnished wood bar and watched the crowd in the mirror behind the fluted wooden columns framing the whiskey assortment. They talked of days gone by over glasses of Guinness stout.

"Remember the time," said Dillon "when the two of us were swimmin' in the Blackwater after a hard day's work with the horses, and our neighbors, the Healey girls, happened upon us, with our clothes on the bank, and all?"

"And being young gentlemen, we marched out of the river to get into our clothes and be decent," continued Rory. "Such a screamin' and hollerin' y'never heard before."

"Oh, Uncle, and didn't y'lay about us with the strap after that goin's-on?" Dillon leaned back in his chair and grinned. "T'was a good thing we were twelve instead of seventeen!"

"And now look at the both of you, all grown up and still schemin' together, like always," said Francis. The cousins had explained to him the Confederate plan, keeping their voices low and their eyes on nearby tables.

"I can't imagine Dillon Stables without Grandfather Fearghus, Uncle," said Rory.

"Thank you, Rory," Francis replied. "That's right, Da died just after you left for the Naval Academy, in '51. You've not seen the place without him. He was 85, you know. He was so proud of having taught you to fence, and to speak rudimentary French." Francis' father, Fearghus Dillon, had served in Dillon's Regiment of the French Army's Irish Brigade. The land granted to the Dillons on the Blackwater was for service to the Bourbon monarchy, and at the behest of the French monarchy in exile in Britain during the Napoleonic years. Rory's great grandfather, Seamus, had served in Dillon's Regiment, and had been on detached duty with La Fayette at the battle of Yorktown.

"Sure, the place remains one of the finest horse stables and breeding grounds in all Ireland," Francis continued. "We still have several entries at Bellewstown each year." The Bellewstown Meeting, a premier, four-day horse event in County Meath, was held each July only eighteen miles from Dillon Stables, on a high hill with a view of the Irish Sea and the Mountains of Mourne. Rory remembered the steep and winding road to the hilltop from his youth.

"Will you go back to Liverpool, now, Rory?" Dillon asked.

"No, cousin, I'll telegraph Commander Bulloch of our progress, and ask him to approach Commissioner Mason for the approval with the delay period. I'm off tomorrow on the train to Galway. Uncle Liam, the freight boat magnate that he is, will have some ideas on potential officers for our new enterprise, I don't doubt."

"Sure, and a chance to see your Aunt Caitlin, who raised you, and even, perchance, Mary Kate O'Shaughnessy, the playmate of your youth!" Dillon Fitzhugh smiled an impish smile.

"Now, who is this person?" Francis asked, interested.

"Only the colleen Dunbrody here would talk about incessantly, when he was a moonstruck lad of thirteen."

"Such lies t'be tellin', cousin," said Rory, "and me a man as good as betrothed."

"And who might the lady be, then?"

"Miss Carrie Anne Eastman, a southern woman of golden hair and considerable intellect."

"Rory, me boyo, you're a sailor for all of that, not settled and stable, as we bankers are."

"And isn't it grand to deal with a banker and not worry he's a gombeen man," replied Rory, referring to the usurers often found in rural Ireland. The evening wore on and they finally saw Rory safely to his hotel, with loving familial goodbyes.

CHAPTER 32
THE TRIAL OF TOBIAS ST. JOHN

Sailing Master Tobias St. John, United States Navy, sat in the flag cabin of *USS Wabash,* flagship of the South Atlantic Blockading Squadron, on station off Charleston. The squadron's commander, Rear Admiral Samuel Francis Du Pont, had turned his lavishly furnished cabin over to Tobias and the defense attorney in his upcoming court martial, Everett Chalmers Winthrop. The court martial was to be held aboard USS *North Carolina,* at Hampton Roads, Virginia.

Tobias, a great favorite of Du Pont's, had served under him for more than a year as one of his most decorated and accomplished officers. Tobias had been charged by the former captain of the gunboat USS *Wilkes-Barre* with malfeasance and dereliction of duty regarding her loss by shipwreck. Du Pont's counterpart in the North Atlantic Blockading Squadron, Rear Admiral Samuel P. Lee, had been obligated to go forward with a court martial upon the recommendation of a preliminary court of inquiry. Witnesses who would have testified on Tobias' behalf were unavailable for the court of inquiry.

Everett Chalmers Winthrop had been a congressman from New York, and had become a leading litigator since he had left elected office. A group of wealthy abolitionists had retained him to represent Tobias in his court-martial. *I'm lucky to have him,* thought Tobias. As he had learned of Winthrop's involvement through Assistant Secretary of the Navy Gustavus Fox, Tobias had always assumed that President Lincoln, who had made Tobias the first black awarded the Medal of Honor, was more than casually interested in the outcome of his trial.

"Let me summarize the current situation, Mr. St. John," said

Winthrop. "Tell me if I miss any particulars. The judge advocate and the court of inquiry had no choice but to recommend to Admiral Lee, the convening authority, that a court martial be held because your witnesses were unavailable for the court's hearing," Winthrop began. "It became a case of Lieutenant Oldham's word against yours. I believe I outlined what may have prompted this unusual action by your former commanding officer."

"Yes, sir," said Tobias. "We were both puzzled as to why he would accuse me of failing to warn him off Frying Pan Shoals when so many of his crew heard me beg him repeatedly to sheer off. He was far too close to the shoal line. You said it might be an affirmative defense to influence his own court-martial which he is to undergo for losing his ship on the shoal."

"True, Mr. St. John," said Winthrop, "that was one of my suppositions. Or, he may be hoping that the witnesses will be unavailable, either stationed too far from Hampton Roads where the court will convene, or dead. It is also possible that he has persuaded other witnesses to come forward who will refute our witnesses' testimony. Or, then again, it may be that he hopes no Navy court will accept a black man's word when it contravenes that of a white man, particularly one as well-connected as Mr. Oldham." Oldham's family was of blue-blood New England stock. Many of its members were leaders in government and industry, and all of them were wealthy, and socially elevated.

"Have we made progress, sir, in contacting our witnesses?" Tobias leaned forward anxiously in his chair.

"Admiral Du Pont has been most helpful in endorsing our requests to the current commanders of our witnesses," said Winthrop, reassuringly grasping Tobias' forearm. "He remembers vividly his service on the six courts-martial brought by Charles Wilkes and his subordinates against one another in 1842. He wants every witness present, in the interests of naval justice."

"He was certainly generous in allowing us the use of his cabin," said Tobias. "Mr. Winthrop, we're going to be closely associated for the next month. I'd be very comfortable with less formality. Please call me Tobias."

"That will suit me fine, Tobias, and I'll ask that you call me Everett. I'm confident that Midshipman Jones and Quartermaster Macgillycuddy are on their way to Hampton Roads from their blockade ship off Galveston," said Winthrop, smiling. "It only takes a week to get them their orders for appearance. Lieutenant Fredericks and Able Seaman O'Mahony are another question. Fredericks is aboard USS *Vanderbilt.* She's in the Caribbean, at last report, searching for *Alabama.* O'Mahony's aboard *Conestoga,* on the Mississippi. It may be difficult to reach them. O'Mahony will have to come around through Ohio. I've sent word to *Vanderbilt* through her collier. We'll hope they coal in time for the message to reach Fredericks and do us some good." Winthrop shrugged his shoulders, his hands palms-up.

The trial was scheduled to begin in ten days, aboard USS *North Carolina,* a two-decker ship of the line that now served as a receiving ship for the North Atlantic Blockade Squadron. Coincidentally, she had been the scene of the Wilkes courts martial in 1842, when she was a fully commissioned ship of the line, in New York City. Now obsolete as a warship, her huge bulk, built to carry 74 guns, was useful for housing sailors awaiting assignment. Her spacious main cabin still made an excellent courtroom.

"Everett, will Macgillycuddy and Jones be credible enough to convince the court?" Tobias was not as confident as he'd like to be.

"It depends on the court's make-up, Tobias," said Winthrop. "If the court includes veteran officers, or, with luck, an officer up through the ranks who once served as a senior petty officer, then a quartermaster like Macgillycuddy will carry a great deal of weight. Midshipmen are fine as corroborating witnesses, but I'd be more sanguine if Lieutenant Fredericks were to appear."

Tobias was lost in thought, speculation, and hope as he retired to his quarters. He saw the test of his word against that of a New England blue-blood as a true gladiatorial conflict. His realism about his chances, as a black man against a member of the Yankee establishment, were sprinkled with the sugar of optimism provided by President Lincoln's stake in his continued success as a naval officer.

The next day, Tobias and Winthrop boarded a dispatch steamer to carry them north to Hampton Roads. Several days later, Tobias unpacked in his assigned cabin aboard *North Carolina,* and Winthrop took lodging at an inn in Hampton.

Tobias' optimism ebbed the next day when Winthrop told him of a witness who would appear for Oldham. "I just learned this morning that Oldham's clerk aboard *Wilkes-Barre,* Witte Van den Herter, will appear. I'll need to depose him."

"I don't remember Van den Herter being on the bridge when I was talking to the captain," said Tobias.

"What is the duty of the clerk during blockade at night?" Winthrop sat with his pen poised.

"We had not yet cleared for action that evening," Tobias responded. "When darkness falls, we go to our action quarters, because we have no warning of blockade runners approaching in the dark. Prior to clearing for action, Van den Herter could have been any where on the ship, as he does not stand a watch. After we beat to quarters, his station is on the bridge as the captain's runner."

"It may be difficult to prove his whereabouts, and therefore, to challenge his veracity as a witness," said Winthrop.

Two days later, Winthrop met with Tobias, shortly after having deposed Van den Herter. "He swears he was on the bridge just prior to the ship grounding, and heard no comment from you cautioning Oldham about being too close to the shoal," said Winthrop. "He admits he was not on the bridge when you asked permission to go forward to the leadsman in the chains."

"How damaging will his testimony be, sir?" Tobias asked.

"I'm sure we'll contradict it, but it will be much more effective if we can contradict it with Frederick's testimony," said Winthrop. "Remember, the weight of testimony needs to be with you, in order to be effective. We're calling Commander French, Captain Alden, and Captain Rodgers, your old commanding officers, as well as Allan Pinkerton, as witnesses to your diligence and attention to detail. I'm toying with calling Admiral Du Pont and Admiral Lee, as well."

That night, in his cabin, Tobias reviewed a draft brief Winthrop had given him, and reflected upon his position. *To have come so far, and yet be poised on the brink of disgrace*, he thought. *The very accusation will stain me for the rest of my service, for many will not credit a black against the word of a white man, no matter what my accomplishments. To have to endure the hatred and condescension of bigots like that damned Fell, aboard Preble. Or those army bastards in Beaufort. And now, this dilettante, Oldham!* Tobias stood and hurled the brief against the cabin bulkhead, in rage and despair. He sank back in his chair, breathing heavily. *Sometimes, I think I'd be happier as a whaler*, he thought. *No, dammit, I won't quit! I'll confront the challenges the navy presents!*

His resolve had a calming effect. *Oh, well, I still have my medal, a moderate fortune in prize money, and my knowledge that my skills and courage are real, no matter what others may perceive. After all, I could be in chains!* He shook his head, uncertain of his future, yet cautiously optimistic.

I wish Rory were here to help me sort through this. His bright, Irish view of everything would be well-applied now.

The day of the court martial, a Thursday, dawned bleak, overcast, and cold, with a hint of snow in the air. All of Tobias' witnesses were present, except Fredericks and O'Mahony. No word had come of them. Winthrop had opted to call Captain Rodgers of the *Wabash*, rather than attempt to call Du Pont. Calling a flag officer might be seen as an attempt to unduly influence the court.

The cabin of the *North Carolina* held a long table just in front of the stern windows. At the table were the nine chairs for the court. Commodore Barclay, the president of the court, would sit in the middle. He would be flanked by a captain, two commanders, two lieutenants, two masters, and an acting master. The Articles of War precluded more than half of the court being junior to the officer being tried. The acting master was the only officer more junior than Tobias.

The judge advocate's polished oak table was to Tobias' left as he faced aft. The judge advocate would advise the court on procedure and admission of evidence, and keep a "true record" of the evidence and proceedings. Tobias knew that the judge advocate would manage the proceedings, the order of witnesses to appear, and recommend a verdict to the court. Had Tobias not been represented by counsel, the judge advocate would have assisted him in questioning his witnesses. While the judge advocate was the "referee" of the proceeding, the president was the ultimate authority. He would administer an oath to all witnesses, rule on all motions, and control the trial process.

When Tobias received Oldham's charges and their specifics, he had surrendered his sword to his commanding officer, as prescribed by the Articles of War. That sword now lay on a small, low table directly in front of the president's seat at the long table. It lay athwartships, its hilt to the port side and its point toward the starboard. At the conclusion of the trial, when the verdict had been arrived at, it would point either at Tobias (guilty) or away from him with its hilt toward him (not guilty).

As the ship's bell rang four times (four bells in the morning watch, or 10:00 a.m.), a solitary gun fired, signaling the beginning of the court martial. Those in the cabin rose. The court members filed in, waiting to take their seats until Commodore Barclay, the president, was seated.

"Mr. Judge Advocate, read the charges and specifications," intoned Barclay.

"Aye, aye, Mr. President. Tobias St. John, Master, USN, you are charged with violation of Article Eight, Section Eleven of the Articles of War, in that, on November 9th, 1862, you suffered the USS *Wilkes-Barre* to run upon Frying Pan Shoal off Cape Fear, through inattention or negligence, by failing to apprise your commanding officer of the proximity of the shoal. You are further charged with violation of Article Eight, Section Nine, in that you were culpably inefficient in the performance of your duty, as specified above."

The judge advocate, Lieutenant Christopherson, turned to Commodore Barclay, who asked, "How do you plead, Mr. St. John?"

"Not guilty, Mr. President," Tobias replied.

"Be seated," Barclay instructed those in the cabin. "Mr. Judge Advocate, please stand and be sworn." Barclay then administered an oath to the judge advocate, in which he swore to keep a true record of evidence and proceedings, and not to divulge deliberations. The judge advocate then swore in the members of the court. They promised to try the case without prejudice or partiality, according to the evidence, navy rules, and their own consciences.

"Mr. Judge Advocate, you may deliver your opening statement," said Barclay.

"Mr. President, members of the court, Lieutenant Oldham charges that Mr. St. John failed to warn him of the proximity of Frying Pan Shoal, and thereby caused the loss of USS *Wilkes-Barre*. He will appear as witness to his charges, and present another witness in support of his charges and specifications. Mr. St. John maintains he warned Mr. Oldham several times that the ship was in peril, and will present witnesses to substantiate his claim. He will also present witnesses to demonstrate his history of diligence and attention to duty in his capacity as a sailing master. Mr. St. John is represented by counsel, Mr. Winthrop."

"Very well, you may call the first witness," said Barclay.

"I call Lieutenant Jeremiah Oldham," Christopherson replied.

"Mr. Oldham," said Barclay, "do you solemnly swear that the evidence you shall give in the case now before this court shall be the truth, the whole truth, and nothing but the truth, and that you will state everything within your knowledge in relation to the charges, so help you God?"

"I do," replied Oldham, with a solemn look.

Tobias had not seen Oldham since the night of the grounding. He looked away, lest his emotions become visible and upset the court. He found himself wanting to beat the man into a pulp. He took a deep breath.

"Mr. Oldham," said the judge advocate, "tell us your recollection of the events of the night of November 9th, 1862."

"We were maintaining our assigned station at the east end of the picket line halfway down the channel that parallels Frying Pan Shoals," said Oldham. "Toward sunset, I remember Mr. St. John saying that we were in three fathoms, and I could ease my mind for her safety."

Tobias leaned over to Winthrop and whispered, "He's twisting my words! I said 'the ship was too far east for her safety.' I begged him to ease to the west."

Winthrop nodded, and placed a restraining hand on Tobias' arm.

"What happened next, Mr. Oldham?" The judge advocate asked.

"I asked for a cast of the lead, and it showed two and a half fathoms, rather than the three Mr. St. John had claimed. I had just given the command to bear to the west when we struck. Mr. St. John panicked and went racing around the deck, looking over-side. I determined that her back was broken and directed the men to abandon ship. I stayed to convince Mr. St. John to get in one of the boats. He was still acting irrationally. Just then, he grabbed me and threw me overboard. He followed, and I managed to grab him as he was sinking, just as a boat picked us up."

"I have no further questions, Mr. President," said the judge advocate.

"Very well. Mr. Winthrop, does Mr. St. John have questions of this witness?"

"Yes, he does, your honor, Mr. President." Winthrop was having some trouble adjusting to the terminology of a naval court. "Mr. Oldham," said Winthrop, "do you recall Mr. St. John cautioning you to move west for the safety of the ship, and do you recall replying 'we'll maintain station for the present'?"

"No, I do not."

"Do you recall him asking permission to go forward to the leadsman in the chains?

"I do not."

"Do you recall him then returning and reporting eight feet under the keel?"

"No."

"Mr. President," said Winthrop, "I have no further questions for this witness at present, but I request the opportunity to recall him."

"The witness is excused, subject to recall," Barclay responded.

"Mr. President, I wish to call Witte Van den Herter, captain's clerk of the *Wilkes-Barre*."

"Very well, Mr. Christopherson."

Van den Herter was sworn by Barclay, and took his seat in the straight-backed witness chair. The judge advocate stood at his table and began his questioning. "Mr. Van den Herter, in your deposition, you said you were present on the bridge just prior to grounding. Is that correct?"

Van den Herter blinked rapidly several times, his eyes magnified behind thick, wire-rimmed spectacles. "Yes sir, that is correct," he responded.

"Mr. Van den Herter, do you recall Mr. St. John informing the captain that the ship was in three fathoms and that he could ease his mind as to her safety?"

The clerk swallowed hard, and glanced toward Oldham, who stared straight ahead. "Mr. President," said Judge Advocate Christopherson, "I ask that the witness be directed to answer the question."

"The witness will answer the question, will refrain from seeking guidance from the officer bringing charges, and will remember he is under oath." Barclay fixed the clerk with a gaze that had turned many a sailor's knees to jelly.

The clerk reddened, tugged at his collar and stammered, "I don't recall Mr. St. John saying anything to the captain."

The judge advocate leaned over the witness. "Is it your testimony that you were on the bridge when the ship struck?"

Another pause. "Yes, sir, that is my testimony." Van den Herter did not look directly at Christopherson, who turned to Barclay.

"Mr. President, I have no further questions."

"Mr. Oldham?"

Oldham reflected for a moment, and then said, "Is it your testimony that Mr. St. John never warned me about being too close to the shoal?"

"I never heard him say anything, sir, but it was dark and the wind was howling and it was hard to hear."

"Thank you. No further questions." Oldham sat down, his face expressionless.

"Mr. Winthrop?"

"Thank you, Mr. President." Winthrop approached the witness chair. "Mr. Van den Herter, how long have you served as clerk to Mr. Oldham?"

"Since he took command of the Wilkes-Barre, I guess about six months," the clerk replied.

Winthrop turned away from the witness, and gazed out the open gun port at the starboard side of the cabin. "And your occupation before that?"

"I was personal secretary to the president of the firm of Oldham and Oldham."

"And was that president the father Of Lieutenant Jeremiah Oldham?"

Van den Herter swallowed uncomfortably. "Yes."

"And for how many years did you serve as the personal secretary to the father of Lieutenant Oldham?"

Van den Herter's brow knit noticeably. "For ten years."

"So you were in the Navy to keep an eye on young Mr. Oldham for his father?"

Oldham sprang to his feet. "Mr. President, I object!"

"I withdraw the question," said Winthrop. "I beg the court's pardon. I have no further questions." Barclay, his mouth open to chastise, closed it, but several members of the court had difficulty in suppressing smiles.

"Questions from members of the court?"

One of the sailing masters leaned forward. "Mr. Van den Herter, what did you do after the ship grounded on the shoal?"

"Sir, I don't recall. It was all so confusing and chaotic," said the clerk.

"Anyone else? No? Very well, Mr. Van den Herter, you are excused. The court will recess until two bells of the afternoon watch."

After a hasty lunch in the wardroom, set aside for the defense attorney and defense witnesses, Winthrop and Tobias stood by the quarterdeck rail and discussed the morning.

"I think we sustained only light damage this morning, Tobias," said Winthrop. "Van den Herter was not a good witness. It was obvious to the court that his memory of events was questionable. He couldn't remember the remark Oldham had attributed to you. He couldn't remember his actions after grounding. And Oldham was obviously afraid to ask Van den Herter if he'd heard any remarks from Oldham. I'm not sure if Oldham rehearsed him, possibly, but it was to no avail. The poor man was so flustered that he was worthless. There'll be doubts in the minds of the court about whether anything he says can be trusted."

"Is the judge advocate going to call anyone else?" Tobias asked.

"There's no one on his list, and his is really the charging officer's list. Christopherson will ask Oldham for a closing statement, as he's not represented, and we'll be up. I'll open this afternoon, telling them what we intend to prove. If we have time, I'll call Macgillycuddy."

"Why isn't Oldham represented by counsel?" Tobias gave voice to a question he'd been puzzling over. "You'd think, with his money and connections, he'd buy the best lawyer around."

"He already has," replied Winthrop. "Ethan Lodge, the best in Connecticut, has been sitting in the back spectator's row. He'll be at the table when Oldham goes through his court martial for the loss of the ship, I assure you. It's my guess that they wanted to appear confident and not overwhelming in this case, not make you the sympathetic downtrodden black facing the big guns of the wealthy. So Oldham gets strategy from Lodge, and appears to go it on his own, letting the judge advocate present his case. It's not a bad strategy."

Tobias sighed, and gazed at the ramparts of Fortress Monroe in the distance. "I think I prefer battle at sea to this exercise."

"Understandable," said Winthrop. "Your kind of battle is assuredly more straightforward. We'd best join the court for round two."

Oldham's closing statement turned out to a rambling rehash of his earlier testimony under questioning from the judge advocate. In addition he emphasized the difficulty his clerk experienced in hearing, owing to the noise from the storm. As Oldham concluded, Tobias noted several court members with puzzled looks. *That's somewhat reassuring*, he thought.

Tobias refocused his attention on Winthrop as he addressed the court, presenting the defense opening statement. "We will offer proof that Mr. St. John warned the captain of the proximity of the shoal, and that the captain failed to timely heed that warning. We will offer proof that the warning was repeated. We will show that Mr. St. John saved Mr. Oldham's life by bringing him to a boat when Oldham had vowed to go down with his ship, out of shame for his failure to keep her afloat. And, finally, we will show that Mr. St. John is an officer of outstanding piloting ability, known throughout the service for his navigational talent, strict adherence to duty, and his courage and fortitude under fire, as evidenced by his status as one of the first recipients of the Medal of Honor. Thank you." Winthrop sat down and whispered to Tobias, "Always keep the opening short, give them a framework, and then bedazzle them with the testimony!"

Macgillycuddy the quartermaster was called as the first defense witness, sworn and questioned first by the judge advocate who established his presence at the helm during the grounding. Winthrop's questions followed.

"Quartermaster Macgillycuddy, did you hear an exchange, a conversation between Mr. St. John and Captain Oldham while you were at the helm?"

"Yes, sor, I did."

"Repeat it please, as best you remember it."

"Mr. St. John, the pilot, sor, he told the captain twice that he should move away from the shoal, respectful-like, and all, but he said we were in only three fathoms and not safe. Sor." He added.

"And how did Captain Oldham respond, quartermaster?"

"He said no Rebel would run in-shoal of him, and told the pilot he was 'faint of heart,' I think he said. And then he told me to maintain station."

"What happened next, quartermaster?"

"The pilot asked permission to go forward to the leadsman, sor, and the captain said alright, and when Mr. St. John came back and told the captain we were in two and a half fathoms, the captain said 'very well, you've made your point.' He was giving me a command when we struck, sor."

"Then what happened, Mr. Macgillycuddy?"

"The first luff, er, lieutenant, Mr. Fredericks, seemed to take charge, sor. The captain didn't say anything. The pilot asked the first if he could fire flares, and then went forward to the leadsman. Mr. Fredericks told the captain the chief engineer had four feet of water in the hold, and had sent his lads on deck. The first told the captain we were listing to port and ready to abandon. The pilot came back from the leadsman and told the captain we were hard aground on a falling tide. The captain said to carry on, and Mr. Fredericks sent us to the boats."

"Was that the last you saw of the captain?"

"Until I looked over from the cutter and saw Mr. St. John swimmin' to the longboat, pullin' the captain with him, sor. That pilot, he's a swimmer, sor!"

"Was there material from the wreck, planks, spars, crates or the like, in the water as Mr. St. John and the captain approached the longboat?"

"Oh, t'be sure, there were all manner o' wreckage, sor."

"No further questions, Mr. President." Winthrop walked back to his chair.

Oldham sat, a stunned look on his face. Barclay fixed him with a long, inquisitive look. "Questions, Mr. Oldham?" He asked.

Oldham gathered his wits with an effort. "Yes, Mr. President. Quartermaster, you testified I was about to order you to steer west?"

"Yes, sor, I believe you were."

"And before that, you didn't hear Mr. St. John tell me we were safe where we were?"

"No, sor, I'm sorry, captain, I heard him ask you twice to move." Macgillycuddy was visibly discomfited to have to contradict his former captain.

"What was the wind blowing that night?"

"Oh, it were twenty-five to thirty knots, captain."

"Was it hard to hear, quartermaster?"

"Oh, yes sor, it were very hard to hear, sor."

"That's all the questions I have, Mr. President," said Oldham.

"Very well, questions from the court?"

A commander raised his hand. "How long have you served, quartermaster?"

"Goin' on thirty year, sor," Macgillycuddy responded.

"Thank you, Macgillycuddy," said the commander.

Barclay dismissed the quartermaster and Midshipman Jones was called. When he was sworn and seated, the judge advocate began.

"You were on watch when the ship went aground?"

"Yes, sir."

"Who do you recall being on the bridge?"

"Well, sir, the captain, the executive officer, the quartermaster, and the master, although Mr. St. John left for a short time to speak to the leadsman. Then, he came back."

"Did you see the captain's clerk?"

"Not that I recall, sir. We hadn't cleared for action, so he wouldn't be required on the bridge as the captain's runner until we had."

"Thank you, Mr. Jones."

The judge advocate sat down, and Barclay called upon Winthrop for his questions of his witness. "Mr. Jones," said Winthrop, "can you recount the exchange of words between the captain and the master just before the ship struck?"

"Sir, to the best of my recollection, Mr. St. John told the captain we were too close to the three fathom line of Frying Pan shoal. The captain was reluctant to move west sir, not wanting to allow room for a blockade-runner to pass in-shoal of us in the dark, but the master came back from the leadsman with a sounding of two and a half fathoms. The captain agreed to moving west, but before he could give the command, we struck."

"Could you hear the exchanges, midshipman?"

"Yes, sir, it was blowing hard, but I was standing right next to Mr. Fredericks, the first lieutenant, sir. And the master and the captain were talking loud over the wind noise."

"Mr. Jones, what did you do after the grounding?"

"Mr. Fredericks had us lower the boats to abandon, sir. I was in the longboat with him. Mr. St. John and the captain were the last men aboard. Mr. St. John called down to us that the captain wouldn't leave the ship. He had us go to the lee side, and lie off, and finally, we saw him wrap his arms around the captain and jump overboard. Then he swam to the boat, pulling the captain. Mr. St. John's quite the accomplished swimmer."

"Did you hear the captain say anything in the longboat after Mr. St. John had rescued him?"

"He said he wanted to go down with the ship, sir."

"Was there flotsam, debris in the water when the master and the captain went overboard?"

"Oh, yes, sir, pieces of hatch covers, planks, spars. It was quite cluttered, sir."

"Is it possible that the captain might have struck his head on debris in the water as they dropped from the rail?"

"I suppose that's possible, sir. I didn't see such happen, but it was fairly dark, just past dusk, and stormy."

"Thank you, Mr. Jones. No further questions."

"Mr. Oldham?" Barclay asked.

Oldham rose, ashen-faced and obviously trying to compose himself after Jones' testimony. "Thank you, Mr. President. Mr. Jones, you say I was about to give the command to move away from the shoal?"

"Yes, sir, you had just said so to Mr. St. John when we grounded."

"And it was noisy?"

"Yes, sir, it was."

"In the longboat, as well?"

"Yes, sir."

"Thank you, Mr. Jones."

The members posed no questions for the young midshipman. Barclay dismissed him and noted the late hour. The court was recessed until Friday morning. The parties and spectators walked in silence through the passageway, out on to the quarterdeck and into the grey of the dying day. "We'll meet for dinner in an hour, then, Tobias?" Winthrop paused before descending the gangway to the pier on which *North Carolina* was secured.

"I'll see you at your inn, Everett," Tobias replied.

Winthrop and Tobias assessed the day over a dinner at the Hampton inn where Winthrop was lodged. "I'm liking the way it went today, Tobias, said Winthrop. "I believe he's shifted his goal from winning this court martial to hoping to win the next, his court for the loss of the ship. He didn't challenge our witnesses when they each claimed he spurned your advice at first to move west. He emphasized instead how

difficult it was to hear. And he also stressed that he was about to give
the order to move west that he should have done earlier. He's in essence
refuting his earlier testimony." Winthrop smiled, obviously pleased with
the course the trial had taken.

"What were the questions about debris in the water for?" Asked
Tobias, clearly puzzled.

"If I can avoid accusing Oldham of outright lies, it will make it
easier for the court to find you not guilty. Officers would prefer not to
publicly pronounce one of their own a liar. If we can offer them the out
that the difference between his story and the story of every other credible
witness could possibly be owing to a whack on his head, they'll take that
as a basis for exonerating you, even though they know in their hearts he's a
mendacious son of a bitch."

"As my friend Rory might say, 'brilliant,'" said Tobias with a
laugh. "You'll win this, yet!"

"We're well on our way," Winthrop replied. "Jones' testimony
that Oldham said he wanted to go down with the ship was perfect! It
refutes Oldham's testimony that you were panicking and running about
the deck, and that he was the one who wanted to abandon. If any of our
other witnesses get here, we'll reinforce that. Fredericks and O'Mahony
were also in the longboat. The final triumph today, my friend," said
Winthrop, clapping Tobias on the shoulder, "was that both our witnesses
testified to your swimming prowess that night. That contradicts his
claim that he saved you! In our closing statement I can now point out
that testimony is clear. You advised early, he responded late, and he was
irrational."

Tobias took a deep breath, and exhaled slowly. Beads of
perspiration covered his brow, even on this chill winter night.
"It's hard for me to let myself have hope, Everett. If I relax, soon I'll be
fantasizing victory, and be crushed if it's snatched from me."

"I understand, Tobias. Just pull gently on that cable of hope, and
hold on until the next good day. It should be a good one tomorrow. We
have excellent character witnesses, and then it will be the weekend, and
that will give O'Mahony and Fredericks two more days to get here. And I
still have yet to cross-examine Oldham. That will give us more time yet."

"Perhaps I'll allow myself a faint hope, then," Tobias said, smiling.

In the morning Winthrop called Captain James Alden, Tobias' commanding officer aboard USS *Active* from 1857 to 1861. "Captain Alden, please describe Mr. St. John's service under your command, paying particular attention to his reliability, attention to detail, and piloting and navigational skills."

"Mr. St. John joined *Active* in 1857. We were detached to the US Coast Survey, and were charting the Pacific Northwest. The Coast Survey is recognized as one of the world's finest cartographic entities. Mr. St. John was known throughout the organization for his excellent chart work. He was a master's mate serving in our master's billet as acting master. He was a fine navigator. We were always sure of our position."

"What about his seamanship?" Winthrop asked.

"He'd come to the navy from whale ships. He was a superb seaman. A very strong swimmer. He once saved two men overboard simultaneously. One of them was a fellow officer, Dunbrody, now sadly, with the Rebels. I saw Mr. St. John and Mr. Dunbrody take seven survivors off a wreck in a gale. Mr. St. John's also an excellent hand-to-hand fighter, and saw action against the Haida Indian raiders in Puget's Sound."

"So, you would be surprised to learn he had to be saved from drowning?"

"I'd be incredulous!"

"When did you last see Mr. St. John?"

"Just after his promotion. On my recommendation, and that of Coast Survey Superintendent Davidson, he was promoted master and commissioned in April, 1861."

"Thank you, captain."

After Alden's testimony, the court took a short recess. Commander Henry French, Tobias' commander aboard USS *Preble*, was called next. "Commander French," Winthrop began, "you were captain of the *Preble* when Mr. St. John took the action for which he later received the Medal of Honor?"

"I was. October 1861. It was the most gallant stroke I'll

ever see! The captain of the *Vincennes,* aground, had misread a signal, abandoned ship, and lit a fuse to his powder magazine. The *Vincennes* was still under fire from the Rebel squadron. St. John volunteered to take the launch, went aboard *Vincennes*, and cut the fuse just short of explosion."

"Did he have trouble finding men for the launch crew?"

"Not a bit, the men knew he'd take them into excitement, and they loved him for it. I had my glass on the boat as it rowed toward the *Vincennes*. They were pulling like fiends and laughing as if they were on a lark. Mr. St. John has a special leadership quality. He'll not ask any sailor to do something he wouldn't do himself. It's enabled him to rise in the navy in spite of his race."

"How would you describe his navigational skills?"

"Excellent, both at sea and inshore. *Preble* had no engines. We were among the shifting sands of the Mississippi delta. We never ran aground. Two others did, and one had steam."

"Would you ask for him again as your sailing master?"

"He's the man I'd want to have."

After French stepped down, the court recessed for lunch. In the afternoon, Captain C. R. Perry Rodgers took the stand. "Captain," said Winthrop, "please describe your command experience with Sailing Master Tobias St. John."

"Mr. St. John was master of USS *Wabash*, my command, beginning in late 1861. His duties included safe navigation of the ship, the squadron flagship, among the sea islands of Port Royal, Cumberland Sound, and Charleston Harbor. Those are difficult waters in which to sail. He did an excellent job. He also commanded several units in our landing forces. He single-handedly subdued a Rebel battery commander, preventing him from exploding the battery magazine and destroying a Union gunboat"

"Sir, if you were to be told that Mr. St. John failed to keep a vessel clear of Frying Pan Shoal, what would your reaction be?"

"I'd be astonished. Such a failure would be most uncharacteristic of Mr. St. John."

"Thank you, captain. No further questions."

Barclay leaned forward. "Mr. Oldham? Members of the court?

No? Very well, captain, you're excused. Mr. Winthrop, call your next witness."

"Mr. President, we call Allan Pinkerton."

Allan Pinkerton, the Glasgow-born former chief of the Secret Service under General McClellan, looked, as always, nondescript, somewhat rumpled, and thoroughly unmemorable. A detective could scarcely ask for a more desirable presence. After Pinkerton was sworn, Winthrop asked him to describe his wartime activities.

"Until November, I was chief of the Army's Secret Service," he said in his Glaswegian burr. "Fer the noo, I have returned tae private life, as an investigator."

"In the Secret service, did you have occasion to work with Sailing Master St. John?"

"Och, aye, I did that, and a finer operative I cannae imagine. We first met at Port Royal, where he helped me establish an intelligence network among the former slave population. I dinnae dare give the details for fear of compromising an ongoing operation, but it was most successful."

"Did you work further together?"

"Och, aye, the next time was in a different State, where he spent quite some time with our agents behind enemy lines, posing as a slave pilot. The resultant loss tae the enemy was three valuable blockade-runners. Again, I dare no' give details. He is a careful, exacting and resolute man, that he is."

"I'm sure the court understands your hesitancy to provide detail, Mr. Pinkerton," said Winthrop. "Thank you. I have no further questions."

Tobias sensed that Oldham was doing his best not to look discouraged. It seemed to Tobias that the court had reacted with favor and considerable interest to the parade of character witnesses Winthrop had arrayed before them. Three seasoned commanders and a secret service chief made a formidable assembly. Tobias cautioned himself against high expectations. *These testimonies are not evidence*, he thought. *We need witnesses from the scene.* He was relieved when Commodore Barclay, obviously weary from two full court days, adjourned until Monday at

10:30 a.m. "How did we do, counselor?" He asked Winthrop hopefully as they left the *North Carolina*.

"Better and better, Tobias," Winthrop answered. "Every one of them painted the same portrait of you; meticulous, strong, brave. There's nothing like consistency to convince a court or a jury."

"We still need more eyewitnesses, don't we?"

"Yes, we do, Tobias, but we bought ourselves two and a half more days for them to appear. If they're not here Monday, I'll cross examine Oldham, and make it last as long as I can. I can also put you on the stand."

"Would that be advisable, Everett? I thought lawyers considered it dangerous to put the accused in the sights of the accuser."

"That is the conventional wisdom, but you would be an exceptional witness. Absent Mr. Fredericks, it would help to have our own eyewitness to all the events. You're the next best thing to Fredericks, at this point. Let's meet Sunday for dinner to go over our Monday schedule. Who knows, they may have arrived by then!" Winthrop gave a broad smile to Tobias, clearly meant to be reassuring. It fell somewhat short of its intent.

CHAPTER 33
EXONERATION

Tobias spent a long introspective weekend beneath the slate-gray skies of Hampton Roads, wandering the streets of Hampton and walking into the countryside to the banks of Harris Creek and the Little Back River. His walking companions were his thoughts of his seagoing career, the waters he'd sailed and the foreign lands he'd seen. *Those times seem now so untrammeled, so free of care and woe,* he thought to himself. *Just 'do your duty' and take each day as it comes. In this war, every step comes with weighty consequence.*

Hampton Village had been burned and razed by Confederates, in August, 1861 under the command of General Magruder, who feared that the village, a stop on the "underground railway", would become a haven for slaves escaping during the war's early days. His fears were realized when the Union seized the village and the area surrounding Fort Monroe and rebuilt Hampton Village, creating hundreds of homes for "contrabands."

Passing soldiers, sailors, and citizens alike would glance at the sight of the tall Negro in the uniform of a naval officer, first an unobtrusive look, and then, a second, bolder glance as the rarity of what they saw registered. As Lincoln had just issued the Emancipation Proclamation, "contraband" residents were particularly interested. Tobias outwardly ignored the stares, 'though he was keenly aware of each. *I will win this battle, yet,* he thought, *'though I miss Monique's guidance. She's sustained me through every risk I've taken; moving from Antigua to New Bedford, becoming a whaler, joining the navy. We've been too long apart.*

Tobias' Sunday was brightened considerably at dinner when

Winthrop told him that O'Mahony was in Hampton, aboard the *North Carolina*, and that he would be a helpful witness. "He thinks much of you, Tobias," said the attorney. "I'd describe his picture of you as a 'sailor's sailor.' He'll be a fine witness."

On Monday, O'Mahony sat in the witness chair, his square Irish jaw thrust before him like the bluff bow of a ship. Winthrop approached the witness chair, his hands clasped behind him.

"Seaman O'Mahony, you were the senior leadsman aboard USS *Wilkes-Barre*, and now in the same billet aboard USS *Conestoga*, is that correct?"

"Yes, sir."

"What abilities does the Navy look for when it assigns a sailor to leadsman's duties?" Winthrop looked at O'Mahony with an encouraging smile.

O'Mahony paused for a moment, leaning back in the witness chair, and then leaned forward, an earnest look on his face. "Sir, the Navy wants a man who can cast the lead quickly, who won't tire out for a long while, and who can read the lead line and the lead day or night with no mistakes. A loud voice helps, too, sir."

"So," Winthrop continued, "strong, fast, accurate, tireless?"

"Yes, sir."

"I'm just a landsman, seaman," said Winthrop, self-deprecatingly, "but from your testimony, a leadsman seems to be the first line of communication with the navigator or pilot in shallow waters. Were you confident Mr. St. John would make good use of the information you work so hard to gather?"

"Sure, now, sir, Mr. St. John spent time before the mast, and then made master's mate and master. He knew what he was about, sir."

"From the soundings you took that night of the grounding, were you concerned about the ship's position?"

"Sure, and I was, sir, and didn't I mention it to Mr. St. John, sir? Respectful-like, of course. We were in two and a half fathoms!"

"What was the master's reaction?"

"Oh, he already knew, sir. And he'd already told the captain, sir. He said as much, careful-like, so as not to disrespect the captain. But I knew, sir. He said, 'I'll pass that word. Again.' And then he told me to carry on, and went back aft, sir."

"Did you see him again, after the grounding?"

"Yes, sir, he came forward to find me, and the two of us took soundings all along the starboard side where we was aground. Steady as a rock, he was. Then he went back to the bridge. The next time I saw him, I was cox'n of the long boat. Mr. Fredericks and Mr. Jones was in the boat and we was waiting for Mr. St. John and the captain. Mr. St. John hollered down to us that the captain wouldn't get in the boat. He told us to get into the lee while he brought the captain down himself. We did, but the captain still wouldn't abandon ship. So we lay off a few yards, and I saw Mr. St. John grab the captain in his arms and jump overside with him. Then Mr. St. John swam to the boat, pulling the captain. The master's a mighty strong swimmer, sure and he is!" O'Mahony paused.

"What happened next, Seaman O'Mahony?"

"Mr. Jones and meself pulled the captain into the boat, and Mr. St. John hauled himself over the gun'l. Then we rowed to the *Dacotah*."

"Did the captain say anything when he was in the longboat?"

"Yes, sir, he said he wanted to go down with the ship."

"You heard him clearly?"

"He said it pretty loud, sir."

"When Mr. St. John and the captain went overboard, was there debris, flotsam, in the water?"

"Yessir, 'twas all manner of planks and crates and oars and such, tossin' all about in the waves, sir."

"Is it possible that the captain might have been struck by such an object?"

"I suppose it could be, sir."

"Thank you, Seaman O'Mahony. No further questions."

Barclay turned to Oldham, who responded before Barclay could ask the question. "I have no questions of this witness, Mr. President."

Tobias looked around the cabin. *No sign of Fredericks. Maybe we can get by without him,* he thought.

The president excused O'Mahony, and Winthrop whispered to Tobias, "I'm going to cross examine Oldham, and then rest. We're in a strong position." Tobias nodded assent, and as he did, glanced up to see Lieutenant McDonald Fredericks enter the great cabin and take a seat in the back row. Winthrop was already on his feet, and speaking.

"Mr. President, we beg to recall Jeremiah Oldham."

"Very well. Captain Oldham, I remind you that you are still under oath."

Winthrop approached the witness with an almost-deferential air. "Captain Oldham, *Wilkes-Barre* was your first navy command, was she not?"

"She was."

"And in your maritime experience outside the navy, have you ever commanded a ship of her tonnage?"

"I have not."

"So is it fair to say that you have only four months experience as a commander of a gunboat or the equivalent?"

"Yes, it would."

"Have you ever experienced shipwreck before the loss of *Wilkes-Barre?*"

"No."

"As charging officer, you've been present for the testimony in this trial. You've heard testimony that Mr. St. John twice recommended moving west from the shoal, and that you, after consideration, accepted that recommendation. Is it possible, sir, that in the noise and wrack of the storm, you misunderstood when you believed you heard Mr. St. John say your position was safe, and that in the confusion of the ensuing shipwreck, precise remarks and events have become difficult to recall?"

Oldham reflected for a moment, and conceded, "I suppose that's possible."

"You've heard several witnesses describe Mr. St. John's concern for your safety after the wreck, and his subsequent successful effort to bring you to the longboat through the storm. Is it possible, sir, owing to the confusion and chaos of the vessel disintegrating in the storm, or owing to the possibility you may have been concussed by striking some debris as you went overboard, that your ability to recall precisely the details of abandoning ship may have been impaired? An impairment, I might add, perfectly understandable under the circumstances."

"It could be," replied Oldham.

"Thank you, Captain Oldham. Mr. President, the defense rests."

"Very well, Mr. Winthrop. We'll recess for lunch, and return for closing argument." Barclay's gavel sounded with a sonorous clap, and the cabin of the *North Carolina* emptied quickly.

Tobias grabbed Winthrop by the arm. "Everett, Fredericks just walked in."

"Have him join us for lunch," Winthrop responded, "but I don't think we'll need his testimony. Oldham just handed us a not guilty verdict, unless I'm completely misreading the court."

They took their lunch in the small compartment reserved for the defense. "I picked the right moment to appear, Tobias," said Fredericks, "I mean from the standpoint of understanding the trial. Oldham didn't look like a man about to win."

"You're right, Macdonald. Everett, here has offered him a way out of being branded a liar, and it appears he's ready to take the bait."

"True enough, Mr. Fredericks," said Winthrop. "Unless I miss my guess, Ethan Lodge, the oh-so-prominent attorney advising Oldham from the background is at this minute suggesting that Oldham withdraw charges and request a medical resignation, for injuries sustained in the wreck of the *Wilkes-Barre*. But, if I'm wrong, and we have to deliver our closing or 'defense' as the navy calls it, here's what I'll say:

"Members of the court, the picture painted here is of two men. The first, an experienced sailor who's ranged the seven seas, served before the mast and risen on his talents to a commission in the US Navy. He's a superb cartographer and navigator, who served in the ranks of the US Coast Survey, the navigational elite. He's a brave man, used to storms at sea, shipwreck, and mortal combat. He's a man who keeps his head while behind enemy lines."

"The second man is an earnest but inexperienced commander. In this, his first navy command, he was unused to shipwreck, understandably confused, perhaps concussed, and certainly devastated by the loss of his ship."

"Whom to believe, members of the court? A Medal-of-Honor

winner, whose shipmates and commanders all paint precisely the same portrait: brave, resolute, expert navigator, cool under pressure? Or an inexperienced man who has lost his ship and who seeks to find justification for it? A man whose reaction to the storm and shipwreck was as confused as that of his only, equally inexperienced witness. This court can only reach one conclusion: not guilty!"

Tobias and Fredericks applauded heartily, as they rose from the table to return to the cabin and Tobias' fate.

"Closing statement, Mr. Oldham?" Barclay turned to the charging officer.

"May it please the court, upon the recommendation of my advising counsel, I beg leave to read the following statement: 'As these proceedings have progressed it has become apparent that my charges were based on errors of perception. The noise and confusion of the storm, the wreck, and the possibility that my memory and judgment were impaired by injury, lead me to conclude, after lengthy consideration, that my impaired memory evoked these charges, charges that have largely been demonstrated to be in error. Accordingly, I request that I be allowed to withdraw all charges and specifications in this case.'"

"Mr. Judge Advocate, have you any comments?" Barclay fixed Christiansen with an inquiring look over the top of his spectacles.

"Mr. President, in my judgment, the interests of justice would be well-served if these charges are withdrawn. In my professional opinion, the evidence shows no inefficiency, nor negligence, nor inattention."

"Thank you, Mr. Judge Advocate. Are there any objections from members of the court to the withdrawal of charges? Hearing none, the charges are withdrawn, and Mr. St. John is fully restored to duty. If I may say so, the navy is the better for the restoration to duty of this fine officer. This court is adjourned."

Tobias, Winthrop and Fredericks burst onto the broad quarterdeck of the *North Carolina*, bathed in rare January sunshine. The defense witnesses, O'Mahony, Macgillycuddy, and Jones, were standing near the rail, having been required to stand by throughout the trial in case of recall. The character witnesses had returned to station, save for Pinkerton, who as a civilian was his own master and an interested spectator for the entire proceeding.

"Congratulations, sir," said Jones to Tobias. "Justice was served!"

"That's so, Mr. St. John," echoed the two Irishmen and the Glasgow Scot.

"Gentlemen, you're all invited to the Inn at Hampton Roads," said Winthrop. "I've engaged a room off the bar for a small celebration. Shall we say an hour from now?"

Later, at the inn, amid toasts and handshakes, Winthrop called for quiet. "I have a telegram here in response to one I sent earlier, after the court adjourned. It's from Assistant Secretary of the Navy Gustavus Fox. He says: 'Congratulations to Sailing Master St. John and Everett Winthrop, Esq. for a well-deserved and just victory. President Lincoln and Secretary Welles add their heartiest congratulations.' Here you are, Tobias, for your scrapbook. Or is it a log, in the navy?"

"Thank you, Everett, for this and all your good endeavors. I'll write to thank the secretaries and the president." Tobias turned to place the telegram in his notecase, and found Pinkerton at his elbow.

"Och, laddie, you can thank them in person," said the detective in an undertone. "I've signed a contract with the executive branch to arrange an espionage mission, and you're just the geordie I need tae do the job. Let's have breakfast in the morning, when the celebratin's done, and we'll talk."

Tobias turned back to his friends and supporters, a faint and quizzical smile on his face. *What has fate in store for me now?* he wondered.

TO BE CONTINUED IN
"THE WAKE OF THE *WOONSOCKET*"

258

APPENDIX A:
SHIPS

Most of the ships appearing in this novel were actual vessels, and most of the officers noted were historical characters aboard these ships. The following are the only fictional ships:

Bosworth: paddle wheel steamer.

Carolina Princess: "purpose-built" blockade-runner.

USS Commodore Truxton: ex-New York ferry boat, now a gunboat.

USS Chingatchgook: "90-day" class shallow-draft gunboat.

Cuirassier - French sloop of war observing Hampton Roads.

Fair Maid of Roanoke: older blockade-runner.

CSS Ocracoke: Clyde steamer blockade-runner, navy-owned.

CSS Old Dominion: One-gun screw tug, Rory's first command.

CSS Rose of Clifton: Dunbrody shipyard-built paddlewheel gunboat.

Santa Victoria: Antiguan schooner.

USS Wilkes-Barre: Octorara-class double-ender gunboat.

USS Woonsocket: Wyoming-class sloop of war, 1500 tons, draft of 14 feet, speed – eleven knots.

APPENDIX B:
MAJOR CHARACTERS

Rory Dunbrody, CSN, and father Patrick, sister Siobhan, brother Tim, Uncle Liam, and the Dillon side of the family.
Tobias St. John, and his family. Antiguan-born former slave, whaler and now a Union sailing master.
Kalama, Kele and son Kekoa - Hawaiian seafarers. Kekoa becomes a master's mate in the USN.

Other Important Characters
"*" denotes an actual historical figure.
* Captain James Alden, USN – commander aboard USS Active in Puget's Sound, later commanding officer of several Union vessels.
* Commander James D. Bulloch, CSN – Directed raider acquisitions in Europe.
* Jefferson Davis – President, Confederate States.

Amanda Devereaux (and her employees)– Union spy and ship owner in North Carolina.
Major Grenville Donovan, CSA (& family)– Confederate intelligence officer and brother of Thomas whom Rory killed in a duel over Carrie Anne Eastman.
* Admiral Samuel Francis "Frank" Du Pont – commanding the South Atlantic Blockading Squadron (and therefore, Tobias) in the first years of the war.
Captain Jean Gilbert Duquesne – French naval officer.
Monique Duvalliere and family – Tobias' lover and childhood sweetheart in les Isles de Saintes.
Carrie Anne Eastman and family - Rory's Southern love interest.
* Charlotte Forten – Abolitionist and teacher from a prominent black Philadelphia family who taught newly-freed slaves in Port Royal, South Carolina.
* Gustavus Fox, Assistant US Navy Secretary.
Quentin Glendenning, CSN – Rory's subordinate lieutenant.
* Catesby ap Jones, CSN – commander of CSS Virginia.

* Lieutenant Roswell Lamson, USN – Outstanding US Navy officer from Oregon whose assignments are often coincident with Tobias'.
* President Abraham Lincoln
Lieutenant Bertram Ludlow, Royal Navy – Blockade runner, bigot and general trouble-maker in Tobias' world.
* Confederate Secretary of the Navy Stephen Mallory – ran the Rebel navy with creativity and determination.
* Midshipman James Morris "Jimmie" Morgan, CSN – his assignments in New Orleans, Richmond and Great Britain were coincident with Rory's.
* Confederate cavalryman John Singleton Mosby. At first a scout for JEB Stuart, he later commands the 43rd Virginia, a famed guerilla battalion that operated near the present Dulles Airport in Loudoun and Fauquier counties.
Archibald Ormsby, South Carolinian naval officer often under Rory's command.
* George Edward Pickett, US Army captain and later Confederate major general. Last in his class at West Point. Charming. Flamboyant. He and Rory cross paths frequently.
* Edward L. Pierce – infantryman, attorney and director of the Port Royal Experiment, schooling thousands of newly-freed slaves.
* Allan Pinkerton – Secret Service Chief for General McClellan and Lincoln's protector. Tobias impresses him with his clandestine abilities.
* Robert Smalls, slave pilot who commandeered the CSS Planter and delivered her to the Union blockade. Later commanded a Union gunboat, served after the war in the South Carolina state legislature, US Congress and South Carolina National Guard (major general).
* John Randolph Tucker – senior US and Confederate naval officer in many theaters where Rory fought. Later an admiral jointly commanding the Chilean and Peruvian navies.
Klaus Dieter von Klopfenstein – aide to George Pickett, formerly a Prussian army officer and duelist, Rory's antagonist.
* Gideon Welles - Union Secretary of the Navy, cabinet adviser to

President Lincoln.

* John Taylor Wood – dashing rebel navy commander. Formerly assistant US Naval Academy superintendant. Commanded a "naval cavalry" unit specializing in the capture of Union blockader gunboats. Gunnery officer aboard CSS Virginia at Hampton Roads. Jefferson Davis' nephew.

Appendix C:
Glossary

Readers of The Chesapeake Command asked for a glossary to be included in this sequel. The author would appreciate feedback as to the success of this attempt.

ABAFT: Toward the stern of the ship, used relatively, e.g., "the gun was abaft the mizzenmast."

ABEAM: beside, next to, abreast. At the side of, as opposed to in front or behind.

AFTERGUARD: seamen whose station is on the quarterdeck.

AVAST: a shipboard order, hold, or stop hauling.

ARMS:

Cannon: Smoothbore cannon had no rifling or grooves inside the barrel, and fired roundshot (solid cannon balls) as well as grapeshot (bags of musket balls) or chainshot (two roundshot bound together by a chain) very harmful to rigging. They were muzzleloaders, and usually mounted on wooden gun carriages with wooden wheels to accommodate recoil. Sometimes, they were on Marsilly or "dumb-truck" carriages, on which the back two wheels were replaced by a wooden bar sliding on the deck to more effectively reduce recoil. They were classified by the weight of their roundshot, e.g., 32 pounders, 24 pounders. These cannon were used afloat and ashore. Swivels were small smoothbores mounted or set in the gunwales of ships or ship's boats and rotated in any direction. Smoothbores were most often mounted in broadside, firing from only one side of the vessel, through a gunport.

Rifled cannon fire shaped shells, either exploding or solid, with rims so that the rifling causes them to spin through the air for better accuracy. They are classified by muzzle diameter, e.g., 8 inch, eleven inch, and inventor or manufacturer, e.g., Parrott, Dahlgren (Union), Brooke, the British Whitworth, Blakely, and Armstrong (Confederacy). Their effective range was a bit more than a mile. Most are muzzleloaders, except the breechloader Armstrong. These cannon were used afloat and ashore. So were howitzers, smaller wheeled cannon with elevated muzzles. Columbiads were huge 15,000 pound guns used in shore fortifications, with a range of three miles. Rifled cannon were frequently mounted as pivots, on tracks secured to the fore or after decks that enabled the gun to be trained in any direction. A pivot might have three gunports through which it could fire, rather than the one customary for a broadside gun.

Excellent sources for some of the above are Paul Silverstone's Civil War Navies 1855-1883 – Naval Institute Press, and Ironclads and Columbiads by William R. Trotter – John F. Blair.

Swords: Sabers and cutlasses were the most common used by Civil war armed forces, and were used more often to cut and slash than to thrust, with a single edged blade. Rapiers, including epees, were double or triple edged and used more to thrust. They were common in dueling.

Sidearms, handguns and revolvers: Very popular was the 1851 Colt .36 caliber Navy Six, a six-shot revolver light in weight and favored by cavalry and the navy.

BEAR UP: in a sailing ship, to sail closer to the wind, or in a steamer, to head for.

BEAT TO QUARTERS: A drum rhythm from the ship's drummer that called the crew to battle stations.

BELL TIME: The striking of the ship's bell to mark the passage of time. Time at sea is divided into four-hour "watches," One bell is struck at each half hour, for a cumulative total of eight bells at the end of the fourth hour. From midnight, the watches are Mid, Morning, Forenoon and Afternoon, bringing the day to 4:00 pm, or "eight bells in the afternoon watch." To preclude sailors from standing the same watch each day, two two-hour watches span the 4:00 to 8:oo pm time. They are known as the First and Second Dog Watches. Four bells are sounded at the end of the First Dog Watch, but in the Second we hear one, two, three, and then at 8:00 pm, eight bells once again. The seventh watch is the Evening Watch, ending when eight bells sounds midnight.

BEST BOWER: The starboard of the two anchors carried at the bow, as opposed to the SMALL BOWER, the portside anchor, which was, peculiarly, the same weight as the best bower.

BLATHERSKITE: In Ireland, a nonsense talker, a useless individual who talks nonsense, or "blather."

BROAD REACH: a point of sailing with the wind abeam or slightly abaft the beam.

CAISSONS: two-wheeled wagons carrying artillery ammunition.

CAPOEIRA: a martial art often disguised as dance and frequently practiced to music, developed first in the slave plantations of Brazil, emphasizing striking with the legs. When slave masters would appear, the participants would subtly shift from confrontational movements to dance form.

CATESBY AP ROGER JONES: the Welsh-named first lieutenant and later commander of the CSS Virginia. "Ap" is a Welsh prefix meaning "son of."

CHANDLERY: the store of a ship chandler, a supplier of goods for ships.

COUNTER: The underside of the after overhang of a ship, below the transom.

CRANK: in a ship, unstable, in danger of capsizing or overturning, particularly in heavy weather, caused by poor construction, design or improper stowage or ballasting.

DAVIT: a set of two small cranes fitted with blocks and tackle to lower the boat slung between them along the side or the stern of a ship.

DRAFT: or draught, the vertical distance between a ship's waterline and her keel. The depth of water a ship "draws" is her draft. E.g., "she drew 22 feet."

DOUSED HER GLIM: put out the lantern or other light showing aboard a ship.

DUN LAOGHAIRE: A port south of Dublin, connected by rail. Pronounced "Dun Leary."

FALLS: the hauling rope part of a tackle. For the tackles lowering boats in davits, the boat-falls or "falls" for short.

FORTIFICATIONS: Forts or fortresses consist of ramparts, the outer walls, surmounted by parapets, upward extensions of the ramparts behind which guns are mounted and fired through embra-

sures or openings in the parapet. Corners of the fortification may
project beyond the main walls in hexagonal outward extensions
called bastions, which contain chambers called casemates in which
guns are housed. Sally ports are chambered entrances with two
doors, an inner door closed after defenders are in the sally port, and
an outer door that then is opened to let the defenders "sally forth."
Redoubts are earthworks outside of main forts and independent of
them.

GALLOWGLASSES: in Ireland, originally Gaelic mercenaries of
the thirteenth century who fought for Domnall mac Domnaill,
brother of an Irish king, against the Normans. They were heavily
armed and armored foot soldiers.

GOMBEEN MEN: Rural Irish usurers who exacted exorbitant
interest on loans to the Irish peasantry.

GROG: A mixture of rum and water served daily to the ship's crew
in the Royal and American navies. Named for British Admiral Ver-
non, whose nickname, after a coat he wore, was "Old Grogham."
Drink too much and you were "groggy." The Royal Navy continued
the custom through the twentieth century, but the Union (US)
Navy discontinued it in 1862.

GUNWALE: The upper edge of the side or bulwark of a vessel.
Pronounced "gun'l."

HAWSE HOLE: The aperture in the bows of a ship through which
the anchor cable passes.

HAWSER: A heavy rope or cable greater than five inches in circum-
ference. Used for towing, some anchor lines or to secure to a dock.

HOGGING: When the bow and stern of a ship droop below
the midship section of the keel, either on a wave crest, or when
aground.

HOKU: In Hawaii, a star.

KAHUNA: In Hawaii, a priest, wizard, minister, expert in any
profession.

KANAKA: The Hawaiian word for human being, man, person,
individual. In the world outside the Hawaiian Islands, frequently
used to denote a Hawaiian.

KEEL: The principal member or timber extending the length of a ship's bottom. The ship's "backbone."

KERNES or KERNS: Irish light infantry, originally around the thirteenth century.

KILO: In Hawaii, a stargazer, seer, reader of omens.

LANYARD: a short length of rope used for a variety of purposes, including the release of the hammer on flintlocks when they were used as firing mechanisms for cannon.

LEAD LINE: a 25-fathom (150 foot) line with a lead weight cylinder attached, used to find the depth of the water. The lead's lower end is cupped and "armed' with tallow, to bring to the surface the nature of the bottom, mud, sand, pebbles, shingles, etc. The line is measured in six-foot lengths or fathoms. The leadsman heaves the line ahead of the ship so that it is vertical as it reaches the bottom. He is positioned in the chains, a platform to which the fore shrouds are attached. The line is marked with specific knots, rags or leathers at most of the six-foot 'fathom' intervals. The leadsman can identify the depth marks by feel, even in the dark. Depths measured by indicators are referred to as marks. Unmarked fathoms in between marks are called out as deeps. "By the mark two" was distinguished by two strips of leather. The "deep six" had no mark but was between "mark five" (white duck cloth) and "mark seven" (red bunting).

The deep sea or "dipsea' lead measures depths up to 100 fathoms. It is extended along the length of the ship and held at intervals by sailors who drop their segment of the line in succession.

LEE: the side of a ship or promontory away from the wind.

LIGHTERS: barges used to convey cargo from ship to shore in shallow waters. They are shallow draft and very steady in calmer water.

LUFF: 1. Slang for lieutenant, from the French and British pronunciation "leftenant." "First Luff" is the first lieutenant or executive officer of a ship. 2. The leading edge of a fore-and-aft sail. To "luff up" is to bring the vessel into the wind so that the luff shivers and the sail spills the wind.

MASSEY LOG: the most accurate rotating log developed in the early nineteenth century, a streamlined rotator with dials towed at the end of a log-line, invented by Edward Massey. It had to be hauled in for each reading, but was remarkably accurate in measuring ship speed. The rotator varied its speed, and therefore its readings, as the ship varied hers.

MOKU: In Hawaii, an island, a ship (because the first European ships suggested islands). Sailor is kelamoku, or in pidgin, sailamoku.

MOULINET: In fencing, a circular saber stroke or swing at head level.

MONKEY FIST: an intricately constructed knot, round, and weighty, attached to the end of the light heaving line first tossed from a ship to another vessel or to a dock. Once the lighter, more-easily-thrown heaving line was in hand, the ship's end was tied or "bent" to a heavier line that secured the originating ship to the other vessel or to the dock.

ORLOP DECK: the lowest deck in a ship. Usually, the location of the surgeon's operating compartment, called the "cockpit." "Orlop" and "cockpit" were sometimes used interchangeably when referring to the surgery.

PA ELE: In Hawaii, a Negro.

PALU: In Micronesia, a navigator-priest confirmed in a "Pwo" ceremony.

PELORUS: an instrument for taking bearings, with two sighting vanes, fitted to the rim of a compass and giving the bearings of two objects from a fixed point, usually a ship or boat.

SASANACH: In Ireland, an Englishman, sometimes, a Protestant. A term of derision.

SCREW: A nautical propeller.

SCUPPERS: drains for the weather or upper decks.

SCUTTLEBUTT: 1. A cask of fresh water for daily drinking use, located in a convenient part of the ship. 2. Gossip. As many members of the crew would use the scuttlebutt and pause during the ship's work day, talk and gossip were exchanged there. Gossip exchanged at the office water fountain is a direct descendant.

SHIP'S BOATS: The dimensions and characteristics of the boats described herein varied with the passage of time and the size of the ships they served. For instance, a cutter, a beamy boat that sailed well, but rowed less well, could be 34 feet long and carry 66 men on a ship of the line or a large steam frigate, but measured 18 feet long on a brig. Smaller vessels had difficulty in hoisting out larger boats using their main and fore course yards. The invention of davits in the 1790s helped the smaller craft to more easily hoist out boats.

Generally, the size of a boat from large to small followed this order: Longboat, launch, pinnace, barge, cutter, yawl, gig, jolly boat, skiff, dory, wherry, dinghy. Double-ended whaleboats of 28-30 feet length came into naval use in the mid 1800s. A quarter boat often was one of the above hung in davits at the ship's quarter or after part.

The following list from the 1817 Royal Navy Rate Book show the variety of boats sizes within small boat nomenclature. It is taken from W E May's excellent "The Boats of Men of War," Naval Institute Press 1999, the definitive work on the topic:

Launches: in 17 varying lengths – 16 ft to 34 ft.
Barges & pinnaces: 8 lengths – 28 to 37 ft.
Cutters: 17 lengths – 12 to 34 ft.
Gigs: 6 lengths – 18 to 26 ft.

Ship's boats were designed for sailing qualities, rowing qualities, or a compromise combination. Rowing configurations were termed single banked or double banked. Single banked boats had one rower to a thwart, seated all the way across the thwart from the oarlock. For wider or more beamy boats, double banking put two men each with

oars, on each thwart. Oarlocks were first thole pins,
upright pegs in the gunwales that the oar pulled against as
a fulcrum, with a lanyard around the oar to secure it.
Next, a second thole pin was added and the oar set between.
Later, notches were cut in a strake above the gunwale and
the oar set in. In 1826, metal swiveling oar crutches were
introduced.

SHIP TYPES: Beginning with the system of the Royal Navy's Lord
Anson in 1751, warships of sailing navies were divided into six divi-
sions or "rates" according to the number of broadside guns carried.
A "first rate" carried 100 guns or more. A "fourth rate" carried from
50 to 70 guns, and was the smallest ship of the line, or line-of-
battle ship. Fifth and sixth rates were brigs of war, sloops of war,
corvettes or frigates carrying up to fifty guns.
Steam power brought additional and changing classifications. Ships
carried more powerful pivot guns that fired in any direction, in addition to broadside guns. Steam ships came to be classified by how
they were powered or armored. Ironclads, sidewheel frigates, screw
frigates, sidewheel or screw sloops, sidewheel or screw gunboats,
and armed sidewheel or screw tugs were some new types. Specialty
vessels, such as spar torpedo boats and hand-propelled submarines
were introduced in the American Civil War. River combat spawned
cottonclads, tinclads, timberclads and rams.
It's interesting to note that "second-rate," now connoting low
quality, originally meant a ship of the line carrying from 84 to 100
guns, with nothing low-quality about her.
SIDEBOY: A sailor assigned to attend the gangway when officers
or other dignitaries are boarding the ship. The rank of the boarding
officer determines the number of sideboys.
SPALPEEN: In Ireland, an itinerant farmhand of dubious reputation or low degree. A rascal. A derogatory term.
STERNSHEETS: In an open boat the section aft of the after
thwart, usually fitted with seats for the coxswain, boat commander
or passengers.
STOP HER COCKS: To plug any below-waterline pipes opening

to the sea on a vessel.

STRAKE: A line of planking in a wooden vessel. The hull is made up of rows of strakes.

TEAGUE: A common Irish surname which came to be used as a derogatory term for an Irishman in the USA and Great Britain of the 19th century, like "mick" or "paddy." The "tea' is pronounced "tay." Sometimes, "Taig" or "Teig."

THWART: The transverse wooden seat in a rowing boat on which oarsmen sit.

TIDES: The states of the tides include: slack water, when the tide changes from ebb to flood or the reverse; ebb, outgoing; flood, incoming; high, the greatest level, and low, the lowest level.

TOP HAMPER: A ship's superstructure and upper-deck equipment.

TRANSOM: the athwartship timbers bolted to the sternpost, constituting a flat stern.

WARDROOM: The mess and common room for the senior officers (except the captain) in a larger warship, or for all officers (except the captain) in a smaller ship. The gunroom in a larger ship serves the more junior officers.

WAY and WEIGH: Way is to be in motion over the sea bottom. A ship has "way" on her, or is "under way." The command for rowers to begin rowing is "give way all." To weigh anchor is to lift the anchor from the sea bottom. "Under weigh" is an incorrect usage.

WAY ENOUGH: A command to stop rowing.

"WILL NAE BE KENT": In Scots dialect, "will not be known."

YAW, PITCH AND ROLL: Yaw is the motion of the bow to the left or to the right of the course. Pitch is the up and down motion of the bow caused by wave action ahead or astern of the ship. Roll is the up and down movement of the side of a ship due to wave action from the side or abeam of the ship.

In addition to the sources cited above, the author is indebted to
The Oxford Companion to Ships and the Sea, Peter Kemp, Ox-
ford Reference; Ship to Shore, Peter D. Jeans, McGraw Hill; A
Sea of Words, Dean King, Henry Bolt; Origins of Sea Terms, John
G. Rogers, Mystic Seaport Museum; Hawaiian Dictionary, Mary
Kawena Pukui and Samuel H. Elbert, University of Hawaii Press;
and Slanguage, a Dictionary of Irish Slang, Bernard Share, Gill and
Macmillan.